BURNT FINGERS

BURNT FINGERS

It's a matter of life and death

MICHAEL ROGERS

iUniverse, Inc.
Bloomington

BURNT FINGERS
It's a matter of life and death

iUniverse books may be ordered through booksellers or by contacting:

iUniverse
1663 Liberty Drive
Bloomington, IN 47403
www.iuniverse.com
1-800-Authors (1-800-288-4677)

Cover illustration by Matthew Rogers
Courtesy of www.matthewrogersillustration.com
All rights reserved.

ISBN: 978-1-4697-8822-7 (sc)
ISBN: 978-1-4697-8825-8 (ebk)

Printed in the United States of America

iUniverse rev. date: 03/21/2012

This novel is dedicated to the glory of God.

For Joel, Melody, Jack and Annabelle.
Here's to an epic adventure through the painted deserts of
Nevada in the hush of night,
driving past a maximum security prison
with signs on the road telling us not to pick up hitchhikers.
Thank you for the best summer of my life.

To everyone held captive by the sensitive issues
covered by this novel, I pray that your Shot at Glory becomes
everything that you hoped it would be.

"Anyone who kills a person is to be put to death
as a murderer only on the testimony of witnesses. But no one is
to be put to death on the testimony of only one witness."

Numbers 35v30

CONTENTS

1   A SHOT AT GLORY

Tragedy reigned as the skies over Higher Pelham quickly darkened. The sunset unfurled its wings over the English countryside in a spectacular panorama of Heavenly majesty, with every tree, field and lonely rooftop splattered with a harrowing crimson glow. The light was fading fast and the last clots of sunlight were dribbling upwards from the horizon; occasionally there would be a haemorrhage in the bank of cloud and a great spool of cracked rubies would pulse in the hush of twilight. From her lofty hilltop Kate Hewitt surveyed the scene on a dreadful day. She was totally alone; there was not another human in sight, only the horses in the field who neighed and bolted in a frenzied, crippling terror.

Kate waited for her mother to answer the phone with a rising sensation of despair.

"Mum?"

"Yes?" She could hear the pressing urgency in her daughter's voice. "What's happened? You're really late, you should have been here ages ago. What's wrong, Kate?"

"I can't find Joy. She's gone."

Alice's heart began to pound. What could have happened to her? Where could she have gone? How many things can happen to a seven year old girl on her way home from school?

"Where are you?"

"I'm coming up the lane that runs down the side of the churchyard, coming up the hill from school. She was walking behind me, a man came towards us, and the next thing I knew they had both disappeared. I can't find her and I've looked everywhere I can think of." Her voice tailed off slightly, as she knew the conclusion that they were both coming to. "I . . . I don't know how long I should leave it before I call the police."

"Stay there, Kate, I'm coming." Alice slammed the phone down and ran. She threw open the door of the cottage and sprinted off into the evening; Kate was close, but too afraid for the safety of her sister to leave the scene and come home on her own. Alice didn't bother to shut or lock the door, and the dog was left barking into the darkness as she ran down the garden path in her thin summer dress and with bare feet. She ran across the village square towards the lane where Kate was waiting for her; the cobbles of the empty streets were cold and lifeless against her toes. The cottage was lit from within, there was smoke rising from the chimney and Alice sprinted as fast as she could through the tiny hamlet which was now shrouded in a dumbfounded silence.

*   *   *

Country life for the Hewitt family was good. They had moved to a tiny village somewhere on the border between Wiltshire and Dorset which was named Higher Pelham, a beautiful little hamlet where nothing seemed to have changed at all in the last few hundred years. Higher Pelham was blessed by many tree lined lanes and ancient hedgerows where an afternoon walk in the heat of the day would be made pleasant again by the overwhelming beauty of the most beautiful village in England. It was only home to fifty thatched cottages with a population of about two hundred, and had a quiet little church with the absurdly English name of St George's and a market square with a few small traditional shops. There was the baker and the poultry; the fishmonger and the butcher; a quaint little farm shop which sold every kind of jam, pie and chutney; a carpenter and a traditional toyshop. It was only natural for a village as quintessential as this one to proudly flaunt Union Jacks at any opportunity, and patriotic bunting was a regular sight in the summer months and during the searing July when the family moved there. The village pub was called The Green Man and it was very small but it seemed as though it would last forever. The central square was given over to The Green Man on one side and the entrance to St George's on the other; there was a long pathway that ran alongside the boundary of the churchyard, with a tree shaded lane leading out towards the other end of the village and the hill that led down to Lower Pelham. On the hillside between the two villages was the tiny train station, Pelham Central, and Pelham School, which because of the remoteness of the twin hamlets served as the only school in the area and as a result it served all age groups, so all of the Hewitt children went to and from school together.

Alice and Geoff Hewitt had moved to the village from a home in Raynes Park where Geoff had made a small fortune with an internet company; wanting to give the children a better life in the country, they had moved to Higher Pelham and Geoff continued with the business from home. The cottage that they had found themselves in was a wonderful and beautiful home, the sort of place where children's imaginations run away with themselves and where a game of hide and seek could last for hours even though the place was tiny. It was Geoff's castle, his slice of the good life, and the Hewitt family's shot at glory after the claustrophobia and haste of city existence. To be here with a young family, they felt, was to live life in all of its abundant fullness, whereas the old house in Rosevine Road was to simply exist and be hauled forwards by the erosion of time, to see only the part of being a human that was constructed of a deep coldness. Raynes Park had been good to them financially but Alice had felt somewhat like a bird in a cage must feel when out of the window she catches a fleeting glimpse of the branches of a tree where a migrating flock has just set off from or listens to the sounds of moths fluttering in the moonlight. She couldn't even really see or hear freedom, but she knew in her soul that it must be close. Higher Pelham for Alice Hewitt spelt out independence. It was her new republic, her unexplored landscape of opportunity and promise and she saw echoes of herself and her family in the meadows, lanes and hills all around the beautiful little village. Being here made her soul sing and dance for joy in the endless beauty and grandeur of the village's matchless serenity and peace. She could lose herself in the meadows and as she breathed deeply the rural air on a searing hot summer day, all she could smell was the delicate aroma of fields of freshly cut grass. Glory.

The children, of course, needed some convincing about the move, being established as they were in their lives at home and having a particular resentment of changing the status quo in favour of the unfamiliar. Catherine was fourteen and very settled in her environment during the troublesome task that she was facing of moulding herself successfully and painlessly into womanhood. She was very firm-willed and headstrong with a formidable character for her young age and it was clear that she had fine leadership qualities which would serve her well in the future. Geoff and Kate were the only ones in the family with dark hair and Kate did not share her younger siblings' freckled faces. Jonathan was ten and he shared his mother's strawberry blond hair colour, and although he was slightly small for his age he was a keen amateur footballer. Joy was seven and a dreamer; she had great cascades of golden blonde hair, freckles and misshapen milk teeth. She was not the tallest girl in her class and that was something which frustrated her endlessly, but by all accounts she was incredibly beautiful and she lit up a room when she walked in. Joy wasn't the kind of girl who was able to concentrate on much and her mother would affectionately say that she had the brain of a butterfly because it would flutter away and it was extremely hard to catch. The Hewitt family's old golden retriever was named Milly. The children were very reluctant about moving away, but when they saw the village and the cottage that their father had just bought all three of them were convinced of its status as the perfect place for all of them to live. The cottage had tiny lattice windows with deep sills, doors crafted from ancient planks of oak and secret compartments in the backs of wardrobes, sections of hallway where the floor would have three steps up and two steps down, sections of exposed brickwork and recesses in the wall where candlesticks used to be kept. There were even rumours of tunnels to the local churchyard where highwaymen would store contraband goods such as lace and tea that their colleagues had managed to smuggle through the watch-points on the coast, but nothing had ever been found.

Magnolia Cottage on Archangel Lane was a thatched house which had become available after the elderly owner had moved away and her family could not be traced. She had sold the cottage fully furnished and used the funds to provide for herself when she moved into a care home. Alice and Geoff promised her that they would take great care of the house and all of its contents. In the hallway stood a huge mahogany grandfather clock and handmade rugs splashed their colours into every room; the ceilings were beamed deep and low and the bookshelves were stuffed with antique editions of classic novels coated with a thick film of white dust. The firelight in the inglenook gave out a warm and hearty glow in the evenings and the cushioned armchair beside it was the perfect place to curl up on a winter's night with a book as the ambiance of the grate reflected cheerfully in the brass of the coal chute and the poker set beside the fireplace. Milly loved to spread herself out on the floor next to the fire and chase the birds around in the garden. Magnolia Cottage had great cascades of roses growing up and around the door, and the dreamy spires of foxgloves in the flowerbeds outside windows so low that they almost managed to reach up to them. The lawns were deep and lush and thickly carpeted in emerald green turf, stretching for a square acre with apple trees and a magnificent magnolia bush in the far corner from the house. Under a sky of a deep and rich azure blue the family would have afternoon tea on picnic blankets on the lawn in the summer. There would be tinkling teacups and ornate spoons of silver, dishes and doilies and glasses filled with lemonade and ginger beer, Milly chasing rabbits around the lawn and carrot and walnut cake for all. It really was an existence almost frighteningly close to sublime bliss.

Everyone seemed to have a different favourite room of the house. The downstairs study was Geoff's pride and joy; he filled the endless bookcases with hundreds and hundreds of books that he collected over the years. Joy's favourite, ironically, was not the only patch that was truly hers as she loved her parents' room more than she did her own. Of all the virtues of that room it was not the extremely low window looking out over the field beyond the garden, or the wisteria crowning the outside of the wall with vast bouquets of purple blossom that almost looked like great bunches of grapes, or the sloping ceiling above the deep and soft four poster bed which enticed her so. It was not the tiny fireplace in the corner that held only a vase of sunflowers now. The room had a trapdoor that when opened revealed a white wrought iron spiral staircase, so steep that it was almost in miniature, winding down to the living room below. It was Joy's favourite place in the whole world to sit and read or think or sing or draw pictures. When any of the family couldn't find Jonathan he was sure to be in the sitting room, curled up with his dog on the sofa which was the best place to relax. Alice loved the bathroom most of all, because in Raynes Park space was at such a premium that they could not afford a house with anything more than a tiny bathroom but this one was huge. Her refuge was the very deep roll-top bath with the golden lion feet at the bottom, and the golden taps and shower attachment that she had specifically chosen because of their ability to be operated by her toes; it was the moment that she saw them when they were viewing the property that she knew that she was for the first time in her new home. The colour scheme of the room was white and gold, and Jonathan was the first to notice that this was the same as the colour scheme for the staterooms at Buckingham Palace. The bathroom floor was chequered with black and white stone, and the walls were painted the most stunningly merry and joyful midsummer yellow, and the low window and deep windowsill were positively buried behind a magnificent crumpled and billowing lace curtain that looked like the train of a wedding dress, the deep ruffles shining as the light cascaded in through the window. She saw it as her escape pod, as though the great mass of white curtain was her parachute and that she would grasp it tightly and drop serenely to Earth when her wings would ignite from flying too close to the sun. In that bathtub, sunken into the vast and womb-like cocoon of hotness, she would watch the steam rise from the surface of the water and curl gently around the spotlights in the pure white ceiling, and the as the bubbles drained off of her skin as she lifted a leg out of the water it made her look as though she were made of glass. Closing her mouth and taking a huge breath, Alice let her head slip below the surface and into the water and enjoyed the tingling sensation of the heat on the skin of her face; diving down there was like a brief voyage into the cosmos. She would keep her eyes open as she loved to see her hair streaming around her head amongst the currents and tides of her own personal ocean and then, bringing herself up and bursting through the surface of the bathwater she would feel like a glittering shooting star, exploding out in a shower of sparkling diamonds. Laughing, she found her once weightless hair plastered to her head, neck, face and shoulders in unflattering streaks and, in a secret act of thrilling recklessness, she would shake her head and spin the bun of hair like a lasso so that great strings of water would shoot across the room. She felt like a great booming firework exploding in the night sky, with sparks emblazoned against the darkness in burning droplets of water.

Geoff had always called her his Venus, his muse. He always thought that she looked like Venus Verticordia by Rossetti, with her pre-Raphaelite cascades of billowing hair and porcelain white skin. Everyone else saw merely a cottage bathroom but to Alice it was her cathedral and the roof was decorated with angels and heavenly trumpeters announcing something magnificent. Theirs was the happiest of love stories, the beautiful woman pursued and won over by her handsome stranger, and the Hewitts had been infatuated with one another ever since they had become engaged when she was nineteen and he was twenty two. He had been a wonderful husband, inventive in his ways of loving her, incredibly supportive in every way, and he took great pleasure in treating her to all manner of good things for no reason at all other than because he loved her. He adored her; they had been made for one another. He was a handsome man, taller and broader than average and strong and fit with a keen interest in playing sports. Alice particularly loved his dark hair. Married for sixteen years and with three beautiful children and a move to a dream cottage in the countryside already, life for Alice and Geoff was as wonderful as it could be.

The children had enrolled at the local school for that September, and had new uniforms to get used to; the colours of the school were red, charcoal and white, and so because Kate was fourteen years old and going into year ten she had a red blazer and a charcoal skirt, whilst Jonathan and Joy were given red jumpers because they were younger. All of the children at the school had red and black striped ties and white collared shirts. Jonathan had become a keen member of the school's football team and would stay late for practice on Wednesday evenings. This was the only day of the week that the children would not make the walk up the hill, past the church and across the village square towards their home, as a group of three.

The Wednesday in question had begun like any other. It was a beautiful day in late September, with a sky of a brilliant blue and with faint windswept cirrus high in the stratosphere, the shining dribbles on the edges gleaming like an Arabic signature. The family had all gathered at the breakfast table as normal, with Joy nattering about what Mrs Ellis was teaching them about the Romans and how much she liked the games that the girls taught her at lunchtimes. Kate had been unusually quiet over the last few months, which worried her family about how she was settling in and making new friends. Jonathan had found it all a challenge that he had risen to magnificently; he had joined in with as much as possible and his easygoing nature and sharp sense of humour had made him popular with the boys in his year-group. In the business of the breakfast gathering, with Milly barking so that nobody would forget to feed her and Geoff spreading his extremely large broadsheet newspaper over the table so that Jonathan had to threaten to empty his cereal bowl over it in order to have enough room to eat, Alice was stressed. She didn't really know why she had woken up in a bad mood, but she would be searching for answers to explain it for the rest of her life.

Joy was a clever girl but she was in equal measure blessed and cursed with a churning bottomless ocean of an imagination. At the age of seven she found concentrating on things very difficult and following a painstaking systematic routine boring and pointless. Mrs Ellis had already informed Alice, who was very keen to hear of her daughter's progress, that Joy would much rather gaze out of a window or draw doodles of characters that she had read about in books than listen to a lesson which was important for her to understand correctly. If she was interested in something that she was learning then it would undoubtedly be a success, but getting her to focus when she was unwilling was a mighty challenge.

The whole family was running late that day. Jonathan had football practice and Alice had been given the task of cleaning and packing his kit which she did just before breakfast, Geoff had a morning dental appointment to keep and Milly was well overdue to have her coat shampooed; she was starting to smell and Alice suspected fleas. She had also wanted to put another coat of paint on the wooden summerhouse at the end of the garden before winter set in, and she had clearing to do in the attic, plus there were a thousand and one things to be done to fix the plumbing in the kitchen.

Finally the time came for everyone to leave; Jonathan raced up the stairs one final time and collected his bag and put his shoes on, Kate gave her mum a hug and a kiss goodbye, Geoff tried to remember where he had left the car keys and Joy sat on the chair reading her book until Alice physically placed her bag in her hands and marched her towards the rest of her family as they waited at the door. She was telling her about an episode of a cartoon that she had seen the previous evening, whilst Alice was frantically trying to make sure that everyone had everything that they needed. They had all left half-full bowls of cereal on the table for her to clear up after them; she was the only one not leaving, so she clearly had time for all that they needed her to do.

As they got into the car, Joy opened her window and called to Alice, who was standing beneath an arch of roses at the front gate with their golden retriever standing beside her in the morning sunshine. Geoff hesitated for a moment, admiring the loveliness of his new life.

"Mummy, do you know where my copy of *The Lion the Witch and the Wardrobe* is? The one from the library at school? Mrs Ellis told me that it is overdue and that I have to give it back to her today or I will get into trouble. Could you bring it to me?"

Alice was aghast. She knew that there was no way that it could be found with so little time amongst the piles and boxes of books that scattered Joy's new bedroom, and that the upstairs of the cottage was a disorganised mess; she was sure that Joy knew that as well.

"No, Joy, I'm not doing that now. You didn't leave enough time to sort the problem out."

"Please Mummy? I don't want to get into trouble with Mrs Ellis."

Alice was getting very frustrated. "How is that my fault, Joy? You didn't think fast enough. I will try my best to find it today if I am not too busy. You need to give me time next time."

"Oh, and can you take all of my teddy bears out of the boxes and put them on my bed with Peter Rabbit? It's just him at the moment, and he is lonely."

Alice's face soured. "No, Joy, that's your job. You do it when you get home. I am not your servant and I have my own things to get done today."

Geoff told the children that they had to go, and Joy waved and kissed her Mum goodbye out of the window. "See you later, Mummy, I love you."

Alice had been waiting for the stress of the morning routine so that she could sit down for ten minutes with a nice cup of tea from her flowery Cath Kidston teapot in the garden. Bliss. She turned away from the car and headed for the house.

"I'll be here when you come home," she called, "now get out of here."

The car carried Joy far away from her mother.

*   *   *

After school Kate walked along the lane as she always had on the way back to the cottage, glancing over her shoulder occasionally to check whether or not Joy was following her. It was the most perfect late autumn day. The leaves on the trees and piling up in the lane were a rustic golden brown, and the wood of the fences, tree-trunks and gates were dappled with the scribbled texture of a nearby winter. The skies overhead, whilst filled with hot blueness and warm sunshine, had small clouds on the horizon and all of heaven was the colour of a bruised fruit. She was checking her texts from Tom, the boy who she had been thinking of for the last week and who had this morning told her that he liked her. What did he mean by that? Did he mean that she was a friend of his, or did he mean that she was not in the group of friends that he didn't like? Perhaps he was judging her reaction so that he knew whether or not asking her to be his girlfriend would be a good idea. She dreamed of the possibilities as she walked along the lane, her heels crunching against the gravel and her skin warmed by the afternoon sunshine flowing hazily through the trees. She pictured him kissing her, but rather than seeing anything in her mind's eye all she detected was the feeling, the sense of soft skin touching as though she was in complete darkness with him. As their lips met in her mind, she felt the most delicious sensation sweep up the inside of her thighs.

She looked behind her and saw that Joy was quite a long way behind, making a crown for her head from a daisy chain. She threaded them carefully and, focusing intently as she did so in the sunshine, she bit her lip and let one of her feet drag slightly behind the other as she concentrated. Her red school jumper shone against the sea of green that she floated in, the smells and quiet sounds of the meadows and fields beyond the wood filling her with a peaceful happiness.

Kate turned back to face the way she was walking. "Keep up, Joy," she called behind her as she put her earphones back in. The rhythms of her music pounded in her ears. She noticed that a man was coming towards her and he was walking extremely fast. The lane was very narrow and she had to stand to one side to let him pass. She took one earphone out as he came close to her body in the small gap between the yew tree and the fence. He smelt of hunger.

"Excuse me, which way do I need to go to get to the train station?"

It seemed like an odd question, as only three trains a day stopped at the village station; one in the morning, at lunchtime and late in the evening. Pelham Central Station was tiny, far from the mainline, frequently deserted and completely unstaffed. It had only one platform and a small covered bench to wait on, and was served by pointless and irregular Parliamentary trains. It was now between the two services which ran at the end of the day, and the stranger would have a wait of many hours. Although it was still warm, once the sun had set it would be a very cold and lonely wait. The man was extremely composed and well spoken. Along the lane, there was a gate to the churchyard, and Kate pointed to it.

"You go through the churchyard and you will come to a road; go left down the road and when you get to the end take the first left and the first right. It's about a twenty minute walk down the hill."

The traveller thanked her, gathered his greatcoat about his body and made for the gate. Kate put in her earphone and carried on her way. She dreamed of Tom again; he consumed her every thought. Would he notice her tomorrow? Was she making a fool of herself? There was something intensely thrilling about the way that in her thoughts he belonged to her and her alone, and she could do to him whatever she wished, to possess every inch of him and to unveil herself to him safe in the knowledge that, in her fantasies at least, he would be completely infatuated with her. Her thoughts landed once again in reality as a huge yellow butterfly fluttered in front of her and sank into the intense greenery of the meadow through the trees. Behind all of the metamorphosis of a young woman engaging in her glorious awakening of a body given a new use, she knew that all she wanted was to have Tom's heart above all else. The rest was a futile game, a joke with herself simply that she could think anything she liked and know nobody would find out. She wanted him to love her, to really love her, and to be bold enough to publicly claim her as his own. Kate was too shy to make statements about herself such as this but she reckoned that she was a prize worth fighting for. She wanted a boy to stun her with his romantic imagination and thoughtfulness. She wanted a boy who would love her fully with no desperate reliance upon the return she could offer him. She flicked through the music on her phone, trying to find something to match her mood, something that was an uplifting end to her day at school but that would not make her dwell on him more than was necessary should she be befallen by some unforeseen disaster.

As she came to the end of the lane where it met the village square, she turned her head to look behind her. The lane was completely empty. She scanned it in its entirety. Joy was gone.

"Joy." Kate shouted her name, but her voice seemed to be stolen by the faint afternoon breeze that wafted through the trees. She called again. Nothing. She turned, putting her phone in her pocket, and began to retrace her steps. What was this, some kind of game? "Joy." Her voice became firmer. "Where are you?" She was only greeted by silence.

*　　*　　*

Leo had been waiting at the end of the lane for hours now. He sat, crouched against a fallen tree in the row that lined the edge of the lane, peering over as he saw the small groups of people coming along the pathway in the late afternoon sunshine. He was perfectly comfortable, hiding behind the uprooted tree with the lice and maggots crawling around in the dry-rot beneath him, occasionally getting into his clothes. This tree definitely had a personality, with its humped knees on the roots and arms and thumbs and knuckles, the gnarled bark like the hide of an elephant's leg. There was something so desperately attractive to him in the smell of decay. He knew that Kate would wait for Tom so that she could say goodbye to him before he was collected from school that afternoon, and that his mother would be slightly late, because he had listened to a conversation that the two had had on the phone the previous night as Kate came home, with Leo waiting by the gate for her to come back to the cottage, listening to every word that she might say in regard to the whereabouts of her sister. Apparently her name was Joy, and she was unfathomably beautiful. He knew that the wait at the end of the lane would be long as he could pinpoint almost precisely a small window of time in which the rendezvous would take place, but the longer he was there the more his senses were heightened. His mouth watered at the prospect of her fragrant, delicate white skin. As he pictured her small arms wrapped around his body he felt an intense rush of ecstatic pleasure, a delicious flutter in his belly. He sat alone, quite still and isolated, pleasuring himself on technicolour fantasies, letting his mind run away with cinematic splendour. Every minute detail concerning colour and texture and sensation was planned out very carefully in his mind and had been for years; within moments the reality could begin.

Then he saw it; a pinprick of red across the green meadow, heading for the lane and coming very slowly towards Leo, like a speck of blood on a seamstress' finger. It was a human, a person; Leo's mouth widened into a smile as the form coming towards him became identifiable as his prey, and the corners of his mouth curled upwards as though it was a cheese knife. The tension inside of him climaxed to an almost unbearably pleasurable level, and his heart thudded violently inside of his chest as he anticipated the excitement that was to come. The butterflies in his stomach flew faster and stronger than ever and as he climbed to his feet his legs became weak with hungry passion. He could barely fathom what was coming. He walked along the lane as fast as he could without running. He let his mind soar away from him as it dreamed incessantly of a compartmentalised anatomy; of elbows and fingers and thumbs and toenails and knuckles and hair and ears and, finally, the remainder. That magnificent, wonderful remainder.

With a jolt that felt like an electric shock, he stopped. It wasn't her. He had made a mistake; instead he was confronted by Kate, coming towards him and fiddling with her phone. She looked up at him and caught him full in the face with her eyes; she must have suspected something. She was definitely onto him and he felt like Icarus, dragged from the skies in his prime and breathlessly torn down to Earth in flames. Wasn't Joy always the one to walk on ahead of her sister? He had assumed that Kate would not suspect anything because it would look as though Joy was slightly ahead of her all the way home, and by the time anyone noticed the two of them would be well on the way to a romantic honeymoon of euphoria. Panicked and shocked, he tried to compose himself and regulate his heavy and fast breathing. She took out her earphone and moved to one side of the lane, looking at him and clearly inviting him to speak to her. He beheld her and felt repulsed; the sickening adolescent skin under her white shirt and red blazer and, going deeper before he could help himself, he saw her legs beneath her school socks and the disgusting final location of any sexual fantasy. For a second, he felt physically ill at the thought of an adult male making love to an adult female; the idea of conceiving a foetus inside of a female body made his stomach churn like dough being mixed in a bowl by a wooden spoon. Forcing the foul thoughts from his mind, he swallowed hard, concentrating with all his might on sounding natural and calm whilst never giving up on what he had come here for. Weeks of work, hours of waiting would all come down to a few seconds, maybe less, of pure and fragile opportunity.

He made up some preposterous question about the train station. He knew that she didn't buy it, but he was too proud to drop his pretence. His heart was pounding the whole time. She directed him towards a gate, put her earphone back in and carried on forwards, her grey school skirt tight against her vile womanly buttocks, swaying as she walked.

And then he saw her.

With a rising sense of emotion in his heart, he beheld little Joy. She was more beautiful than he had ever imagined a human being could possibly be, the very personification of innocence and heavenly, matchless loveliness. Her teeth were freshwater pearls, her eyes were vast oceans that he swam and dived for starfish in and her hair was the meadow behind her, the grasses swaying restlessly and as clearly as if each strand was crafted from solid gold. Her skin was completely blemishless, as wholesome and faultless as a hymn sheet from which he would sing proudly. She was like a cherub from the painting on the ceiling of the Sistine Chapel, her skin shimmering with the gloss of tangerine gold and her whole being infused with the fragrance of abundant life. He ignored the virginal red school jumper and the charcoal plaited skirt, but instead saw her robed in a miniature wedding dress, with none of the polluted corruption of a woman, a virgin bride laid out for him on a platter of fresh flowers of the meadow, all encased beneath a silver dome which he alone could lift up and enter into. He gazed on her in love as he hurried towards her and, swimming in the never-ending sea of his affections and hunger for Joy, he threw himself back and let the pounding waves crash over him, not caring whether or not he would drown. He was so happy that he thought he was about to burst into tears as all of his dreams came true at the same time; love overwhelmed him completely.

She raised her head to look at him as he approached her and as she held the incomplete daisy chain in her hand, she opened her mouth to speak. Leo slammed his entire left fist into her mouth to silence her and used his right to hold her firmly by the shoulder and lift her to the gate to the churchyard, his fingers in an iron like grip which dug very deeply into the skin of her shoulder. Before he lifted her feet from the track she dragged and scuffed the gravel which made a trail and a quiet sound. Just before they disappeared into the gap in the ancient, tangled hedgerow he glanced for a split second back at Kate to make sure that she had not waited for Joy; she was walking along and facing away from them, listening to her music and daydreaming. The plan had worked, it was unfortunate that she had seen his face but he now had his prize and all that it meant was that he would work harder to leave Higher Pelham with no trace as soon as the job was done. He had considered doing it in the lane but there was no correctness, no sense of sentimentality to that; no, instead he would do it where she could be his and his alone, for she was too beautiful to be shared. He wanted to dignify her with some privacy.

Joy's lip was bleeding and she had lost a tooth from the punch. Her eyes blazed with fear and terror, and as soon as he found a dense thicket of trees on the boundary of the churchyard, he drank in the euphoria of his orgasmic triumph. With his hands trembling from delighted passion he placed his right behind her ear and his left on her jaw and snapped her head anticlockwise as hard as he could.

Now, finally, it could begin. He felt as though the glitter of a shooting star flowed through his veins and that his spine was made from a single bolt of lightning. There would be no more resisting, no more waiting, no more shame. Joy belonged to him now.

2 THE DAWN OF DARKNESS

As soon as the little girl was confirmed to be missing and the search party had been deployed, the investigation into what had happened to her had to be given access to the very heart of her family and her home in an attempt to understand where she may have gone. The detective assigned to the case was a man named Albert Fish, and Jonathan noticed that he was extraordinarily tall. It was quite a shock to come home from football practice after being collected by his father to find the detective in his house and rumours from Kate of his sister being taken by someone. Fish had hollowed out eyes and a bristly moustache, and a manner of interrogation whenever he spoke, even to accept Geoff's offer of a cup of tea. He was accompanied by two police officers whenever he came into contact with the family and they had gone as far as to cordon off Magnolia Cottage as a crime scene because this would protect the privacy of the residents and attempt to preserve the house exactly as it had been when Joy disappeared. Jonathan and Kate would not be going to school in the morning, that was already decided, and they hoped that she would be found quickly and unharmed so that their new life in Higher Pelham could continue without delay.

The detective seemed especially concerned with Alice as she had been alone in the house when Joy had vanished.

"What happened this morning, Mrs Hewitt?"

"We all had breakfast together as usual, my husband had a dental appointment to keep so he drove the children to school and I stayed here."

"And that was the last time that you saw her alive?"

Alice paused. With a stomach churning horror she went back to that morning in her head and revisited the final words that she ever said to her daughter. Joy had told her that she loved her, and then vanished forever. But she could not let her bad mood that she had woken up with sound suspicious.

"Yes, that was the last time I saw her." Alice suddenly became indignant. "Everyone else in the family saw her after I did, so maybe the others would be more helpful to your investigation, especially Kate. Kate claims that she saw the man who took Joy."

"I will come to her in good time, Mrs Hewitt; at the moment I am dealing with you."

"But I have already told you everything that I know."

"I understand that you are new to the village, and that you are originally from South London."

"Yes we are."

"Do you consider your family to be popular in the village? Are you well liked, and are you an integral part of the community? Is there anyone here who would have any ill feeling towards you or your children?"

"No. Nobody. We have settled in very well."

"And this is the first time that Joy has run away?"

Alice was aghast. "She hasn't run away, detective, she has been abducted by a man who wants to sexually assault her and murder her."

Detective Fish's eyes widened. Alice's desperation was obvious.

"Kate, if I could come to you quickly; did you ever actually see with your own eyes the man in the lane touching your sister?"

"No sir."

He turned back to Alice. "You see my dilemma. We have no evidence whatsoever that she was taken by anyone and we have no indication of whether or not she is held captive or is dead. We only know that she is not here and she should be here. Now, if we could please focus on what we do know without speculation; has there been a problem with your marriage recently? Any arguments? Was there anything between yourself and Mr Hewitt that would make Joy uncomfortable with living here?"

Alice was scolding in the tone of her reply. "That's ridiculous. She is seven; she's not some moody teenager who is rebelling against us by running away. She has been taken and is being held captive by a paedophile. Our marriage is perfectly happy and we have no problems at all."

"And you are sure that she has never run away from home before? No problems of alcoholism or violence between the two of you, either against each other or your children?"

"That's not relevant."

"Mrs Hewitt, you are not cooperating with my questioning as I had hoped you would. I understand that you are distressed by the disappearance of your daughter but you really must answer my questions with direct answers. Has she ever run away from home before?"

Alice raised her voice and began to shout at him angrily. "I am offended, Detective Fish. How dare you come into my home and ask me such inappropriate, irrelevant and stupid questions! If you want to prove to me that you actually intend to find my daughter, I think you had better ask Kate what she saw."

He scribbled some notes in his book, checked that the Dictaphone on the coffee table was still recording and invited her to sit down in her mother's place.

"I need you to describe him to me as best you can. Everything that is relevant, everything he said to you if he spoke."

"He was taller than me; I would say about 5'8". He was wearing a black coat, very long, which seemed odd on a warm afternoon. It was soft, not leather, and he had a hat on. I think he did, I think he had a hat on. He had blue eyes and he had stubble all over his face. I don't really remember the shirt but I think it was white. We met in the lane and he asked me the way to the train station on the hillside. I pointed through the churchyard, and told him the way he needed to go. When I next looked round he and Joy had both disappeared."

"Was anything suspicious until you noticed that they had disappeared?"

"Yes, he was walking very fast towards me. When he saw that I was looking at him he stopped dead. The question about the train station didn't really make sense at that time of day, and he wasn't carrying anything so he couldn't have been going far."

"Thank you. Alice, one more question for you, if I may. Is this the first time you have lost a child?"

Every muscle in Alice's body went cold and the cells in her bloodstream had the thrilling sensation of pieces of crushed ice.

"Yes, Detective."

"No other children have been harmed in your family? No others have died in your care?"

"No, Detective."

"Then would you mind explaining to me why you failed to respond to a direct question by telling me that you and your husband suffered a cot death of a young son before Joy was born? I have seen your medical and criminal records, Mrs Hewitt. I know that you had a second son, David, and he died at the age of approximately two days in suspicious circumstances."

*   *   *

David's heartbeat of a life had marked Alice's real transition into adulthood. Grief is not a competition, but in some way a stillborn or deceased newborn child trumps everything because there are no happy memories to look back on with a smile. Instead there was a vast and gaping hole in Alice's heart as she constantly strived for something which she could never have, something that might have been and something that should have been. But David became instead something that never was, and Alice and

Geoff were grieving for someone they did not know. He had been born perfectly healthily and with a good birth-weight but two days into his life his heart simply stopped beating. Nobody knew why and whilst they were still determining the cause of death the Hewitts had been questioned by social services before being given counselling. David was cremated as a victim of Sudden Infant Death Syndrome. Alice and Geoff had been traumatised by the questioning and they knew that this had led them to have a particular hatred for interrogation. What was everyone's problem; why did they jump to the conclusion that the parents would harm their own precious children?

Some time later Alice received a call on her mobile phone from a number that she did not recognise, and she assumed that it would be the police bringing news of them finding Joy. This would be important news, whether that was good or bad. She answered, and it was Matthew Brady, the editor in chief of the *Envoy*, the most popular tabloid newspaper publication in Britain at the time.

"How did you get my number?"

"I was contacted by a source who claimed to be your mother, Mrs Hewitt. I am very aware of the sensitivity with which your family must be treated at this time and I am very sorry for any offence that may have been caused in my contacting you, but I have an offer to make you."

Alice was slightly taken aback at his boldness and the speed with which he struck up a conversation; his voice had an extraordinary warmth to it, and he sounded as though he had been a family friend for a lifetime. He was very softly spoken and Alice did not notice that he was pushing an agenda until she began to listen to the words he was using. It did not sound anything like a business deal, but she knew that it was.

"I am not going to sell my story. The answer is no."

"Wait. That's not what I meant. No, Mrs Hewitt, I am prepared to offer some money to be put up as a reward in exchange for information about your daughter's disappearance. If it leads to her safe return we will be prepared to be very generous to the people who know where she is."

She motioned for Geoff to come and join her and she switched the handset to speakerphone so that he could hear, and then continued.

"What do you mean by 'very generous', Mr Brady?"

"Our reward would be up to two million pounds if the information given leads directly to Joy being returned to her family safely, and up to one million pounds if it leads directly to the conviction of those responsible if it turns out that she has been abducted and killed."

A silence cloaked them both as they huddled around the phone. It was the dreadful mathematics of death, and they were both profoundly disturbed by the fact that he had factored into his calculations the fact that she could be dead, and what that would mean in financial terms. It was very sobering to think that everything about their little girl had a monetary value, and that her brains and bones and muscles and blood and hair and skin and jellies and glues and tubes and veins and organs were valued in finite amounts of cold hard cash. If this crime was a theft, her stolen life and virginity had now been reduced to commodities.

"I would like to remind you both that this is the biggest reward that has ever been offered by a British tabloid in return for information about a crime. We care very much about the safety of this nation's children and we would like to do what we can to speed up the judicial process. We ask only in return that we would be publicly identified as the donors of the reward fund, nothing else. No funny business, no tricks. We just want to be a part of your fight to get her back. My publication stands up for the rights of parents to protect their children and we want to prove that to the nation by standing by you the whole way and giving you as much support as you want and need. We believe that our offer would be very tempting for a friend or relative of the kidnapper and that they would be very likely to do the right thing and turn in the guilty perpetrator."

Geoff and Alice agreed to call him back, and deliberated over the decision for some time. Alice was seeing a new side of her husband that she was not familiar with; he was so gentle in her memory, but now he was agitated with a hunger for justice and a subtly hidden desire for revenge against the person who had put them through the most unbearable suffering.

*   *   *

Out in the churchyard, some of the sniffer dogs had come across a freshly moved section of earth in amongst the headstones. Detective Fish had initially thought that it was a recent burial in an assigned grave but when the vicar was called to identify the most recent plots to be disturbed they had a dreadful dawning of realisation that it was not a plot that had been marked out by the gravediggers. With some of the search party holding lanterns above the diabolical scar in the ground which was beneath them, they identified it as a possible resting place for the girl they were searching for and the workers began the morbid duty of starting to dig. It was a gloomy, richly Gothic sight to behold; a churchyard, in the dead of night, with only the antique glow of the lanterns and the silvery shimmer of a full moon to illuminate the fresh soil. The ravens were rustling in the foliage. This was no place for a child to die.

She revealed her secrets around two feet below the surface, with her back to the sky. She was naked, wrapped up in a huge black coat, and the clothes were not buried with or near the body. She was the colour of steel, and she had pieces of soil under her fingernails and eyelids and embedded in her golden blonde hair. The rescuers were stunned by the completeness of the corpse and the way in which it had not decayed at all after being buried in the soil for one hundred hours. Gently the workers raised her out of her grave and Detective Fish touched her on the leg. She was as cold as stone. The whole thing was emotionally exhausting and tragic beyond belief; a seven year old girl, in the prime of her childhood, butchered by a madman for his own sick ends. It was clearly murder, for there was a lot of damage to the neck and some finger-marks on the face. The first conclusion they came to upon seeing her was that she had been violently strangled.

They lay her down on an old tarpaulin and began a brief process of identification using a DNA testing kit. They had been given access to Joy's dental records by the family and all of the Hewitts had taken blood tests and swabs from the inside of their cheeks to help with the process of identification. They also performed some toxicology tests on her flesh to determine whether or not she had had been preserved by chemicals which kept her body so intact.

The hour was late. Back at Magnolia Cottage the phone rang, a hollow drilling against the still silence of the cottage. It pierced through the atmosphere like a bullet from a gun, and Alice and Geoff both felt their hearts skip a beat. Their eyes met, and they both took a few shallow, long breaths; both knew what was coming and understood that the moment that they hoped would never come had arrived. Alice thought of her daughter's face, of Joy's infectious smile and how her eyes used to sparkle like fireworks. They had been expecting dozens of phone-calls from their friends and family offering comfort and support, but they had also been expecting a far more gruesome call and by some mystical telepathy they were both absolutely certain that they knew that the time had come. This was it. Alice walked into the kitchen and slowly reached for the telephone receiver.

"Hello?"

"Mrs Hewitt?"

Alice swallowed hard.

"Yes. It's me."

"Mrs Hewitt this is Detective Fish. We have found your daughter." There was a silence which seemed to last forever. "I am very sorry."

Every muscle in Alice's body seized up. She closed her eyes and she dropped the phone with a clatter on the flagstone kitchen floor. Alice let out a cry from the depth of her gut which spoke clearer than words could of the moment that her very soul was split down the middle. The cry was long, loud and extremely deep, wrenching her stomach and sounding as though her bowels were being wrung out like a wet dishcloth. Geoff, having been able to deduce exactly what had happened, ran into the kitchen and he held her tightly as she sobbed and screamed until the colour began to drain from her lips. They just stood there, held together in a tight embrace in the kitchen of Magnolia Cottage, as little Jonathan looked between the wooden slats of the banister, out of the sight of his parents. He knew little of what had happened and yet it was an inescapable truth that his sister had been killed by an unspeakably evil human being who had single handedly ruined their small slice of Utopia.

Jonathan watched as he saw his father pick up the phone again, check that it wasn't damaged, and call Detective Fish back. Alice could not stand the pressure of the wait for news of her daughter's fate and simply wanted to hide away from the truth, but Geoff wanted to know straight away exactly what had happened to her.

"Detective Fish? This is Geoff Hewitt."

"Mr Hewitt, hello. May I take this opportunity to offer you my condolences at this difficult time."

"Thank you, sir. Have you found the body?"

"Yes, Mr Hewitt, we have."

"What happened to her? I want to know everything that you know."

Albert took a deep breath. "We found the body approximately fifteen minutes ago and used a portable DNA kit to identify her, which is not very accurate but we can tell you that we are as sure as we can be that it is her and there are no other females in this area who we would be looking for at this time. The body of any child we find is probably her, but the DNA does appear to match. The body was found in the grounds of St George's church in the village. We know that your daughter sustained sexual injuries and that the body was disturbed several times after it was buried."

Geoff sounded composed and calm, but inside he was breaking.

"How do you think he killed her?"

"We are still working on that investigation but she has some bad damage to her neck. The spinal cord looks like it is severed and there is major damage to the muscle tissue of her collar area. It looks probable that the method of murder was either a very violent strangulation, or she may have been hanged. Other than her genitals, we don't think she has any other notable serious injuries."

"And the body was found intact?"

"Yes Mr Hewitt, there were no decapitations, mutilations, that kind of thing. If you are asking whether or not she was raped, I am afraid that we have found evidence of a sexual motive for the attack. She is in very good condition considering the amount of time she was buried for. We are working on the assumption that it was an attempted rape and that she struggled or screamed, so the attacker panicked. He may not even have intended to kill her. We have very little to go on as there has been little time since the discovery but we are assuming that the attacker saw her as more of a lover than a murder victim. He has profound psychological issues, we can see that already."

By morning Higher Pelham and the surrounding area was filled with journalists. The police had cordoned off the grounds of the church and there were seven police cars parked around the tiny village square; there was a tent which was visible from the lane erected over the place where they had found the body, a brilliant white stain on the reputation of Higher Pelham that would never be removed, and a reminder of the innocence and virginity that had been stolen from Joy in that place. One of the fields of the village was taken over by vans with satellite dishes and aerials on the top of them, broadcasting images of the crime scene around the nation and the world. The police continued their investigations and hours and hours passed as they deliberated on who may be responsible. It was an agonising time for the Hewitt family.

*   *   *

There was a knock at the door of the cottage, and Geoff rushed to open it to see who it was; perhaps they had caught him. It was Detective Fish.

"May I come in, Sir?"

Geoff obliged and invited him and the two policemen into the living room. As he held the door open, he noticed that the police car outside still had the blue flashing lights turned on.

"Where is your wife, Mr Hewitt?"

The sternness in his voice took Geoff by surprise. He had expected sympathy, but he was met with a wall of sharp coldness. He looked at the detective blankly, and so he explained what he had come for.

"There is something else that I have to question her about. It is extremely urgent and I need your full cooperation."

Alice was upstairs, trying to find a cake tin that was the right size for the Victoria sponge that she was going to bake for the children. Geoff stood at the bottom of the staircase and called up to her, asking her to come down and saying that the police had arrived. The group of men could hear rummaging and finally she emerged, looking so utterly magnificent as she descended the staircase that Geoff honestly thought for a split second that she would declare to them all that she was ready for her close up, and that the policemen were not policemen at all but instead a throng of adoring fans.

She offered the men a cup of tea, as this had been such a regular occurrence throughout the last few days that she thought that nothing they could say would shock her. They all firmly declined; obviously they were not planning to stay in the cottage long. Alice smiled at them sweetly. "You're early, boys," she purred, "perhaps if you came back in a few hours I would have found this cake tin and we could all share it together." Even Geoff thought that this behaviour, considering that she had so recently been told that her daughter had been murdered, was incredibly bizarre and out of character. For the first time in their marriage Geoff Hewitt wondered if his wife was keeping a secret from him. Detective Fish ignored her and, confused, she walked towards him as he prepared to say something that he had obviously said countless times before.

"Alice Hewitt . . ." She could feel the solid anger in his voice. He sounded almost hurt, angry that he had been stupid enough to be deceived. Why was he using both of her names? She sat down on the sofa before she was invited to. "I am arresting you on suspicion of the murder of Joy Hewitt on 27th September." She was dumbfounded, paralysed with shock for a few seconds. She felt a rising panic clamour over her as Fish's assistants approached her and pulled handcuffs out of their pockets. "You have the right to remain silent, but it may harm your defence if you fail to mention when questioned something that you later come to rely on in court." One of them wrenched her hand as he pulled it up towards him, and with an abhorrent sense of smothering finality they attached the brutally heavy silver bracelet to her wrist, twisting her arm around to clamp her wrists together behind her back. Alice was no longer listening, and instead was sobbing and crying out in pain, and Geoff was loudly protesting her innocence behind the men. "Anything that you do tell us may be used as evidence against you."

As they led her to the door Geoff ran behind, frustrated by his own helplessness. He demanded to know on what evidence they had detained her, but they told him nothing. Alice felt a heavy hand on the back of her head, pushing her to a crouch and forcing her into the back of the car. She shot a desperate glance at her husband as she sat inside in the split second before they slammed the door, wishing she could run up to him and throw her arms around him again. He stood with Milly, holding her by the collar as she began barking and growling ferociously at the policemen, her husband and her dog filling the doorway to the cottage that she had always dreamed of living in; the roses that had billowed around the archway so beautifully during the summer were starting to die. The car took Alice far away from her husband.

Because the village was so small the nearest police station which had a suitable cell was a considerable distance away. She asked them what was happening throughout the journey down the narrow country lanes but they didn't answer her once, saying that they would explain when they arrived. Handcuffed and helpless, she stared out of the window of the car with tears streaming down her cheeks, thinking of Joy and of the fugitive who was on the run and looked likely to avoid justice for his crime.

*   *   *

When they arrived at the station, Alice was taken into a room to be interrogated further. She was provided with an attorney by the state because she had told them that she could not afford one; the reality was that she was so sure that the case would fall through that she did not see why she should waste her own money providing herself with one. She was asked to sit at a table with her lawyer; Detective Fish and his assistant sat on the opposite side. Alice Hewitt was experienced in grief, and her reaction was just the same as it had been with David almost a decade before as the initial shock and agonising sadness gave way to a violent anger. She knew that they did not deserve this and that it was outrageous for her to be questioned again. Back then she had hated pregnant women with a blazing passion and now she hated little girls and their mothers because she knew that she deserved what they had but that her shot at glory had come to nothing. She looked at the detective and the lawyers sitting with her with their steely faces and she hated them too. The room was sterile and sparse, with white tiles and a throbbing, harsh strip light on the ceiling. Alice did not wait for Fish to speak first.

"You have to explain to me all of the evidence which you have seen that made you think this was a good idea."

"Alright, Mrs Hewitt, that is quite enough of that. I will explain."

"Is there something wrong with your head, Detective? I didn't do it. Catherine has provided you with a detailed description. You need to be chasing him, not wasting your time on me. Every minute I spend here with you the killer gets further away."

Fish took a sinister tone, and leaned forwards over the desk. He did not have to shout.

"Catherine is not the only witness that we have received a testimony from."

Alice was confused. "But she was the only one with Joy when she disappeared."

Fish smiled at her. "Only if you assume that we accept what you have told us as the complete truth. And, Mrs Hewitt, I'm afraid we don't."

Fish went on to tell her exactly what had happened in the investigation so far. He had been greatly moved by the tragic stories of Alice and Catherine, but the other villagers had been less rosy in their descriptions of what had gone on that afternoon. Sixteen different people had claimed that they had seen Alice Hewitt sprinting barefoot across the square in early evening towards the crime scene, and four of those claimed that she had been carrying a knife in her hand when they had seen her. Mr West who lived next door had been out trimming his roses when Geoff had driven the children to school that morning and he had claimed that Alice had a malicious tone in her voice when she spoke to Joy, and that getting to know her over the summer he had detected a side of her character which was impatient and angry. Others had accused her of shouting at the children when she was shopping with them on the high street or at the village market. Alice was deeply troubled, not only by the daunting task before her of verbally fighting her way out of a corner but also of the fact that the sheer adoration that she felt for her children, the amount that she cherished each of them, seemed to have gone completely unnoticed by a cruel and judgemental local community whom she had wrongly assumed would be on her side.

She was held in the cell overnight, and it was the longest and bleakest night of her whole life. She barely slept as the barred night looked in on her. In the morning the station received a phone call from the police force in Higher Pelham. An arrest had been made, as a man was found trying to board a train out of Pelham Central who exactly matched the description that had been given to them by Kate. A fellow traveller declared that he had seen him fleeing the churchyard and discarding a heavy shovel in a meadow of long, swaying grass. The man, a twenty eight year old named Leonard Faulkner, was eventually caught hiding in a sewage hole in the ground a short distance from the main road and confessed to the murder upon his arrest, claiming that the escape attempt was a game of cat and mouse with the police which had given him enormous pleasure. They had summoned Kate to an identity parade at dawn, and she had picked the suspect five consecutive times in a row amongst actors and with the order constantly changing. She was not even fooled when they removed him altogether twice in a row and gave her a line up of innocent men. They looked as though they had caught their man, and he was swiftly charged with the murder and rape and Alice was free to go.

That evening Alice had a bath to calm herself down. She tried her best to make it as peaceful and relaxing as possible, with a double helping of lavender bubble bath and a big bath bomb to ease the nerves. She put candles around the floor of the bathroom, some of them scented, and turned out the lights so that the whole room glowed with the ambience of candlelight. Dipping her toe into the water, she breathed out deeply as she felt the hotness wrap itself around her feet.

Alice felt herself sinking into the bathtub, not wanting to reach the bottom and feeling a wrenching disappointment when her spine came into contact with the solid enamel base. She tried to plunge her head beneath the surface of the crystal waters and lose herself for a few seconds amongst the stars but somehow now that Joy was gone the weightlessness seemed to have lost its sparkle and the constellations and orbiting planets eluded the reach of her fingertips.

Once she was in the bath she felt that the candlelight which seemed like such a good idea as she was filling the tub now gave the whole bathroom, her favourite room in their dream cottage, the wretched aroma of a shrine in a funeral parlour. Everywhere she could see the disintegration and fragility of the mortal human body, the vibrant pulsing hue of death. In the bathtub she ran a finger down her abdomen until she came to the scene of the crime on her daughter's body, where her virginity and femininity had been abhorrently stolen from her and which was now filled with chemicals to stop the folds of skin and flesh being overcome with grave worms writhing and wriggling beneath the surface. The great billowing ruffled curtain in the window which reminded her so much of her bridal triumph now became instead resplendent of the lilies that would surround Joy's absurdly small coffin on a dreadful day. Even in the steaming hot water laced with lavender bubbles, her skin felt cold at the thought of her beloved dying in a lonely churchyard and being left there rather than being back, safe and warm in her bedroom at Magnolia Cottage where she belonged.

As she climbed into the four poster bed that she shared with Geoff, it seemed smaller than she had remembered it and the sleeping form of her husband, gently rising and falling to the rhythm of his breath, seemed closer to her than she had expected. She climbed beneath the sheets and rested her head on the pillow next to him; his fragrance filled the whole room, but he was facing away, silhouetted very faintly against the dim moonlight coming through the window. Higher Pelham was dark.

Unsurprisingly, sleep eluded her. Rolling and tossing and turning like some doomed ship on a stormy sea, Alice could not get comfortable and get her mind away from the horrors that had befallen her wonderful and beautiful little girl. It was unfathomable to her that Joy was dead and gone, and she found the finality of it all so chilling. When sleep did eventually come, the dreams were filled with the ghoulish spectre of death. In one of them there was a happy scene where Alice was bathing Joy as a young toddler, perhaps two years old, her golden hair splashing around in the water, laughing and shrieking as the water covered her face in a picture of joy in Rosevine Road in Raynes Park. Joy would urge her on, encouraging her to drench her again with the jug, scooping up the bathwater and unleashing it all over her little face. They sped up, getting faster and faster and more and more agitated in their movements which every time would be an exact repetition of the one before, as though they were not humans at all but instead clockwork robots. Alice had just dumped the jug all over her and went to fill it again, all the while looking at Joy's eyes and not the hand that she was using to fill it with, but when she brought it back to splash her again it was not a jug at all but an electric kettle full to the brim with boiling water. Before she had time to react the clockwork had taken over, the key in her back involuntarily and mechanically spinning slowly and she poured the entire kettle full all over Joy's smiling face. She screamed loudly as the pain sank into her, beneath the skin and muscle and blood, right down so that even her bones were wet. She shrieked, but this time it was from agonising trauma rather than joy, throwing her neck in circles, spinning her head from side to side in a hopeless attempt to somehow shake the heat away from her. The scalding hot steam from the kettle rose gradually and touched Alice's hand, searing through the skin, causing her so much virtual pain that she could feel herself thrashing around in her bed, causing her to drop the kettle into the bathtub. As the plug and the wire hit the water the whole bath now became a shower of sparks and lightning bolts as Joy's body was electrocuted and the skin began to singe and fry. She looked at her daughter's face and it was blistered from the first injury from the kettle, and it bubbled and swelled beyond recognition as she screamed and shouted. Geoff had heard the commotion from downstairs and she could hear him sprinting up, battering the locked door until it eventually swung open. His face fell as he saw the scene laid out before him, his wife kneeling beside the tub and their daughter's char-grilled and blackened corpse, quiet and still, burnt to a cinder in the bath. "What have you done to her?" His voice trembled with shock and disbelief, but also with grief and love. Kate and Jonathan followed him into the bathroom, followed by Mrs Ellis and Alice and Geoff's families, and then by the villagers of Higher Pelham, and then following them were the judges and a jury and the media. Their bathroom was filled with hundreds and hundreds of people, all of them saying the same thing in unison, "what have you done to her?" Soon it was no longer a bathroom at all but more like a vast Roman amphitheatre with grandstands filled with crowds, all of them staring down at Alice and the bathtub. "What have you done to her?" Alice began to shout her innocence at them, tears streaming down her cheeks, shouting and screaming the same line over and over and over again. "I love her. I love her. I love her . . ." She looked back at the bathtub behind her and saw that it was filled with ash and fading sparks, and Joy was gone forever.

She sat upright in her bed, in the middle of the night, trembling and agitated from her heart right down to her fingertips, crying uncontrollably and breathless with shock. In her nightdress she had to get up and walk over to the window, to crouch down and look out over the view and see the stars blazing far above. It was all perfectly still, as distinctive as if engraved on silver. Everything was silent: the hillside that led down towards the river; the fields behind their cottage; the fences and hedgerows and their own lawns with the apple trees in the corner of the plot which the children so loved to pick from and use the fruit to play cricket with. The whole serenity of the garden and the stars seemed to relentlessly mock Alice as though the scene was tormenting her with its peacefulness. The moon was full, sending streams of steel ribbon through the trees and the thatched rooftops of their neighbours were perfectly still and hushed in a deathly silence. It was ghostly.

The next morning, Alice received another telephone call. The woman introduced herself as Valerie Whiting, His Britannic Majesty's Secretary of State for Justice and Human Rights, and she had a warm, strong voice. She was calling from her offices in Whitehall, and said that she had learnt of the arrest and that she was personally offering her sympathy on behalf of the Home Secretary for the mistake by the police force. Mrs Whiting had offered a substantial amount of compensation for the inconvenience as this was turning into an extremely high profile case, and also to ask her of any conversations that she may have had with a man named Matthew Brady. Alice told her that he had offered up a million pound reward in exchange for information that would lead directly to a successful conviction, but the Secretary responded immediately to tell her that was not what she had meant.

"Did he say anything to you about the restoration of the death penalty in the UK? Anything at all?"

Alice was stunned. "No, madam Secretary, he did not."

"He has told me that he is planning to put a petition on the *Envoy* website that will call for the criminal to be the first person in this country to be executed for his crime since Allen, Evans and West on 13th August 1964. The death penalty was formally abolished for all crimes including treason and piracy in 1998 in line with a human rights treaty in the European Union. From February 2004 the UK has been required to leave the Council of Europe in order to reinstate capital punishment. If successful, the campaign Brady is planning will lead to a Bill being presented to Parliament to vote on and if passed by both the House of Commons and the House of Lords, the murderer will be put to death."

"He will be presenting a Bill in Parliament? He's a journalist, can he do that?"

"No, Mrs, Hewitt, the Bill will be presented by a Member of Parliament who supports it, usually a Cabinet Minister. I am calling firstly to let you know, as my fears that he may not have told you turned out to be correct, and also to gauge whether or not you would support a Bill if it ends up coming to that. I believe that it is currently recorded in opinion polls that seventy per cent of the public are in favour of child killers being executed for their crimes."

"Madam Secretary, is there a Cabinet Minister who would be prepared to support a campaign for execution?"

An uncomfortable silence clogged the phone line like tar; Alice could not see Mrs Whiting, but she could tell that she was thumbing her pearl necklace and looking out of the window at the Cenotaph, trying to build courage.

"Yes, Mrs Hewitt. The Bill would be presented by me."

                    *   *   *

Detective Fish had told them that the trial of Leo Faulkner was so high profile that it would have to take place in London at the Old Bailey, and Brady had already clamoured to offer Geoff and Alice hotel accommodation for the duration of the court proceedings. The following day they received an extraordinarily gracious telephone call from Daniel Huntley, the Prime Minister, saying that he understood that the case would be a historic one and that he would very much like them to come to Downing Street when they were in London so that he could offer his personal condolences.

The date came around fast and three days before the trial was due to begin Jonathan and Milly went to stay with Geoff's sister in Bristol. Alice, Geoff and Kate all went to London on the train, their first class tickets a gift from Brady, and Kate and Alice had never travelled first class before. It was a surreal experience to be making the return journey from the one that they had made in a car, following a removal van down country lanes on the last day in May, as a family of four once again. They got off the train at Waterloo and took the Jubilee Line two stops westbound to Green Park, and found their way to the Mayfair Hotel on Stratton Street. There were gleaming black limousines on the road outside and uniformed footmen opening the doors for them; the lobby of the hotel was a palatial sea of polished black and cream stone. Their rooms were beautiful, extremely modern in their decoration and very different to the idyllic tradition of Higher Pelham, and on the dressing table hotel staff had left a bouquet of flowers and some champagne on ice, with a card signed by all of the staff giving their condolences after the bereavement.

The purpose of their visit to London only truly sank in when they received a call from Reception saying that the Prime Minister's limousine was downstairs and was ready to collect them and take them to dinner. Geoff looked at his wife and pondered for a second the remarkable journey that they had embarked upon. "Are you ready, darling?" She looked into the mirror and adjusted her diamond earrings. "Yes. I'm ready." The car whisked them along Piccadilly in the darkness towards the shimmering neon of Piccadilly Circus, and then down Haymarket and Trafalgar Square where Horatio Nelson reached high into the deep violet sky, finally turning down Whitehall towards Big Ben in the distance and turning in through the armour plated gates onto Downing Street. There was a large crowd of people outside, and an explosion of flashbulbs greeted them as they stepped out of the car and onto the pavement outside the most famous front door in the world. Alice was keen to head straight inside but Geoff allowed himself a split second to listen to what the gathered crowd of journalists were shouting at him.

"Mr Hewitt, how do you react to the rumours that Leonard Faulkner will be executed if he is found guilty?"

"Mr Hewitt do you think that the justice system has failed your daughter?"

"Mr Hewitt should the Prime Minister resign if the law is not changed?"

He was taken aback by the nature of the questions. How big would this case become, and how deep would the division in opinion eventually grow? Surely the death of his daughter was a terrible personal tragedy but little more, and he was shocked that this event would turn into a political storm.

Downing Street was exactly as they had imagined it. The three terraced houses, interconnected by countless passageways and corridors, a vast and sometimes incoherent jumble of awkwardly arranged rooms which did not seem to follow any order of logic, architecture that seemed to have spawned and grown rather than being designed and built as a tangible whole. The policeman opened the door for them on the inside and his colleague guarding the door to the street turned to Alice. "Mrs Hewitt, welcome to Downing Street." Inside stood Daniel Huntley, and he commanded their reverence and respect before he had spoken a word. He was young; elected at forty five, a charismatic and youthful injection into the Conservative Party that had been badly needed and he was an outstanding orator who was famous for making rousing speeches across the world. He was also the first Afro Caribbean Prime Minister and because his wife Charlotte was Caucasian they were the first mixed race family to reside in Downing Street in the country's history. He had been accused by Brady of playing on the black vote and they had run the controversial election night headline of "Whatever next, a black King?" Valerie Whiting was standing next to Daniel, with Mrs Huntley behind her. The entrance hall was beautiful, with black and white chequered tiling on the floor and ornate oil paintings everywhere.

Mr and Mrs Huntley, Mr and Mrs Hewitt, Catherine and Valerie had a four course meal in the Small Dining Room of Number Ten. The family ensured that they thanked their hosts for their kindness and support since the mistake was discovered, and were grateful for the encouragement that they were receiving in the build up to a very high profile trial. Mr Huntley was particularly interested in Catherine and her courage and maturity in promising to testify against the paedophile.

The Prime Minister took a sip from his glass of wine and Alice wondered how it had ever come to this with such blistering haste. "You understand, Catherine, that if you put in a particularly courageous performance in court this week you will be directly sending a man to his death?"

"She knows," Geoff answered for her without looking up from his roast lamb.

"What are the views of your family on the death penalty, Mrs Hewitt?" asked Mrs Huntley. She was very beautiful and evidently took a great deal of care and attention on her appearance, and to hear her discussing something so grisly was a sharp contrast to her perfectly coiffed hair and scarlet lips. Alice opened her mouth to answer, but Geoff opened his first and she gracefully put a forkful of parsnip in to save her embarrassment, but feared that she had failed.

"Obviously," he said, hesitating for a second to swallow a piece of potato, "if it turns out that this man is responsible for the death of our daughter then we would want to see justice done to the fullest extent. He deserves the maximum that the law can give him, and perhaps even then the law is too lenient on the most serious of criminals. Catherine understands exactly what is riding on her testimony. We believe that this man has surrendered his human rights and that the way forward for this country is to promote the rights of the victim above the rights of the criminal."

Mrs Whiting evidently supported him completely. "Hear hear," she said, slapping the table gently with the palm of her hand. Alice opened her mouth again and began to tell the Prime Minister that she was concerned that the line between justice and mob rule was being blurred, but Geoff interrupted her. "Excuse me, Alice," he said, looking directly at Mrs Whiting, "I have not finished speaking." Hurt and offended, Alice did not want to cause a scene at dinner with the Prime Minister, so she let it go and closed her mouth again.

3   RENDEZVOUS

At the cabinet meeting on the first morning of the trial, the ministers discussed the things that had been on the table for as long as they had held their positions; immigration, the tax rate on the richest, foreign policy towards the United States and what on Earth they were going to do about Honduras. As soon as Parliament resumed after the Christmas break the proposed bill to restore the death penalty would take priority and would be implemented as quickly as possible. Valerie Whiting and Daniel Huntley were both interrogated as to the exact nature of the situation unfolding before them in the proposed overhaul to the justice system; they confirmed that they had had talks with *The Envoy* and knew that they were planning a petition, and if the timing was right they could beat them to it and announce a vote beforehand then they could claim that the Tabloids were attempting to cash in on a Parliamentary process and that the Government had responded perfectly to a very pressurized and sensitive situation in light of such a shocking crime. However there were some parts of the press which were not sympathetic to Huntley's handling of the crisis so far and saw him inviting the Hewitts for dinner as at best a cheap PR tactic to garner extra votes and to create Huntley's Conservative brand as the political party to represent the British family and to be taking the side of the victims in the justice system.

"I need you to know that a vote is inevitable and I will be wholeheartedly supporting the restoration of capital punishment in the UK when it comes to it. We need to be clear on this, Prime Minister, and it is the right thing to do."

"I don't know if I can do this, Valerie," he said. "Right or wrong, it is a total revision of the moral backbone that this nation has built over the last hundred years."

Her eyes blazed with passion and anger. "You have to. There can be no time for cowardice in the face of doing what is right because it will lose us political advantages. Some things are too important for that. I know that this needs to happen. It is about democracy, it's about listening to the views of the public; there has not been a single occasion since abolition when the nation as a whole has not wanted it back."

"I think it's too risky. What about Europe? We will be evicted from the Union if this legislation goes through. Brussels won't allow it."

"To hell with Brussels," she sighed, "it's about what is right for us. We are servants to the British people and we need to represent them, not the EU. If we leave then we leave, and we bow out in a blaze of moral glory."

Huntley raised his eyebrows. "It's not on your watch, Valerie. My reputation is on the line here. My Premiership will be remembered for this if it goes wrong."

"I'll be your fall man if you need me to be. You should know that I am planning to resign if this vote is not passed. Which is why I told you that I want to present the debate in the Commons and argue the Government's case; this isn't going to look as bad for you as you think it is. We win, and we share the credit. We lose, and I resign for moral reasons; and it can be up to you to appoint me to something nice as compensation. For God's sake, Daniel, don't send me to a convent, but I want to do something similarly subtle if the gamble doesn't pay off. Something foreign, perhaps. Be inventive, and remember me when you get re-elected. I believe in this with my whole career, and I will risk everything to make sure Leo Faulkner gets killed in retaliation for what he did to Joy Hewitt."

The "movement for law change" or MLC as it had been seamlessly branded was heavily supported by Matthew Brady and the *Envoy* newspaper, so much so that Alice had noted that there was a considerable amount of debate to be had over whether or not the media had instructed the public to feel outraged by the events or whether the media was simply reacting to and reflecting the strength of public feeling against Faulkner. On the morning of the murder trial the entire front page of the newspaper was devoted to the formal launch of the campaign to reinstate the death penalty to the UK, inviting readers to sign a petition which would be presented to the Government in support of their cause. A law dating all the way back to August 2011 meant that any petition with a hundred thousand signatories, however trivial, would be debated in Parliament with the potential for a Bill to be put forward as well. On the morning of the trial, four hours since the petition went live, Brady and his publication already had three hundred and seventeen thousand people willing to be named as supporters of the campaign. Whilst the campaign went by the name of the MLC, the Act of Parliament which they hoped to pass into law was known as the Restoration Bill.

Following an emergency change in legislation after being pressurised by Brady, the judge had allowed television cameras and press photographers into the courtroom during a murder trial for the first time in British history. Regulations against the use of recording devices in the courtroom had been waived by the authorities and as a result many of the people in the public gallery were holding up cameras and mobile phones to the bullet-proof screen which protected the defendant from the wrath of the mob. Outside the Old Bailey friends of the people who had made it into the public gallery, many of whom had queued on the street from 4am, were calling newspapers and television networks attempting to auction the footage and photographs off as unique amateur material, or "citizen journalism" as they had branded it. Many of the group were competing with the professional journalists inside the building for payments and exclusive deals.

Across the road, riot police were monitoring a crowd that had gathered along Newgate Street and were concerned that the protests against the defendant would become violent and aggressive. Some of the crowd were carrying banners emblazoned with messages for him such as "burn in Hell", "I hope you rot" and "justice for Joy, punish him". All of the attention, particularly of the media and the politicians, was on the banners and shouts of the crowd that specifically described the ways in which they wanted Leo Faulkner to pay for what he was being accused of should he be found guilty. One banner screamed "kiddie fiddlers should fry", another implored the judge to "give him the jab" and some of the protesters were playing games of hangman with chalk on the pavement. There had been some accusations in the more liberal media that even though the public gallery inside the courtroom was to be on a first come first served basis in the pursuit of complete neutrality, people were more likely to be admitted if they held extremely strong views in favour of the death penalty.

It was as though the golden figure of Justice standing proudly atop the summit of the building in her supreme authority was holding in her hands not a sword and scales, but instead parcels of food and a cup of water, and the people amassed in the street far below her were desperate victims of a famine in a scene of Biblical desolation. When the van arrived with its blacked out windows and armoured exterior the line of police was suddenly overwhelmed and several of the protesters forced their way out into the road ahead of the vehicle. The desperation in the faces of the crowd, the sheer crippling hunger for blood, and the relentless urging for retribution to be poured down from Heaven in an overpowering display of damnation for injustice, surged through the people like a wildfire in the same way that it had grown in the public psyche like a cancer. People began to hurl eggs and other missiles at the van, and members of the public abandoned the vacant expressions unique to London's public spaces and replaced them with outbursts of pure, unrestrained hatred. They fought for his downfall with the same strength of instinct that a victim of a great and tragic disaster would fight for survival. The van eventually made its way through the crowd as the police regained control of the situation and took Leo to his appointment with the law.

*　*　*

Leo stood in the dock, calmly ready to face down the jury. He looked more bored than defiant; his face flashed between expressions of contempt and a twisted satisfaction at all of the fuss that his obsession had caused. He smacked his chops, fiddled with his fingers, cast menacing grins at the women in the jury and, as Catherine waited to speak against him, shot disapproving looks at her small breasts and her bum. He could not believe his luck. He could not have dreamed of the success that could have befallen him and that his lone fantasy could have triggered such an overwhelming rush of public anger.

Finally, the moment came that he had been waiting for; Alice and Geoff entered the courtroom and came to take their seats. He smiled at them both, and gave a little wave as he slouched against the podium. When they responded only with steadfast and dignified silence as they took their seats, Leo became irritated and annoyed. "What?" he shouted, mocking the family, "You finally came to see the show? Do I not even deserve for you to look at me?" The courtroom erupted in shouts of anger, cries of disgust and loud booing. At the invitation of Geoff, Matthew Brady had joined the family in the front row of their side of the courtroom.

"All rise." The judge came in and took his seat, and the court sat down again. A policeman asked Leo to swear on the Holy Bible, and he did so. He didn't sound particularly convincing.

"Mr Leonard Richard Faulkner, you are accused of the abduction, rape, murder and sexual interference with the corpse of seven year old Joy Hewitt from the village of Higher Pelham which occurred on the 27th of September of this year. How does the defendant plead?"

Leo leaned forwards in the dock and his mouth curled upwards into a wicked grin. "I did it, I killed her".

Alice gripped her husband's hand, with tears streaming down her cheeks. She had known what was coming but she never quite had summoned the courage to face up to it until it presented itself to her in this way.

"Am I to take that as a guilty plea, Mr Faulkner?"

Leo said nothing, and simply laughed as he stuck his middle finger up at the family.

"Why did you kill her, Mr Faulkner?" asked the Judge.

Leo looked directly at Alice as he replied. "Because she was the most beautiful thing I have ever seen in my whole life. I had to do it. I couldn't let the opportunity pass."

There were two King's Counsels present and each was assigned the task of cross examining each of the witnesses, rather than the traditional method of trial which used a prosecution and a defence. The evidence was overwhelming, the defendant was adamant that he wanted to plead guilty and it was such a high profile case with such an inevitable outcome that even if Faulkner had wanted a defence attorney he would have had trouble convincing one to represent him. Assuming that there was no miraculous intervention which meant that he could not be found guilty the defending lawyer's career would have been ruined and they would have possibly been at risk of an attack from the mob.

The three witnesses to be cross examined were to be the defendant, Catherine Hewitt who was the only person to see the killer at the time and place of the crime, and Detective Fish who had examined the corpse and had conducted the investigation. The Detective was the first to take the stand. The KCs took turns to ask the questions; Kate could not stop staring at their black robes and ceremonial wigs.

"How did she die, Detective Fish?"

"After close examination of the corpse of the young girl we found that her neck was very severely damaged. She was found with multiple fractures to her vertebrae and her spinal cord was snapped, which we believe was the cause of death. She had stretch and friction marks around her neck and this would suggest that the defendant forcibly strangled her with his bare hands. We have never found any evidence of a murder weapon and believe that the crime was committed by a lone killer using no equipment of any kind. We are as sure as we possibly can be that he had no accomplices and that he killed Joy Hewitt with his bare hands.

"We are confident with approximately 99.9% certainty that Joy Hewitt sustained sexual injuries after she was killed rather than when she was still alive. She had some internal injuries, the details of which I have here in front of me, but I believe the description of the extreme injuries to the lower abdomen of Joy Hewitt will cause great distress to those who knew and loved her."

He handed documents to a policeman who in turn gave it to the members of the jury who reacted in hushed and shocked silence. Looking over to them, Geoff concluded that they must have contained photographs from the post mortem examination. He did not want to, but he pictured in his mind the tangled mass of flesh between her legs, blood flowing and the innards visible like some seething blossom of lunacy. He wondered as he sat on the bench whether or not he wanted to see the pictures and he genuinely could not make up his mind as to which option would be less painful.

"Can you prove that this man is sexually attracted to young children, Detective?"

"In addition to the analysis of the body we raided the home of Leonard Faulkner on Tuesday 9th November and found pornographic depictions of children on the hard drive of his computer. These were in excess of three hundred thousand articles, and they were very extreme in their nature. I cannot think of a reason other than sexual attraction to children which would compel the defendant to own such material."

"Something which is going to need explaining to us is why it was that Joy Hewitt was found after almost one hundred hours in the ground with such a remarkably low level of decomposition. Detective Fish?"

"Yes, she had very little decomposition. The human body begins to decompose within four minutes of death, and Joy did not show very many of the typical signs at all. Some of her internal organs had collapsed, and some of the flesh around her vagina was rotten, but her torso, limbs and head was remarkably intact. I have the toxicology report here, and it reveals that her skin contained high levels of formaldehyde, methanol, ethanol and other solvents."

"Do we know where she was taken in the time between her disappearance and her discovery?"

"No sir. We have speculation to go on and sadly nothing more than that. Traces of Mr Faulkner's semen were found on her body and in the place where she was buried but there were no other pieces of forensic evidence linking him to a particular place."

Kate was called to the witness stand and began to speak against Leo when asked what had happened on that terrible day.

"I was walking towards the end of the lane and I noticed a man coming towards me."

"And where was your sister at this time, Miss Hewitt?"

"She was behind me."

"I see. Did you get a clear look at the man that you talk about?"

"Yes I did. I looked at him fully in the face. He seemed lost and he asked me directions to the train station. I explained the way to him, and we looked at each other the whole time."

"And there were absolutely no other people that were in the same area at the same time as the three of you?"

"No sir."

"You're sure?"

"I am."

"Is that man in the courtroom today, Miss Hewitt?"

"Yes, he is. The man I saw approximately ten seconds before my sister disappeared is the defendant."

There was a murmur in the room as the audience understood the gravity of the situation and what it meant for the man in the dock.

"Catherine, do you think that there is any possibility that you could be mistaken, and that it may have been someone else of whom the defendant merely reminds you?"

"There is absolutely no possibility of that at all. It was him; I have never been more certain of anything in my whole life. And I'll thank you to address me in the courtroom as Miss Hewitt, please Sir, we are not on first name terms yet."

She could tell that he didn't think anything of her because of her age; in years gone by she would not have been trusted because she was an underage girl. Kate was determined to not be overlooked and ignored, especially with something so important. She had a point to prove and she had always been stubborn and belligerent. Leo was smiling in approval at the exchange and he mockingly called Kate a "drama queen" when she had made the comment about not being on first name terms.

"Close your mouth," she hissed. "I hate you and your life depends on my testimony, so back off and shut your face."

The courtroom was tense, and it was filled with voices as the two spat insults at one another. The judge brought the room to order and the lawyer continued his cross-examination.

"Was it down to negligence that your sister was abducted? Did you let her out of your care, even for a second?"

Kate was convicted with a boldness that defied her age. "The reason that my sister was abducted was because the rat in the dock is a sick child killer and he decided to kill Joy to fulfil his disgusting fantasy. I did nothing wrong and I could have done nothing to stop him. He is guilty, not me."

"But did you let her out of your care, even for a second, Miss Hewitt?"

"It depends on your definition. If walking a few metres ahead to encourage her to catch up, and taking your eyes off of her for a second is not caring for her, then yes. But I would argue with you and I am completely sure that I personally fulfilled all of my obligations to look after her. Besides, we were kids walking home from school together. I am fourteen. I'm not old enough to be responsible for anything yet so by default that also means that I can't be accused of neglecting to fulfil obligations that I never had. I can't vote, I can't drive, I can't drink alcohol, but you think I can be accountable for my sister's disappearance? It wasn't my job to look after her; I was doing it because there was nobody else there to do it for her."

"Miss Hewitt," said the KC, "let me be very clear about this. We know that the defendant has confessed but that does not mean that he is guilty of this crime. We owe it to your family and to the children of this nation that we are absolutely certain that we find the right man and that Joy's killer is not still at large.

"Did anything strike you as being unusual about Joy's behaviour on that afternoon? Was anything out of the ordinary?"

Kate seemed slightly confused by the question; in her mind all that she should be asked about was the glancing moment when she had locked eyes with Leo, the fleeting and fragile second when she laid eyes on the face of the man who killed her sister.

"She told me that she was very happy that day because her teacher had been teaching the class about the Ancient Egyptians, which was something Joy was interested in. That was what she told me when she met me after school. She was walking behind me on the way home, slower than usual, which seemed a bit strange. She was making a daisy chain to put on her head. There was nothing else that I can think of except for that."

"Miss Hewitt, do you believe that there is any reason why your sister would have been especially vulnerable on the afternoon of her death?"

She went over every aspect of that day again in her head, for the thousandth time. Every tiny moment of that normal day now became a monumental event in the life of her family, and the pressure on her memory was enormous.

"No. No more so than usual. It was a perfectly ordinary day."
She paused, deep in thought and then something sprang to her
mind. "I found it very strange that the murderer was wearing
such a large coat on such a warm day."

The final witness was the defendant, Leo Faulkner, to be
aggressively cross examined by the KCs acting as if they were the
prosecution. It was a quick trial, and the verdict seemed extremely
predictable which affected the nature of the questions.

"Mr Faulkner did you murder Joy Hewitt?"

"Yes Ma'am."

The court murmured with outrage and disgust. Leo loved it.
"Why?"

"Because I fancied her, she turned me on. It was something I
needed to do to get sexual satisfaction."

"What happened after you killed her?"

"I buried her in the churchyard, just as deep as I could dig with
my fingers, and then I left a whole red apple on top of the dirt so
I could find her again. Catherine, the reason why I was wearing
such a large coat was so that I could take it off to wrap the corpse
in and so that I could escape without anyone recognising me. I
visited the churchyard as often as I could, and I would shag her in
the bushes. I like the coldness."

"I see. The Detective seems to think you embalmed her. Did
you act alone?"

"Yes."

"Where and whom do you get your knowledge of embalming
fluids from?"

Leo grinned abominably. "Play fair, my Lord. I need some
secrets. You can't have all of me. Some things are just for me to
enjoy."

*   *   *

As the jury retired to consider their verdict, Alice went to the
bathrooms to relieve herself. She went down the long corridor
and opened the door, and the bathroom was empty except for a

woman standing at the sinks and staring into the mirror. They recognised each other immediately; the other woman was Lillith Faulkner, the mother of the defendant. Alice quickly went into the cubicle and used it, trying to take as long as possible so that Lillith would leave without them seeing each other again, but when she emerged the old woman was still there and it was clear that she had been weeping. She was washing her hands, and Alice went over to the sinks to do the same. She could not help imagining Leo as a child, with his mother teaching him and instilling in him an ethical compass of good and evil, right and wrong—but exactly where had the failing come? Was it a biological disorder that he had inherited which made him want to have sex with her dead daughter, and were the same satanic chemicals channelling their courses through Lillith's veins as well? Had she failed in her basic duty as a mother to infuse in him a basic sense of morality which would have prevented the murder, and had Lillith's negligence indirectly caused Joy's death? Lillith turned to Alice with a look of grief welling up in her vast, bottomless eyes. She had the ashen face of a mother who knew that her issue was about to die, a sensation which Alice had never known; Joy's death had come to her as a shocking surprise, not an agonisingly long and painful legal process with a dreadfully predictable conclusion looming on the horizon. Lillith asked Alice to pass her a towel, and she looked around to see a pile of them on the counter beside the sink she was using. She passed one over; Lillith used it and thanked her, then left. As soon as the bathroom door swung closed she leant her back up against the wall and collapsed into a plunging precipice of emotion, her body becoming so weak that she slid down the wall until she was sitting on the floor. She sobbed and sobbed for what seemed like hours; the most confusing aspect of it all was that she simply did not know what she wanted in return for the death of her child. Did she want the other woman to apologise? Or was it instead that she felt an odd connection with her, that she felt empathy towards the other mother and her own traumatic battle? She could not decide whether or not the two of them should be best friends or fierce enemies; all she felt was the power of grief and anguish thumping through her ravaged body. Finally composing herself, she took her place in the courtroom again as the jury returned to deliver their verdict. The Old Bailey was used to controversial decisions lasting many hours and even many days, but the jury for Leo Faulkner took thirteen minutes before they returned to deliver the verdict to the judge. The one thing this case lacked was doubt.

"Members of the Jury, have you come to a decision?"

The foreman responded steadfastly. "We have, Your Honour."

"And was the decision unanimous?"

"Yes, Your Honour."

"Very well," he said, seemingly bewildered at the speed of the decision making even though it was one of the more obvious mysteries of his career, "How do you find the defendant, Mr Leonard Faulkner, who is charged with the abduction, murder, rape and sexual interference with the corpse of Joy Hewitt on the 27th of September of this year?"

"We find him guilty on all counts, Your Honour."

A few people scattered across the courtroom let out cries of joy and relief as the spokesman delivered his line and stepped away from the stage, but the room did not erupt in triumphant, delirious joy. Lillith Faulkner buried her head in her hands and the Hewitts were so utterly convinced of his guilt that the moment was devoid of all surprise. Their primary concern was not whether or not he was guilty of the crime against their daughter but instead what would happen to him as punishment for it, and because of this the verdict itself was merely a formality.

"Mr Faulkner, I am forced by the law to delay your sentencing. I hope that we can all appreciate that these are untested waters in the criminal justice system and that we must wait for the final decisions on the restoration of capital punishment before we can be sure of exactly what will happen to you. I am recommending you to the Secretary of State for Justice and Human Rights for execution, although if the law is not passed you will not be able to lawfully serve this sentence. You will be sentenced to a bare minimum of twenty five years in prison; no parole is granted for any reason until twenty five years from this date, and the sentence will only be altered to make it more severe, not less. If the new legislation is brought into law then you will be the first prisoner executed in this country under that law. You showed no remorse whatsoever, and have insulted and abused the grieving family of your victim. You have shown an extremely disrespectful attitude to this courtroom and you have behaved very badly under the supervision of the police.

As for the crime itself, I have no doubt that you are an extremely dangerous threat to the security of the general public. You were chillingly efficient and organised in the planning and preparation for your crime and you set out with premeditated intent to kill and rape a defenceless child. It was a despicable act and you showed a disgusting contempt for human life. I fear that you will never fully understand the magnitude of your crime against the Hewitt family and the way that you have destroyed the domestic life that they so enjoyed before their move from London to Higher Pelham. You chose your victim, stalked her, followed her and groomed her so that you could fulfil your devilish desires. You are an abomination of human sexuality and you should never again be allowed to have access to children. You will be denied this access as long as your life may endure.

"As far as I understand it you will be accommodated in HMP Belmarsh, in a single cell in isolation from the rest of the prisoners, and identified as a category A inmate and Exceptional Risk. Because of the psychological disturbances that we discovered in the evidence and also because of any attempt to jeopardise your possible execution you will be placed under the strictest suicide watch of any inmate that Belmarsh has ever held. You will be the first to discover your fate, Mr Faulkner. In case we must prepare ourselves for the maximum penalty being imposed, may God have mercy on your soul."

Alice was crying as Leo was led below in handcuffs, but Geoff was staring straight ahead with steel in his eyes. The prisoner was shouting something at them but it was hard to distinguish his actual words as he was led away, but because it was directed at them rather than the judge or jury Alice assumed that it was abusive rather than a protest of innocence and so she had deliberately tried to blur the noises when they reached her ears. They had expected great cheers and relief in the courtroom as the prisoner was lead away, but instead there was a hushed and ghoulish silence, because of the foreboding sense of the unknown justice system that lay ahead of them kept the audience quiet. When he was gone there was a bustling as everyone prepared to leave the courtroom.

Outside, the Hewitt family lawyer was reading a prepared statement to the enormous throng of assembled press. Geoff and Alice had written a pair of statements, one for each potential outcome of the trial so that they would be given some privacy when the verdict was read out. It had been devised predominantly by Geoff because it was suggestive of a support for the death penalty for Leo but Alice had eventually given in and signed the statement too.

"Our family would like to thank the British public for their support for us at this difficult time. We have experienced a tremendous loss and trauma but we are incredibly proud of the determination and maturity displayed by our daughter Catherine when she took the stand to testify against Leo Faulkner. We have lost our beloved Joy, our priceless treasure and our ray of light, but we are comforted by the support we have received from each and every member of the public who has been thinking of us and praying for our difficult journey. No little girl deserves to be killed and sexually assaulted and so we are grateful that justice has been done by the verdict that was delivered today. We are pleased that the jury came to a unanimous decision and that we can move on with our lives with the knowledge that the killer of our daughter is safely behind bars and that he cannot harm children again. We understand that there is some controversy about the sentence that may or may not be passed through Parliament in the coming weeks but we feel that it is a journey this country must make together. We want to see justice done, not only for our family but for every family who have experienced a loss like this, and we are working closely with the British Government and the King and Queen to secure a revision in the law to adequately deal with extreme crime against the most vulnerable people in our society."

"So I spoke to the Prime Minister," began Brady as they left the courtroom together, "and he told me that he entertained you for dinner on Saturday evening at Number Ten, Downing Street."

"Yes," said Alice, "he was very kind to us. It was very generous of him to invite us to his home to give us his condolences."

"Don't you see?" Brady interjected, clearly showing a well seasoned cynicism of politicians and their motives for doing the things that they did. "He is trying to soften the blow. He knows that Leo was guilty and that it would trigger a petition for the death penalty as we know that he definitely did it. If he releases this to the media then it will look very good for him, and he will get away with not passing the Bill without having to endure people branding him as insensitive and damaging his image. Number Ten is his workplace, Alice, not his home."

Alice lowered her head and kept walking. "I am choosing to believe that he did it out of the goodness of his heart because it is a high profile case. He needed us to know that we had his support before the trial. You can choose to believe what you want to, but I know that we have the Prime Minister on our side whether the Bill is passed or not."

The preparations to the Bill were made in advance by Valerie Whiting, and once two million people had signed the online petition Matthew Brady and Geoff Hewitt delivered the Prime Minister at Ten Downing Street and the process of delivering ultimate justice for Joy finally gathered momentum. There was a throng of journalists outside Number Ten for Geoff Hewitt's second visit, just as there had been for his first, and many of them were demanding to know his opinion and reaction to the seismic changes rocking the justice system which would soon come up for debate in Westminster. Geoff Hewitt let it be known that he was a proud supporter, whilst Alice was much more hesitant for more blood to be spilt.

Whilst Valerie was confident, the Prime Minister was very sceptical of their chances of success. He had made an unwitting remark in the corridors of the BBC studios when he had not switched off a live microphone, and the quote had made the front pages. "Government is a big operation; it's like a supertanker. It cannot be turned on a sixpence, no matter how hard you try."

The incessant march of the months through autumn towards the withering morbidity of winter beyond it continued ceaselessly, even though the Hewitt family felt as though the whole world had come to a shuddering halt on the 27th September. November the Fifth was a particular landmark date in the calendar that the family loved, and it reminded them all of the magnificence of childhood. In London they would take the train to Clapham Junction after school as soon as darkness fell and all five of them would take a big bag full of sparklers and glowsticks to celebrate with a few thousand perfect strangers the execution of a traitor in 1605. At points along the journey the railway line would have enough of a view to see the London skyline on a special night and the fireworks would emerge above the rooftops; great bursting explosions of gunpowder, in an uncountable number of luminescent colours, huge celestial dandelions filling the sky with colour and vibrancy. As the sparks slowly faded the endless black canvas of Heaven would be dyed every shade of the rainbow as the paint bled and smudged to make an exhilarating splash of colour, like chalk on a pavement in the rain. Getting off and coming out onto St John's Hill, they would turn right at Debenhams and follow the crowds, thousands of them, onto the relative open darkness of Clapham Common and the huge public firework and bonfire display and a regimented family tradition.

This year was different, obviously, due to the fact that Joy was now gone. She loved that day so much; the wrapping up warm beneath a starlit sky, the glow of the fire on her cheeks and the bursting shimmer of sparklers which danced in their delighted eyes. It was a uniquely British thing, a strange and morbid celebration of failure, an obsession with burning and gruesomely torturing a traitor to the crown and a thanksgiving of the preservation of an ancient system of government which had been long since abolished. Nobody cared about any of that nowadays though, it was merely the jewel in autumn's crown and a wonderful opportunity for fireworks and parties and good cheer. But something was definitely different in the air over England that night, as memories of the events that had gone before were freshly exhumed by the Faulkner case. The unusual celebration came at a poignant time as the nation knew that the grisly secrets of the Tower of London could be recreated as early as the New Year in Belmarsh Prison.

The four of them stood around a bonfire in Higher Pelham, staring into the embers and trying to pretend to all of the others that they were not hurting on the inside. Kate was definitely too old to make a guy with her father, but the parents had humoured Jonathan and let him make a huge ball of newspaper and stick a picture of a human face to it, finally mounting it atop a scarecrow-like figure and sitting him on the summit of a huge pile of firewood that they had gathered in the garden. Standing back to admire his handiwork, Jonathan had a chilling shock when he saw his father light the base of the pyre and take up a pitchfork, impaling the figure and slashing at the shirt in an incredible display of passionate aggression. Finally, when the flames around the base were licking high enough to need no more kindling, Geoff put the pitchfork through the side of the head and pushed the body downwards, holding the face in the middle of the consuming flames. The firelight was bright enough to see clearly the expression on his father's face, but Jonathan didn't want to look.

The reason that Joy loved Bonfire Night was because it truly signalled the beginning of Christmas. November in Higher Pelham was exquisite, with the lanes being filled with deep drifts of scarlet and gold autumnal leaves, and the deciduous trees were dappled with brushstrokes of flame endowed on them by an Almighty paintbrush. The evenings were drawing in earlier and earlier and the villagers would often put candles in their low front windows, casting their flickering glow across the cobbles of the streets outside. The fields outside of Higher Pelham were cleared of crops, and the shadow of a frost would dance around the light of the old lampposts and the roof of the Hewitts' car would glisten like a carpet of diamonds.

December was a beautiful month; the village became once again a picture postcard scene of rural England, with thick snowfall covering the hillside by the school and some of the smaller roads becoming impassable because of snowdrifts. Everything reverted to a wonderfully archaic existence when the winter months were at their most brutal; with all of the advances of technology and the changing nature of childhood it was very comforting to the Hewitts to look out of their front windows and see children making makeshift sledges and dragging them towards the notoriously steep Pelham Hill, emblazoned against the anonymity of the snow in their brightly coloured coats and knitwear. The shire horses had been moved from the field behind the cottage to a warmer venue with shelter and plentiful food, and the middle of the village square was now dominated by a magnificent and enormous Christmas tree from a nearby wood which was illumined with white lights which shone like a net of diamonds and each branch was adorned by an ornament made by a child at the school. Although nobody had given out any expressed instructions, a huge majority of them were impromptu tributes to Joy and prayers for the new laws on punishment of crimes against children. Some of them urged God's action on ending the chain of death, others called on Him to "defend the innocent and see justice done" and to "uphold His perfect standards". The family were touched by the tribute, but it had transformed a beautiful Christmas tree, once a symbol of such overwhelming joy and of family togetherness, into a vast token of death, a great idol of vengeance and tragedy, a wedge of pain through the Hewitts like the wooden stake through Dracula's heart. The whole village was in danger of becoming something of a souvenir, a relic of one terrible day in September, a town unable to shake off its gruesome history, an English version of Salem. Alice knew that the tree had died when it had been decapitated, but she was sure that it was growing every time she saw it. The village was so beautiful and picturesque, and now so famous, that many local photographers and artists came to shoot for Christmas cards and chocolate boxes; the snow-covered ivy in the hedgerows, the proud red-breasted robins in the forests and fields, the snow on the thatched roofs and the stonework of the church and war memorial. Alice's favourite one was a scene looking west, down the Hill, and at a moment during dusk when all of the lights were on but darkness had not fallen sufficiently for the distant hills and fields beneath their dazzling blankets to be obscured, with the snow in the foreground thick and textured and gradually fading down the cobbled street. The line of cottages and their quaint little thatched roofs were bathed in a glow of homely light and from the chimneypots gently and gracefully rose thin wisps of wood-smoke.

Christmas Eve was an unusually difficult day. The family had gone to church in the morning, not because of any religious feeling of obligation but instead because it was a place where the community would all be gathered together at a very sensitive milestone in the journey forward beyond their time with Joy. Alice and Geoff did not believe in God, but they understood, respected and this year were desperate to believe in the message of hope preached by the church and the importance that it placed on being a good person. Following the tension in the village following the disappearance and the level of suspicion within the community, there was a great level of compassion on display for the Hewitt family and they were warmly welcomed to the Christingle service. In the evening, as the frost began to gather on the cobbles and an unripe moon shone through a faint halo in the frozen dark sky, the choir gathered together to sing Christmas carols in the glow of the old Victorian streetlamps. The Christmas tree was the focal point of the village just as it had been for hundreds of years and all of the cottages were decorated with beautiful white lights; no garish neon colour in sight, just strings of bejewelled fairy lights that pierced the darkness like diamonds. The sound of traditional carols sung by the choir assembled outside the entrance to St George's shone like a vigil against the darkness of the world, a reminder of the beauty that lies beyond the tragedy. Eventually their voices faded and blended back into the night, and Higher Pelham was silent once more.

Beside the fireplace in the sitting room, the Hewitts underwent a tradition of their own, sitting around the hearty ambience glowing from the grate and eating walnuts and oranges together as they told stories beside the Christmas tree. The tradition had been to tell one another ghost stories but this year that could not continue as the stench of death clung all too heavily to their new home. Because of the pending changes in the law their whole lives had an air of morbidity. Kate could not look at the stockings over the fireplace, just hers and her brother's, because she feared that if she did the floodgates of emotion would be totally uncontrollable.

Alice and Geoff Hewitt were not talking as openly and honestly as a married couple should. Their attempt at normality and of setting an example to their children in how to move on after the death of a loved one was failing, and they could not bring themselves to face it. Kate had always expressed a wish to skate on the village pond when it had frozen over. But tonight, in the first moments of their first Christmas as a family of four again, the hairline cracks in the ice snaked their way across the glittering surface and eventually the ruptures in the polished veneer became irresistible and the ice broke away.

4

THE SANCTITY OF LIFE

Rose and Fred Hewitt, Geoff's mother and father, had travelled down to London for the trial and subsequent debate on a relentless pilgrimage in search of justice for their granddaughter. It was unthinkable that she was gone, so soon after welcoming her into the world and seemingly immediately after the move to the country that they had all yearned over for such a long time. They walked together up the steps of the exit from Westminster Station and stared upwards at the towering beauty of Big Ben. The gold inlaid on the roof glinted in the sunshine and the stunning and delicate intricacy of the ornate clock face impressed them no matter how many times they had seen it before. Fred was more nervous than his wife, and Rose placed a steady hand on his wrist as they stepped out onto the ancient and mottled pavement of Bridge Street. A newspaper vendor was handing out the *Standard* to London's commuters as they exited and entered the station and Rose took one from him, noticing the fact that they locked eyes for far longer than the fraction of a second he was used to for all of the others he had served that day. She was fully aware of her celebrity status and she hated every second of it, although it must surely be nothing compared to what Alice must be experiencing. The other Mr and Mrs Hewitt were travelling with the convoy down Whitehall as the interest of the crowd was too intense to allow them to use public transport.

As they walked towards Parliament Square, Rose glanced at the front page of the paper. It was a photo of Daniel Huntley and President Gonzalez giving a press conference in the Rose Garden of the White House. The visit by the Prime Minister to Washington had originally been to commemorate an anniversary of the deaths of British and American forces who had died together in World War III, but the journalists in the conference had unwittingly steered the conversation towards Joy with questions for the President on his opinions of the British policy towards the death penalty. Gonzalez had told them that "my personal opinion is that people who kill children for sex have voluntarily denied themselves their own human rights and do not deserve to live." Daniel Huntley made his position on the situation clear by reaffirming that he would support the notion if it is passed by Parliament but that he would not actively influence the vote because he believed that the present justice system was working well enough to get the job done effectively. The headline of the *Standard* ran with his closing quote of his response to the question; "My loyalty is to the status quo". Scanning the article, she noticed that Valerie Whiting was quoted without source as being "furious and ready to resign". Much was made of the severity of the situation in the Commons as Huntley cut short his visit to Washington DC and flew back to London for the debate. The trip had been planned far in advance, well before the murder of Joy Hewitt, and the Foreign Secretary had expressed a concern that the sudden departure of the British delegation from Washington without giving the President any form of formal apology may harm the bilateral relationship between the two nations which had been so strong during the War. President Gonzalez had been Governor of California before winning the White House and under his command the state had executed more criminals than any of the others, taking the morbid title from the long term champion of Texas for the first time in its history.

Perhaps the most striking aspect of the move of their son and his family away to Higher Pelham with Joy had been hidden from them and was revealed only now; London's insatiable churning river of human life, that ceaseless and bottomless ocean of mankind which never stopped reinventing itself and surging relentlessly in all directions at once. There were people of every colour and creed, race and religion here; the city was built on human foundations and it was impossible for an outsider to determine whether there was something incredible or tragic happening to the community of the city, the millions of strangers who interacted with one another every day. The first two things which the Hewitts noticed was the number of foreign languages floating in their ears and the completely unique smell of the London Underground which clung to their nostrils and the peeling paint and grouting of the walls of the endless tunnels winding beneath the streets.

Fred and Rose walked across the road to the centre of Parliament Square which had become something of a makeshift debating chamber of its own as the crowds had assembled on the grass for the monumental day in the Commons. It was not a large group, for the majority of demonstrators and protesters had gathered in Trafalgar Square, but the police were there keeping an eye on things and some of the individuals were having heated conversations about the fate of Leo Faulkner. Rose introduced them as Joy's grandparents, and perfect strangers from both sides of the argument embraced them with tears streaming down their cheeks, the grief of a nation etched with every anguished look on every face in Westminster.

Across the square Fred spotted a motorcade coming out of the junction with Whitehall and towards the entrance to the Palace of Westminster. The centre of the group of cars and motorcycles was a gleaming Jaguar limousine which she knew must belong to the Prime Minister. On the bench in Parliament Square, deep in the infancy of winter, Rose held her husband's hand tightly. It's time to go inside, she said to him. Fred sat on the bench, quite motionless and silent, having a moment to himself as he gazed at the western facade of the Abbey.

Composing themselves in the public gallery as they prepared for the debate, Fred and Rose sat with Geoff and Alice Hewitt as they saw that Valerie Whiting was sitting next to the Prime Minister on the front bench, looking through her papers. She was wearing, somewhat distastefully, a blood red double breasted suit with a sterling silver necklace and diamond earrings; the effect, whether intentional or otherwise, was that every eye in the House had been inescapably drawn to her. Huntley was sweating slightly as he sat next to her. Whiting was perfectly composed, preparing for her performance in the moment that she knew would one day come to define her career. She was gambling in the highest sense, staking her full reputation on the outcome of the Restoration Bill.

The Speaker, John Allitt, called the house to order and the completely full chamber became quiet and settled; not even the Opposition benches, which were normally loud with anger and heckling, uttered a sound as the House prepared for the debate. Whiting was the first to speak, and she stood assuredly at the Dispatch Box. As she cleared her throat she knew that the whole world was watching. It was a lonely moment.

"Ladies and Gentlemen, my Right Honourable friends, we are here today united in one purpose. It is time for us to stand together in our common goal of sending a signal to the society in which we live that there will be no tolerance whatsoever for people who commit the gravest of crimes against the most vulnerable and innocent of the citizens of this nation. This country has a proud history of justice and freedom and we must uphold that today by retaining our age old objective of ensuring that crimes go suitably punished. Nobody has the right to do what he did. Nobody has the right to take a life and devastate a family. This man has nothing within him that could ever be a positive contribution to society, and the British taxpayer has better things to spend our nation's money on than food and shelter for murderers in prison.

"Joy Hewitt was seven years old when she died. It is a tragedy beyond belief that she was killed by a stranger in her village who snapped her spinal cord with his hands by breaking her neck so that he could have sexual intercourse with the corpse. My Right Honourable Friends, we must agree on this that it is time for liberal sentencing to end once and for all and for a life to really mean a life. It is our duty, your duty as MPs, to end this man's life because it is the only way that we will really bring some closure and justice to the family of Joy Hewitt.

"We are all beyond doubt that it is the overwhelming will of the British people to have Leonard Faulkner executed for his crimes against children. We are also, incidentally, completely certain of the guilt of Leo Faulkner and therefore it is simply not a credible principle to oppose this Bill on the grounds that we cannot guarantee that an innocent man will not be put to death in this case. He has been psychoanalysed by the very finest in the field of psychology and I can assure the House that Leo Faulkner is of completely sound mind. The crimes were committed because of his sexual orientation combined with his desire to corrupt and destroy, not because of any mental illness. The people of this country want us to send a message to criminals which says that if you are going to commit the most heinous of crimes on our islands, you will be chased, you will be caught and you will pay for what you have done. We must send a strong message to both the innocent and the guilty that justice in this country is a priority for our Government and that we will do all that we can to ensure the protection of our citizens.

"This is about deterring would be criminals from committing their crimes, but there is more to the debate than that. The opposition to this Bill will be strong, undoubtedly, and will argue that there is no evidence to prove that this will deter violent individuals from committing crimes against the most vulnerable of individuals in our society, but to focus on that is to miss the point.

"What this debate comes down to is the fact that we need that oldest of Conservative values which tells us that we should have a small Government and a big society. It is clearly the will of the people that the death penalty is restored to this country as our highest punishment for the most severe of crimes and we are not a Parliament which is doing its job if we are willingly ignoring the majority view of the people of the nation which we are representing here and instead pushing through our own legislation which reflects the interests of the minorities. Tomorrow will be a sad day for democracy in this country if we fail as a Parliament to listen to the constituents that we all are here to represent."

William Sutcliffe was the Labour Leader of the Opposition, and he took it upon himself to lead the pro-life arguments against the Government. Huntley knew that he would make a strong appeal to the rebellious Conservative back-benchers, and that whilst Sutcliffe did not have an overwhelming following it would be enough to cause him embarrassment. For the Prime Minister it was a question of the reputation of the Government and unity within the Cabinet as well as a question of principle. As Huntley collected his thoughts, Sutcliffe began the response.

"Whilst I congratulate Mrs Whiting on her passionate and assured delivery on her arguments, I would like to remind the House that there is far more at stake here than the settling of one case of a crime against a girl from Higher Pelham. It goes far deeper than that. As you make your vote today I urge you to consider what a vote in favour of the death penalty would mean for the United Kingdom. Under the convention of 1998, it is illegal in European law for any of the member states to uphold the death penalty against its citizens for any reason, effective from February 2004. This would mean that we would be forced out of the European Union based on the sentencing of one criminal. This would cause many millions of pounds worth of damage to the British Economy on the understanding that the UK may not enjoy the current levels of trade and positive international relations with other members of the EU, including G8 nations such as Germany and France. Three and a half million British jobs depend directly on the UK's inclusion in the European community. These islands have always been geographically isolated from the rest of the continent and it is not in our best interests to implement the death penalty so that we are isolated ethically, diplomatically and financially as well. Finally, Mrs Whiting, I need you to promise me something."

His voice became grave and hushed, as the gravity of the situation increased as the hour drew nearer.

"I need your reassurance to myself, and this House, and the people of this nation that you have not waged this campaign with Matthew Brady and the Hewitt family in order to promote a pursuit of vengeance as a result of a personal vendetta against the murderer Leonard Faulkner. I promise you that although our opinions of the way in which we should punish him greatly differ, we agree on the notion that his crime was a vile abuse of an innocent child and he is an abhorrent disgrace to society. But the reason why I will be voting against this motion is the fact that I cannot be sufficiently reassured that it is not a bloodthirsty and sadistic campaign to see him suffer because of your own wish to feel some sense of vanquish against an enemy of the state. Mrs Whiting, I do not believe in luck and I do not believe in karma. I believe that justice and retribution are fundamentally different things and that we need to be very aware of that crucial difference when we are punishing our criminals.

"It is of the most opportune importance that we define our terms absolutely. I would like to remind the House, Mrs Whiting, that you are evoking the idea of justice based on quid pro quo, based on an eye for an eye. But is what we are proposing to do to Leonard Faulkner equal to what he did to Joy Hewitt? For example, did he tell her that he was going to commit the murder up to forty years before it was actually committed, a crime that the US state of California is guilty of, and was under the now President Gonzalez? I am assured by the detectives and the judge in the case that this was not someone who knew the family and that she had genuinely no idea of what would happen to her on her way home from school that day. Joy probably learned of her fate in the last five seconds of her life. That is the first difference between Joy Hewitt's death and Leonard Faulkner's. In the time that she was being stalked and followed, the time when Faulkner was planning to murder her, she was not held prisoner and incarcerated whilst she waited for the crime to be committed against her, always waking up in the morning not knowing whether this new day would be her last on Earth. Furthermore, he was not a public and democratic figure who was killing in the name of other people who he represented in Government. It was not a public servant who was being paid to do his gruesome task by the taxpayer. He was a loner and a criminal with a very unusual and specific fetish. There is no way that we can realistically replicate that when executing people, and we should not attempt to.

"Finally Mr Speaker I am encouraged to speak to the House in order to do a little boasting, of which our nation never does enough. We have been a beacon of freedom and justice in this world for hundreds of years. We have had dark moments and shadowy moments of shame which blight our past but on the grand scale we are a very successful and well established democracy and we have championed the cause of freedom and justice across the world. We have seen tyrannical governments and racist dictators overthrown and replaced with parliaments and assemblies which represent the wishes of the people whom they represent and to whom they must be held accountable. I understand that it is the will of the British people to have Leonard Faulkner executed but I suggest to this House that it is simply not a strong enough argument to rely upon. We are facing the destruction of our reputation in this capacity if this law is passed and organised murder is committed on a national level. We will have no moral leverage to rely upon when dealing with terrorists and rogue nations, no standing in the United Nations and expulsion or resignation from the European Union, and state-enforce barbarism is not the way we should be looking to enforce an end to tragedies such as the case of Joy Hewitt. This plot for revenge in a bid to deter criminals will fail. The reason that I am against the death penalty is because it is fundamentally wrong."

Valerie stood up again. "Thank you for your response, Mr Sutcliffe, but firstly I would like to argue with your point about the proposed withdrawal from the EU. I have no interest in surrendering the moral policy of this nation and this Government to Brussels. You talk of financial implications, but ignoring the overwhelming will of the people that we are here to represent in favour of being dictated to by the EU is far too high a price to pay. We spend forty million pounds a day on our inclusion in the European Union and our contributions to the Council of Europe, and we spend many millions more of taxpayers' money on housing and feeding a prisons population which exceeded one hundred and thirty thousand for the first time this year. I suggest to the House that all of this money could be better spent. Leonard Faulkner is the perfect candidate for execution and we need to do the right thing, not buckle under the pressure of an outdated and useless bureaucratic machine which is not able to benefit our country in any way. Rather than London following Brussels, when it comes to moral standards perhaps it should be Brussels following London."

"Mrs Whiting, I do not believe that the right course of action is to justify your own desire for revenge against the criminal in the case which has fuelled this debate with arguments concerning financial streamlining. You are assuming that a reduced prison population is automatically in the interests of this country primarily because of the reduced prisons budget. This shows a scandalous contempt for human life and you are trivialising it, reducing it down to a commodity and an inconvenient expenditure for your Government to clamp down on. Even if you were correct, you are failing to recognise that potassium chloride is an extremely expensive drug; I don't think that your shambolic NHS budgeting system would stretch to that. You would be quite a Government if you bankrupted the Health Service so that you could kill British Citizens. I suggest to you, Mrs Whiting and the Conservative Party, we should be upholding the value of human life in these Parliamentary votes, a duty which is the noblest of all the tasks to which we have been assigned.

"Furthermore, I am convinced that Leo Faulkner is guilty but that does not mean that he deserves to die." There was loud scorning from the benches when he said this. "Others in the future may not be convicted on such firm and sound evidence.

Death is a permanent punishment; there is no hope of acquittal, no hope of meaningfully pardoning people. The reputation of our country would be ruined forever if even one criminal was unjustly put to death because of this law. Life is important and life is worth protecting, no matter whose life it is. She talks about small Government, but this Government is playing God."

*   *   *

Since the day of Leo Faulkner's trial at the Old Bailey in London there had been a fierce public outpouring of anger against both the criminals who commit the most heinous of crimes against the most vulnerable and innocent of people, and the politicians who refused to make exceptions in the law for what they deemed an exceptional case. Over two and a half million people marched on the London from all around the country on the day of the vote in the Commons, determined to change the views of the people who represented them. The permanent protesters in Parliament Square opposite the Palace of Westminster increased tenfold and their banners were, for once, in total unison. They no longer jostled for attention with their demands for gay rights or an end to the Government's relaxed laws on immigration, or the tax system and a call for the end to British troops being used in the war in Honduras. Instead all of the other issues were temporarily forgotten and all of the protesters were united in a single purpose; to end the life of the killer of Joy Hewitt, and to inflict upon the condemned man a penalty so severe that it would recognise and protect the value of the life of a child.

The Parliamentary voting got under way shortly after dawn on the morning after the end of the two day debate. It was a dull morning, a low and cloudy sky oppressed the city and a greasy mist was hovering above the brown waters of the Thames. Streetlamps stayed on unnaturally late and the Palace of Westminster's Gothic splendour cast a jagged silhouette against the dark sky as the orange lights from within glowed and shone varicose reflections across the surface of the river. The Metropolitan Police had uncovered a splinter cell of a terrorist group who had vowed to recreate the attack on Parliament of 1605 if the vote was not passed. As the Prime Minister and his Justice Secretary shared an armoured limousine on their way to the vote, they knew that this would be one day that they would never forget. Alice and Geoff Hewitt were both due to appear in the public gallery again, and the news channels had already been showing two hours of live coverage by the time the first MPs arrived.

The previous night the protests had been long and violent. The statues in Parliament Square were defaced and some of the police line buckled under the surging, churning mob; the metal barriers that had been put in place were pushed back and some of the riot police were forced to use tear gas to disperse the crowd. There was a death, but it was not Leo's; one woman was crushed in a stampede as she found herself in a group trying to break down the door of Westminster Abbey and mounted police personnel forced the group away with batons and electric tasers. Finally the centre of Parliament Square was the scene of a huge bonfire, which the protesters claimed symbolised the funeral pyre of British democracy if the Bill was not passed, and the thick black smoke sailed through the darkness like the haggard spectre of plague seeping through London's skin. The warm orange glow from the burning banners and flags which illuminated the underside of the cloud echoed the cold electric blue of the screens of cameras and mobile phones on which people were recording images of the protests and using social networking to provoke and entice unrest.

In Trafalgar Square the following morning protesters had erected makeshift electric chairs in the fountains and on the steps of the National Gallery. Other groups had brought industrial amounts of food colouring with them and had dyed the water in the two fountains blood red, which was a shocking sight to behold. The murky waters of a dark scarlet foamed and frothed as the jets of crimson water shot upwards, casting a cerise mist across the Square and tainting the skin of the crowd in a scene reminiscent of the tomatoes of Buñol. Nelson's Column had been transformed into an enormous set of gallows fifty metres high by an especially brave and well prepared group of protesters who had attached great tree trunks to the side of the statue using ropes, pulleys and a hijacked crane; the police had ordered them to stop and had threatened to use force but some of the group were lying down on the top of the beam like the photographs of construction workers in New York in the 1930s. This highlighted the absurdity of the way that the British state values human life far above common sense, because as soon as there was a living human in the way of the police machine the whole offensive ground to a creaky halt. As soon as there was a protester on top of the plinth, shouting obscenities and rallying the troops with a megaphone as he put an arm around the huge likeness of Nelson, the control of the Square was fully in the hands of the protesters. Trafalgar Square became the centre point of the campaign against the liberal punishments of the justice system and it was here that the TV corporations interviewed protesters to appear on their news programmes, and most of the high profile campaigners would converge here, beneath the Gallows, to give their views which meant that it was where the majority of the protesters wanted to be. It was an iconic sight, having people interviewed with the camera low towards the ground and pointing upwards with the shot filled with sky, and having the protester on one side of the frame and Nelson's Gallows on the other. It was an image that filled front pages across the country and featured on news programmes across the world.

A huge crowd had gathered outside Buckingham Palace and were taunting the King and Queen. They had also positioned themselves all along the Mall between the two sites, so the area that was used as a private road for state visitors and ceremonial processions was now a campsite where protesters demanded that Leo Faulkner be executed after being found guilty of the murder. The police force was woefully overstretched, and there were tense nerves on the front lines of the disputes as many were afraid that a peaceful protest in pursuit of justice for Joy would turn into a mass riot and that violence would spread without mercy. Some left wing extremists had even issued the King with a death threat in the eventuality that the law was rejected, and they were swiftly caught and tried for treason. Daniel Huntley was determined to show the people that he had not lost his grip on power, even if there were times when he did not particularly believe that himself. These were dark days for the United Kingdom, and it was all in great danger of becoming a lynch mob, that the trophy of power would pass from the stifled order of the Constitutional Monarchy to the unruly and untamed crowd culture of a hysterical people. They all rallied around Westminster as the vote was underway, and a huge number of journalists, TV crews, and helicopters descended on the area to watch the crowd demand their way, a vast and churning sea of faces and bodies, of all colours, classes, races, beliefs and political views, all wanting the same thing. Some of them were holding banners carrying photographs of Joy that the family had released when she was missing, and others were carrying imaginative tokens of the execution chamber such as enormous inflatable syringes and lassos of hangman's rope.

Local supermarkets had sold out of many things which were red, as well as food colouring for the fountains. Some of the protesters had paid the butchers for the blood from their animals, and balloons filled with blood were launched at several high profile targets. One of them was launched through the railings of Buckingham Palace, landing in a spectacular red splash on the forecourt, and others splattered the sides of Big Ben as they were launched from Westminster Bridge. Valerie Whiting was lauded as a heroine for her contribution to the campaign, but William Sutcliffe's car was spotted speeding along Whitehall and was promptly drenched in pig's blood. Matthew Brady only stepped in to appeal for calm amongst the protesters for his cause when someone in Trafalgar Square was apparently bored and frustrated by the lack of carnage and set off a fire extinguisher in the face of a policeman as he patrolled the crowd.

With the proposition and formation of the Bill by Whiting and her team there was a decision to be made about the name of the law itself and the terms with which Faulkner's unique new brand of crime would be described. Brady had been quick to volunteer his thoughts on the matter and had said that he liked the ring that "Joy's Law" had to it, but Alice was happy to defy Geoff on this topic and had said in a hasty interview outside the Old Bailey that she hated the name and that she would do everything she could to have it called something else. It was of enormous importance to her that she should remember Joy, and especially Joy's name, as a word forever associated with abundant and glorious life. It should forever be a word that evoked images of freedom, love, health, and unending beauty. Lending her name to a law that was in place to execute criminals would, by contrast, infuse the memory she had of her daughter with blood and gore and mementos of her unnaturally grisly end in a country churchyard. There were a great number of laws that could have been put in place in connection with what Leo did to her; laws that gave parents access to the addresses and identities of paedophiles, greater powers for community leaders to name and shame, making psychosexual counselling compulsory for people whom were suspected of these crimes, and stripping criminals of the right to anonymity and new identities upon release to name but a few. But Alice would not budge, and Joy's name would not be going on any of them. Eventually she and Valerie Whiting brainstormed and come up with the name of the crime that he committed as "Crimes against Childhood". It worked because whilst rape, murder and sexual interference with a corpse were three separate crimes that already existed, they united to make something worse in the way that genocide and war crimes united to make a Crime against Humanity. It spoke of a different scale, one where the crime was not so much simply against Joy Hewitt but also in some way against every seven year old girl in the country, that his crime was against the community and the nation as well as his specific victim. The conditions of the law were that the criminal had abducted and murdered a child under the legal age of sexual consent, that the primary motive of the attack was for sexual reasons and that this had happened on more than one occasion. Leo had never killed a girl before Joy but he had been wanted for other rape charges against minors and so he just about scraped qualification for Crimes against Childhood. At first it was thought that only Crimes against Childhood, Regicide, Terrorism, Assassination and Crimes against Humanity would be punishable by death because the Government wanted to make the distinction between murder and an exceptional murder for an unusual or highly dangerous or disturbing reason. The phrase "exceptional cases of murder" drew immediate parallels with the phrase "cruel or unusual punishments" from the American Constitution in the press and there were rumours that President Gonzalez was still not satisfied with the reforms to the law as he was not convinced that enough criminals would be executed to make the penalty worthwhile as a deterrent.

The Bill had passed seamlessly through the first two readings in the House of Commons after it had been drafted by Valerie Whiting. Finally the third stage of the vote was complete and all of the 650 MPs in the Commons had walked through the doors which split them into two groups, one for the Bill and one against it, and the Speaker was ready to announce the results.

"This House has hereby voted on the enacting of the Bill for the Restoration of Capital Punishment. The Bill is read a third and final time and the House is divided: Ayes to the left, four hundred and six."

The Conservative benches erupted in cheers and shouts, and nobody waited for Allitt to finish his speech. News commentators cut across him to explain the result of the vote and when the news was announced to Trafalgar Square a few seconds later millions of people, from Nelson's Gallows to Buckingham Palace and Parliament Square, exploded into a huge celebration of unrestrained euphoria as the news of the vote sank in. It was a vast and proud carnival of death, with children dancing in the streets and revellers plunging into the freezing red water of the Trafalgar Square fountains, overcome with laughter and joy.

John Allitt dutifully finished his speech even though he knew that nobody was listening to him. "Noes to the right, two hundred and forty four. The Ayes have it. I hereby declare that the question is accordingly agreed to and I recommend it to the House of Lords where if the vote is successful, it will be passed into law with immediate effect. The House is dismissed."

Valerie Whiting had screamed with delight and spontaneously hugged the Prime Minister on the front bench as the benches behind them erupted in triumphant celebration when they realised that their bid had passed on to the next stage. In the public gallery, Geoff Hewitt punched the air and let out a roar of aggressive satisfaction at the news, but Alice stayed in her seat and stared out of the glass window at the room far below them, the majority of MPs cheering and celebrating in ecstatic jubilation and some others holding their heads in downhearted defeat. A good day for democracy, no doubt, but a bad day for humanity's birthright to life. Alice did not know how to react; firstly she thought that it was all very premature because this would be, at best, the halfway mark of the MLC campaign. But also there was something so unjust about it all, so vulgar and tawdry about the triumphant revelling in the death and destruction that had befallen the UK ever since Leo Faulkner had begun to stalk their daughter. There was no end to the circle of death in this result, no closure, no sense of the pain ceasing upon the news of more bloodshed, and Alice saw it that if Joy could not be exhumed and restored to life and if there was no form of institutionalised justice which would undo the hurt that this experience would cause them then they should end the circle of death and cease the killing. Something sickened her in the way that death was somehow joyful because the man deserved to die. Was every death not a tragedy, the foulest of all fates to befall an individual and the darkest hour of human civilisation? It was Alice's firm and clear belief that the grim demise of a person, no matter how evil or abhorrent, should never be an opportunity for jubilation.

5

WASTED

The day after the Commons had voted to pass the Bill, an emergency session of the House of Lords had been scheduled and they would vote with the prospect of telephoning Belmarsh Prison the same afternoon and giving the order for Leo Faulkner to be executed. The House of Lords had garnered itself something of an unfortunate reputation amongst the British public, with many seeing them as hopelessly out of touch with the country that they held a powerful veto over and as being very carefully planted in positions of authority by a Government who decided who would be given peerages allegedly in exchange for voting loyalties, or more scandalously, cash donations to the political parties. They had a famously atrocious attendance record for turning up for votes and debates and most of them were on the executive boards of giant corporations in the City and the general consensus amongst the public was that they saw their duty to the nation in the Lords as an inconsequential and trivial chore. Seven hundred and forty six of them were eligible to sit, and following a tempestuous day in the Commons and on the protest lines it turned out that every single one of them made the trip to London to vote on the Restoration Bill. It was the busiest assembly in the House of Lords in one hundred and three years.

Because of the fact that the Commons Vote had been more exhausting and traumatising than they had anticipated, Alice and Geoff had asked for Valerie Whiting to phone them when the results of the vote from the House of Lords which was due that afternoon. As they were in London, the Hewitts had decided to take the train from Waterloo and stop off at Raynes Park to have a look at the old house, to satisfy the memories. Crossing over Westminster Bridge under a sky of granite grey, Alice stopped on the side of the pavement to look out over the railing. All around them tourists were swarming and street entertainers were shouting and singing, Alice could hear at least a dozen languages being spoken by the technicolour faces and because of the impromptu food carts around the side of the road the air had the very strange aroma of slightly burnt honey-roasted cashew nuts. Someone thrust into her hands a buy one get one free voucher for West End tickets. Alice looked over the side of the railing towards the London Eye and Somerset House, with her back to the Gothic grandeur of Parliament and the men and women deciding the fate of their daughter's killer, looking far down to the swirling and churning waters of the Thames. At first Alice thought that the foamy whiteness of the wake of river ferries lacing across the shining surface of the Thames made it look slightly like marble, but she realised that it had none of the purity and beauty of white marble as the river was a disgusting shade of brown. The January wind over the river blew cold and blunt, and it was sad to see that the cheer and heartiness of Christmas had evaporated from the city like the smoke from their cottage chimney in Higher Pelham. Geoff caught Alice looking down at the water, hypnotized by the swirls which looked like syrup resting on ice cream, her hair being blown about her head wildly by the freezing wind. The clouds were cracked.

"Do you ever think about jumping?"

Alice stood back up and turned to him, looking him full in the face out of shock at what he had just said. His face was the colour of ash and his eyes were glazed and distant, almost as though he was looking completely through her and up towards Hungerford Bridge. She had never, ever thought of that; he had to know that she would never do that to him, and Jonathan and Kate, and until earlier in the year, Joy as well. It was an unthinkable act of desperation and selfishness and a place of despair that she would never reach. Alice stood on the bridge, completely stunned by what he had said to her. It was a horribly morbid and tragic question to ask and subject matter to think about considering the fact that the life of a man to whom they would forever be inextricably entangled by the silken cords of destiny was being held on a knife-edge in the building behind them, but also it was a question that he should never have needed to ask her. A husband's duty is to know his wife's state of mind so well, for them to be so close that he would never be in a position where the question would need to be asked at all. That January afternoon on Westminster Bridge, she scared herself by not recognising her husband for the first time in their whole marriage. In those words he revealed himself to her as a stranger.

She shook her head and she spluttered her answer back at him. Her heart was churning as fast and as coldly as the water of the river far below, and her voice was hollow with disbelief.

"No, Geoff. No I haven't thought about jumping."

He looked far out towards the bend in the river behind which St Paul's Cathedral and the Leviathan Building both hid reclusively. There was a yellow glaze in his eyes, a weariness the colour of ash, a cold and bitter frustration. The process of waiting for months to hear what would happen to the man who had killed his daughter was an exhausting and draining ordeal. His eyes were distant and reminded her of looking into the eyes of a stranger. She didn't feel as though she knew him any more after he had asked her that most disturbing of questions. Quite naturally, she assumed that his senseless question spoke of a deep hurt within him and a cleverly veiled anguish which could claim his life with self harm or suicide. Wondering what he was thinking was no less distressing than hearing the evidence in the courtroom about what had happened to Joy.

They finished crossing the river and took the pathway beside the Aquarium, beside the London Eye and made a right turn towards the footbridge which led them to the entrance to the station. Waterloo was one of those places which never seemed to change; the faces on the enormous concourse were completely interchangeable, dashing about in the most extraordinary parade of human life, the heartbeat of this great city, with young male commuters clutching briefcases and rucksacks and the women in smart skirts and pearl necklaces, but the actual architecture of the place seemed eternal and the commuters themselves were simply furniture. Old women would gaze from ripened eyes on the scene which appeared to them as a painting by Lowry, a scene of total anonymity even though every one of the hundreds of faces was on show for all to see. Over in the centre of the concourse was the great station clock and beneath it young lovers were embracing as intimately as possible given the very public setting; whether they were kissing to mark a passionate reunion or a tragic separation was unclear. Alice was suddenly very aware of the band of gold around her wedding finger as she looked at them, running her thumb over it as her thoughts took her back to the early days of her marriage when she would come here to meet Geoff after work as a surprise. She was troubled by the fact that she did not recognise him on the bridge, and hurried forwards and held his hand tightly as her coat flared slightly. His fingers seemed smaller than she thought they would be and they seemed to slip between hers. As she caught up with her husband Alice glanced over towards the people beneath the clock. Were they kissing hello or goodbye?

The roof was as filthy as they remembered, with strangely deformed pigeons hobbling around the floor on stumps, looking to scavenge the contents of the brown paper bags dispensed by the numerous sandwich counters around the concourse and the occasional corrugated brown cups which had been placed on top of an overflowing bin. A few teenagers were sat on the base of the statue of Gerald Harper, the British sprinter who had died in a plane crash following his gold medal in the 200m at the Olympic Games in 2024. The departure board was a dizzying sea of black and orange, listing endless numbers and times and destinations which Alice would occasionally recognise with a heartfelt pang of sentimentality, and the inhuman and computerised voice would announce the imminently departing train with exactly the same steely and empty emotion every time. To the residents of deepest rural English Utopia it seemed horribly deprived of personality, all very impersonal and the coldness of the digital displays troubled her. All of the trains were a familiar blend of red, orange and white and the companies were still fighting for space both on the gargantuan advertising billboards and the temporary shop booths that had been arranged messily across the concourse.

Alice and Geoff pressed their Oyster cards down on the circular yellow readers and walked forwards through separate barriers and onto the platform. They boarded the train to Chessington South from platform 3 and sat on the right hand side, with their windows facing the vaulted cathedral like ceiling of the station and the Eye beyond it. After a few minutes which everyone spent staring at the other passengers and reading the newspapers, the train rolled into motion. The journey was so ingrained in them; once someone leaves London, it seems as though the city does not leave them. Geoff looked earnestly at the scenery around him; the wide river of railway tracks of which they sailed down the middle, the sleepers and gravel stones and rivets and davits blurring into a broad whole as the train gathered speed. They passed the MI5 Building, Battersea Power Station and brief glimpses of the Thames. It was when they got to the outskirts of Clapham that they really appreciated the fact that they were going home to their countryside bliss with all of its space and freedom and the new life they had chased which so rightfully should have worked out perfectly. The endless ocean of tiny brick terraced houses, one of which they used to fit into as a family of five, stretched as far as the eye could see with stifling monotony. Gloomy windows all faced onto one another and the small enough houses were slowly converted into flats and in the insatiable quest for space the houses would sprout bristling skylights, heightened ceilings and tiny turrets. The vast forest of chimney pots spread out before them as far as the eye could see. It was shocking to them, even though the time that they had lived here had been so very recent, that the rows of houses stretched so far and wide, street after street, on and on.

Between Clapham Junction and Earlsfield, Geoff's phone rang. He answered, and as he had expected, it was the Justice Secretary. The conversation very quickly turned to the result of the vote as Geoff was worried about losing signal on the train and Valerie Whiting did not really have time for small talk after such an important vote. He recited the vote to his wife as he heard it from the Secretary.

"There were five abstentions, Mr Hewitt"

"Five abstentions."

"And three hundred and seventy Lords voted in favour of introducing the death penalty to the UK."

"Three hundred and seventy in favour."

There was a long silence and then Geoff began to cry uncontrollably in the seat closest to the window. Everyone in the carriage began to stare at him, whilst Alice's mind raced as she tried to keep up with the numbers. She knew that there were seven hundred and forty six in the House, and three hundred and seventy five had been counted already. Her brain whirred as she took the information in. Three hundred and seventy one. It was three hundred and seventy one. The campaign for the death penalty had been rejected by the Lords by a single vote.

Geoff and Alice got off of the train at Raynes Park. The sky was creased like tinfoil and the wind was picking up; soon they would have to head home, but they had some unfinished business to attend to. The station was elevated above the road and so Alice and Geoff carefully walked down the stairs from the platform together, exiting through the same barrier and turning left down the long tunnel that led beneath the tracks towards the main road.

As the couple exited the tunnel Alice glanced over and watched the people in the window of the coffee shop, hidden from her by a transparent and impenetrable barrier; a young couple were drinking hot coffees from big mugs behind the glass, and as Alice saw this she was suddenly made aware of the bitter winter wind sweeping through the area from the direction of Worple Road. As she watched, the girl raised her hand and put it up to the side of her lover's head, with her thumb on his cheek and her fingers behind his ear. With the thumb she stroked him tenderly and slowly. Alice thought of the violent marks left on her daughter's head, the storms of passion which killed her in the same tender gesture and then saw the love in the eyes of these two young dreamers and saw how different it was, the delicacy of it all, the intimacy in a very public coffee shop in winter and the display of love as it should be, as if she was passing a museum rather than a place where living and breathing souls collide. She thought of her daughter, her precious and beautiful Joy, and how she would never reach the age of this pair; Joy would never have a coffee with her boyfriend and would never become the attractive young woman Alice could see now. The pair in the window had a long and a beautiful future ahead of them, and they were a picture of happiness. If Alice didn't know better she would have thought that the glass in the window was gradually getting thicker and thicker. Geoff had headed off again, with his chin against his chest, striding up Lambton Road towards his old home.

Turning right, they came to the small road of terrace houses that they used to call home. Geoff got there first, and Alice came behind him, her hair blowing messily about her head. It was the sort of road which you can walk down the centre of with no need to worry about the traffic; a sombre hush prevailed and even though the street was so close to the centre of Raynes Park the quietness was powerful enough to have a strong and noticeable impact on them, and rather than the commotion and fluidity of Coombe Lane. As well as an opaque quietness there was a sombre stillness in the heavy air. The trees which had once bloomed loudly with life along each pavement down the sides of the small road were now frail skeletons which withered with the curse of mortality, reaching up from the ground like the haggard hands of a corpse, furnished with mottled grey veins running up the length of the trunks. The thousands of individual clay bricks which were used to build the terraces had always flourished in their memories as a radiant deep red, but now they wore a horribly anonymous grey beneath a darkening sky. Gloom reigned.

Walking forwards, Geoff and Alice eventually came to the front of number 85, Rosevine Road. It was a beautiful little house, a cramped but idyllic little slice of the terraced anonymity of South West London. They had made it a very modern and professional little thing, with a kitchen of chrome and dark wood that was a thousand miles away from the traditional idyll of Archangel Lane. If houses could be proud, this one certainly was; through a decision made by previous owners it had become the only one in the terrace with a painted exterior, which led Jonathan to rather proudly refer to his home as The White House, in an erroneously naive and accidental boast of incredibly grand ambition. The roof was a rich shade of terracotta red, and it had a little chimney and a beautiful front door of duck egg blue with frosted glass windows. There was a large number 85 above the doorway etched in glass. The fence was a small line of wooden stakes and the garden—if a garden it may be called because of its astonishingly tiny size and Capability Brown would have been severely impeded—was a favourite of Kate's when she was small enough to be able to run around it. There was a miniature flowerbed in the centre in a diamond shape and white gravel surrounded it, which she used to run around at full speed and pretend that this tiny slice of a street in London was her own vast hedge maze, perhaps in Hampton Court or Longleat. She imagined herself running down the pretend avenues of vast hedges and immaculate lawns in a blue and white dress chasing a rabbit with a pocket-watch or running away from a deck of cards.

Number 85 faced directly down Trewince Road and gave a commanding view of the whole street, which just like Rosevine was a quiet little road of terraced brick houses, although none of them were lucky enough to be white. It too was lined with small trees and pristine little gardens, and there had been a great excitement and awe amongst the children when some of the officers of the Metropolitan Police had asked Geoff for permission to set up a small surveillance camp in the front room of the Hewitt family home in order to record the movements of certain residents of a house in Trewince Road of whom they suspected serious criminal activity. In a horrifically ironic and disturbing premonition Geoff and Alice wordlessly remembered at the exact same moment the time when a particularly malicious and cruel Kate had told Jonathan and Joy about Capital Punishment. Joy, aged five, had asked the policemen what was going to happen to the men because she was worried that they would be hauled to the Tower and literally beheaded by an axe wielding King in some bizarre public relations initiative to promote law and order amongst his people. The man had told her that she could sleep easily because "nobody gets executed any more, we don't do things like that to people now". Today, after the vote, his word still stood true, but only just. That fact did not enable Geoff Hewitt to sleep easily at all, but instead was the most disturbing thing he had ever heard.

There were builders in, and a large yellow skip was in the road outside of number ten so people kept coming out of the house to load building materials into it and the van parked next to it. With a smile they both saw that number seventeen was as neglected as ever and the decay of the exterior was progressing nicely. Leafless vines of ivy climbed up to the roof and the windows were abandoned to curtains of grime holding out the light. Nobody had lived there in years. It was a very quiet street but occasionally a car would come by and perhaps someone would come down the road on foot; Alice's heart seized up as she saw a mother pushing a pram down Pepys Road at the end, just as she so recently had herself with Joy and had wished that she could have done with David. They stood on the pavement on the opposite side of the road; Rosevine only had a single row of terraced houses on one side, for on the other were large brick walls marking the gardens of the last houses on the neighbouring roads and the vast windowless brick facades of the edges of the terraced houses themselves. The couple faced the whole of the long terrace and watched in silence. They were both very nervous of being recognised and of looking suspicious, lingering as they were on the other side of the street and looking at the row of houses in a place which was no longer home. They looked at their own old house so closely, imagining the children in the front two bedrooms; Kate and Joy in the room with the big bay window and Jonathan had the tiny bedroom with the window above the front door, which he was initially very unhappy about but in the end decided that he loved because he could 'keep watch'. At the time they had felt desperately unhappy and miserable, yearning to break free of the stifling claustrophobia and live in the tranquillity and beauty of the quiet countryside but now, retrospectively, Rosevine Road was just as much of the paradise that Higher Pelham had boasted proudly of but had failed so spectacularly to deliver to them. Truthfully Alice hated this home, hated this road and hated her life here, but given the wrenching pain of the loss of her daughter she thought that the biggest tragedy of all was the fact that she did not appreciate perfection when it was presented to her, instead she chased it out of the city and halfway across England. It was a blissful way of life and she didn't even realise it. She looked up at the big bay window of her daughter's bedroom, picturing her asleep in her bed behind the great mass of curtain that blocked the house off from their prying eyes. The Hewitts were unwelcome now.

Once they had seen their old home and were satisfied that it was time to move on, they headed back towards the station and began the train journey home which was long and complicated. They headed back into Waterloo to collect their bags from the hotel, and then changed trains at Richmond, Reading and Castle Cary, finally arriving in Pelham Central on the late train which arrived at 23.49. Needless to say, it was a very long day of travelling. The fact that the village was almost completely unreachable from London and the North was the exact reason why they had chosen to move there the previous spring.

That night in London the atmosphere was of a dumbfound silence. Following the success of the vote in the Commons they had a large amount of confidence in the result of the vote in the Lords, assuming that they would uphold the wishes of the Government and most people saw the result as reasonably predictable. When it was revealed that the current system of life imprisonment would be remaining and executions would not be performed on British soil, the national reaction was quiet shock rather than violent bursts of outraged indignation. The pro life movement, which had been all but drowned out by the media storm and the voices of powerful politicians as well as the uproar in Trafalgar Square, quietly and finally took their moment to be heard as they set off a firework display from The Leviathan, the tallest building in the world which stood on Bishopsgate, in huge bursts of pure white light. The glass building shone like a vast vigil candle, a steadfast symbol of life amongst the surging, baying mob of bloodthirsty protesters demanding the head of Leo Faulkner. Whilst the pro execution campaign seemed to explode in irregular, unpredictable and spectacular outbursts of enraged demands for law change, the anti execution campaign shone a small and steadfast light which never quite burned out, a still small voice which vowed to protect and uphold the life of any man, no matter how evil or condemned he may be. A banner was unfurled from the suicide railing on the observation deck on the Leviathan's roof, which was not visible from the naked eye from street level and so was shown on TV programmes from news helicopters. The letters were made from painted handprints, and the banner read WE ARE NOT MONSTERS YET. Human rights charities saw it as a very important victory for the progress of civilised societies.

Soon enough the family received letters from Buckingham Palace and Downing Street. Alice was the one to read them, and she opened the letter from the King first. Alice's fingers swam over the envelope, trying to comprehend the magnitude of this single piece of paper. Whilst having never particularly nurtured a huge ambition to specifically receive a letter from the King, she knew that these telegrams were meant to be a celebration of life, a paper monument to a life well lived and honouring longevity, whereas instead this one was in tragic memoriam to a life snuffed out at an unjustly young age. It seemed such a shame, in a way, for the King to have given her this under the circumstances that had befallen her.

Dear Mr and Mrs Hewitt.

It is with great sadness that I learn more and more of the suffering of your family at this time of tragedy and unspeakable loss. Due to my role in the constitutional monarchy of this country I am unable to comment on the developments regarding the proposed restoration of the death penalty, but I will say that I admire the bravery and resilience that you have shown in the face of a terrible crime. It has been with a sense of great pride that I have seen a young mother and father refuse to be defeated by the evil of one man and stand so bravely for justice and the rights of this nation's children. The British people are very proud of your considerable achievements for your daughter's memory. You have the sympathy and prayers of both myself and my household at this difficult time.
With every best wish.

Yours sincerely,
His Majesty King William V

Daniel Huntley had also written to them to explain that his party would not be supporting an appeal against the decision in the House of Lords and that as far as he was concerned the case was closed, but he did take the time to wish them all the best and again offer his condolences for their loss. It seemed perfectly genuine; there was no talk of relying upon their vote in the next election, just of how horrible Joy's death was. "Thank you for trying to end the suffering of other families who may in the future be faced with the same heartbreaking circumstances as those you have come to be familiar with in the last few months." He said that he would be supporting "Joy's Law", which was an idea suggested by Geoff that would allow parents to demand access to sensitive information about people they suspected of being sexual criminals. Alice had eventually relented and agreed to compromise on the use of her daughter's name in legislation, and it was passed through Parliament as the first law of the new session.

Over the coming days and nights Geoff would spend more and more time in the village pub, often on his own. He would never tell Alice that he had gone to The Green Man, but in honesty she did not need telling. His secrets were written all over his face in great calligraphic squiggles, every line and pore and freckle and blemish screaming of his guilt. Alice found it almost amusing that he would bother to lie to her when it was so obvious.

He had always been the one to do all of the shopping for the family, and the shopping list was a carefully organised labour of love which he had always taken on as his role within the household; the paternal instinct to provide for his wife and children had somehow always meant more to him that just simply being the breadwinner, and he felt that in addition to the financial provision he had to be the one who would bring home the food that his family would eat. It was a deeply masculine appeal that only he seemed to understand.

Because of his insistence on meticulously planning and organizing the shopping list and the family budget, Alice did not have any realistic way of deciding or limiting what was being bought at the supermarket every week. Even after the death of Joy, the family was too big to survive on the produce of the small parade of shops that lines the high street without travelling further afield to buy everything that they needed. When Geoff was working in his study or was away on a business trip she would search for his wallet, but he always took it with him everywhere he went. He was fiercely protective of his finances and paranoid that people were checking up on him.

One morning when Geoff had taken Kate and Jonathan to school Alice found it, lying on the kitchen counter. They must have been late, just as they had been on the morning of Joy's death. She opened it and found the receipt from the supermarket inside. The total was £309.43, which was roughly double what she had been expecting; looking down the list of items she saw that he had bought a huge amount of alcohol. Was this why he had suddenly become so secretive when it came to finances and bank accounts? Was this why he had been so obsessive when it came to organising and arranging the cupboards? There were bottles of whisky and vodka, multiple six packs of beer, endless bottles of wine, cases of rum, some gin and finally a bottle of brandy nestling between the toothpaste and the tins of tuna. As she looked at the list of items that her husband had bought from the supermarket that week Alice's mind raced. What did this mean? Was he selling it on for a profit? There certainly did not seem to be a vast stash of alcohol in any of the obvious places where she would have expected him to keep it. The following morning she woke up early and searched the house but did not find what she was looking for. It was a special day, but she barely noticed. He didn't leave it at the end of their bed as he had done when Joy was around. The special morning became the special afternoon, and Alice walked the dog through the frozen meadows, the crystallised clouds of breath clinging to their faces as they walked together along the edge of Pelham Hill, looking down on the silent world below.

Geoff, meanwhile, had visited a cocktail bar in Bristol and he did not keep track of the time. Rooted to his bar stool in perfect solitude, he held the shot glass to his mouth and tipped it back. He saw bursting supernovas, felt the exhilaration of a skydive rushing through his veins, soared up through the stars and touched the roof of Heaven. The buzz fizzed and crackled in his throat in a strong, thumping aftertaste. He had never until now considered the reasons why the lure of alcohol was so impossible to resist, but it simply made his existence more euphoric and made him realise how monotone the world was without the compulsive appeal of intoxication. Drinking felt like the opposite of going colour-blind. What else was there to live for? What other source of pleasure, what sense of purpose could be attained from the worthless treasures that plagued the modern man? The relentless pursuit of them was exhausting and depressing and compared not with the rushing, indefatigable relief that surged through him when the alcohol hit his brain cells as though they were a line of dominoes. He had wondered how far down the road he must venture before he should be considered an addict, but then he looked back the way he had come. The Western world and its relentless obsession with enlightened freedom and democracy was so unimaginably oppressive, far more so than his freeing and liberating attraction to pubs and off licences. He had wondered what alcohol could offer him, but the attraction was more in what it could remove. To ask what it could offer was to miss the point entirely; to see its beauty you had to consider the alternative, for the world was so dark. He was already an addict and he had been since he had been born. He had been born into a society which was addicted to political correctness, which enforced oppressive and outdated laws some of which were enshrined in the legal system and others were so socially unacceptable that they may as well have been. Workers were simply paid slaves. Those not in relationships were failures, only slightly worse than those who were married but childless. Taxation was socialised theft. Insurance was a compulsory form of gambling. Mortgage payments were a slower and more inconvenient way of strangling yourself. Normality and fashion had to be adhered to more stringently than any totalitarian regime's crazy restrictions. Television was king. It was impossible to go down a high street without seeing the ruthless demolition of culture and individualism and the construction of commercial behemoths and massive conglomerations in its place. Capitalism was simply being offered the choice between multiple corporations which were all exactly the same, exploiting and repackaging as they went. Supermarkets owned your soul with every ring of the till. Parents worked day and night to support families who hated them and then scraped together enough for a pension, then they died just as ingloriously as they had been born. Individualism was suppressed as much by capitalism as it was by communism and Geoff felt an outburst of resentment every time the Government reminded the British people of their liberties. As his eyes rolled back in his head, fizzing and bursting with the chemical ecstasy, Geoff could not believe that anyone would ever have the audacity to call him free. The world was drenched in bleakness.

What the hell was wrong with everybody? What possible reason could there ever be to not drink alcohol?

The hour was late, and Alice had been in bed a while as she heard the key turn in the front door of the cottage. She had not been intending to wait up for her husband but she was unable to sleep without him next to her if she did not know where he had gone. She didn't know what the time was; the cobbled streets of Higher Pelham were silent, the candle flames all extinguished and the shuttered windows dark. There was no moon. The fire in the sitting room had burnt down to a dull glow, and the flush of the embers flickered in the very bottom of the grate. The silence was so vociferous that it was as though she could hear the midwinter frost falling on the fields and woods outside of the village. The children were dreaming, undoubtedly; she could almost hear Jonathan's imaginings of breathless cliff-tops and magical castles and Kate's visions of swimming with dolphins in lagoons made of gold. Milly was in her basket downstairs, keeping warm beside the ruins of the fire.

Geoff opened the bedroom door as quietly as he could. As she watched him, her eyes barely open but her spirit vigilant, she thought that she could detect some staggering as he moved. He whispered her name but she did not respond, clutching the pillow tighter and keeping perfectly still. He undressed and climbed into bed next to her; she did not know if he had been to the bathroom to brush his teeth and getting into bed was the first thing he seemed to do. She was in her nightdress and he was naked, and a smell seemed to fill the room as soon as he walked in, creeping out of his every pore and crawling between the bedclothes. Geoff smelt strongly of a thick and rancid concoction of alcohol and vomit. His yellow eyes rolled around inside of his head and his skin had a dusty complexion that had not been there before. She waited until he had fallen asleep, that his raspy breathing was steady and frequent enough to know that the metronome of his unconscious had taken over, before she turned to take a closer look at him. It was an exceptionally dark night, but she felt as though every line and feature on the face that she had loved so deeply for so long was illuminated from within, and she was intimately aware of everything. She raised a hand and let it hover over his face so that she could feel his breath, the gentle tickle feathering against her skin, and gazed in dumb wonder on the wreckage of her husband. What had become of the family that she had spent the past sixteen years building? Inside his wounded spirit she could feel a storm raging, a vast tempest churning in the palm of her hand as she held it a above his eyes. He always slept better than she had, but she was beginning to think that it was because of the alcohol and not because of any sense of peace. She looked over towards the wardrobe, and there was a chest next to it which she had used to store blankets in for the winter; now that they were on all of the beds to guard against the cold weather the chest lay empty. It had on it a huge, gleaming steel padlock which she had never noticed before. Happy birthday, Alice. Thank you for being my wife. Instead his eyes were closed and his voice was dormant.

When morning came she asked him if he had remembered to buy her a birthday present. It was a moment of revelation as he admitted that he was drinking more than he used to, telling her that he did not have enough money left over to buy her a present because of the increased amount that he was spending on booze. "Sorry, darling," he called over his shoulder as he left the cottage on his way to the pub. He quite clearly did not regret what he had done; he was simply accepting the inevitability of the fact that an increase in alcohol meant a decrease in disposable income. It was simple mathematics, and Alice was clearly an idiot for thinking that there was more to it than that.

Over the coming days Alice noticed that, when she would get up and get the children ready for school, Geoff was waking later and later. On the weekends he would stay in bed for much of the day and wake up around lunchtime, if not later, and he was often too tired to wash or shave. The lullaby of alcohol was mesmerising, hypnotising him into a bleak trance and he was beginning to see that there was a beautiful symmetry in the kaleidoscope of addiction. He drained the magic out of every bottle and they began to pile up in the recycling bin like the Tower of Babel.

The agonising pain of having a daughter stolen shot through Geoff's body as though his bloodstream was made of acid. He was corroded and tarnished, and he needed the alcohol in him to give him a sense of life, a spark of spirit to make it through and endure the unending heartbreak. With every glass bottle of delight that he emptied he was filled with courage and pleasure, and as the cans were thrown away he felt completed again. The skies above crinkled like tinfoil and the whole world shrank and echoed as though Geoff had his head underwater. He saw colours, sparks, shocks, spins, flames and stars.

Before the murder the last thing that Geoff saw at night was the beautiful face of his wife, and the first thing he saw when the sun rose and the day began was also Alice. From the night of her disappearance he saw Alice's familiar form morph and transform into the face of his daughter as the light in the bedroom was extinguished, and her angelic features were etched against the tangible darkness in the room with the squeal of chalk on a blackboard. Her face haunted and penetrated his every thought, waking and sleeping, and after a night of heavy slumber she was there to greet him when he awoke. He pictured the parts of her that he had never seen and the occasions and memories that he had never experienced; Joy would appear to him in varying degrees as an old woman, a mother with small children, a moody teenager, a university student and a headstrong career woman. The most touching and heartbreaking apparition that he saw of her was little Joy, his little intact maiden, clutching his arm as he led her down the aisle, her cheeks as flushed and glowing with life as the bunch of roses and lilies in her bouquet, with her handsome prince staring steadfastly ahead, refusing to ruin the wholesome reward for which he had waited for so long. But before they ever reached the handsome young man ahead of them the bedroom of Magnolia Cottage became once again a sickening charnel house and the corpse of his daughter was there to greet him when morning came.

The pain that was the sharpest in his gut was the fact that he knew that a man was with her when she died, at her moment of greatest vulnerability, but it was not him as it should have been. He was robbed and mugged of his masculinity and parenthood, castrated by the man who had had his gluttonous fill of Geoff's exquisite daughter. The pain was bottomless and infinite. Alcohol, that old friend, helped him greatly to endure the unendurable. He began drinking at all hours of the day, having a lager for breakfast and drinking swigs from a vodka bottle that he kept in the glove-box of the car whenever he had to drive somewhere; at first it was only for when he was alone as the glove-box was lockable and he would hide the key, but eventually he became bolder and began to take great gulps with Kate and Jonathan in the car as well. Whichever combination of members of the Hewitt family were in the car together it had always been a crucible of great conversation and happy chatter, but with this new dark habit the children became effigies of stone, staring straight ahead in uncomfortable silence. The fizz of the vodka colliding with his brain and ricocheting through his skull distracted him from any desire to talk to his family. Alice did not know about this; if she had known that he was endangering the lives of their children and could not make him stop she would have been forced to tell the police, and it was a truth that Geoff knew. She had never been afraid of her husband in her entire life, but she now found herself unable to confront him about the drinking.

But drink he did. Every loaded bubble in the champagne glass stung with ethereal pleasure as it slammed against his bones and nerves, rupturing his neutrons and charging his bloodstream as alcohol's sweet symphony was etched on his soul with all of the orgasmic, prickling, addictive, throbbing pain of a fresh tattoo. The hangovers would glow like a sunrise in the lobes at the front of his cranium, burning brightly behind his eyeballs. In his bed, wasted and barely conscious, he knelt by the streams of trickling alcohol and scooped great handfuls into his mouth, he laughed in delirious wonder at the sensation of it flowing down his oesophagus as he inhaled. The world's blandness, its tasteless lack of colour, was the faintest of memories now that his bloodstream sang like the crystal champagne flute did when he circled the rim with his finger. Zzzing.

The clear and cold winter skies above Higher Pelham burnt with the colour of ethanol.

6

MELANCHOLIA

Once the Movement for Law Change had come to the end of the road, the time came to bury Joy. The family had waited as long as possible, firstly because they were made to as the forensic tests on the body were being completed with an unprecedented thoroughness because of the nature of the historic case, and secondly because they wanted to end their love affair with Joy and move on from the trauma now that the vote in Parliament had gone through and they could finally say goodbye in peace. The whole time that the battle for Leo's life was going on they could not properly see the case as closed and finished, and in a situation over which they had no control whatsoever they took great pride and pleasure in choosing the exact circumstances of when and how they would end the saga. They would finish it with Joy's funeral and not Leo's; she was a thousand times the human that he was, and she deserved the very best.

She had been preserved in a vast cocktail of chemicals because of the nature of the examinations on her and the investigations into what had happened, so when it finally came to the funeral spring was close. Snowdrops carpeted the forest floor in the woods surrounding Higher Pelham and the fields were sprouting the first crops of the year. The trees were gathering leaves and the meadows were slowly returning to flourished life again, and the apple orchards which had not seen any growth on the branches over a long and cold winter slowly began to regain their sense of vitality.

The night before the funeral, Alice finally summoned the strength to look at what he had done to her daughter. Geoff had already seen the corpse and Kate had not wanted to, whilst they refused to allow Jonathan to because they decided that he was too young. She was being prepared for burial in a small room in the funeral parlour, containing only the coffin and a row of cabinets below a worktop with a washbasin and mirror to one side. Either side of the head of the coffin were two vast arrangements of lilies, great bursts of white fragrance clothed in white and green, and the flowers looked like the trumpets she would surely be listening to as they saluted her entrance to heaven. Above her head was a small and simple cross on the windowsill. The undertaker came in and bowed his head respectfully, maintaining a silence, and slowly and carefully lifted the lid off of the coffin before leaving Alice and Joy to be alone together.

"Hi sweetheart," she said quietly. Joy's face was cloudy and marbled with the rusty silver hue of death and her eyes were closed. Even though the undertakers had been careful to make her face as presentable and recognisable as possible Alice could still see a huge finger-mark on her left temple. Her hair had been washed and no longer had huge clumps of soil in it and her lips were now a deep wine red. She was dressed in a long white dress with an extremely high and frilly neckline that covered everything below her chin, and she had a single fresh sunflower in her hands. Alice could not bear the silence, so she began to speak to her daughter.

"I miss you, Joy. You look like they have taken good care of you." She took her hand; it felt like Plasticine. "I love you and I am so very proud of you. I'm sorry that I was angry that last day. When we are busy sometimes we forget that we love each other, and I am so sorry about that."

She realised as she looked upon the face of her daughter, the second attempt that the Hewitts had made at a third child, she realised that she had been wrong to think that David's death was more painful than the death of a child she had come to know and love. She would give anything to relive that experience now, for if Joy must die, it was surely better for her to die without seven long years of loving attachment to the family before she was ripped away. The happy memories they shared together were intricately connected to the brutal and violent way in which their precious child had been killed. If Joy had died as a newborn baby the grief would have been excruciating but it would have been endurable. This moment, sitting beside a seven-year-old's open coffin, was surely the worst thing any mother could endure.

"I bought you some things," she said, opening her bag. There was a tiny wooden box which contained her first tooth, something stupid which mothers feel the need to keep because it is a part of the child which has grown inside them. She also had her favourite stuffed toy which was a rabbit named Milo, a blade of grass from the garden of Magnolia Cottage, some of Joy's favourite plastic jewellery and one of Milly's old collars. Finally she took out a framed photograph of the family, on a wonderfully happy day, and gave it a little kiss. Geoff looked luminous, full of life and love and laughter. Kate was pulling her best model's pout and Jonathan was tickling Joy whilst trying to stop his parents from seeing him do it. Joy was smiling with such effort that her eyes were small slits in her wrinkled face and her wide open mouth was filled with wobbly milk teeth. The Hewitts had a 50p rule which meant that any of the children caught ruining a photograph with intentionally ridiculous faces would be fined for arson. Alice smiled to herself, because the photograph really was hysterical. Joy was always guilty of that crime; there were literally thousands of pictures of her pulling obscene faces at the camera a split second before the shutter was pressed. Geoff had deleted them as soon as it happened, and Alice regretted letting him now. What a souvenir of a young and innocent life! She opened her purse and found a 50p piece to add to the pile, stroking her thumb over King William's face as she did so.

"You'll never believe he sent me a telegram," she whispered. Ha! Who'd have thought?

She stood up to leave and placed all of the items in the coffin, feeling as though she was interweaving precious and magical gems amongst the bandages of an ancient mummy in a pyramid. Alice did not believe in God, she did not believe that there would be any use her daughter could make of these items after her death, but it was a great comfort to her to place them next to her daughter's corpse. Milo and the others belonged with Joy. Finally she leant over, gave her daughter a kiss on the forehead, and wished her a good night's sleep.

The Hewitts had tried their best to cut all ties with the Envoy and Matthew Brady, but there was still a huge media presence on the village green when the funeral began. The square was filled with a huge crowd from all over the country and tragedy was in the air as the hearse drove through the village towards the ancient splendour of St George's. The blackness of the mourners' clothes and the procession of cars shone radiantly, eclipsing even the multicoloured bouquets that spelt out her name leaning up against her white coffin. The crowd was silent as the cars passed, throwing flowers into the road and onto the hearse and limousines, united together in outrage and a quiet, seething sadness in the face of a great tragedy.

No press were allowed into the church itself by orders of the family; a handful of reporters were allowed in on the condition that they surrendered their recording equipment on the doors. The service was simple and short. Jonathan and Kate read a poem for her and the vicar preached a sermon on 1 Corinthians 15 and the glorious future for the human body when Christ returns, a vast and immeasurable harvest of pure and abundant life and a physical resurrection promised to everyone who loves Jesus. There was not a dry eye in the church when he described how it would feel for Alice and Geoff to wrap their arms around Joy's healthy and restored body in the New Creation. It was impossible to now determine how painful it was for everyone in the village to see the heartbreaking contrast between that day to come and the situation they found themselves in today, burying a seven year old girl who had died in shockingly violent and sadistic circumstances at the hands of a sexual predator.

Afterwards they buried her coffin in the churchyard that she had been murdered in. It was tiny and made of oak painted white with gold inlay on the edges, and had been strengthened and padlocked closed so that there could be no chance that her body was exhumed again to be ruined once more. One by one, all of the people who loved this little girl came up the coffin and kissed it goodbye; Geoff's encounter was particularly touching as he stroked and patted the dead wooden lid as though it was his daughter's own face, as though it had magically become infused with the wondrous hue of vibrant and overflowing life.

As they prepared to lower the coffin into the graveyard Alice stepped forward, surrounded by the lush and living promise of spring and laid a single red rose picked from the flowerbed of their new home on the lid. Joy was then slowly and steadily lowered into the ground. Kate and Jonathan found themselves holding hands for the first time since Kate was six, and all of their relatives and friends had tears streaming down their cheeks as it sank out of sight. The earth was cold.

Afterwards the whole village seemed to gather together at The Green Man as the news stations outside broadcasted their reports to the studios in London and other cities across the world. Jonathan heard several American accents; the news channels had been fascinated with this story as President Gonzalez had attempted to influence the Prime Minister on the issue yet a huge number of Democratic voters were staunchly opposed to the justice system in their own states and welcomed the sentence passed down to Leo Faulkner. Geoff and Alice were in the pub until very late because they had wanted to meet as many of the crowd as possible, strangers who had come to bid farewell to a girl they never knew. The public reaction was of great comfort. Alice stood in the doorway of the pub, greeting people as they arrived and as they left and she was constantly being embraced and shaking hands with everyone; Geoff, however, sat at a solitary table by the window gazing out over the square and towards the churchyard with that dreadful glazed look in his eyes and pint after pint of lager was being emptied at the table. Nobody dared approach him because they had nothing to say to him and he seemed almost trancelike to the point where people wanted to leave him to his memories, sitting alone in the corner. It was a difficult day and the people wanted to let the Hewitt family do their grieving in the way that they found the most comfortable for them, but Alice was furious with her husband. She was seething with anger at him for being what she saw as disrespectful to the members of the public who had come to support the family in their hour of greatest need. He stayed at his table for the whole evening and did not speak to a single person, not even members of his own family.

That night in the cottage, when the last of the well wishers had gone home, Geoff Hewitt descended the tiny staircase and sat in his favourite chair beside the inglenook, gazing into the flames as he stroked Milly as she came to lie down next to him. His eyes never moved, not even once; he had not shaved in days and all about him clung an air of hopelessness and despair. The love and life in his heart had been extinguished and his reason for living was as perennial as the seed of a dandelion, scattering across the fields behind the village, rootlessly drifting.

Alice closed the door, knowing that a long and difficult day had gone by and that she could now rest and she came into the sitting room and saw her husband staring into the flickering embers. He had an almost empty bottle of whisky in his hand and his dark eyes were the colour of cloudy blood.

"I thought you were very rude today, Geoffrey."

He looked up at her and made eye contact for the first time all day. On their wedding day he had promised to love and cherish her forever, but she had felt the power of his promises fading away, slowly but surely, more and more every day.

"You will not take that tone with me."

"The whole village had come out to support us, to show us their love and solidarity, and you didn't even speak to anyone. No hellos, no goodbyes, no thank-yous. You just sat there drinking, being miserable. Do you think that that will help you move on?"

He stood up and filled the inglenook with his presence, casting huge shadows across the floor as the light of the fireplace flickered behind him. His face was dark but not motionless and she caught a strong smell of alcohol scattered across the air as she saw the bottle still in his hand. He was holding it tightly with his dirty fingers wrapped around the neck.

"Shut up, Alice."

She was quite shocked by his response and took a step backwards. Outside the latticed windows and above the sleeping village the stars were unsteady.

"What did you say to me?"

"I told you to shut that hole in your face."

"Don't speak to me like that, Geoffrey. I am your wife and I deserve your respect."

Without warning he threw the bottle from his right hand against the wall as hard as he could. It smashed against a Willow Pattern plate that was hanging from the stonework and both fell to the floor loudly. Alice was horrified and frightened, and thought of her sleeping children.

"What are you doing?"

"You have been so self righteous ever since Joy died and today was too much, Alice. You have no right to tell me how to grieve."

"I understand that you are angry with me but I think it is very important that Jonathan and Kate do not hear us arguing. I never pictured myself having that sort of family. Now close your mouth and let them sleep."

"You know what, Alice? I think you still have some explaining to do. I don't think anyone ever told me the reasons why you were acquitted by the child protection people after David died. I wasn't with you when his heart stopped and I am running out of reasons to convince myself that you didn't smother him or something. I don't know where you were the afternoon that Joy disappeared and I never will. Do you know what that has done to me? And do you remember the last words you ever said to our daughter?"

Geoff's face was suddenly possessed by a terrifying animation of hatred. He appeared to grow in the firelight, to rise far above Alice and loom over her tiny body. He slapped her as hard as he could and she found herself on her knees a split second later, reeling from the pain to the side of her face.

"Geoff, please. Please stop."

He towered above her like a huge skyscraper, the windows dark and the countless floors shrouded in gloom. He kicked her hard as she knelt before him and she climbed to her feet as fast as she could, standing in front of him again and holding her hands up to try to defend herself. It was like closing the front door of a house to stop it being destroyed by a nuclear bomb. She walked away from him slowly; both of them were breathing hard, and Geoff had the shadow of a tear trickling down his left eyelid.

With no signal he flipped again, running at her as fast as he could, his teeth gritted from the wrenching pain, raising his hands at her. She let out a strong shout and tried to make a break for the kitchen, but he caught her hand in his and pulled her back. He sent the coffee table flying with a flick of his wrist, leaving a trail of scattered magazines and broken china and alcohol stains all over the floor of the sitting room, and reached towards the fireplace. He grabbed at one of the pokers, a sharp weapon of gleaming brass, and began to hit her on the head with it drawing blood above her left eye. The poker fell to the ground with a clang and he tried everything else; he clawed at her face, scratched her skin and threw his fists into her cheeks and neck. As he hook her head in his hands and made a lunge to bite her ear she melted away from him in his hands; she was different now, morphing into a stranger beneath him, her skin malleable like glowing hot metal. He saw a hellish figure, a face that he recognised from a previous rendezvous. Pulling at her arms, he noticed that she had grown a small tattoo on her left wrist; a skull and crossbones with the phrase "death is inevitable" etched underneath. She was no longer Alice, but Leo. He punched him in the face as hard as he could, letting out a great roar of ferocious anger and frustration, vowing to kill him himself where Parliament had refused to. Leo fell to the ground and Geoff stamped on his face repeatedly, landing his heel in the centre of the fiend's face and drinking in the satisfaction that he felt as the blood spurted into the pile of the carpet. It felt like he was a child again, splashing in puddles in his wellies and watching the water splatter on either side of his glistening feet as he kicked with unrestrained joy. Leo climbed to his feet again and Geoff punched him, screaming and shouting something about paedophilia.

As the two of them stood together, clinching and grappling in the way that boxers do when they are too close together to fight, Alice reached her neck up and gave her husband a kiss, and Geoff was stunned by the similarity in passion and adrenaline between fighting and embracing. She caught him cleanly on the lips, captivated for a second, plunged once again into the memories that they had spent half a lifetime building together, remembering the first time as the stars had exploded in her belly all those years ago. As she kissed him, all that she could taste was her own blood. She was in agonising pain and she panted hoarsely as she trembled into his chest, her cheeks wet with tears and sweat. His shirt was slightly open and as she collapsed against him, hurting and exhausted, her bleeding nose nestled amongst the sparse hair dusted across his pectorals. He was strong, much stronger than she was, and she never stood a chance. They stood there, held together in an extraordinary stillness and not really knowing how to continue, like two actors who had run out of script. The moment that they spent in that peculiar embrace together seemed like an eternity, and Alice touched his hand with her fingertips, stroking him gently and slowly, trying to calm him down by charm because her physical resistance had done nothing to defend herself. She traced invisible pictures on his skin, tender and terrified.

"Alright darling, alright. That's enough now. That's enough now. Don't forget who we are. Don't forget how much you love me."

They were both panting and breathless, standing still in the middle of a chaos strewn sitting room with debris everywhere and the smell of spilt alcohol burning like acid inside her nostrils. He began to cry, but his weeping was more because of anger than sadness; his lips trembled and his face was moist with tears, but his teeth remained clenched and his tear-filled eyes were focused straight ahead. He spoke with the resoluteness of a mountain range.

"Our children are bastards, and you are not my wife."

*   *   *

That night was the final time they ever shared a bed. Geoff and Alice had not made love since the murder, mostly through Alice's choice because she could only imagine Leo and Joy taking their places. In her head her husband's body moulded into the paedophile's, his hair changing colour and the shapes and contours of his muscled skin transforming beneath her hands and between her legs like clay beneath the hands of the potter. Her own body, her temple to motherhood, lost its breasts, the hips shrank down to how they had been when she was a child and her calves and thighs lost their womanly definition. She told him to stop, but he didn't. She just wanted to lie there and go to sleep, withholding her body from him as some kind of sexual blackmail, but he was having none of it. He would thump her in the breast, pull her hair and claw at her face to make her lie on her back with her legs open; her legs felt like the hands of an enormous clock, but it was no longer half past six, and as he heaved at the hands, wrenching them apart, she felt as though the cogs and wheels and springs and bolts inside of her were going to explode out in a disastrous wreck of crumpled metal. She scratched at his face to get him off but he slid a hand up her back, clamouring at her flesh like the silken cords of the grave threading around her and pulling her down. With that hand he pulled her so that she slammed her back into the mattress and against her pleading and begging, he set about relieving himself.

When he had finished, the silence in the bedroom roared. Alice's motherhood had died on the 27th September and her womb felt like a deserted wasteland within her, the lush fields and forests concreted over, and her ovaries were now cold pebbles rather than the succulent fruits that they once had been. He fell asleep quite fast; he always had. In the daytime Alice had been strong, coping well, holding conversations and being able to speak on behalf of her family with a boldness and dignity that defied her circumstances, but at night she had been plagued with insomnia. Geoff, however, was a hollow shell of his former self in the daytime but seemed to sleep very peacefully at night.

With her bruises still shining in the darkness, she reached a hand over and let it hover a few centimetres from his face once again; without touching him she clenched him tight, held his whole spirit within the palm of her hand. His chest rose and fell gently and regularly, almost mechanically, denoting sleep.

"My love," she whispered into the night, too quietly to disturb him, "what is happening to us?"

He would beat her more and more regularly over the coming days. Jonathan and Kate would always be asleep when he did it, so she would get a burning dread in her heart as she made sure Jonathan had his bath and his mug of hot milk before bed, and as she went into Kate's room to kiss her goodnight Alice's heart would be pounding. She would try to hide from him, but he would always make a way to find her and hurt her. She frightened herself by how quickly she would get to the stage where she would not want to shout or scream or even fight back because she was afraid of waking up the children. She tried her best to only be in the house whenever Jonathan and Kate were because she knew that he would retreat and want to be alone like he had done at Joy's funeral, to go off into his own little world where his only companion was a bottle of whisky.

It was with a dreadful sense of inevitability that she would wait for him to begin. It seemed strange for her to acknowledge it but it wasn't actually the fighting that she found the most difficult thing of their now disastrously fragmented relationship. The fighting was bad, but the stomach-turning apprehension was worse. Often she would take Milly for a walk around the village after dark and would time it very precisely so that Geoff's aggression would be thwarted when it was at its most vicious fury. Even though spring was close the evenings were still dark and by the time she needed to leave the house the skies above the village were encrusted with stars. She had at first wanted to avoid the churchyard because the gruesome scene had instinctively triggered in her a feeling of fear for her safety and a sense of revulsion at the way her daughter had been raped and butchered there. It was a haunting place, a chilling place, but now that Joy was there and Alice's home had become a place of dread, pain and heartache there was a peculiar solace nestled amongst the gravestones.

The very earth beneath her feet seemed to sing a wonderful song of Joy into the enormous darkness. She was a part of that place, a feature of the landscape and an intrinsic ingredient in its beauty and majesty, her youthful loveliness preserved forever in the biology of the churchyard. Milly understood the mood and sensed the undercurrents, slowing down and sitting in silence at every available opportunity. The headstones bore a passing resemblance to human figures sitting bolt upright in the dimness, the ghastly spectres of death and mortality which used to terrify her in the days after the murder, but now that she could put an angelic face to one of them she was greatly comforted. It was a beautiful night, and she would much rather have spent her time in the company of Joy than in the company of Geoff. Looking upwards, she noticed that the trees in the darkest part of the churchyard had enough growth on them to blot out the shimmering starlight as the branches met above the middle of the pathway. The atmosphere over the village was saturated with wood-smoke as the villagers enjoyed one final open fire of the winter season before the evenings became lighter again. At this hallowed hour on the dawn of springtime the woods seemed to stretch out eternally in all directions, and Higher Pelham in its ancient tradition and bygone timelessness was the only trace of humanity on this gigantic landscape. The time came for her to return to the cottage, and as the glow from the windows grew brighter in Alice's eyes she felt her pulse quickening and her breaths becoming sharper and shorter. It was time to face him once again.

Eventually, Geoff's heavy drinking and ruined body clock had an effect on his work, and he was no longer able to maintain the company. His suppliers and distributors ceased business with him and his company closed down after missing numerous deadlines which had led to a slowdown in profits.

Alice was terrified of Geoff, but the loss of his job was an unignorable truth which could not be put aside as it concerned her deeply that the family would not be able to financially provide for themselves unless action was taken soon. Alice began applying for jobs in neighbouring towns but the countryside was not a place where much business was done, meaning that as she did not have any agricultural knowledge or experience she was unable to find employment. The fairytale of Higher Pelham still burned brightly in Alice's exhausted mind, the eternal promise a faint song on her bruised and bleeding lips; she dreamed of opening a bookshop or a coffee shop, either in the village or if she needed to relocate in order to chase profits she could establish the business in a nearby town. She imagined herself in an apron, baking cakes and scones for a living, growing wonderfully ripe by spending hours and hours getting lost in the ancient volumes which were messily stuffed into the bookcases in her shop, with comfy armchairs and deep and low beams above, perhaps a log fire over the winter to tempt the punters in. She had in her a brilliant ability to cling to hope and optimism when life seemed unendurably tough, and she refused to give up and surrender her faith in their better life away from London. Glory.

Geoff did not respond to any of her suggestions for financial stability. She was becoming increasingly frustrated with his new lethargy and his inability to concentrate on anything except for alcohol. If she was honest with herself she did blame him for losing his job and the company folding in, but she did not have the strength or courage to confront him over this. She believed that he had weakened his inner resolve and the strength of his character ever since the death of Joy, and there was an aspect of him that she hated, that pathetic tendency that he had which she had never noticed before which meant that he simply gave up at the earliest opportunity when things became difficult. He loved to take the easy option when he was faced with a problem or a decision to make, which was not a trait which she recognised in him, that cowardice and the hope that alcohol would defer the unpleasantness in his place. What kind of a man is that? His daughter was murdered but, ghastly as it was, Alice felt the need to move on and build a future for herself and her family without ever forgetting her beautiful Joy. She would always have a very central place in her mother's life, but there was no denying that she was now dead and that Alice had longed for the funeral as a landmark to close the case, to end her agony and to bid her Joy one final, poignant goodbye. Geoff did not want to move on and he smashed his brain cells halfway to oblivion by drinking bottle after bottle of whisky before bed. Alice hated him for it.

Jonathan had a football match one Wednesday after school, and the memories of the 27th September distressed Geoff so greatly that he emptied a bottle of vodka during his breakfast at 1pm. He then went back to bed, vomiting all over the floor and collapsing into a fit of unconsciousness which meant that he was unable to collect him as he had promised to. Jonathan waited on the field in the rain, refusing the offers of a lift from the other parents so that his father's journey would not be wasted. An hour and a half after the final whistle was blown his mother arrived in the car with a black eye and a big apology for him.

Being too incapacitated to collect his son from a football match was the final straw for his wife. She could handle the abuse against herself, but she refused to jeopardise the quality of life of her children. This was partly because she had an irrational need to prove her credentials as a mother and partly because she felt that they deserved no less having suffered the unimaginable agony of spending their childhoods as a trio and entering adulthood as a duo. There was something horrifically sinister in the way that Joy had been the last to join the Hewitts and the first to leave them, stolen by a madman.

She faced him without cowardice, but it was only because she was talking about Jonathan. She told him how unacceptable it was to treat him that way, to allow him to suffer for his alcoholism. Geoff told her that she did not understand, that there was nothing he could do about it and the phase would pass and their lives would return to normal in no time. She could sense a rising anger in him, and tenderly told him that she still loved him in an attempt to diffuse the bomb.

She suggested to her husband that he was an alcoholic and that he needed counselling in order to control his addiction and the detonation that she had been waiting for occurred. He stood up with a feverish haste, knocking over the chairs and throwing the table up against the Welsh Dresser which smashed half of the china plates piled up on the shelves. He grabbed her by the throat and lifted her off her feet, throttling her, and slammed her body against the tiled floor. Alice rolled over and scrambled up to her feet, only to find him there again and ready for her, bringing a deluge of fists and fingernails ripping into the skin of her face, the face that he had fallen in love with a lifetime ago. He had tears in his eyes as he did it and she spluttered a few words of anguished desperation to him as she tried to dodge the punches. "Geoff, Geoff, you're killing me!" He chased her out of the kitchen and up the stairs, growling with menace and focusing his eyes on her like Milly did when she was hunting birds in the garden; she grabbed the mobile phone she had left on the sofa as she ran, presumably to call the police. He roared with rage, and the tears were suddenly gone.

She rushed into the upstairs bathroom and tried to pull the door shut behind her, but before she could bolt it he threw a foot between the door and the frame. He pummelled the door with his fists, finally throwing it open, and burst inside to devour her. He grabbed her by the lapel of her dress, filling his fists with great clumps of material, and threw her into the bathroom wall with all of his might. He held her against the mirror, smashing his clenched fist into her mouth and breaking the glass behind her head with the force of the impact leaving cracks like lightning bolts splintering across the smooth glass surface, delicate and fragile as ice. The bright white spotlights in the ceiling began to pulse and throb, and as she opened her eyes all she could see was a stabbing platinum gleam.

She came to her senses as the dizzying blur of colour and light gradually came back into focus. He pushed into her again, lifting her slightly and slamming her back flat against the wall, which cracked a few of the tiles and sounded like the massive tail of a whale slapping against the surface of the ocean. He thrust his face into her neck; she thought that he was biting her but it turned out that he was kissing her breasts. With his left hand he bent her leg so that her knee was adjacent to his body and reached up to her secret parts and her knickers, trying to peel off her garter with his fingers. She shook her head and whispered "no", at which point the kissing did turn to biting. He took a great chunk out of her breast and moved up to her neck again, holding her hand tenderly as he pressed her arm up against the wall, finally taking her right earring in between his bloodstained teeth and wrenching it as hard as he could. With a great cry of pain she felt the steel hook of the earring rip through the flesh of her lobe and come away in his mouth.

Alice ran out of the bathroom and he chased her into the bedroom where they were meant to be sharing one another's bodies every night, an unbreakable union of flesh and love sealed with their wedding rings. She stood at the top of the tiny iron spiral staircase; the trapdoor had, unusually, been left open that day. Running forwards in one final thrust of aggression, he punched her squarely on the jaw and felt her bones crack beneath his knuckles; she was probably unconscious as soon as his fist came away from her face. It was a dull, hollow thudding sound, like an empty wooden rowing boat bumping against a jetty. She was sent into a spin without being thrown backwards, her eyes closed and her face bleeding, and slipped and fell through the trapdoor and down the staircase into the living room. Her limbs and torso slammed against every iron step, bouncing and spinning as she fell, finally cracking the back of her head on the bottom step. She crashed down to Earth just had Lucifer had, blasted by the Almighty's heavenly thunder and wearing the scorch marks on her flesh as though each cut, bruise and broken bone was an item of jewellery. She landed in the middle of the room, sprawled out like a great stranded starfish, her smashed arms and legs spread out like a swastika.

Kate was the first one to find her mother on the floor. She was not conscious and she was not breathing but Kate could find a pulse by pressing her fingers against her mother's neck. She shook her by the shoulders and gave her mouth to mouth, pumping the oxygen in and massaging her mother's chest but nothing seemed to be working. Geoff appeared at the top of the staircase, blood covering his knuckles and an earring in his teeth. He let out a great roar, jumping down the tiny iron staircase three steps at a time, but Kate was undeterred. She shook her mother's shoulders and rubbed her cold fingers and thumb across the skin of her face repeatedly until she could feel the gentle and unmistakeable whisper of a human breath from the bleeding lips.

Her father towered over her, but she would not move. She told Jonathan to go and call an ambulance, but her father told him that if he did he would kill him. With an admirable calmness Kate simply spoke over him, quietly, telling him that she had nothing to be afraid of and that she should do the right thing, even if it was against the will of someone that she loved.

"You won't tell anyone. I'm your father."

She could not be sure if he was begging or if he was instructing her of how she would react. They both knew that Kate could not reasonably stop him, and that he could kill Alice if he wanted. He had done most of the work already, but Kate's only defence was to implore his last sober shred of decency and love; if there was any goodness in him at all he would not harm a child and deny a critically injured woman her right to an ambulance.

"You're not my father, you're a monster. Stand down."

He moved in for her and she could smell the sharp zest of vodka on his breath, and his eyes were sunken and pallid. He raised a bloodied fist and spat out Alice's earring.

"You remind me of someone," she shouted at him, "I see it more and more every day. Do you remember anyone else who liked to hurt people because it made him feel better?"

She stood her ground, with one foot on either side of her stricken mother and her face just centimetres from her father's. He was sweating and wheezing, but she would not move. Kate's eyes blazed with a steadfast and determined hatred. "Stand down."

The paramedics arrived and Jonathan showed them into the sitting room, where Kate had positioned herself between her parents. Alice was the colour of asphalt. They loaded her onto a stretcher and carried her away into the back of the ambulance which had been parked outside. Higher Pelham was far too small of a village for a screaming ambulance speeding through the tiny streets and lanes to go unnoticed, and people were gathered outside the cottages wondering what was going on. Kate could imagine their inaudible whispers of hearing shouting and screaming from the house late at night. She turned back to her father again.

"You'd better run," she hissed at him, "I can't imagine what they would do to you if they found out that you were a wife-beater."

7   THE VICTIM'S VISITANT

Alice awoke in a hospital bed, blinded by the pulse of the platinum light that was beating down from the strip bulbs in the ceiling. She remembered having a conversation with a nurse, but not the topics and subjects that they covered, before realising that she had been cruelly tricked by the numbness of the coma and suddenly fathoming that she was not nearly conscious enough to manipulate her mouth into forming words and sentences. It was a very strange sensation, and she felt as though she was made of lead, and her limbs were agitated by the marbled texture of death. As she gradually awoke, the very first thing that she did was to inspect every inch of her body to see how it was different and what had changed in her absence. Her right wrist was bandaged and the arm was heavily bruised and discoloured, and she had cuts and scratches across her shoulders; she could not move her neck to see any more and realised that this was because she was wearing a neck brace. If she could see her face in a mirror she would have been shocked at the scratches and claw marks on her neck and jaws, the bruising around her eyes and her ripped earlobes.

Alice's body did not feel like it belonged to her, but instead that it was with a strange feeling of weightlessness that her spirit rested on or above her flesh rather than residing within it as it had always done before. She did not know if she had been given any anaesthetic, whether she had had an operation, or how long she had been unconscious for.

There was an envelope with the word "Mum" written on it on the table next to the bed, but Alice couldn't reach it with her shattered hands and arms. When a nurse came she made a sound, any sound, to get her attention and to ask her to open it and read whatever was inside to her. The nurse came, wiped her face and lifted her left hand so that she could grasp the card by herself. She looked at it and saw a photograph of rays of sunshine bursting through the banks of cloud billowing up above a beach, with the light reflected on the perfectly smooth calm of the sea.

Dear Mum,

I am sorry that this isn't as exciting as a telegram from the King.

Get them to call me when you are ready to have visitors and I will come in and see you. Dad's not here anymore, he has been taken away for what he did to you and you will probably be visited by a women's charity to protect you from him in the future. They keep asking me where you are and what has happened, but if they didn't know that then there would be no reason for them to call. It's dumb. The police asked me what he did to you, and I told them. It's like nobody knows how to deal with it when something happens until I turn up and tell them what I saw. I am looking after Jonathan and Milly for you, and we are living with the family of Jessica Connelly from Jonathan's class at school until you come home. Jessica's mum says that they are praying for you and they will have a party when you come back to HP. Jelly and ice-cream, the lot.

Keep going, stay strong, we love you. Let me know if you need anything.

Kate

It was a remarkable thing to receive from a fourteen year old. It marked a transitional point in their relationship, for it felt like only five minutes since Kate had been a tiny baby and she had relied on Alice entirely for everything that she needed in order to survive. Far from being helpless, Kate was instead fast becoming the matriarch of the family as it disintegrated like a sandcastle swept away by the gleaming shimmer of a foaming wave rushing towards the shore. As the waters receded the sand was left with only an indentation where the castle had once proudly stood; after sixteen years of marriage, sixteen years of painstakingly building a family, it had taken less than ten months for it to be destroyed and to leave no trace in the silky wetness of the refreshed sand. They were back where they had started, her bruises the only memories of the time that she had spent sharing her life with Geoff Hewitt. They were treasured relics, beautiful souvenirs, and it would be strange to let them go and surrender them to the past.

When Alice was more accustomed to where she was, Kate and Jonathan came to visit her with Mrs Connelly. She came in and wished Alice well but then left her as long as possible alone with her children, sitting instead on a chair in the corridor outside of the ward. Jonathan was upset by what he saw, but Kate knew the importance of holding it together in even the toughest of circumstances. Alice was visited in hospital by a woman called Grace, a representative of the domestic violence charity Refuge, who explained to her that there had been concern from the neighbours about the state of the Hewitt marriage, prompting an investigation which led them to interview Kate and confirm their suspicions that her fall down the staircase was not quite the accident that it seemed.

Alice's recovery was slow and steady, and she kept in regular contact with the children as her progress sped towards her being well enough to leave the hospital. Grace told her the full extent of her injuries which Geoff had inflicted upon her during the abuse; it transpired that she had suffered internal bleeding on her stomach and liver from being slammed up against the wall so many times, three broken ribs and a crack in her skull from hitting the bottom step of the iron staircase. She had a thick scar on the back of her head and numerous lacerations, scratches and marks all over her skin.

*   *   *

Having been so recently demoted from a Death Row Inmate to merely a prisoner in the maximum security wing of the prison, Leo Faulkner was struggling to adjust to life on the inside at HMP Belmarsh in Thamesmead in South East London. He saw it as a humiliation to get the downgrade, to be in every sense reduced and simplified, his masterpiece abridged. He began a very complex treatment programme to reduce his testosterone levels and to regulate his sexual urges, which began with cognitive behavioural therapy. The members of staff at the prison were not permitted to perform psychological therapy on him because he had been declared completely sane; this was important because he had been put forward as a candidate for execution based on his sound mind. Instead the modifications that they attempted to make to his character were based on altering his sexuality to a less dangerous and poisonous orientation. His therapist, a woman called Veronica, appeared ignorant and out of her depth, but the reality of it was that she wanted to hear the words she could guess actually coming out of the prisoner's mouth. Her job was to heal him, to reduce his likelihood of reoffending and to increase his chance of being healthily rehabilitated and becoming a contributing member of society. That was some mean feat, a daring gauntlet to contend with.

Her questions were bewildering and senseless. She asked him what the paedophilia felt like inside of him, asked what the texture felt like on the inside of his skin when he saw a little girl. She asked him whether he thought it was the same feeling, the same lustful and urgent sensation that every other sexually mature person experiences through arousal. Is the experience identical every time you are stimulated? What colour is paedophilia? What does it feel like when you touch it? What sound does it make when it roars and closes in for the kill, prowling around as cruel as a wolf slinking out of the thickets, homing in on the wounded and the weak? Veronica asked him to draw the feelings he had when she showed him some of the photographs that the police had given her from his computer. She gave him a pencil which was not fully sharpened, but he asked for crayons. He drew paedophilia with a childlike imagination, a vast rainbow of swirling colours and waterfalls of gushing, churning passion. When he was asked to draw it as an animal he drew it as a jellyfish, a smooth lobe of enamelled white brain and strings of tentacles twirling outwards in dazzling pulsing contractions. It seemed appropriate and it made a lot of sense to both Leo and Veronica. There is a beauty in paedophilia, tenderness and splendour in the connection between the man and his young virgin, but this graceful and majestic creature has a sting which is very often fatal. Leo's life had been ruined, and Joy's life had been terminated in a painful and brutal manner. Beautiful and fragile but extremely destructive; they both thought that this summarised his condition quite well.

In addition to the varying degrees of failure experienced of the therapy, he also had *Treatment*, which was something altogether different. It was termed Treatment in perhaps a reference to fleas or ringworm, a clever gesture by the prison authorities to reduce his humanity and re-brand him as a parasite; the removal of something unhealthy and mutated, the correction of an integral part of his identity because it did not fit in with the common notion of what it means to be a full and acceptable human being.

He was given drugs which amounted to a chemical castration. The medics were legally obliged to tell him that it was merely an action of suppression as they could find no cure for the sexual arousal he experienced when exposed to young children, but that they had to distort the effects of the testosterone meandering and coursing through the tissue of his brain. They came in small blue pills which he was ordered to swallow with his breakfast. After the first week he refused to take them any more, and the response of the Prison Governor was to crush the pills up, strap the killer down and inject the crushed remnants of glistening blue powder into his bloodstream. He could feel the sparkling shower of pharmaceutical medicine ingraining itself into his body with the sensation of having the lit tip of a sparkler forcibly inserted into one of his arteries. He felt manhandled and humiliated, with his masculinity and sexuality strewn under the microscope in such a crude and pornographic manner, becoming public property and no longer his own private possessions. It was the closest he hoped that he would ever come to being raped.

It was a normal day; he had the humiliation of the injections in the morning which was followed by an hour of exercise. He was relaxing before the session of cognitive behavioural therapy when he was summoned at a time when he was scheduled to be locked away in isolation. Leo looked up as an officer came to the cell, and spoke to him through the bars in the very small window in the huge metal door that protected him from the hatred of the other prisoners.

"Inmate Faulkner, you have a visitor."

Leo was struck by a sense of shock and surprise, and then dread. Was this someone who had found out where he was being held by watching the news and had come to abuse him? Was it a journalist, coming to find an insight into the mind of a child killer?

"Follow me."

He stood up and followed the guard out of the cell and down the long corridor. Leo was told to sit down at one of the windows along the long line of seats which faced out into the agoraphobia and exposure of freedom. Other prisoners were talking with their loved ones through the phones at the sides of the window and all of them gradually looked up when they realised that he was there.

The guard directed Leo to his seat and invited him to wait. "We will send her in." So it was a female. He was suddenly completely overcome with a stirring of passion from the depth of his groin; perhaps it was a *little girl*.

A prisoner was sitting next to him as he waited for his visitor, talking to a man on the Freedom Side. He would not stop staring at Leo, dumbfounded by shock and revulsion. They were all allowed to watch television in the canteen when they were eating, and because of the cameras at the trial, the protests and the vote in parliament during the first part of his incarceration there was not a single person in Belmarsh, as in the entire country, who did not know who Leo Faulkner was. The paedophile stared back, asking what his problem was. "Bastard," was the stony reply. "If the government is not going to do you in then it looks like it's up to us now." He pointed to the guard who was taking of his handcuffs. "As soon as he sleeps, as soon as he turns his back, you're dead meat."

As he looked back through the window, Leo saw Alice Hewitt standing on the Freedom Side and as he turned his head she pulled her chair back and sat down in front of him. He was staggered, and for a few moments was completely silent in a stunned shock. Out of everyone that he could have possibly expected to come and visit him in jail she was at the very bottom of the list; he could think of no conceivable reason for her to want to come and see him here. She was wearing a white double breasted coat and her blonde hair was tied back in a bun at the back, with a diagonal fringe coming down at the front. She was wearing lipstick and faint eyeliner and was decorated with an earring on one side, a small and delicate teardrop of glass which was suspended on a tiny string of diamonds. It was a very sharp contrast to the strong brutality and drudgery of the prison and the rugged, scruffy and grimy masculinity of the other prisoners. She had a cut above her left eyelid and her temple was bruised, and the right hand side of her head was quite deliberately covered with her hair. Because Leo was in isolation for his own safety he had been escorted to the visitor's window for the conversation and the guard stood between him and the other prisoners with a police truncheon in his hands.

She leaned forwards, pursed her lips and picked up the telephone receiver, suggestively staring at him and wordlessly inviting him to do the same, because she clearly wanted to speak to him. Leo picked up the phone and Alice waited, staring straight at him and waiting to hear what he had to say to her.

"Well this is a surprise."

Alice raised an eyebrow to him and remained remarkably composed.

"You're telling me."

They sat in silence. Leo flashed her a wicked grin, chuckling to himself and mocking her misfortune. A grieving mother only exaggerated his sense of triumphant achievement and his overwhelming pleasure at what he had done; he was afraid that the memories would fade, but now that Alice was here they all came flooding back in an overwhelming deluge which jolted through him like an electric shock. Alice had a quiet and steely determination to uphold her dignity in the face of this monster and to be strong for Joy's memory.

"You know," Leo said, leaning forwards and licking his lips, "You had a very beautiful daughter."

She knew that he was not finished but she interrupted him anyway as a deliberate sign of disrespect.

"Yes, I know. I'm aware of that. She was a great beauty and I loved her fully."

Leo's reply was intended to be totally emotionless, but he failed to control his trembling voice as he answered her. His head was flooded with memories and fantasies about his triumphant victory of the flesh, the most erotic moment of his life, the moment when the floodgates of passion were thrown open for the briefest of moments and he was drenched in a deluge of orgasmic power. His lips quivered as he broke into a grin.

"That is why I had such a good time raping her."

Alice narrowed her eyes, trying to look into him and unsettle him a little. "Well," she said, almost jokingly, "there doesn't seem to be any doubt that we got the right man."

Leo smiled at her. "It was worth it, Alice. It really was." He shrugged slightly, breaking eye contact. "Obviously I would have preferred it if nobody had ever caught me and I could have done it again," he laughed as he looked at her once more. "Maybe Kate could have been next. Maybe she could have been the lucky one. You tell her when you tuck her into her bed tonight that I am sorry that I chose her sister over her. She must be so disappointed that she's still a virgin. You realise that she's past it now, at almost fifteen, and it must have been such a disappointment to know that I was more sexually attracted to her sister than to her. The rejection must have been heartbreaking."

Alice kept incredibly serene. He was a strange little man; she had seen him in the dock at the trial but she had never got a proper, good look at him. She had, in honesty, been expecting a giant of a man, a prowling beast of red blooded masculinity, whose rampant sex drive could not be tamed or limited to just adult women. Instead he was a waif like, scrawny little rodent with mannerisms not altogether human. He was effeminate and ghastly, with the unhealthy and ghostly hue of darkness around his eyes. His tattoos made him look cheap and dirty. She was determined to win and she knew that he was trying to break her down, and she would not grant him the satisfaction of destroying her again. Inside she was a ruin, but on the outside she was a mighty castle.

"Does it depress you, Leo, to think that you could die in this prison, in your cell in isolation?"

"Alice, when was the last time that you saw Joy naked?"

"What about the fact that you will never again be allowed near a child?"

"You know I did. I really did. I owned her for the final moments of her life. I've never seen anything quite as beautiful as her. It felt so good, so satisfying and rewarding to watch her die underneath my hands. Her skin was soft, even after I had killed her, just like a velvety and warm head of a rose. That's what I love about children, the fact that they are so small."

"You will die here, hated and alone, having thrown away your whole life because of the fact that you are a sexual freak who can't reign in his own disgusting and feral urges. You are worse than an animal."

"I could never have sex with an adult woman. Like you, for instance; how many pregnancies have you had, three? Your hole must be so loose and wrinkled, like an overripe fruit which is all flabby and shrivelled. It disgusts me to even think about what you must look like without your knickers on. I think I might vomit and then slash my throat; nobody deserves to see something that rank." He gave her a ghoulish grin as he mocked the nation's attempt to kill him. "I'd rather be fried on an electric chair than see you naked."

"You know, Leo, I heard that you are the most vulnerable prisoner this jail has ever had, more susceptible than anyone else to be attacked, molested and even murdered by your fellow inmates. It must be a nice prospect to wake up every day knowing that if one of the guards falls asleep or suddenly decides he doesn't like you you're very likely to be killed."

"I'm surprised that you and Geoff managed to create a daughter as beautiful as Joy. You're both so disgustingly ugly. Of all the people I could have raped, I am genuinely surprised that it turned out to be her given the gene pool she was drawn from and the tainted stock in the stable. Not exactly a thoroughbred racehorse now, are we Mrs Hewitt?"

"I think rape is a little bit less fun if you're not on top."

"I think rape is a lot more fun if the other person is dead."

They stared each other down in a tense silence. The air was heavy, stagnant and cold. A few minutes of silence passed between the two of them, one a maximum-security and high-profile prisoner, one a beautiful woman, a former mother, who was on the right side of the glass boundary, the perimeter of freedom. Leo broke the standoff.

"Alice, why did you come back here? Have you not won already? I'm in jail, you can forget all about me." He looked up and pointed at the guard, and then he knocked on the bullet-proof glass window that separated them. "I can't get you any more. I'm staying here for a very long time. You can just forget about what happened and move on and I'll be here, waiting to die, just like you said, revelling in my break for glory. What on Earth possessed you to come and visit me?"

Alice gave a small laugh of sarcastic outrage, took the phone receiver away from her face as she looked away from him, and then brought it back as she once again composed herself to speak to the killer.

"You have no idea, do you? None at all. I can't forget you, any more than I can forget Joy. I think about her every morning when I wake up and every night when I go to sleep. Every second that she is not in my home, in her school, in our family, in our village, in the same room as me, I miss her and I hate you a little bit more. She will never grow old, Leo. She will never become the woman that we planned her to be, that she was made to be, that she should have been. You stole that from her and you stole that from all of us. That second of selfishness ruined all of our lives, yours included." Alice pressed her fingers aggressively against the glass and began to raise her voice. "Every single day that goes by and I think of her, and I love her, and I miss her, I think of what you did. I can't forget you any more than either of us can forget her and the way that she died. You are coming with me to my grave."

"Oh it was more than a second." he interjected. "I like to get things right. I slept in the hedgerow on the corner of Archangel Lane three days after you moved in and I never left. I would watch her in the garden, playing with her brother and sister and you. I planned it all very meticulously and it took a lot of my time, much more than just a second. I can tell from that comment that you're pretty ignorant and you have no idea about the finer points of planning a murder. You are an intolerably stupid woman."

Leo paused for a moment and narrowed his eyes, apparently deep in thought. "What happened to your face?"

The eye contact was immediately broken and Leo sensed that he had struck a raw nerve.

"I was riding my bike and I fell." She raised a delicate hand to her forehead and fringe which covered the wound and it was unclear whether or not this was the intended purpose. "It's nothing."

She looked back at him, apparently studying his face in close detail for the first time. His eyes were set back into his head, with dark circles around them that seemed to have nothing to do with tiredness or the light in the room; the eyes had a dark and foreboding evil around them and the actual irises themselves were an electric and bionic blue. Looking at his eyes reminded her of the photos of Rasputin in her history books at school, where even the most passing of glances appeared as a haunting and bone-chilling stare, of windows on a soul containing unspeakable evil. He seemed to be permanently unshaven, with messy and rough stubble across his cheeks and neck, and great tufts of chest hair climbing out of his shirt. His skin was greasy and dirty, and although his hairline was receding and he had an enormous forehead his hair was wildly tousled. Obviously she guessed that the conditions in prison were not such to keep him in peak aesthetic condition but it was a look of scruffy ruggedness that she had remembered from the courtroom and he had a deeply disturbing presence, with more than a hint of psychological abnormality and madness. She pondered his name, which meant *lion*; he had none of the majesty of his namesake but there was the same sense of raw physical power about him, the same instinct to hunt and kill and the same disparity from the human race. Staring deeply and thoughtfully into him, Alice was unsure of whether he was extending or reducing her understanding of what it is to be a human. From an evolutionary point of view, she wondered, was he a terrifying prototype, a hellish vision of what happens when perfectly normal sexual feelings are driven out of all control and breaking out of the confined space within restrictive boundaries that society would call the normality? Or perhaps, as her instinct told her, was he more of a relic and a psychological antique, a man so basic in his primeval and prehistoric filth that he had not yet advanced and evolved far enough to warrant being called a human? She knew that he was a vile monster, but she was unsure of whether he was horribly more or horribly less of a human than she herself was; the depth of his feeling for Joy certainly transcended her own, and with morals and goodness out of the question it seemed as though she may have been mistaken and that he may in fact have been more. His fingers were pressed far more firmly into the electrical current of humankind and he felt a fuller force of the sexual kaleidoscope than she ever did.

"In answer to your question, the reason that I came here to see you is a matter of unfinished business," she said, looking at and then pointing to the guard who was standing watch, slapping the truncheon against the palm of his hand. "It is very important to me that I know what they are doing to you here. I want to see justice being done to you."

"Ah," said the paedophile, his eyes gleaming in the halogen lights of the dungeon ceiling. "You wanted to see them hurt me."

Alice took a second to ponder his response.

"No. I don't need to see you bleed or weep. I know you won't apologise or show any remorse so I have stopped wanting you to in the vain pursuit of happiness. I know you better than you think I do; I know that you are the kind of man who watches other people cry and hurt rather than feels any of that himself. I thought that seeing you here would be helpful to my recovery from the murder of my daughter because after today I will know that you are in a secure jail cell and will never be coming out. I asked the officers if I could see your cell but they refused to grant me access because it is not safe and my counsellor said that it would probably damage me more." Alice looked him deeply in the eyes as though she was examining an insect under a microscope. "I understand that you are on drugs," she said.

He looked unnerved. "How did you know?"

"Because they told me that it is against the law to discuss your medication with you, but I am beyond caring about that. So come on, tell me what they are doing to you. I want you to tell me everything."

"They won't tell me what it is," he said, "but they are blue tablets. I think I am growing tits." He cupped his chest and pressed his breasts together to make a cleavage. "It must be to reduce my testosterone; my liver is killing me."

Alice did not appreciate the reference to death given the ordeals she had been through. She thought that it could have been a backhanded dig at her but she refused to give him the credit for it. She stared blankly ahead, wishing she had never asked, and he continued his obscene and bizarre monologue.

"You said that you don't expect me to say sorry and so you have stopped waiting for me to. But have you stopped wanting me to? Are you here to punish me with the guilt that you expect me to feel when I'm confronted by the mother of my victim?"

"I'm not pressurising you into a guilt that you don't feel. Either way, you're dying here; it makes no difference to me. It isn't as though you feeling guilty will make Joy come home to me tonight and magically repair all of the damage you have done. You feel as much or as little guilt as you like, but I'm here to see for myself the results of your crime and to try to find out some of the answers that I have never had resolved, questions about what is going on in your psyche to make you think that killing and then raping a seven year old girl is a good idea."

"I like getting inside people's heads too," he grinned. "I find it interesting. It's almost as much fun as it was to get the anatomy lesson that I did from your daughter's corpse. Her blood tasted like the sweetest honey, like the teardrops of angels, like water from the wells of Heaven. My only regret about killing her is the fact that I didn't bottle some of her fragrance and wear it as a perfume so I could always remember the way that she smelled."

"You have dehumanised her enough, Leo," Alice spat at him down the phone line. "If you think you are going to break me you are wrong; you're wasting your time. Don't even try. She is a wonderful and beautiful little girl and you can't do anything to change that."

"Was," he replied sternly. "She was. You may need reminding, but she's dead now. Don't take my achievements away from me. Past participles please."

She didn't reply, she just stared at him angrily.

"Do you hate me, Alice Hewitt?" He had picked up on what she had said to him before and wondered how fully she had meant it.

It took all of her inner strength to look him in the eye and lie. "No, Leo, I don't hate you any more. I am above that now. I am a demonstration of all that a mother can and should be, of putting my personal reactions to one side and doing what I should be doing and in the way that is right, not what feels best for me. If I hated you I would collapse into a wreckage of what I used to be, a ruin of bitterness and anger and reminiscence and regret. I am better than that; I owe it to myself and to Joy to be strong and to not let you do more damage than you already have."

She flashed him a sarcastic little smile. "Nice try, though."

"I have a question for you, Alice," he smirked, "were you disappointed that they didn't kill me?"

Alice held her stare. She was not having fun, but she knew that her visit was extremely worthwhile and she was not wasting her time here speaking to the man who had butchered her daughter.

"Before I give you my answer, I want to know how prison life is. Would you have preferred it if they had executed you? Which would have been the merciful option?"

"Ooh, you do tease me you do! Fancy asking me that."

Alice raised her eyebrows at him and tried to hide her bewilderment as best she could. "I don't understand."

"Yes you do," said the fiend. "You do know what you're doing, I'll give you that. I think it's *filthy*. You're trying to turn me on by talking about torture and death; you know it warms me up."

For the first time in the conversation Alice genuinely could not hide her revulsion, outrage and disgust, and she felt as though she was going to vomit, like her stomach was being wrung out through an old Victorian mangle. She calmed herself down as quickly as was possible; he was a maximum security prisoner, graded A with exceptional risk, and was on self harm and suicide watch, so there was no possible way for her to hurt him. The only weapon that she had was her tongue. She was worried about being stereotyped as the hysterical grieving mother who was incapable of self control and was glad that she did not take the opportunity to explode at him. She did, however, find it a bit surreal coming from a lot of violent fights with the very strong and masculine Geoff to seeing a pathetic little man hiding behind bullet-proof glass and steel bars as much protecting him as protecting the little girls of England. The contrast between the two was quite startling.

"Tell me the answer, Leo. Are you glad they didn't kill you?"

"You know what, Alice? In a way, no I'm not. We haven't had prisoners executed since 1964. It would have been a wonderful way to end my life, to have me exit the stage after putting in such an outstanding performance. You know what I'm missing out on? I never got to be a martyr. I never got to go down in history as the first prisoner of a new generation to die for doing a crime so terrible that they had to change the law just for me. I never received true infamy. I was never given the recognition that I so deserved because they stopped short of giving me the ultimate punishment, and the ultimate reward, for my crime. But you must be disappointed. You must think that it is a shame that I was never killed in quite the way that your daughter was. Does it upset you to see me breathing and talking to you? Do you ever catch yourself daydreaming about my body, about it being dismembered and robbed of the sparks of life which were endowed to my veins by my maker?" He pinched the skin on the hand that he was holding the phone receiver with as she looked on through the window, as though he was actually proving to her that he was a fully living and healthy human being. "I have never thought about the ways in which they could have done it. But you know Alice, I was reading about the methods they use in the USA. Did you know that in Virginia they will execute you by lethal injection, unless you specifically ask for another method which means you can choose between electrocution, shooting, hanging or lethal gas?"

"I spoke to the Justice Secretary and the Home Secretary," Alice interrupted him, "and you would have been killed by a lethal injection. There was a concern that your death would be misconstrued as some kind of morbid achievement, so there was no negotiation permitted. It seems they knew what you would be thinking."

Leo continued as though the phone line had been severed and he could not hear her, but he knew for sure that she could hear him. "I think the best would have been electrocution. I like the idea of having my flesh toasted slightly, maybe if we're lucky having my hair singe. It must be thrilling to have pure energy shooting down all of your nerves. Death is a thrill, Alice, I could see that from Joy when I snapped her neck; it's like being swept off over the edge of the Victoria Falls. It's terrifying, I imagine, but there is an indescribable exhilaration to it and the adrenaline rushing through you as you tumble and the wind steals your breath must be incredible."

"You know, Leo, I have a confession to make. Geoff wanted you dead, he really did. I saw it in his eyes before he fell asleep every night and as soon as he woke up again in the morning. He hates you from the bottom of his soul. But I'm not the same. Believe it or not, I don't think that executing you would have achieved anything; there is no way to resurrect Joy, there is no way to repair and rebuild our family now. Enough people have died because of you. The only way to end all of this, to really end it is to lock you away into a little cell in Belmarsh and never think of you again." She knocked on the glass again from the Freedom Side. "Every day I must try to forget you, I am only going to win this battle myself. Your part has been played, you have no use to the world any more. You're never coming out of there, so justice has been done. I am not a bloodthirsty person, Leo, so I can be satisfied without seeing your coffin."

"Lethal gas is not any fun for anyone, but firing squad seems to be a good way to exit. I wonder if they would manage to get me between the eyeballs."

Alice was getting annoyed with his apparent inability to conduct a conversation with anyone. Every time that she tried to navigate the topics of discussion and steer the responses that he made he would dig his heels in and come up with something so completely irrelevant that it would derail her efforts to make sense of him. It was a deliberate tactic, and he would always go back to something disgusting and usually concerned with death or the female anatomy, something to shock her and revile her as cheaply as possible. There must have been some kind of pattern here, something that he wanted to avoid confronting, but perhaps she was mistaken. Perhaps he was really that primeval and feral, so incredibly disturbed mentally that all he could do was talk about the insides of Joy's body and picture Alice naked in front of him. It was a chilling thought, to consider the psyche of the man who had stolen her daughter from her; one thing was for sure, Leo was deeply and fundamentally misunderstood by the whole of society, but she knew somehow that it was not a flaw of the community that there was no place for him in modern England. He did not fit, and could never fit, and so by a methodical conclusion she decided once and for all that the only way to deal with him was to abandon the paedophile to eternity in prison.

"Goodbye, Leo. I have everything that I came for. I've told you all that I can."

"You're leaving so soon?"

"Yes, yes I am. It's been quite long enough."

"But I was having so much fun!"

"The only fun you'll be having now is in permanent isolation in your maximum security jail cell. You are an evil man, you have been dealt with correctly and I am comforted by the fact that Joy was the last victim you'll ever have, the last person you will ever have control over for the rest of your life. The world is a better place without you, Leonard Faulkner."

She hung up the phone, picked up her handbag from the floor and stood up to leave.

"I hope your family burns in Hell, Alice Hewitt," he called after her as she disappeared out of the door and out through the corridor into sunshine and freedom. She didn't hear him because of the thick glass but if she had she would probably have told him that it was how she already felt. That day would be the last time that the two of them would ever see each other again. Their lives, which had come together in the most tragic and infamous of circumstances, now separated again as though they had come to a fork in the road and had selected different paths, and her association with him was gone forever.

There was a delicious freedom in her return to Higher Pelham, in abandoning him to his grimy, dingy cell, in knowing he would never be released to hurt her and the rest of society ever again. She knew that he would probably think of her, and that he would definitely spend the rest of his days in Belmarsh thinking of Joy and dreaming of her death and his triumphant rape of her unhappy remains. But there was a peace that surrounded her on her journey home. There was a wonderful sense of a new beginning, a feeling of spring as the cold days of winter and death were now behind her, as painful as they had been to live through at the time. There was no need for him now; it was as if an enormous and heavy shackle had been released from her ankles. As she walked down the tree-lined Archangel Lane towards Magnolia Cottage, with the dappled sunlight splashing across the cobbles and the roses blooming around the door of her home, she knew that she was free. In the bath that night she skimmed the edge of space, the edge of Heaven, just as she used to when she had first escaped with dastardly audacity from the prison of Raynes Park, when she was whisked away the spring before on the hope of a better day. Weightless once more, she gazed out on the vastness of the constellations and the astounding majesty of the galaxies, and saw a comet whiz past her just eluding the reach of her fingertips. She recognised it as both Geoff and Leo all at once; a moment of great danger and damage had befallen her, with craters and scars on her broken body from the glancing impact, a wounded soul was left behind. Both of the men orbited her in great curving arcs, sweeping brushstrokes of God against the skies of royal blue, being so extremely close to her that it was difficult to distinguish where one ended and the other began. The tails of their shooting stars were blended and intertwined. But when the time came the men were guided away, pulled out of their proximity to Alice by the gravity of the orbit and dragged across to the opposite side of the solar system leaving her in immeasurable emptiness, with just the sparkling dust from their shimmering trails in her fingers as a memento of a dreadful day. Now she could soar freely, and today was a new moment at the beginning of a never-ending future. Alice, and Catherine, Jonathan and Milly, knew that clear skies were now overhead and there was a delicious sense of inevitability, a sense of optimism, a firm assuredness that the unguessable future they were stepping into would be a beautiful one. Higher Pelham was now, finally, the Utopia that it had promised to be.

It was a slim shot at glory, but it was a shot all the same.

8

A HUMAN ZOO

Belmarsh was a vast and labyrinthine cathedral to criminal justice. The perimeter walls were garlanded with circles of razor wire and electric fencing, not particularly unlike the wreaths that had appeared on the doors of the cottages in Higher Pelham at Christmas. The vast brick wall was studded with gloomy watchtowers, and the guards prowled around them like ferocious and predatory wolves, as bleak as famine and as cruel as plague, their guns and dogs ensuring that the nightmarish congregation remain in their places.

It was, at the time, the most high profile prison in the country and the one which was given the biggest budget for security and housed only the deadliest of criminals. Every prisoner was male; because of the higher proportion of male offenders they had a different classification system and were graded A-C, and these were then in turn assessed on the potential risk they posed to the public in an escape scenario. Inmate Faulkner was categorised as an A and exceptional risk, both to the public at large and also of himself becoming a victim of witchhunts and lynch mobs if he ever made it onto the Freedom Side. The inmates who made up Belmarsh's hellish ensemble were inventive and extreme in their particular signatures of violence and hatred. Some were high profile prisoners there for terrorism against the state; others for treason; others still for espionage and war crimes. Then there were the freaks who were not as ambitious in scale more than made up for it in terms of gruesome sadism; monsters who had grilled babies upon rusting old gridirons, cannibals who had advertised for lovers in lonely hearts columns and then peeled their smashed bones clean in the candlelight and madmen who had rampaged a trail of destruction across dozens of strangers in cold blood. There was a psychiatric wing and Belmarsh staff were rigorously scrutinised on their ability to understand and restrain even the most difficult of inmates.

Being in permanent isolation gave Leo a completely different experience of Belmarsh than that endured by his fellow prisoners. The showers and toilets were communal; no doors, no cubicles, no privacy. Leo was escorted by guards wherever he went and was never allowed to be alone for a second unless he was securely locked in his cell. This included the long and lonely walk down the endless corridors that gave the impression of Escher's artwork, where you could wander past the barred cells for an eternity and still end up exactly where you had started from. From the day that he arrived, Inmate Faulkner knew that he was hated. As he was shepherded down the corridor to the exercise yard he saw flailing hands protruding from the continuous row of metal bars, strips of faces and leering, fish-eyed taunts. He genuinely did not understand the jeers and shouts from the other prisoners when they saw him; nobody was here without having committed a heinous crime, and none of them were righteous enough to be considered for parole for decades to come, and yet at the same time they had distinguished him as being different to the rest of the group because his crime, whilst it may not have been the most extreme and gruesome, was a sexual fantasy that had claimed a seven year old girl's life. Quite aside from this, he was also puzzled because if he had been executed (as some of them had demanded through the bars) this would surely have opened the floodgates for other murderers and child killers to be executed as well, and some of the souls on display here would have been stolen by the state. It was worth noting, he thought as he was confronted by a growling, screaming gargoyle of a man, that Leo's case was one which employed delayed sentencing and it was surely not too unfathomable for the courts to systematically go through their backlog of abhorrent monsters and execute them for crimes committed before the law was passed. He never expected a triumphant fanfare, but he was surprised that the hatred on the Captive Side was just as hostile and filled with anger Trafalgar Square had been.

The architecture of the prison was an extraordinary paradox of stark, sterile, sanitary design and unhygienic filth in the bowels of the criminal underworld that would only be survived by the fighters. When he walked into the bathrooms with the escort he would try not to touch anything, and try not to breathe the poisoned air. The bathrooms would stink of masculine piss, the uniquely acidic and rancid fragrance of uncleanliness seemingly coming from the dribbling stalactites of rust dripping down the back of the urinals. The stench crawled inside of the inmates' nostrils and festered there, sticking to the skin and turning the stomach.

Leo found that he was dealing with a great burden of disappointment as he adjusted himself to life in his new home. Rather than a fanfare, he found himself welcomed into the banality of anonymity and he could not help feeling that his shot at glory had come and gone, wasted and spent. His cell was three paces long and two wide. He had a cold metal bed frame, a very thin mattress and pillow, and an itchy grey woollen blanket on it to wrap around him at night, a table and chair and a toilet bowl set into the floor. The cell was whitewashed and had a high window looking out on slices of sky, and on the opposite wall, a crude and brutally heavy metal door. The world had changed forever and it now had five thick steel bars etched across its surface.

The food in jail was predictably detestable. Inmate Faulkner was forbidden from dining with his fellow prisoners for his own safety, so instead meals were delivered to his cell and put through a padlocked hatch in the door. He would be given slices of white bread and a puddle of jam, perhaps a cup of tea with his breakfast and meat with vegetables for dinner. Because he was one of the men in permanent isolation he knew that the staff had prepared his meals separately from the other prisoners, and on more than one occasion he found what he thought looked like the bubbling glue of saliva on the side of the plastic tray, dribbling down into the almost luminous macaroni. For his own safety he was on suicide watch as well as having to eat alone, so he was rarely given any cutlery. When meals were impossible to eat any other way, such as soup or gruel, he was given inadequately flimsy and blunt utensils which were little better than his hands. The corners of the table were perfectly rounded like the type of furniture that you would find in a nursery school, and he had a reinforced CCTV camera in his cell which was monitored constantly. He was given no shoelaces, nothing around his wrists, nothing metal or sharp, no neckties, waxy bed sheets that were designed not to rip or shred and extremely limited access to everything which was outside of his cell.

Lying in bed every night, Leo was not short of time alone to think about the situation that he now found himself in. He felt his way around the cold metal frame, drinking in the starkness of his new existence through his fingertips, and closed his eyes and imagined his coffin. He thought of what it would feel like, what it would be made of, the dimensions and the smoothness of the wood. He felt the elaborate cushioned interior of the coffin of a rich and beautiful purple, and pictured the ornate garlands of flowers a few inches above his face. He was not delusional; in his visions of his burial there were no weeping relatives, no great outbursts of emotion, perhaps just a solitary priest blessing his departed soul in a windswept and rain lashed cemetery. Perhaps he would have been cremated or buried in the walls of the prison itself. One thing which was certain was that he would not be entitled to the right of a free man to refuse his organs to be donated to the NHS. His blood would have been immediately drained in the execution chamber to top-up the dangerously low supplies suitable for transfusion, and his organs would have been removed and transported in boxes of ice to the nearest transplant stockpile. Whilst he had done his best to preserve Joy's appearance her innards had been too far decomposed to be able to offer her organs to those needing surgery as her parents would have wished, so they had lobbied the Health Secretary and the Justice Secretary to add to the Restoration Bill being voted on that executed criminals would have their organs forcibly donated to the register upon their death in the chamber. It had been the Hewitt family's attempt at bringing life through the tragedy that had affected their daughter and a somewhat fanciful attempt to bring a counterargument against the pro life concerns that the new law would bring a downward spiral of death to an already tragic situation. State sponsored health, vitality and life coming directly through state sponsored death was a romantic notion and a public relations dream for the politicians, undoubtedly, but he failed to see that it would take off in real life. Who would want to be infused with the flesh and tissue of a man who had accommodated within his body the spirit of a child killer or the meticulous fantasies which flooded his brains? If your diseased heart was transplanted with a heart which had pumped a circulatory system flushed with adrenaline caused by thrilling sexual arousal at the sight or thought of a naked child, would you not be disturbed and distraught, your flesh creeping with the idea of the heart within you polluting and tainting you from the inside out? It was a stupid idea, an idealistic opportunity by the Government for some good PR given the popularity problems they would have once they started killing criminals, and deep down Leo knew that nobody would have wanted any part of his body to be transfused inside them. But then again he had never had leukaemia or kidney failure and he did not know the procedure of transfusions and how much choice—or lack of it—was afforded to patients over exactly what would be put inside them. If it came down to life or death, would they care?

Perhaps his corpse would have been donated to scientific research in another attempt to bring some goodness out of the wretched abhorrence of his execution. He imagined himself aiding Egyptologists in their quest to discover the mysteries of the ancient Royal Dynasties by having his corpse mummified. He could feel the magical energy exuding from the bandages which entombed him, a deep and mystical connection to the Pharaohs of past millennia, the stone sarcophagus containing his mummy and the gems and artefacts between the bandages and pressing against his dry, papery flesh. The jelly of his brain had been dragged out of his skull by a hook through the nose and all of his organs pickled for eternity in Canopic jars with mathematical precision.

Whatever happened to him, he knew that in the event of his very premeditated and deliberate death many things were knowable and predictable about what the reactions would be. There would have been glee in Westminster, with Government ministers gathering in Parliament with looks of satisfaction on their faces and a quiet determination to move forward without the European Union, in every sense a group of islands off the coast of the Continent. There would probably have been a public outcry at his death and marches and protests in response, but it seemed likely that there would always be a stronger and louder voice calling for the most extreme and high profile criminals to be killed to retain some sense of just sanity in the sea of chaos that had engulfed the Hewitt family in the wake of his destructive sexual conquest. He imagined Huntley and Whiting sitting together in Number Ten, popping open a champagne bottle to celebrate as his heart ceased to beat, raising a toast to his termination.

The days and months rolled together as Leo marched relentlessly forward towards the magical and symbolic target of Year Twenty Five. He didn't care what the date was or which year it was because to him they were all the same. None of that mattered. He had no clock, and therefore he had no time. He had no calendar or diary, and therefore he had no date. Because he was forbidden from coming into contact with any of the other prisoners, he did not need to share their routine and he had no structure to his day. Nobody who worked at Belmarsh made any deliberate attempt at making his life difficult; there was no sadism, no attempts at revenge, no pleasure taken in the torture of the inmates, but instead the whole operation with its military sense of precision and rigidity was a very elaborate exercise in public protection. Life, with all of its glory and intricacy, had been blunted and sterilised beyond recognition. The only reason why they were locked away in the prison was to stop them from being able to hurt and kill innocent people in wider society, and there seemed to be a lack of punishment in that. It was of course much more than a mere inconvenience that he would never see the outside world again in the remainder of his lifetime, but that was for the public's protection and not a through a sense of penalty issued to the killer. It was a strange predicament to be in; isolated but not punished, restricted but not tortured, and there was not a person at Belmarsh who did not daily ponder on the full meaning of justice and who did not constantly wonder if it was being administered to the fullest of its definition.

The other prisoners with whom he shared this hellish dwelling, though, were less kind than the restrained guards and wardens.

There was one occasion where Leo was showering, watched as always by his guard, who needed to make sure that the prisoner did not harm himself or launch some far fetched escape plan, but at the same time wanted to avert his eyes from the naked convict. He always had to be alone, whilst the rest of the inmates crowded together in a wet bundle of humanity, a seething mass of skin and hair and tattoos and muscles and genitals, a great heaving sponge of flesh herded into the showers like cattle to be disinfected. There was a sense of dignity that the Captive Side always robbed of an inmate, and showering in front of other people was second nature to him now after his first day where he was stripped naked for a medical examination and his head was shaved against his consent. Consent and dignity were clothes that only needed to be worn away from here, out in the world which had no order and lacked structure and rigidity. It was not for their own enjoyment that they were permitted to shower but a rigorously enforced hygiene ritual which ensured that illnesses did not spread and the men did not become unhealthy because of unclean conditions. The maximum security prisoners were given solo showers throughout the day and the other prisoners were left with a small window of time in which they would all cram into the showers together. For Leo this was a highlight of his day and he enjoyed the feeling of being drenched in the water which was as cold as ice and sent a thrilling chill though his skin as it touched him, because as his skin tingled with the animation of the water and soap running down him onto the tiles between his toes he was reminded, against all of the odds, that he was still alive. As unlikely as it seemed, his soaked flesh was still infused with the magical sparks of life. When he was wet the ink of his tattoos turned from blue back to black and he loved the way that they looked; it was as if they were brand new again, as if the buzzing sound of the needle had only just fallen silent.

He finished soaping and rinsing himself, turned the water off and wrapped the towel around his waist. He had probably had the final private shower of his life before he had entered prison and as a result he had lost the instinctive shyness that he had before of people seeing his naked body. He had never been left alone and the feeling of needing to be in private simply evaporated. Walking with his guard back through the bathrooms, he came to the row of sinks and mirrors at which one of the other men was shaving. He was very large, with a torso packed with muscle, and gave Leo a look of pure seething hatred.

"I know you," he said, eyeing up the guard as he turned to Leo, "you're the one who raped the dead Hewitt kid." Leo quickened his pace, and the guard drew closer to him.

The man made a sudden swing at Leo, slamming his fist against the side of his head and he fell to the floor, the guard too dumbstruck to react. The prisoner shouted obscenities at the paedophile, yelling that he wished that he had been hanged, and as quick as a flash he released the safety catch on the head of his razor and made a sweeping slash at Leo's throat. The guard was too slow; he rushed to shield the prisoner from his attacker by crouching over him as he lay on the tiles but ribbons of blood were already unfurling into the grouting. Leo lost consciousness, with a gaping wound to the side of his neck and upon hearing the commotion other prison guards came to find them, holding the attacker back and trying to revive the sprawled victim. The guards quickly started to question their colleague, and he insisted that he had done everything that he could have done given the speed of the attack but the others suspected him of having a hatred of paedophiles and letting the attack happen. He vehemently denied this accusation, but another thing which had to be quickly learnt when entering Belmarsh was that there sense of hierarchy within the staff was as strong as it was within the group of prisoners. He had not been negligent, but his innocence did not mean that the young guard was not going to be heavily blamed.

Leo was taken into the treatment room at the prison and his wounds were attended to; nobody understood how the attacker was able to get so close to him with only one guard there to separate them. It was a particular type of place which bred magnificent legends and fanciful tales of bravery, and the fable of the attack in the bathroom was soon the talk of the canteen. Only when everyone was lauding the attacker as a hero and the very vocal disappointment when it was rumoured that Leo's condition was stable was it clear that even amongst this flock of rapists, murderers and cannibals Inmate Faulkner was intensely despised.

Leo's wounds were serious but not untreatable, and he had the gash stitched up and was allowed to have a male nurse come and administer treatment and pain relief to him once he was fit enough to return to his maximum security cell. For the first time he was allowed visitors other than guards, the most unusual and probably unwanted of whom was Rev. Peter Scripps, the prison Chaplain. He was responsible for the pastoral care of the prisoners and was usually only dealing with the most vulnerable and mentally unstable of inmates and, whilst his crime caused ripples of shocked outrage across the country, it took a few years and an attack from an angry criminal for him to be considered worthy of a visit from the Chaplain.

Peter was a small man, old and with thinning white hair, kind eyes and horrific dress sense. The very first thing that Leo noticed about him was the fact that he had an unusual amount of hair sprouting from his ears; the second was the cardigan. He was an old man who had lived a life very different from every single person imprisoned here, and Leo did not accept him into his cell with any great sense of optimism as to what might be achieved by the rendezvous. He didn't expect him to understand, however kind his intentions may have been. If Belmarsh had been a theatrical company the shambolic casting of Peter Scripps would have been enough to close the production. Until he saw Peter he had thought he was the only misfit, the only freakish outcast that could be found in this place.

He was polite enough to knock on the reinforced metal door of the maximum security jail cell. Did Leo somehow have a choice in the matter? How utterly surreal. Peter asked his permission to sit with him on the thin mattress, clearly intending for this not to come across as an interrogation. Nobody had ever asked him permission for anything ever since that Wednesday in Higher Pelham. Leo was the one to begin.

"Are you here to reform me?"

He was about to add something to his question to boast about his wild character, like a horse in the West which was impossible to break in, but Peter beat him to it. He could tell that this would be an interesting and bizarre interaction.

"No, Leo, I'm not prepared to give you years and years of intensive therapy, because I can't be bothered. Reformation is down to you. We'll help, but we can't do it for you. I am here to see how you are doing."

He stroked the thickening scar on his collarbone. The stitches were beginning to come out and the blood was congealing like a jelly setting in the fridge. It seemed an odd question to ask a man who was beginning a very long spell behind bars.

"I've been better." He looked at his companion. "Do you think I am evil?"

Peter did not drop his serious and sympathetic look. "No. Why do you ask that?"

"You're the Chaplain, aren't you? Were you the one who left the Bible on my bed when I moved in here?"

"I am the Chaplain, but the Bible was left for you by the Gideons, a charity which provides for people who sleep in public or Government buildings. Have you used it at all?"

Leo could not help emitting a small snort of laughter. "No mate, not me. I am the wrong kind of man for that."

Peter raised his eyebrows. "Oh yes? What kind of man do you have to be to read the Bible, Leo?"

"What if I told you something really dreadful?" he said, with his lips curling into a dastardly grin. "Something to chill your bones and to make you shudder with horror and fear? I have done a terrible thing."

"This is the highest security jail in London, sonny," he replied with a knowing expression of morbid sincerity. "I very much doubt that you could shock me."

"No no," interjected Leo, determined not to let anyone blunt his glory, "my crime went down in legal history. It was one of the worst."

"I know you, Leo," he said. "I have known who you are and what you have done ever since I first laid eyes on you. I know that they tried to give you the jab and it was voted through Parliament. I know that you are sexually aroused by children. I know that you have taken lives and abused young girls. I don't try to investigate criminals here but at the same time, there was a time when everyone in the world knew who you were."

"If you knew me," said the paedophile, "you would not waste your time on me, you would not have overlooked the fact that I am quite clearly not a good person and quite clearly not in the kind of prisoner that you will have any success in reforming."

"Do you think that you are beyond help, Leo?"

"I don't want to be helped."

"Sometimes we are in desperate need of help but we don't realise it. I don't think you are a waste of time. Here's a story for you, Leo. Here's the most important thing that anybody will ever tell you in your whole life. You were created to be in a perfect relationship with God. He made you because He loves you, and there is nothing about you that He does not know and is not able to forgive. But along the way our relationship with the Father who made us became broken and spoilt. Some of the things that caused this were deliberate actions on our part, things that we do on purpose to be selfish or cruel. Some of them were parts of our characters which simply fall short of the gauntlet of glory that God Himself laid down for us in His perfection, which cause us to fall short of his standards. Finally, some are just because the world we live in sucks and we are caught up in the collateral damage. God is a King of justice." He paused, and looked around the sterile cell. "Everyone in this place knows a thing or two about being on the wrong side of the law. In here we are punished for doing things that fall short of the world's standards, extreme crimes that the whole of society decides are outrageous and unacceptable. But in terms of our relationship with God, we only have one judge, one standard to meet. Sadly for us, it's a standard of absolute perfection and absolutely nobody passes the test. If God is perfect then He by definition cannot tolerate imperfection coming anywhere near Him, because it taints and stains Him. Did you see the World Cup Final ten summers ago? Do you remember when England won, and James Kelly collected the trophy from the Empress of Japan? You saw how dirty Kelly was, with his shirt covered in sweat and mud and how beautiful the Empress looked in her traditional Japanese costume. Now just imagine if he had run up to her, this tiny woman, and given her a great big hug as he wrenched the trophy out of her hands. The gloves she was wearing were perfectly white, pristine and beautiful. That outfit would have been completely ruined, stained with mud and smelling of sweat, and he probably had a nosebleed too! There is so much identity wrapped up the clothes of these two; him in his England kit, leading his team out as their captain, and her in her traditional clothes, symbolising the nation that she has come to represent. If they hug, she loses a lot of that identity. She is still the Empress if she is dirty, undoubtedly, but she loses a lot of dignity and glory. She becomes a lesser version of her role if she is covered in mud and sweat because she is defined by her beautiful traditional clothes. It's the same with God. He is defined by the clothes that he wears, clothes made of power and beauty and glory and perfection. Sadly, we can be defined by our clothes and they are not as wonderful as God's; our clothes are made of selfishness, greed, lies, sadness, loneliness and hurt. The two don't go together. His perfection is defined by the fact that everything that is imperfect is banished from His presence. If Heaven is a bucket of water and Earth is a bucket of sewage, Heaven can come to Earth without changing anything but if Earth goes to Heaven, even a spoonful, then both buckets become sewage. God can't allow that to happen."

Leo could not have looked any more disinterested if he had tried, but he did catch himself listening to Peter's words.

"This leaves God, the King of the Universe, with a dilemma. I want you to picture Him agonising over it, wondering what to do. If He lets the imperfection in, He can't be perfect, it simply isn't possible. But if He banishes it away, He can't be perfectly loving and forgiving. He turns into some kind of insane dictator, hell-bent on power and glory and, in honesty, he becomes a tragic loner." If He is the most perfect of all things, because He made all things, then He can't be in contact with anything else because nothing else matches His standard. If you can never be with Him, He can't love you. Not really; He can't love you if you are banished out of His presence. But somehow He does, with a love that never ends and that can survive all things, a love set down before the foundation of the world. So here's what He decided to do to solve the puzzle. Because there was no way that we could ever reach Him, He decided that He needed to come and find us. So He decided to throw off His traditional Japanese dress and run onto the pitch and give the football captain a great big hug. He sent His son to die on a cross, executed as a criminal, even though He was the only human being who ever lived in all of history with a clean record both by the standards of Earth and the standards of Heaven. Most can manage one, but nobody else has managed both. You know more than most people what it feels like to face execution, but He faced it as the only person out of all of us who had a perfectly clean record. He died a death that was meant for us. God is the source of all life, and being cut off from Him means that rather than being immortal, we wither away and die instead. We all die, eventually, Leo. We get sick, we have diseases, we have accidents and make mistakes, we get hurt, we let each other down, we are mean to each other, and in the end we die. The whole world is ripe with decay, and it is because the whole world is to varying degrees cut off from the love of God. It was the love by which we were conceived and created, so when we lose it there is a big effect on us. It's like a computer having the plug pulled; although it may be able to hang on for a bit if it has a good battery the lifeblood which it needs to survive has been removed. Eventually it will shut down. The countdown clock starts ticking for the first time. But instead of us dying, instead we have been given the chance to reconnect to the mains. It was His son, Jesus, who ended up taking that consequence for us; a consequence which involved being cut off from the love of God which we need to live forever in a perfect world, and instead suffering the pain and shame of execution. What that means now for us, is that if we choose to trust in Jesus and accept that He took the punishment on our behalf, we are invited to reconnect to the mains again and rejoin the family of God, meaning that we can live eternally with Him, in the way that He designed life to be lived. It's a life of wholesome fullness, a life of eternal joy and vast, wonderful abundance."

"Piss off, asshole," Leo shot back at him once he had finished his long monologue, "and before you start banging on about your own little breed of insanity, with talk of voices in your head and castles in the sky, I have one thing to tell you. There is no shame in execution. It's not humiliating or degrading. It is the crowning glory of a life well lived, of a man who had an impact on world. A man who mattered. That's why they didn't pass the Bill through Parliament, it was because they didn't want to give me any glory by killing me as a martyr."

He stopped speaking and his eye contact dropped immediately. As much as he tried to revel in it, it was very clear that he was uncomfortable talking about his proposed execution. He seemed so downhearted and disappointed with his sentence; perhaps the attacks and insults were getting to him. He was angry with Peter, and something inside of him was deeply offended by the notion that he could be loved after all that he had done, not least loved by some fanciful fairytale which held no logical truth and which existed to make the attractive shimmer of a damned world gleam that little bit brighter. It was nonsense, of course, whimsical drivel which made no sense to anyone with any ounce of intelligence. The man believed that the world had been made in six days by a maker who had crafted the whole universe like it was a piece of pottery; it didn't take a lot of brainpower to realise that there was no way that could be true. And the idea that the world was four thousand years old was offensively laughable. How dare he? What about fossils, and mathematical calculations about the speed with which the universe expands, and dinosaurs, and evolution? There are some things that we cannot know, Peter had said. There are some questions which we must simply speculate over, which we must debate, rather than knowing as absolute, scientific truth. The secular theories over the origin of the Universe were not absolute truths but scientific speculation. But Leo knew. He knew that the world had been made billions of years ago by the big bang; he knew that the universe was a melting pot of chemicals and elements and it had all come together in a brilliant, purposeless accident. There was no direction, no sense of destiny; that was all the result of humanity's collective imagination left unpruned. But again Peter dared to challenge him; can you know that for sure if you weren't there to see it happen? Peter couldn't, it turned out, and so his solution was to trust what the Bible said because it was written by God, an eyewitness to the creation of the world, something nobody else can claim to be. How magnificently absurd and deluded this fool was.

Leo found himself not merely ignoring the message that Peter had given him, not simply letting it wash over him and appreciating the sentiment whilst quietly refusing to make any response to the myth of a divine rescuer loving him, but instead he was seething with a fiery indignation and fierce anger. He was consumed with rage because of the man's senseless ideas, and something about what he had said made his very spirit erupt in fiery fury.

Peter still visited him in his cell every day, and a guard stood watch to protect him every time the two men came into contact with one another. Each and every time that Peter showed an interest in Leo he was met with abusive hatred, and the paedophile was somehow aggravated, somehow irritated by the Gospel and the Chaplain in a way that he simply was not by anything and anyone else. Peter was puzzled by this; he had a great deal of experience with other prisoners on Leo's security, isolation and suicide-risk levels. In fact the only thing that was even remotely unique about Inmate Faulkner was the fact that he had caused so much controversy and the major political storm which followed had come as close as was possible to having him executed for the crime that he had committed. Peter knew how to approach angry prisoners sensitively, but the anger within Leo was of a level that he simply had not prepared himself for. He screamed and shouted and hurled expletives at Peter, but the calm and steady stream of love which flowed out of him could not be plugged; there were some occasions where the guard needed to restrain him from assaulting the Chaplain as his rage was allowed to fester in his flesh. Living, and being thrown into Belmarsh with the countless other inmates, had leeched all of the infamy out of him. Leo hated it.

The truth of it was that Leo was surprised, which made him explode with rage. He remembered his encounter with Alice Hewitt as she spoke to him through the glass from the Freedom Side, and how she had made a noble but ultimately failed attempt at dignity and graceful restraint, but had regressed into insults and telling him about her satisfaction at the justly severe nature of his treatment. That was fine; he could deal with being hated. He could handle being scorned and rejected and despised, and he relished in the way that the people had marched in a sea of human hatred demanding his death. He understood and fully appreciated the way that the other inmates had treated him, insulting and abusing him, but to do what he had done and to get *grace* in return simply did not make any sense. It troubled him deeply.

"Are you offended by the idea of sin and judgement, Leo? Does it unsettle you that the world is broken and is suffering so much?"

He didn't say anything in reply. He was growing to hate these interactions with Peter, and he knew that it was only a matter of time before his violent impatience got the better of his cool temper.

"If you are, why don't you look at it this way . . . in a single question, what do you think it is that God owes you? What do you think you are entitled to be awarded by the one who made you? Before you answer, think about the fact that He created you for the very simple purpose of enjoying your company and that there was no obligation for Him to bring you into existence in the first place. You were created by grace and commissioned in love. Does He owe you life, even another millisecond of it on top of what he has already provided you with? Does He owe you health? Does He owe you happiness, love and joy? Having answered that, does it make you think about the fact that He *does* love you in a different way? Was life itself not a phenomenal gift to give someone, let alone all the extras He has given you along the way? Is that how you see it, or are you only seeing your existence in a prison cell?"

Instead of hatred, what Peter offered was an onslaught of love, against which Leo could not defend himself. It was an offensive and ludicrous theology which went against everything he stood for and believed was possible. That affected Leo deeply and he felt a stirring hatred deep within him that he felt that he simply could not ignore. What was there to love about a paedophile, a man who had killed an innocent seven year old so that he could have sex with her corpse? How was it possible that he was cherished and adored by his maker and that even when he was at his worst, when he was in the process of killing Joy with his brain and flesh filled with impulsive surges, the love of Christ which promised to rescue him and restore him back to the glory which was intended for him never failed, ceased or grew faint? How could that be? Something about the story of a man on a cross filled him with anger. There was an irrationality about it that haunted him, the idea that an innocent man should be given the execution that he himself was denied and that the guilty people in the world who had ever fallen short of a perfect standard, all of the men in this prison, would be given the opportunity to go free in his place. He was deeply offended by the idea that a man could commit a terrible and violent crime against someone else, could live an appalling life and be a disgusting individual and yet be welcomed into an eternity in paradise in the arms of their maker. On the other hand, a perfectly good person who had lived a wholesome and virtuous life would be condemned to exclusion from God's presence because of a decision that they did not make during their time on Earth. It conflicted with every sense of justice and logic that he had within himself; every moral fibre of his being rejected the idea.

The thing which infuriated him most about Peter was that he had an annoyingly smart answer for everything and he knew precisely what he was about to be asked. It felt as though every thought that passed through Leo's head had been second guessed and that he was incapable of coming up with a completely original thought, an idea that nobody else had ever had. The smart answer for this particular question was to refer back to the two standards of justice that there are; Heaven's justice and Earth's justice. Earth's justice depends on what you do, and this was the one which Leo was relating to. But Heaven's justice relies of who you know and who you trust, and since the cross there is only one crime by which we are judged: the crime of living selfishly and rejecting God's rule over us, or the act of righteousness of choosing to trust and follow Jesus and accept the gift of restored life that He gives with it. We are now judged on nothing else at all, for everything else is second to whether or not trust Jesus as your Lord and Saviour when God looks at your criminal record and decides whether or not you are clean. He had never heard anything more outrageous, unjust, miraculous and absurd in his whole life.

The problem with Belmarsh, he was finding, was that it was a place where the prisoner had an unlimited amount of time to think. The words of the Chaplain were like seeds, their germinated sprouts crawling through the folded flannel of his brain like the grave-worms should have done, and soon the idea was taking hold of him and he simply could not let it go. For a few weeks after the first conversation he was incapable of thinking about anything else and he wondered for a moment, with the stress of a possible execution, permanent isolation and abuses at the hands of other prisoners, whether or not he had allowed his sanity to drip and trickle out of his skull without even noticing.

9

THE FREEDOM SIDE

Leo Faulkner grew old in his cage, largely forgotten by the outside world and the MLC's aggressive pursuit of their goal of killing prisoners was abandoned. Over the intervening years there were references in the news to the landmarks in the law that were made in the Joy Hewitt case whenever there was another child murdered, and the attacks on him in jail were reported in the tabloids and occasionally the media would cover events such as either an anniversary of the attack or Joy's birthday with a documentary about the case, but in broad terms the insatiable appetite for vengeance, the public's view of the relationship between blood and justice, ebbed away with astonishing speed and the momentum of the campaign was never recovered. The sentiments of the public were the same as they had been that winter, but it would be a very long time before their concerns would be taken seriously again, and the Executionists knew that they had missed the best opportunity that they would ever get.

There had been young girls murdered for sex before Joy Hewitt, and undoubtedly there would be attacks after he had long gone, but for some reason the wildfire of feeling that swept the nation that winter burnt fiercer than emotions stirred up for any case before it and was unlikely to be seen again. Other Prime Ministers did not invite the parents of other murder victims to Downing Street, and other newspaper editors did not give the family full financial backing in exchange for a campaign for dramatic changes in the law. Whilst the residents of Higher Pelham were immediately suspicious of the parents and their accusations led to Alice Hewitt's arrest, the public were united in their support for the family and their outraged hatred of the killer. Brady had tried to use the momentum of the campaign in other areas of the newspaper's interests but it had never again achieved anything close to the same effect. Journalism industry insiders were puzzled as to what aspect of the case had caught the public imagination with such spectacular effect but there seemed to be no obvious answer; the case was not totally unique in any way and he had only killed once even though he was guilty of other sexual crimes. One academic in a news interview caused a minor political storm by claiming that it was because Joy Hewitt was a young white female, the personification of innocence and vulnerability, implying that the public as a whole had a racist outlook and were more horrified by crimes against young white girls than young black boys.

Alice Hewitt was the only visitor that Leo ever received in his time at Belmarsh Prison. His mother was the only living relative he had left, but she had been too ashamed to visit him for the early part of his incarceration and had wanted to avoid connections to him in the wake of the hatred to which he was exposed. Alice was desperate for closure, for a solution and explanation as to what had happened to his brain, but Lillith knew that her curiosity would forever remain insatiable and there would be no explanation he could possibly have given her which would have satisfied her and justified what he had done. Knowing this, she stopped waiting for him to explain. Lillith grew older as the years gently eroded her, finally dying one cold winter having never understood the raging sexual storm brewing inside of her son. In her will she left him her flat, a modest little place in east London, and one of Lillith's friends had custody of it (and the revenue for the rent which was being paid on it by the new tenants) until the time of Leo's release in the far future. She clearly had more faith in him at the time of her death than the justice system did. The only contact he had from her was a letter from her solicitor telling him the legal arrangements of the property.

Over the years, Leo and Peter formed an unlikely friendship. The killer knew that although he did not have any immediate interest in what it was that Peter offered him, this was a man who took an interest in him as a person and who was always happy to listen to what he had to say, regardless of what it was. During his time behind bars Peter Scripps was the only man who addressed Leo Faulkner by his first name.

The assaults on the inmate were regular throughout the serving of his sentence; he was punched, gouged, scratched, stabbed and scalded by the other prisoners and he had been considered for relocation to another prison or to a psychiatric ward even though he had never been declared insane. The motivation for these moves was that other, low risk jails would have fewer dangerous inmates who would be less likely to attack Faulkner. This would be because their sentences would be shorter and they would have a real hope of release which would discourage them from bad behaviour. Mulcahy had begun proceedings to have him moved to the category B HMP Wandsworth on the other side of London, but he received severe criticism from the tabloid press (led by the *Envoy*) after beginning legal action against the guards at Belmarsh after he deemed them to be not doing enough to protect their most famous inmate. The view of the public, however, was that the guards were doing far too much in the way of protection and that Faulkner should be left to suffer at the hands of others as Joy Hewitt had suffered because of him. Outraged by the retention of the current justice system Valerie Whiting had resigned from her post as Secretary for Justice and Human Rights, just as she had promised to, and taken the quite unrelated job of the British ambassador to China; a post of extreme difficulty given the war between the two alliances a short decade before. It was a smart move from Huntley, in the twilight of his Government, because China and the United States had both pressurized Westminster to pass the Bill and adhere to their own moral guidelines in accordance with the conditions of loans and arms and trade embargos. Whilst the relationship between the Governments was very bad, the Chinese welcomed Whiting with open arms as a champion of their cause in the British Parliament. Three years after the defeat of the MLC campaign through Parliament, the pro-death Conservatives lost the general election and William Sutcliffe became the new Labour Prime Minister. The pro-life campaigners were angry that Huntley's Government had attempted to restore capital punishment and the pro-execution campaigners were angry that he had failed in his bid to kill Leo Faulkner, so he lost votes from all sides. With the transfer of power Ryan Mulcahy lost his job as Prisons Minister and the momentum for protecting Leo Faulkner was lost, meaning that he stayed in Belmarsh for the duration of his sentence. He had been hated by the prisoners from the moment that he had been incarcerated there, but with the attack where his throat had been slashed he had caused a great deal of frenzied accusations to fly amongst the staff with regard to incompetence, and some of the prisoners were even complaining to the Government about the fact that the staff appeared to be letting the violence happen. When Ryan Mulcahy began to talk of legal action against them, the outpouring of accusation turned simply to a union between every single person at Belmarsh in one common aim; each and every one of them hated Leo Faulkner, the paedophile and necrophile, with a passion that blazed as hot and bright as a supernova.

Amidst all of this, the senior board of the prison, which included the parole officers, looked on Leo with a great sympathy. He had not requested to sue the staff of the prison, and he had been awarded £2,500 in legal aid to pursue his claim from Ryan Mulcahy without ever asking for it. The beatings continued, and they intensified in severity and frequency as the prisoners became angrier and the guards garnered a reputation for allowing them to happen. Whilst that was not entirely true, they certainly did not make any great effort to go out of their way to prevent them from happening.

Whilst everything seemed to be collapsing in on him, Leo found a very steadfast friend in the Chaplain. Everyone else was too disgusted or intimidated to be seen with him, but Peter never gave up on Leo. At first he had been very hostile to him, the frequent visits angering him so furiously that there was a day when he had snapped and unleashed a punch into the middle of Peter's face as soon as he mentioned the word "love". He had been taken away with a broken nose and treated by the doctor, but came back the very next morning with a dressing on his wound and began again the process of befriending the man who everyone else stayed well clear of. Leo was so shocked by the fact that he had not rejected him even though he had been violent against his visitant; there was not an ounce of revenge or anger in Peter's body, and he seemed to be the last person in the country who did not feel this way against the man who had killed and raped a child. He was so shocked that he was instantly disarmed; Peter had already forgiven him long before he had ever been offered an apology. How could that be? What did this frail little man have within him, what inner strength which was capable of forgiving an attacker with such ease? Peter seemed to be the only one in the prison who was physically smaller than Leo and the only person that he felt he was capable of intimidating, and all of his anger seemed to come out on Peter in physical and verbal assaults. But now he had been completely disarmed with his pacifism. It was mesmerising to watch; Leo was simply too dumbfounded to be angry any more, he was desperate to know what had caused this man to be so frail in body but so mighty and towering in sprit.

His mind had been on the lunacy of the Gospel and its otherworldly and ethereal justice system for some time before he began to consider it as a thing of truth. A war zone such as Belmarsh, with its own unique conglomeration of trenches and barricades, demanded and placed tremendous value on alliances and the unlikeliest of friendships.

Peter was lucky in the fact that he did not need to convince the huge majority of the inmates of Belmarsh that they were guilty and in need of redemptive forgiveness. On the Freedom Side it was harder to convince people who had always seen themselves as good that they were in fact falling short of the perfect standard that the King of Heaven required to be accepted into His presence on virtue alone. Slowly, Leo was beginning to see that he was in desperate need of a divine rescuer.

One Christmas Day a few years later, Peter was doing his rounds of the cells. The prison was under the minimum level of supervision so that the staff could go home to their families and many of the prisoners had loved ones come to visit them, but Leo was not amongst their number. Alice Hewitt was the first and last visitor that ever bothered to come and see him. He had been permanently estranged from his family for years already by the time he had come to murder Joy, he was a loner who obsessively collected child pornography and because of this the majority of his interactions with other non-virtual people came through stalking and molesting little girls. Leo spent Christmas Day the same way that he spent every other day, sitting on his bed, thinking and spending time remembering what it was like to be on the Freedom Side.

He was quite alone, because all of the other standard grade prisoners had gathered in the canteen where the staff had agreed to broadcast the King's Christmas Speech and a good number of the men were wearing Santa hats for the occasion. When hope is gone the survivors still never falter from certain rigid traditions and characteristics of the world outside of the prison wall; there was a structure, an order, a hierarchy and a resolute formation to the particular microcosm in which they found themselves. It reassured them all, gave them a fleeing sense of purpose when there seemed to be none. However hopeless their situation was serving long sentences, the sense of society which is inherent to all human beings was brought to the jail by every new prisoner and retained by every existing one, and in their strict and rigid observance of complex social structures within their damned community they expressed a level of humanity which their doubters and accusers on the Freedom Side would have argued that a murderer or rapist could never have possessed.

Peter knocked on the steel door and gave Leo a hearty smile through the service hatch. Leo got up from his bed and nodded to the guard who unlocked the door using a massive bunch of keys. "Good afternoon, Leo," said Peter. He was unusually cheerful. "Merry Christmas to you."

"Happy Christmas, Peter," he replied, slightly surprised that he was choosing to spend his time on Christmas Day with the prisoners on his day job. Surely he had places that he would rather be, and had people who he would rather be with on this most precious of all days? He was, after all, one of the very few men in Belmarsh who was still free and still his own man. He put it to his friend, suggesting that as this was probably his most sacred day of the year that he perhaps had somewhere better to be. He wasn't even watching the King's Speech, which was unthinkable to Leo as he felt like the only man in the country not able to take his place and connect with the whole nation for ten minutes each Christmas Day.

Peter's reply made him think. He said that he knew that Christmas Day was enshrined in British culture as the most important holiday of the year, and the one in which the retail industry made probably half of its money and the economy got a boost which was welcome for everyone. Christmas had been branded and mass produced, commercialised and commoditised, driven more by money and its position in the middle of winter than the religious celebration on which it had been based. Christmas was now a roaring beast which had far outgrown the confines of its origins, mutating and swallowing more and more of the commercial sector each December and growing further from the true meaning than ever before.

Peter explained that there was nothing at all which was not miraculous and heart-warming about Christmas and its true meaning, but it was not the cornerstone of the Christian year. Christmas was a time every year when the birth of Jesus Christ was celebrated, but God's great gift of grace was only truly unveiled at Easter. The destiny of the human race relied on Easter Sunday, not on this beloved relic of a nation which had long since lost its unquestioning faith. Leo was curious and receptive, but not ready to comply with anything that Peter said. He was grateful to have companionship and a conversation to share with someone else, no matter how absurd that conversation may turn out to be. This one was on a different level of lunacy to most.

Peter began in Genesis, a good place to start, with God creating the Heavens and the Earth. He listed off all of the magnificent things that God had made, a vast and lush tapestry of creation which contrasted sharply with the bare and dull walls of the jail cell in which he was hearing the story. The blank white walls were the canvas of the tale and in Leo's mind they became illustrated with the beauty and the wonder of the things which Peter began to tell him about. There was a mesmerising quality to his voice, a soothing calmness in his words.

He looked at the walls and found himself blinded by the first light in history, a light so brilliant and white and pure that it rendered him breathless. It had no source, and did not shine, but instead the horizonless ocean seemed to radiate energy and warmth. With a great slash the sky was divided into a firmament above and the surging waters below, rolling and raging in tempestuous impatience. The water gathered into different places beneath the starless sky and a perfectly empty Earth began to take shape; vast, multicoloured valleys and plains of nothing but dust and rock. It was an incredible idea to behold.

The skies stretched above Leo as he looked upwards, smooth and perfectly dark, as deep and empty as coal. Light was all around him but it was not coming from the sky. For billions of light years in every direction lay vast, blank, bare cosmos. He saw the days and the nights separated for the first time, heard in Peter's voice the first day there had ever been, listened to the glow of a brand new sun. He heard the first whisper of the crescent moon, held in its place as the king of the night time, but the thing which gave a really lasting impression on Leo was the carelessness, the inattention and almost boredom with which the stars were created. "He also made the stars." He listened to them in Peter's voice, their twinkling glory, their majestic splendour and the greatest illustration of distance available to a human being. He heard the swoosh of the Milky Way curving across the hemispheres in a great arc, the pinholes to another world and the features of Heaven which have bewitched civilizations ever since the foundation of the human race. They were an afterthought. They were made with a spontaneous click of God's fingers. If he were writing the Bible as a hoax, would Leo not have decided to boast a little in the way in which arguably the most impressive feature of the universe came to be? The gargantuan distances, the mesmerising nebulae and supernovas and constellations, all expertly and painstakingly arranged and orchestrated for us to admire and to make the existence of a god undeniable so that he may be praised forever? Leo questioned Peter about this as he read it to him, and in the discussion it became evidently clear to him that this was not Genesis' approach at all. The message was clear: God does not need praise, He is not some desperate attention seeker, but instead love is something we choose to give Him out of thankfulness. He proved that He is perfectly capable of existing without the adoration of his creations by doing just that before we were made. He wants us to love Him; he doesn't stomp his feet and scream and shout like a toddler would. It's very fanciful, Peter claimed, that man thinks that he can somehow endorse or enhance the majesty of his maker simply by recognising that He is there. Even if we had never been made God would be just as glorious and the stars would be just as magnificent even if we were never around to see them. Leo saw the glory of God as integral to His character and identity; He simply could not help but make the stars in the spectacular way that they are, because He is not capable of being any less than that. God is central to our identity, but we are not central to His; we are worth more than we would otherwise have been because He chooses us. Peter continued to describe the different animals which now roamed and inhabited the Earth in all of their wonderful beauty and intricacy, and the walls of the jail cell were covered in every kind of mammal and fish, bird and reptile.

Leo simply could not let the strongest of his disputes with Creationism go unanswered any longer. It was such an enormous barrier to his belief that he could not endure any more until the mystery was solved. He told Peter the fact, the concrete and solid fact, that the universe had been created by the Big Bang and that we could definitely know that scientific fact because it was possible to measure the size of the cosmos and the speed with which it was expanding. Given speed and distance, it was relatively simple to calculate the amount of time and it was a period vastly longer than the one Peter was advocating. The numbers of Creationism simply did not add up or make sense. His response was very simple and very assured. He was not in the least fazed by the apparently conclusive counterargument.

"You are making assumptions, Leo, because that's what science is. Science is looking at the evidence and making the conclusion yourself based on the most likely outcome. The evidence is that the universe is expanding at a constant speed and therefore it must have been billions and billions of years ago that it was all together in the Big Bang. But this is God we are talking about. He illuminates the heavens with starlight from billions of different solar systems with the snap of his fingers. This is the God who created the incredible intricacy of the human inner ear, so who says that He must stick to our rules? Is it provable, without any human being having ever witnessed it, that the universe has always expanded at the exact same speed that it is expanding now? Is it so unbelievable that an incredible and omnipotent God would be able to create the world exactly as we see it now, and that the timeline of history did not necessarily start at the very beginning?"

Then Peter read the part where God created the first man. When he had finished, Leo noticed that it was the first time in the description of creation in which God had chosen to describe His work as "very good". With all of the majesty and wonder of what had gone before—the eye of the stallion, the rainbows and sunsets, the patterns of snowflakes and the glitter of the shooting star, the hush of twilight, the colour and texture of strawberry flesh, the technicolour fishbowl of a coral reef and the rose erupting into bloom—the rest was merely "good". Of everything that he had made, the Maker was most satisfied when He made the human being. Leo Faulkner was His greatest masterpiece, the peak of God's career, the King of Heaven's magnum opus. He had not made Adam as a baby; he had made him as an adult, a fully grown man. Did that mean that planet Earth was also fully grown upon its creation, complete with fossils, set in a universe midway through expansion and containing a partially eroded Grand Canyon? If you were prepared to accept that God made it all because He wanted to, was it a particularly large stretch to advance to the conclusion that He would have it within His power to scatter a few dinosaur skeletons in the ground, exactly as we found them when they were discovered by humans? If we were not there to see it, how can we be absolutely sure?

Bearing this in mind, Leo was dumbfounded when he heard about the way in which Adam and Eve had lived in a perfect world but had squandered their shot at glory. God did not make us to be programmable like robots, Peter said, but instead He chose to endow us with the gift of free will, which He knew would open up the possibility of humanity never knowing Him and never having a relationship with Him. But it had to be done, for a relationship with no freedom is no relationship at all.

Looking into the past showed Leo the fact that the relationship with God was broken, which was what Peter had been telling him in a previous conversation. But then Peter turned Leo's attention to the future and what God had offered him, flicking through the Bible to 1 Corinthians chapter 15 which was close to the back. Peter knew that this was the passage read out at Joy's funeral, but Leo was blissfully unaware. What was Leo's understanding of Heaven? It was an untrue myth, a fairytale to stop children being afraid of fragile mortality, a crumb of comfort when a grandmother dies. It was a fanciful, far fetched legend which saw lights at the end of tunnels, floating outside of the human body and eternity being an otherworldly, ethereal congregation of wispy, cloudlike souls. None of it was physical, so none of it was real.

As he had heard before, the execution of Jesus Christ had been offered as a sacrifice for the fate that the whole of humanity was relentlessly heading towards, which was death. The letter in the Bible had been written by a man named Paul, a man who had been the biggest enemy of the early church and who had taken enormous pleasure in exterminating Christians with all the monstrous zeal of Adolf Hitler, throwing them to lions and burning their bodies. He was specifically on a journey to Damascus to butcher people who loved God when God himself interrupted his life to win him to salvation. He then became the most influential writer of the New Testament, the last half of the Bible, and Peter burst with enthusiasm—"don't you see, Leo? We are so quick to write ourselves off, and the world calls us failures, but can you think of a person who would be worse at that job than St Paul? Was there a single candidate in the whole world who would have done a worse job than him? God has a million and one more obvious ways of doing things than the ways He chooses but that's not the point; instead He is doing a great work in the world and He chooses us, with all of our faults and failures, because He wants to invite us to be involved. Also Paul can be under no illusions that he doesn't deserve even an ounce of the glory; it helps us to recognise God's identity."

For the first time in any of their conversations Leo's mind was working faster than Peter's. Perhaps it was the shiny blue pills, but the neurons in his brain were spinning and the cogs and machinery whirred as he contemplated the gravity of what was being said. Leo was a child killer and a sex offender, and he had thought that his prospects and his future had been executed without him. Paul had been committing genocide, and yet he was central to God's plans for the future. Could it be that the river of grace was flooding down as far as him? Could it be that the offer of redemption was available to everyone regardless of the skeletons in their closets? Could it be that there was nothing he could have done and no crime he could have possibly committed which could have invalidated the restoring power of the cross of Christ?

As he had done beforehand, Peter explained that death is unfortunately an inherent aspect of the DNA of humankind; if we are born into Adam's family tree then we will die. We are mortal and we are built for corrosion and ruin, a faded image of the grandeur gone by. But the second man, the Second Adam, offers us adoption into his family tree instead, which means that we will be like Him and, instead of inheriting ruinous decay, we will inherit magnificent and abundant life. Life as it was meant to be experienced, restored once again to God's magnum opus.

Following the resurrection of Jesus from the grave, Leo learnt that He invited people to follow Him; following Jesus in life would mean that they would also follow Him in death. What He got, they would get too. He was gloriously resurrected from the dead, in a physical body which had no ghostly qualities at all, and after his death he ate and drank with his friends, talked and walked with them, interacting with five hundred people. The very first Easter Day was not the ghostly spirit party which Leo had imagined it to be in the fairytales, where the whole human dies but it is only the soul which receives an afterlife. No; all of Jesus went to the cross, all of Him died, and all of Him was raised to life again to rescue the world. And it was not only restored to life only to grow old and die again, for the inherited curse of mortality was now broken. Jesus was healed of his scars and was recognisable as the man He had been on Earth but an improved version with his blemishes and weaknesses gone. Leo would have the chance to follow Him and to have his own weaknesses in his ravaged and ruined body miraculously dealt with; his collapsed veins from previous drug abuse, the scar on his neck, the dreadful sexual urges which he had been a prisoner to all of his life; all would come under the wonderful Kingship of Christ and he would be, finally and physically, free.

The depiction of Heaven which Peter was telling him about was vastly different to the one which he had in his mind since childhood. There was nothing ethereal or ghostly about this new

Creation, a vast harvest of life following a long winter of death, and it enchanted him. There would be no shade of the Heaven that is embellished in Western culture for centuries, the notion of gates made from pearls sitting on clouds with angels wearing togas and vaporous outlines of human souls hovering like clouds in an endless sea of intangible apparitions. The problem for the Corinthians, the people to whom the letter was addressed, was much the same as the problem for Leo; he had spent his whole life rigidly clinging to the notion that the human soul and the human body were completely unconnected, even opposite, concepts. But looking at the Biblical passages, this idea simply vanished between the words on the page; it was not at all what he understood from the letter when he read it with no external ideas in his mind and tried to simply place a meaning on what was being said. If there is no future for the human body and the Heaven which we are all commanded to hope for rests on a gargantuan gathering of fleshless, invisible spirits, then Christ himself walked out of his tomb as a fleshless, invisible spirit and there was no physical resurrection for him. The trouble with that is that the entire theology of the Bible rests on the promise that the sins of the world are forgiven because of the atoning death and resurrection of Jesus Christ. Paul's argument was that it simply is not possible to separate the spirit and the body, for they are intrinsically and permanently connected. If all that happened that first Easter Sunday was that a human body was left to rot and the spirit of Christ was raised from the dead as a mystical puff of smoke, then that was not enough on which to base the salvation of the world. There had to be a firm, sound, physical victory over death. In a thrilling moment of revelation, Leo realised that there was.

This was the Gospel which touched Leo, the story of real good news for his real and ravaged body. It was the knowledge that he had been made to look like God and that perfection itself was the blueprint of humanity. With a rushing sense of glorious awe he realised that life on Earth was infinitely more than he had anticipated; he was more wretched and lost, doomed and ruined that he could have ever imagined but also God's grace was more wonderful and infinite, bottomless and everlasting than he could ever have comprehended. It stretched across the universe and reached even someone as tiny and lost as Leo. It was simultaneously the best and worst moment of his life, to know the vastness of his guilt but to know that the grace of God was enough to rescue him and to present a child killer as the beloved child of God.

On Christmas Day, in a maximum security jail cell in HMP Belmarsh, Leo's life changed forever. The last thing that Jesus had come to do was to organise another religion. Instead the purpose of his visit to Earth was to show us what life in a relationship with God should be like. He came to demonstrate love in a powerful way, a controversial and unlimited way, not like anything we could have seen before or dreamt up ourselves.

His mind was fixed on Joy and never left her side when Peter had been telling him about the wondrous beauty of humanity. It was not until this Christmas Day that he had understood that killing a child was wrong. Why could it not be wrong? Obviously the family would be worried about her suffering, but Leo was the only one to have set eyes on her in the final moments of her life and he knew that she did not experience pain. In fact he doubted that she experienced anything at all; she set eyes on him a few short seconds before her life ended, and she certainly did not remember the trauma of being raped. He had ended her life in the same way that poultry may have their necks wrung to extinguish their animation, and he was quite certain that it was instant and completely painless. Given that at the time he thought that humanity—Joy included—was an accidental speck of unimaginable anonymity and insignificance in a world ruled by arbitrary randomness, surely there was nothing wrong with killing her? All she consisted of was a conglomeration of chaotic cells, blood, bone, skin, hair, organs and jellied brains, hastily assembled by one hundred and eighty five million generations of accidental chance. Her very existence was not in any way predetermined or endowed with the majesty of order and logic; instead the weak had consistently given way to the strong and after billions of years of mutations and evolutions, Joy finally and randomly appeared. She was not created; instead she was an extremely complex version of an ape, which was an extremely complex version of a vertebrate mammal, constantly adapted and mutated since the original common ancestor for all biology of a single celled bacterium. Whether or not it was true did not matter; fact or fiction, a beautiful spellbinding wonder or a troubling falsehood, humanity contained no glory whatsoever if its construction had no predetermined purpose. However carefully Geoff and Alice had planned her, Joy was an inconspicuous accident. If this was it, if life was all there was, what on Earth was wrong with raping a dead child? If the law of evolution was king, why did people have such an outraged objection to him exercising his physical dominance over the weak just as had been practiced for billions of years? He was not surprised at the outrage but he could not understand it; surely the instinct of Geoff and Alice to selflessly protect their young would be detrimental to the instinct which had ensured the success of their species through the ages, the ruthless mentality which had seen humans dominate? He looked down at verse 32 again. "If there's no resurrection, 'we eat, we drink, the next day we die' and that's all there is to it." Kill children if you want to, why does anything matter if there is no order, no sense of hope? But something in him was stirring and protesting against this bleak conclusion; and deep inside himself Leo knew that he was made of more than just dust.

But there was something for which he had not accounted, and upon realising it the abhorrence of his crime dawned on him with a horrible reality. It was not the suffering that he caused her but the disrespect and the sacrilege that he committed against her dignity, a dignity that she had inherited from her Father. That was his crime against Joy Hewitt all those years ago, for she did not deserve to be raped by a murderer because it was the exact opposite of the glory for which she had been painstakingly made. Peter directed him to Psalm 139; "For you created my inmost being, you knit me together in my mother's womb. I praise you because

I am fearfully and wonderfully made; your works are wonderful, I know that full well. My frame was not hidden from you when I was made in the secret place. When I was woven together in the depths of the Earth, your eyes saw my unformed body." Joy had been crafted by a loving maker in His divine image, intended for eternal glory as God's masterpiece, and he had stolen her precious and flushing hue of life for a brief sexual buzz.

With an intense gravity he realised the significance of the crime which he had committed against the Hewitt family and against society as a whole. For the first time in his life he stopped seeing himself as the victim of misunderstanding and felt remorse and regret for what had happened to Joy; it was not about him any more. There was something bigger, something distinctly external, to be concerned with now.

"Aim for Heaven," Peter would say, "and you get Earth thrown in with it. Aim for Earth . . ." his voice trailed off into silence as the two men sat in the cold, sterile cell, a place of hopelessness and destruction and despair. Peter smiled. "You'll miss. You have nothing to lose at all and everything to gain. It's a journey worth every step."

*　　*　　*

After many years, the day finally came; the magical and long-awaited milestone of Year Twenty Five finally arrived. Leo took his place in the interview room and members of the parole board filed in slowly. There seemed to be hundreds of them; it was many more in number than the jury who had initially condemned him. Most prominent of these were the new Justice and Human Rights Secretary, who had taken a break in his busy schedule in Westminster to come and determine the freedom of one infamous individual, and the country's leading psychosexual therapist.

"Inmate Faulkner," began the chairman, "you were charged for the abduction, murder, rape and sexual interference with the corpse of seven year old Joy Hewitt in the village of Higher Pelham twenty six years ago. You were initially sentenced to death but this was reduced to life in prison when Parliament failed to pass a law restoring the death penalty for crimes such as yours. You were not eligible for a bail application until you had served twenty five years in permanent isolation, which is why we are here today because twenty five years have hereby passed since your trial."

He turned to the Chaplain. "I will begin with you, Reverend Scripps. What is your assessment of the Inmate's time in His Majesty's Prison, Belmarsh over the last twenty five years?"

Scripps was emphatic in his response. "Inmate Faulkner has behaved impeccably behind bars for the duration of his sentence. His first year with us was difficult but we managed to overcome the problems with violence and antisocial behaviour. He integrated well into the community here and he never once gave me any reason to suspect that he would reoffend. I saw a complete transformation in his character and the old Leo that we knew at his trial and during the beginning of his sentence. He was not the same person at all."

Next to testify was the nurse. Veronica was long gone but her replacements had seen Leo make great progress over the years. "Inmate Faulkner did not initially respond well to the treatments, especially the neurological and pharmaceutical methods which were used, and we have records of him refusing to take castration medication at the beginning of his sentence and the medical team having to use force to make sure that his testosterone levels were lowered. He did not respond well to the cognitive behavioural therapy, until around the time when Reverend Scripps told us that he converted to Christianity. He was more open to the questions which we posed to him and we immediately noticed a difference in his willingness to comply with the treatment. He was suddenly very remorseful about what he had done and he was desperate to allow us to change him so that he would not be in the same position with a minor ever again."

"Do you agree with this, Reverend Scripps?"

"Absolutely. He showed an immediate understanding of the Gospel and he understood that he was forgiven by God but that did not mean that he was forgiven by the justice system in this country. He had a sudden revelation that he should not be behaving as he had done, and he felt a pragmatic desire to pay off his debt to society by being incarcerated in this prison. He showed full and immediate remorse for his crime."

"And was he ever told the details of the drugs that he was given?" he asked the nurse.

"No, he was never told the ingredients of what he was given. Because of the laws in place at the time of the conviction he was told that the effects of the treatment are reversible and are not a guaranteed success; we have no way of actually removing his sex drive and his attraction to underage girls. There is a small chance that he must live with this temptation for the rest of his life." She gave Leo a quick, knowing glance. "By the way, they were cyproterone acetate tablets, and you were being given 300mg per day. We monitored your liver toxicity levels and we reduced the dosage to 100mg when we realised that you were vulnerable to liver damage."

Leo felt slightly numb. He had wondered for years about what it was that they were thrusting into him through a syringe every morning, but now that he knew there was something so indescribably dull about what she had said that he wished that he had never found out. The truth has no zest to it at all; it tasted like a mouthful of ash.

"What are the chances of Leo Faulkner reoffending upon release?"

The nurse told him that the chances were extremely small, that his willpower would be enough to counteract the heavily reduced levels of sexual urging in his system. Scripps' answer was much more direct and confident. "Zero," he said.

The conversation went on and on; it was not that the chairman was purposely trying to find a reason to keep Faulkner in jail, but he would interrogate the prison staff about every aspect of the prisoner's character and behaviour, and the staff would always reply with high praise for his transformation and the new and rehabilitated man that he was turning into. There had been a remarkable transformation from within which was very clear for all to see. When he had arrived in jail, he had been hated first by the prisoners and then by the staff, but a quarter of a century had come and gone since then and the staff had been entirely replaced; Peter Scripps was the only one who had been there since the beginning of Leo Faulkner's sentence, and he was about to retire having extended his working life specifically to see the end of Leo's sentence. There was a slick sense of seamlessness in the stories that each of the members of staff were telling and the way that it all intertwined together with no conducting or dictation. It was clearly not fabrication because of the way that it stood up under the intense interrogation that it was subjected to; Leo Faulkner was a changed man.

"Well, Inmate Faulkner," said the chairman, leaning back in his chair with an air of satisfaction, "by all accounts you have behaved impeccably in this prison facility, and have spent twenty five years clearing your debt to society for the murder that you committed. I have spoken to the psychotherapists working at HMP Belmarsh and they have said that they categorise you as a prisoner with an extremely low probability of reoffending. Prison life has not been easy for you because of the other prisoners but the people who have assessed your capability for release have been very impressed by the way that you have adapted to the regime of this institution."

"We have come to a decision, Mr Faulkner. You will be free to go, released on parole, having behaved so well for the duration of your sentence so far. Congratulations."

Leo reeled with shock. He knew that he had not broken any of the rules but he was taken aback by the prospect of being set free. In the seconds that followed he felt a rush of relief surge through his flesh, the alternating current massaging his body from his temples to his toes.

"Here are the conditions of your release, Mr Faulkner; you will be able to have a new identity because of the nature of the high profile case which put you behind bars all those years ago. We are going to permit you to change your name, and we will destroy your criminal record under the Spent Convictions Act because of the wave of public feeling against you when the trial was being completed. We will not be funding any cosmetic surgery that you choose to have done but if you do decide to have this course of treatment we believe that it will be very beneficial in terms of moving on with your life without the fear of abuse for your crime from members of the public. Your identity will be a state secret to enable you to have a chance to have a normal life when you are rehabilitated but there will be restrictions. The Prisons Service will have access to your new identity and if you attempt to gain employment working with children, however indirectly, you will be sentenced to five years in jail even if you do not commit any crimes against the children. Your presence in a school or any other institution for children will be considered a crime in itself. You will be forbidden from obtaining Criminal Records Bureau police clearances for working with vulnerable people, and if you do reoffend by sexually assaulting a child you will be given another life sentence from which you will never be freed and never considered for parole. You have one chance, Inmate. Do not let freedom pass you by."

Leo decided upon the name Richard MacGregor. Richard was his middle name, and MacGregor was the name of an old family friend who had died long ago with no known relatives. His favourite verse from the Bible, 2 Corinthians 5v17, was being personified in his own transformation: "Now we look inside, and what we see is that anyone united with the Messiah gets a fresh start, is created new. The old life is gone; a new life burgeons!"

The cosmetic surgeon had eyes that shone a great kindness. The room in which he did his work was just as sterile and clinical as the prison had been, but Richard felt a soothing calmness about it all. Something was deeply correct about the way that this had all worked out. David Shipman was a very attentive to his clients. The spotlights on the telescopic lamp which reached over the chair in the middle of the room, and there were rows of various metal instruments gleaming menacingly laid out with mathematical precision.

Richard and the doctor had a long discussion about what would be done to his face upon release. He would have his nose completely reconstructed to add a different shape to it, have his ears replaced with slightly smaller ones, and have surgery on his teeth to change the distinctive shapes of the front of his smile. He would have the colours of his eyes changed from brown to blue through the use of contact lenses and he would change the lengths of his vocal cords to alter the tone of his voice. The distinctive tattoos were to be removed with lasers, and he had a few moles which had distinctive shapes which would need to be removed. He had his tattoos peeled off slowly and painstakingly and replaced with patches of clean white skin; gone were the skull and crossbones on his forearm, the rose thorns on his ribcage and the Grim Reaper's scythe on his shoulder blade. The surgery was painful, and some of it was undertaken using a general anaesthetic, which included the opening up of his throat and the facelift which made incisions around his hairline. It was a long process, and even after the date of release had gone by Richard decided to stay behind bars at night because he wanted to leave Belmarsh only when all traces of Leo Faulkner had been utterly obliterated.

There was something undeniably beautiful about the way that the scalpel hovered above his sleeping skin in the seconds before it was put to work. This was far from a normal task assigned to Dr Shipman, and as he began he could not help saying a mental obituary to Leo the killer. There was a new person within, a reborn spirit beneath the same membrane, and he felt the same rush as he imagined a surgeon must feel when they perform a caesarean incision, that their steady hands and anatomical expertise would play a part in bringing abundant new life gushing through the opening. Richard's skin parted like the Red Sea beneath the smiling blade of the scalpel, and Shipman briefly became Moses, an architect of freedom leading a slave out of exile and back to the land that he had been promised by God an age before.

The vocal chords were an incredibly delicate piece of engineering that used all of his skill and talent. The steel instruments prickled through the pulsing flesh like a soldering iron, rewiring the current and fastening the loose cables back to the circuit board. His davits were moulded supplely; they glowed white hot beneath his steady fingers and a gentle flow of sparks ebbed faintly onto his gloves. The surgeon kept his visor down and the mask across his mouth. It had been revealed in the trial that Leo had abused and assaulted young girls before his conviction, even though he had never murdered anyone before Joy Hewitt, and during the attack one of the girls gave a very detailed description of his genitals which included telling the police about his foreskin. Whilst he was having the surgery for everything else he also decided to have a circumcision, to distance himself from the assaults that he had committed in the past and also to echo the religious symbolism of the operation, the new treaty which Abraham made with God and a physical token of the change which he had undertaken internally. This, declared his flesh, was a new man. Leo Faulkner and his monstrous past were gone forever.

The recovery period was about a week; he spent it behind bars, and he was not permitted to leave the cell for any reason, not even to use the bathrooms or eat, because it was extremely important that none of the other inmates had any contact with him at all. He rested his voice and did not speak, spending most days lying in bed so that he could rest his body and allow it to fully recover.

Finally, after so many years of waiting, the time came for him to leave. Once he could walk comfortably without pain or hesitation Peter came back to the maximum security cell for the final time, to help him "pack his bags". It was a tiny and simple room, a room he had lived in for almost half of his life, and a room in which his life had changed beyond recognition forever. It seemed odd and bittersweet; from the moment when he had heard that he would not be murdered by a vengeful state in retaliation for a crime he had committed against a seven year old girl he had longed to be free, longed to walk across the mighty partition which held him on the Captive Side and to resume his life where he had left off. He doubted that he could do it without the love and encouragement of Peter, but he was assured that he could. Peter had his own secrets to reveal, for he was dying of stomach cancer. He had been working as hard as he could to stay at Belmarsh to one day see Richard released, and now that he had waited so long the day came as Peter had only six months to live. Richard asked him why he was not scared of dying, and his response was something that he would never forget. Peter's wisdom astounded him. "My dear friend," he began, "I am not truly alive yet. Why should I be afraid of going home?"

Peter delivered a line which he had been expecting to deliver more than two decades beforehand. "Goodbye, Richard." The man who had changed him and saved him and the man who was himself dying gathered up his belongings and prepared to leave Belmarsh forever, the two of them side by side as they stepped into the sunshine together. The world was waiting.

10 AGORAPHOBIA

Freedom was a new and beautiful thing. It was as incomparable to life in Belmarsh as Heaven is to life on Earth; the sheer raw power of that most audacious and conspicuous of birthrights endowed to humanity, a vast and bottomless reserve of euphoria that Richard could draw from whenever he wished. There was no possible way that he could have prepared himself for the sensations that he would be exposed to upon his release, and he felt as he had when he had first found out about the glorious truth of his eternal destiny: both tremendously excited and blissfully unprepared for what he was about to encounter, for there is no means by which the captive mind can wrap itself around the pure and unadulterated concept of true freedom. Explaining freedom to him was like describing snow to a child who had grown up in the wilds of the Kalahari, exotic lands of spice and mystery which afforded them no possible means of experiencing first hand the wintry beauty that is infinitely different to how any description of it may be. Freedom was the song in Richard's weary throat after all these years of darkness and despair, and the texture of the skies creased and crumpled beneath his fingers.

Richard did not know where to begin with his new life, for the outside world was so overwhelming at first. He was more alone than he had ever been inside his cell in permanent isolation, with no trace of his old name, no contact with his family and no record of his former way of life. Keeping his cover secure was absolutely paramount to his survival and this was a truth that he knew he would never be allowed to forget.

He decided never to go back to Higher Pelham again. It would be too incorrect, too disrespectful, but most of all he feared the loss of control over his body. The rivers of passion that channelled their courses through his veins and ignited them like strings of fibre optic cable were sure to be stirred by the erotic memories of his moment of triumph a quarter of a century before. If he saw another girl of the same age he genuinely was not able to predict what his instinctive reaction would be. He had been in a jail cell for twenty five years and he had had contact with males only, and he wondered if such a long period of sexual abstinence would have buried the animalistic hunger deep within his psyche or whether he would instead be starving and wanting to gorge his fill with record speed and gluttonous aggression to make up for lost time. He did not want to feel that way again, he did not have any plans to reoffend but he was terrified that he would need far more than simple willpower alone to defeat the demon within him.

The whole world was spread out before him with a glorious and thrilling sense of endlessness. There seemed to be no limit, no boundary, no restriction to the freedom that he had encountered as soon as his release was finalised. Just as the soldiers of all three World Wars had given the strange and exotic foreign lands which formed the backdrop of battle familiar nicknames to relate to the motherland, so too did Richard rename the world in relation to what he had become accustomed to. Areas within Belmarsh had nicknames too amongst the prisoners; in the same way that the trenches of the Somme had been given street names to appeal to the instinctive memory, the row of cells in the jail where the prison uniforms were distributed was named Saville Row, the prison guards' offices were called Westminster and the exercise yard was named Elizabeth's, rather ambitiously after the Olympic Park in East London. He struggled not to reverse the tradition and compare the houses to cells, but with nothing to reference his new surroundings to it was a very difficult thing to behold and fathom the environment in which he now found himself.

For a while he stayed in London. It was dizzying and exhilarating, the hedonistic sense of freedom and opportunity clinging to his soul like ivy to the trunk of a tree. This city had been the scene of such intense hatred against him and an ultimately unsuccessful surge forwards into new and unguessable legal territory, the backdrop of protests and marches showing the public outrage at his crime and, ultimately, the city in which his life should have ended as soon as the House of Lords passed the Restoration Act which would have seen him executed in Belmarsh. He had no idea of his way around any more because the city had changed so much, but he managed to find his way to the base of the Leviathan Building, just a short walk from St Paul's, and took the lift to the top after buying a ticket for the Observation Deck on the 490th Floor. He gazed out across the Thames Estuary to the East with the aeroplanes lining up over the coastline, at altitudes lower than the roof of the building, as they came in to land at the new airport on Sheppey more than fifty miles away and he could clearly see the coastlines of Essex and Kent as he gazed through the suicide railing which had once flown a banner celebrating the preservation of his life by a merciful Parliament. He felt a deep sense of connection with the landscape far below him, the tiny streets as wide as a strand of human hair, the vehicles and pedestrians completely undetectable on a scene a mile below which appeared smaller than on a map of the City. He followed the South Coast with his eye, round Kent, and finally gazed out across the English Channel towards an invisible France. The air was wonderfully enriching and it had a distinctive smell to it, a smell only a truly free man can know. Looking around the crowded Observation Deck, he saw a father holding his son up to the railing so that he could see the spectacular view stretched out far below them, marvelling at the surreal experience of having parts of the view obscured by the topsides of clouds and helicopters. The man was holding his child in a demonstration of a powerful type of love, manhood as it should be, the wonderful and precious gift shared between a father and his son. The man's strong hands holding his boy's delicate small fingers and arms held with them a great beauty that Richard had never truly known.

Out of curiosity, and to complete his journey, he visited all the places which had been landmarks in his previous life and his eventual transferral to jail. He stood on the pavement across the road from the Old Bailey where hundreds of people had assembled to show him their outrage and abhorrence at his crime, jeering and screaming in protest as he arrived for his trial. He didn't go inside, but he could easily have done and maybe he should have. Perhaps he was afraid that he would not recognise the theatre of his greatest performance. He smiled to himself as he remembered Kate's incredible courage, facing him down and doing her part in his doom at the tender age of fourteen, and reflected thoughtfully on the place where he had scorned the family of his victim with such contempt.

He went to Trafalgar Square, too; he took the 453 to get there and it was still just as slow and horrifically overcrowded as he remembered it. A part of him expected the Freedom Side to have used the long years of his incarceration to carefully and systematically remove all of the problems of the world and it was with a slight disappointment that he saw that the state of the Earth was much the same as it always had been. Coming to terms with the intense proximity to anonymous Londoners after the sparse loneliness of his single cell, touching their bodies with his, he glanced at the *Standard* that he had picked up when he had got off the tube. He turned to the World News section and he saw the article on New Palestine's Presidential election, and Israeli terrorists setting off a car-bomb in the capital to coincide with the polls opening. Some things never change. He stepped off of the bus by Admiralty Arch and stared upwards at the towering height of Nelson's Column, guarded by his four lions, and tried to soak in the significance that this place had all those years ago. He saw the people walking calmly across the square, both businessmen in tailored suits and baffled tourists trying to unfold a crumpled map, and then closed his eyes and pictured two million people roaring with hatred, burning effigies of him, scaling the Column and transforming it into an enormous token of organised, state sponsored death. He pictured the banners and the megaphones and the photographs of Joy Hewitt, the roaring crowd baying for his blood, the foaming scarlet of the fountains, and the thirteen people who had died as a result of the public anger in attacks of mistaken identity. It was like trying to remember the faintest of dreams, for the faces were blank and all that remained in his memory was the sensations he felt at the time.

Looking over towards the closest of the two massive fountains, he saw a little girl leaning over the side to lay a hand on the surface of the water which had once gleamed a rich blood red. She was facing away from him and she was holding her bottom in the air as she knelt on the stone edge of the fountain. A flash of ankle. A glimpse of shoulder. Hair, fingers and shoes.

Skin.

Richard had all but lost his ability to judge people's ages having seen so few of them for such a long time but his instincts had always been stronger with children. He guessed that she was about three years old. There were very few children about; she was one of the youngest. What day was this? He was not used to it mattering, for he was such a high profile prisoner that his records were kept up to date so meticulously that he had no need for keeping count of the days that passed. Furthermore, he was on strict suicide watch and for a great deal of his time behind bars he did not have permission to use pens and sharp pencils which could have been misused as weaponry and as apparatus for use in self harm. He realised with a sudden shock that he did not have any idea what day it was and what that meant, whether schools were in session or whether the transport network was running a reduced service.

He looked down at the newspaper that he had picked up, and saw that there was a date printed on the front page. Tuesday 29th April. What would have come so naturally to a regular person had been to him a perplexing challenge to hunt down a reclusive source of information, and he was momentarily terrified by his lack of acclimatisation to the world around him. It was a weekday, and the businessmen in the Square were on their lunch-breaks. All of the children over the age of three were at school. The confusion over which day it was had distracted him from the fact that he was getting an erection after seeing the flesh of pink knickers, as though the three year old had carelessly etched her autograph across the jelly of his brain. His heart was pounding and he was breathing faster than he should have been. After all these years, Richard was still stirred physically when he was confronted by his mind transforming a group of children into a sexualised menagerie of passion. Their alteration inside his mind was completely involuntary and absolutely disgusting to him now that he had changed so much during his time in prison.

He turned away, tears prickling at the insides of his eyelids. He had not prepared himself at all for how difficult this would turn out to be. He had expected the feelings to simply evaporate the moment that he had decided that he no longer wanted to abuse children, and that when he wanted to shut it out of his head he would be able to simply move on and forget that any of the mess that had gone before had ever happened. He closed his eyes, looking up to Heaven and pleading with his Father and Saviour to remove the grotesque feelings that stained his flesh but he could not remove the indelible image flashing across the insides of his eyelids of him biting into the shoulder of the young girl as if she were an exotic fruit, the sweet juices trickling down to his chin.

The young family had a dog with them, a black Labrador, and he ran up and began sniffing around Richard's feet. The family called him back, but eventually they realised that they would have to come up to the dog and bring him away from Richard because he was not interested in retreating on his own. Richard was using the guard dogs of Belmarsh as a point of reference and he expected the Labrador to jump up and bite him, but that was not all that he was nervous about.

"Hello," said the mother of the family, "I'm very sorry about Chester. He's very friendly really, he won't hurt you." A small silence came between them, and the woman smiled awkwardly. "Holly," she called to her daughter, "come and say hello to Chester's new friend."

No, God, Jesus, please, please, no. Holly came bounding up to them, her golden hair shimmering in the sunshine, and held her mother's hand as she stroked the dog. "Hello," she said, but Richard could not bring himself to look at her; he was breathing through clenched teeth and his heart leapt inside of him. He tried closing his eyes as he heard her voice as she spoke to her mother, but her corpse was indelibly painted onto his eyelids. It disgusted him, and he begged Jesus to let him be free of it, but he was terrified to learn through experience that the current of arousal surging around his bloodstream like power around an electrical circuit was completely involuntary. He left Holly with a strained smile but he knew that he could not keep on running forever.

He went into a clothes shop on Oxford Street but he had to leave immediately as the children's-wear section was right by the main entrance and some of the mannequins were being dressed in the new summer ranges. Some of them were only partially clothed and some of them were not being used at all so they were left naked in the corner, which aroused Richard as he looked at the shining plastic skin. The insensitivity of the staff was barely believable.

Richard thought that coming out of jail would have been the beginning of a new life of anonymity, far removed from the old temptations that used to plague him; the shock of being released was a tragically difficult thing to become accustomed to. He had promised himself that, in line with his faith, he would not place himself in compromising situations which would lead to him being tempted and vulnerable to regressing back into the habits that he was determined to be rid of. Being in jail and given so long to do little other than think had made him extremely familiar with the man that he now was, with all of his glorious flaws and faults, and he knew what positions and situations he needed to avoid if his clean record was to be maintained. He did not care about the criminal courts or about his new blemishless record that he had been given under the new identity but instead the promises that he had made to God, that he would change his life to realign it with the purpose for which he had been so fearfully and wonderfully designed. It wasn't about legalism or obligation, far from it; he simply was making the change from living for himself and feasting on his sexual fill of children whenever he felt like it to living for Jesus and the behaviour that such a matchless relationship inspired in him. He was free of the premeditated wish to kill children and he thought that this alone would be enough to see him through but instead he was discovering that he needed far more than this to restrain the feverish desire that resided within his loins being stirred when confronted by a tempting situation that he could not avoid. Then of course there was the issue of other people being unaware of how he felt, because there can surely be nothing more unexplainable, nothing that inspires less sympathy, than a battle of his own meek willpower against the almighty and uncontrollable forces of sexual arousal by children. Had Holly's mother known the thoughts and feelings surging through Richard at the time she would never have let her come close and may even have gone as far as to light her torch and reach for her pitchfork in the very Square where millions campaigned for his death, but whilst paedophiles were demonised above all others there was not any form of counselling session where it was truly *safe* for open and honest feelings about this to be addressed. He found himself completely alone in that respect; alcoholics could find solace in an AA meeting, and the overweight could talk freely with a group of like minded individuals who would encourage one another, but the best place for people addicted to sex with children to congregate would be a jail, and in years gone by people had campaigned for much worse. Richard was absolutely alone in this struggle and there could be no other way. He doubted that someone would be insensitive enough to gorge on a huge chocolate cake in the presence of an anorexic, yet because his addiction was perhaps the ultimate taboo there was no possible way of avoiding the confrontation with an inappropriate situation that he knew he should not be in. How could he have possibly told her what was happening? With a heavy heart and a tortuously bleak outlook on the future of the Freedom Side, Richard realised that he was more of a prisoner now than he had ever been in his life.

In an attempt at disobedience of his fate he did all of the things that a free man should do in London. He climbed the Monument and got a certificate declaring his achievement. He lost himself in the wonder of the majestic masterpieces in the Tate Britain and came face to face with the Rosetta Stone at the British Museum. He laughed and cried at the beauty of the spoken word at the Globe. He walked from Roehampton to Richmond across the biggest and most beautiful park in the city and drank in the view of the skyline from the highest hill. He listened to the madmen rant their hearts out at Speakers' Corner, and stared in glorious and defiant triumph at the green in the middle of the Tower of London. He decided to take a look at Westminster as well, walking down Whitehall and crossing the road at the Cenotaph to have a look at Downing Street. Huntley and Whiting were long gone, but he had not read his *Standard* carefully enough to know the current residents. Pulling it out of his bag again he flicked through until he found a photograph of a white man named Oliver Cotton leaving Number Ten accompanied by a headline which criticized his policies on tax reform. Richard was struck by a wonderful thought; could he be eligible to vote at the next election? Might he for the first time in his life be permitted to take the great and enlightened burden of democracy upon his humble shoulders, shared with the rest of the society to which he suddenly belonged, a right that he had been denied as a berated criminal? The Freedom Side was infinitely more hostile, complex, wonderful, frustrating, beautiful, confusing, bewildering and uncomfortable than he could possibly have imagined and his withdrawal from it had amplified its every curse and virtue. He felt like a man who had just been cured of blindness being taken straight to a fireworks display as soon as his sight had been restored. The world was now indescribably more luminous in every way than he had ever experienced before his incarceration.

Going back to claim the flat that he had been bequeathed by his mother, he came across a group of schoolgirls as he rode the DLR. He knew that there was no way he could avoid confrontations with his demons every day, because it was extremely difficult to be free and to engage with members of the public in a normal way yet simultaneously avoid times when he would be tempted by the urges which had killed Joy. He sat there perfectly still as they chatted and laughed and shrieked behind him, the embodiment of youth and vitality and happiness, with Richard struggling to suppress his yearning hunger within him. He looked out of the window of the train as they passed Canary Wharf and a tear ran slowly down his cheek as his face was reflected in the raindrops on the outside of the glass. His eyes were filled with skyscrapers but his mind was filled with knickerless schoolgirls whilst his heart was filled with Jesus. It was a horrible collision which was extremely disturbing to him. He could receive no counselling or guidance on his release because it would surrender his identity and so he had to suffer in unendurable silence instead. He cast his mind back to the times when he had been in church and the clergy had offered prayer ministry to the congregation; how could anyone be deluded enough to think that he was included in that? They would tell him that "there is no problem which is too big for God to deal with" but it would be almost laughable if it wasn't so tragic; there was nobody who would be able to help him, and there are some things which must remain unsaid. He was tested and stretched more than he thought was possible, and he did not understand why his considerable willpower was not enough to see him through. Over the coming days he was tempted by all kinds of things; the penduluming of a recently vacated swing, school uniforms in the shops, the sound of children in passing cars as they drove by with the windows open. There was a particularly provocative billboard advertising children's television on his way home and he tried his best to bow his head and walk on by without letting the temptation take hold of him, but it was with a sense of heartbreaking dread that he noticed that his pulse was jumping inside of his chest. Once it crept in, it was impossible to remove it despite his feverish prayers. He was bound by his sexuality, enslaved to it, crushed beneath it. It felt as though he was having his head forcibly held underwater, his passionate yearning seeping into his every orifice and pore, screaming without anyone there to hear him, so preoccupied with halting the deluge that he was sickeningly disorientated. The whole thing, in a word, was tortuous. Why? Why did it have to grip him so tightly when his willpower was pulling so strenuously in the opposite direction? He thought of Romans Seven Fifteen, a verse that he had learnt from Peter: "I've spent a long time in sin's prison. What I don't understand about myself is that I decide one way, but then I act another, doing things I absolutely despise."

Richard tried to join a church so that he could continue to nurture his fledgling faith, but it was extremely difficult to find a church in London which taught the Bible faithfully and did not have a thriving children's ministry. With an agonising sense of irony he realised that his preconception of church when he had been jailed all those years ago as a cold and miserable place which the elderly and terminally ill used as a divine insurance policy, where ancient people found company in ancient buildings and where women in pearls with blue rinses had held a warm up party for their funerals had been woefully incorrect. London's churches were filled with abundant, wonderful life. All of them were filled with young people, families where the parents were in their late twenties, and the children whom he could not ignore. After sitting through an entire service gazing at a child who reminded him of Joy and realising that he had not taken in a word of the sermon, he knew that something had to change. He was so desperate to be taught from the Bible and to worship his maker in the church family which he so deserved but with a heavy heart he knew that he could not be in a community without facing the issues of lust which had to remain his secret until the day he died. He deeply missed that institution of jail, the rigid timescale and the definitive hierarchy, and being free was giving him withdrawal symptoms as though he was undergoing rehabilitation for drug addiction again. He looked at every bank and jewellery shop he passed with a sense of opportunity. Perhaps he could persuade the justice system to welcome him back home with open arms.

He realised that his plan to rehabilitate himself was unfeasible when the summer ended and Halloween came around. Even when he was finding it difficult out in public he knew that he could come home and escape his temptations, for the secret was in removing himself from the situations which he found arousing, but on this evening they came to him. He was locked up in his little flat, hiding himself away and he would hear the doorbell ring. He would sit in his chair watching the television, shivering with sexual frustration and trying not to peel off their multicoloured costumes in his mind. They kept returning, kept coming up the staircase and ringing the doorbell so that they could ask him for sweets and money. It felt to him as though each and every one of them was little Joy, coming back from the dead to ask him to groom her. Tears ran down his cheeks with a feverish and heartbreaking agony; he so desperately wanted to honour God and to do the right thing, but that beast lurking within the very depths of his body, that orgasmic and urgent need for what was forbidden, could not be quenched as easily as he had anticipated. His mind wanted to do what was right, but his body quite undeniably wanted to do what was evil.

One day after visiting the city again he had come into uncomfortably close proximity to a girl and her father as they watched a performer in Covent Garden, and so he had preserved his integrity and taken the decision to come home early. As he got off the train, there were a group of youths with baseball bats waiting behind a brick wall. He lowered his head. They began to stop talking and start walking.

Richard picked up his speed. They matched every step he took. Eventually he began to jog and then it accelerated to a sprint, but the boys began to chase after him and soon they were gaining on him. They were shouting things at him as they ran, but he did not bother to stop and listen to what they had to say to him. One word that he could not escape, however, drew shocked attention from the few people who were witnessing the exchange. They yelled it at the top of their lungs and it was unignorable, even though he tried his best to shut it out as he began to run away from them. Paedophile. You disgusting bastard, you like to shag little girls, don't you? With every word they shouted he tried to increase his pace.

Richard was old. His lungs were seizing up in painful contractions and he felt as though his bronchioles were about to ignite. With his breaths becoming more shallow and drawn out he finally tripped on the kerbstone, his exhausted body slamming against the road and his vision blurring as it was filled with nothing but phosphorescent sky. He wheezed sharply, rolling over against the burning pain in his muscles and tasting the dribbles of blood that congealed between his teeth.

As his vision gradually steadied, he saw the group of figures approaching him with their feet pounding against the vertical pavement so that each footstep echoed through his broken flesh. How could this be? How could they have found out that it was him? They towered above him with a terrifying brutality, and the stark nakedness of their physical power over him rendered him in a breathless state of thrilling awe. As the first of the baseball bats crashed against his skull, Richard was suddenly reminded of Joy once again, and her little eyes transfixed on him as she surrendered to his terrifying superiority. One of the bats caught him square in the jaw and he felt his teeth dislodging and breaking away from the bone beneath; now, in a painful episode of irony a quarter of a century later, Richard was the one who was submitting to his superiors who held him at their mercy. As the blood flowed it gave him a calming sense of connection with her, of sympathy for her, of empathy with her agony that she had suffered beneath his body. One of the bats slammed into his collarbone and he thought of his own execution, the death that the whole nation never quite managed to make come about, and how unfitting that would have been. The blows made him sorry whereas the injection would have made him a proud and defiant martyr. For all the talk of punishments being made to fit the crime, nothing seemed to fit better than this, experiencing the unique cocktail of extreme sensations that Joy had been exposed to all those years ago. Contrary to what that lunatic Whiting had proposed in the Commons on that forgotten day, there is more than simply a choice between jail and death. There is no justice without remorse, and there is no remorse without empathy for the victim. The nation had been waiting for justice for Joy Hewitt for over two decades and now finally it came at the hands of a group of thugs with baseball bats.

Feeling the aroused superiority of a group of youths unleashing a torrent of torture against his battered body was oddly calming. It was with a sense of peace that he surrendered. A quarter of a century of shame was being poured out on him at the beginning of his new life, and it seemed that he had never been as alive as he was when he was having the life pummelled out of his broken body and watching it ebb into the grit which was pressed against his cheek.

Eventually someone witnessed the attack and the thugs ran away. It was many precious minutes before an ambulance arrived to rescue the stricken and broken body in the middle of the road. Richard fell out of consciousness and he did not feel himself being lifted onto a stretcher and loaded into the back of an ambulance. He did not hear the screaming siren as he was rushed to hospital and he did not see the lights on the ceiling flash past his face in one long and continuous stream, like the beads in a rosary.

Strapped to that hospital bed, with all of his wires and tubes penetrating his skin as he drifted in and out of consciousness, Richard learned that timeless lesson, the unendurably agonising reality that he had unwittingly taught the Hewitt family all those years ago: freedom, with all of its boasts and audacious claims of glorious enlightenment, falls short of the heights for which it dares to soar. That most wonderfully ambitious of humanity's attempts at idealism, the instinctive hunger within everyone for emancipation and liberty, that loftiest of ideas in literature and politics, the opium of the masses for which incarcerated men become so excited that they can barely sit still or hold a thought in their heads, all of its virtuous goodness and moral might ends here, in a hospital bed, where a free man blew his cover so that other free men could do with him as they pleased. Before him now was not a shimmering meadow of luscious and abundant life but instead a desolate valley of aridity and disenchantment. Had he known what the Freedom Side would have been like and how it would have treated him he probably would have summoned the rebellious strength within him to attack a guard and lose his appeal for parole. Freedom's withered corpse did not seem worth the effort. The last thought to cross his mind was that freedom was like Jesus; it had been executed in his place, it had to be surrendered in order to secure his release and it had to die to preserve his life.

Richard's eyes closed. Some birds were meant for cages. Freedom is not free.

11 REDEEMING LOVE

With both Geoff and Leo gone forever, the Hewitt family endured the storms and trials and moved onwards in the pursuit of the better life that had brought them to Higher Pelham in the first place but which they had been unable to make more than an elusive and cruelly intangible fantasy. Twenty five long years came and went before eventually news reached the Hewitt family of the fate that had befallen their old nemesis, the child killer Leo Faulkner. Alice read with raised eyebrows of his conversion to Christianity and his impeccable behaviour behind bars and of the parole board's unanimous decision to ensure that the sentence was carried out to the minimum of their requirements. It was with an intense shock and fury that she read in the *Envoy* of a story of a plastic surgeon, who no doubt had been given an enormous sum of payment by the newspaper, breaking the news to the British press that he had been asked by the Prisons Service to change the appearance of the paedophile in accordance with the new identity that he had been given to protect his human rights upon leaving jail, through a series of gruesome and very painful operations on his face. The surgeon seemed to be of quite a stupid nature by the way that he articulated himself in the article that was printed, claiming that he had massive moral discrepancies with what he was being asked to do but he did his job in an attempt to get rich by releasing the information for extortionate fees. As she read it Alice was puzzled and she couldn't see how it was logical that a doctor would deliberately go against all of his principles just to make some money from the tabloids. Surely he would have refused? Something within her led to the conclusion that some secrets had not been revealed. Was the doctor tortured or blackmailed by the mob or the press? Did he have a secret of his own to conceal? As Alice's mind raced she thought that perhaps the only reason for a doctor to abandon his principles quite so spectacularly would be because he wanted to shame someone else for suffering with the same condition of sexuality as him. She considered that he wanted to deflect the accusation onto the only child abuser he knew, but then she scolded herself for her loose grip on sense and logic. The *Envoy* had printed the new name of the criminal as one Richard MacGregor, who was living in East London and an address was printed in the national publication to name and shame him. Alice was shocked at the thought that he could be walking the streets with a new name and a new appearance, until the next day when it was reported that several men by the name of Richard MacGregor were alleged to have been attacked and had their homes and cars vandalised. A mild frenzy swept the nation and the MP for Dumfries and Galloway, Richard MacGregor, even had to issue press conferences denying any connection and drafted in extra protection from the local police force. Kate took a deliberate disinterest in the stories of Leo's misfortune as it brought back bad memories for her and she distanced herself from it all as much as was possible in the midst of a media storm by the far right tabloid press. All in all thirteen innocent people, Joy not among them, had been killed during the campaign to execute Leo Faulkner, beginning with the woman trampled to death outside Westminster Abbey and ending with a paediatrician and his family who were being chased down a motorway in a case of mistaken identity which had led to a high speed car crash in which the five of them were killed. They were known as 'Leo's Thirteen' and did not include his direct victims or his long suffering mother who had died of a broken heart. Finally, the mob got their man, and the victim confirmed to be the person formerly known as Leo Faulkner was battered by a group of youths wielding blunt weapons in a street in East London. He was taken to hospital with severe head injuries and multiple broken bones and was not expected to survive the night. It was many things, but the least of them was justice. Joy's murder was not avenged by boys shouting insults and spontaneously attacking a man who had spent a quarter of a century attempting to atone. Even with this disturbing development, the family could not move on, and they were a very different family at the end of Faulkner's sentence in jail than they had been on that warm September afternoon.

Alice had taken some temporary jobs doing reception work in doctors' surgeries and schools, then moved on to do care work for elderly people in care homes. She had divorced Geoff through several conversations with lawyers and the police, and because he had been convicted of Grievous Bodily Harm he had been issued with a restraining order and was never allowed to see her again. The divorce was finalised through all their representatives, and it was a great burden lifted from her shoulders that she never had to lay eyes on him throughout the whole process. He served time behind bars for the assaults that he had subjected her to and she had considered visiting him in prison when he was serving his four months, the same as she had done with Leo, but she did not have the same conviction to find answers as she had done with the killer. His sentence was reduced from a year on appeal because of the completely unique domestic circumstances that surrounded the break-up of the marriage, but the mitigating circumstances did not improve his relationship with the children. Alice received a financial settlement, and the family moved out of the village so that she could sell the house and the money could be split between them. She did not find it difficult to convince the courts that her children should not be given to an abusive father and she was awarded full custody, and the children would visit Geoff at Christmas and his birthday if they chose to.

Whilst Geoff had been in prison Milly had lived with Alice, Kate and Jonathan, and when he was released Alice offered her to Geoff as an olive branch to show him that there were no hard feelings and as a slight act of compensation after she was awarded the custody of the children. It was also a cunning way of appeasing the increasing tension with Jonathan, who claimed to have no interest in seeing his father again and his mother did not want to appear to be keeping him and Geoff apart in order to break the conditions of the custody; when Milly moved in with his father, suddenly he could find it in himself to visit regularly. The beautiful big dog, no doubt, greatly helped Geoff to deal with his loneliness and she became his new companion, the one to share the rest of his life with. He never remarried and spent his days trying to rebuild his career from a small flat in NW20, and Milly lived to the age of twelve before dying peacefully in her sleep as Geoff gave her a long warm cuddle in front of the television on a winter's night. She was the only member of the family who carried on after Joy's death in the same way as she had before, the embodiment of innocence and blissful naivety. She had a long and happy life and was much loved, and had spent the years that she had loved in return easing a great deal of suffering endured by her family.

A few months after the murder, Tom Ferguson had nervously asked Kate to be his girlfriend. She was a traditionalist and would not jump the gun and do the deed herself; if it didn't come from him then it wouldn't be fitting or correct enough to build her fairytale on. She also knew that he would relish the chance to prove his bravery by pursuing her in the right way, the way that she felt she deserved, to be prized as a treasure and pursued by her man in a noble and romantic fantasy which she was proud to still have faith in. Kate and Tom were sweethearts all the way through their teens and both went to study at Edinburgh when they were eighteen. In their second year they shared a house together with some of their friends, much to the disapproval of Alice who thought that danger of a break-up under the same roof with contracts to honour would be unnecessarily painful, but the strength of their relationship proved everyone wrong. Kate was a determined and capable young woman now, ferociously ambitious and a naturally gifted leader, and she relished every opportunity she was given to prove the virtuous content of her character. She let the doomsayers speak as loudly as they wanted to; silently and steadfastly, they knew the truth. Because of warring parents, moving away from the village, custody battles and testimonies in court they knew that their relationship had survived too much to be split by arguments over the electricity bill. Both of them loved Edinburgh; they loved University life, the social scene, the academic challenge, the delicious freedom that came with pure and limitless independence and, of course, the breathtaking grandeur of the city itself. It was the place that they had come to know and love as home, a spectacularly perennial backdrop to their defining years as young and impulsive spirits. In the ancient landscape they found echoes of themselves, their spirits reflected in the hills and stone and trees and lights.

Edinburgh, how do I love thee? Let me count the ways . . . I love thee to the very depth and breadth and height my soul can reach. The experience of University was indescribably fantastic. Up all night. Making preparations to travel the world. Dreaming big dreams of who they were and who they wanted to become. They had the power to choose for possibly the final time in their lives, for the future belonged to them and only them. Barbecues on the lawn, and sharing a home with one hundred and thirty nine other people whilst in Halls. Scotland's ancient capital beneath their fingertips. Not paying full price for anything. Outrageous and outlandish ideas for fancy dress. Boiling the kettle for the late night rush to complete essays as all of the housemates sat on the sofa in their sleeping bags madly trying to reach the word limit before morning. Hedonistic nights of dancing until sunrise. Stumbling into a stranger in the bar and that moment of glory when, like Benedick and Beatrice, you both realise that you are soul-mates. University was a magnificent experience, the golden days of Tom and Kate's lives, and it enriched and enhanced their characters more than they would ever realise. They were made in Edinburgh, the fabric of their character was painstakingly stitched together by every experience and memory of being a student. It was glorious.

After three incredibly happy years at Edinburgh University Tom fulfilled his obligation as a gentleman and proposed to the love of his life. After the graduation and with a wonderfully empty and opportunistic future ahead of them they decided to build a life and family together. Alice, who throughout the whole thing had been convinced that disaster was just around the corner, found it hard to believe that it had all worked out so perfectly for her daughter and Kate had taught her a great deal about the value of optimism and trust and love and hope after an unspeakable tragedy. She only realised when she caught herself scolding Kate for being so loving and trusting of Tom when she believed that he was using her and not as sincere as he promised that in fact Geoff had stolen from her an ability to see a relationship with a man as a good thing. From that moment she was determined to put that right and to overcome her insecurities, whereas Kate was still strongly denying that the experiences had stained her. The moment when Alice really was able to bury her husband's ghost and put the abuse and heartbreak behind her was when Tom came to visit her and take her out for dinner in order for him to ask for Catherine's hand in marriage. In that moment Kate and Alice swapped roles; Kate was a sceptic and inherently suspicious of people in her nature, seeing the worst in them and assuming that they were setting out to prolong the agony of the family. Alice regained her trust in men, believing once more that the romantic dream is alive and well and that the world is filled with goodness whilst only being sprinkled with pinpricks of darkness. Tom taught Alice a great lesson in that abuse is only really over when the victim is able to completely forget all about their abuser, not when the bruises fade and the perpetrator is led away in a police van. Geoff had been tormenting her for years and years, but now that Tom and Kate were engaged suddenly Geoff's taunts had fallen completely silent.

Kate was far too strong to admit it, but she was in desperate need a rescuer. She had wanted a little sister ever since she realised that she was an oldest child. The disappointment that she had expressed when Jonathan was born and she slowly realised that he may not wish to have dressing up competitions with her nor did he share her dreams of being an equestrian gold medallist was a laughing point for her parents for years to come. Her joy at Joy's birth and the way that she was the perfectly nurturing and encouraging big sister had made the edge of the tragedy even more sharp when it had been her who was the only one with her when Leo struck. She had been consumed with guilt and regret and her mother was sure that her bullish nature and attitude was down to the fact that as she could not control the circumstances of her sister's demise she needed to compensate by controlling as much of the rest of her life as was possible. Kate herself would have said that because her parents had done such a terrible job of coping with the crisis that somebody needed to take charge but the role was sadly unfulfilled by anyone else.

Three years after the wedding, Kate fell pregnant. Nine painful and illness-ridden months later, she was overjoyed to give birth to a baby girl. She was just as beautiful as Joy had been, a smiling butterball babe sculpted and crafted from pure love itself. When deciding on a name, Tom and Kate decided on the only word that had kept them together, the only word that had enabled Alice to endure for as long as she had and the only thing that had enabled them to survive in the face of such destruction. They decided to call their daughter Hope. Three years later she was followed by a son, William. The family and Alice all moved into a four bedroom semi detached house just outside of Reading, in a quiet little cul-de-sac called Salem Crescent. It wasn't Magnolia Cottage, but it would do. The dream could resume now.

Jonathan had been deeply affected by the murder of his sister and had found his teenage years very stressful and difficult. He was very good at suppressing the feelings initially and because his family was imploding they found it difficult to notice him amongst the emotional wreckage. He had been feeling fine and had done well in his GCSEs, but when it came to staying at school after 16 to prepare for University he had struggled immensely to make any sense of his life having lost his sister and all but lost his father. His AS levels were a disaster and he suffered from a deep depression and had considered suicide and self harm many times, but somehow the memory of what had happened to Joy became both the reason for and the solution to his anguished problems; how could he reasonably choose to damage himself in this way when the Hewitt family had already been so utterly broken by death and destruction in years gone by? He received counselling and cognitive behavioural therapy and managed to recover his academic grades sufficiently to get a place at University in Leeds, and it was there that he had come into his own, had rediscovered his passion for life and had experienced a golden age of glory days. He was now thirty five, had a good job in the technology business, and was doing well enough to make Alice immensely proud. He was single and lived alone, and had been remarkably unlucky when it came to romance, often being slow to gather the courage needed to pursue women righteously and had a tragic habit of realising that he was deeply in love only when the opportunity had already passed him by. He was not unhappy, but he was waiting patiently and counting the years as they slipped erroneously past, wondering if and when his turn would ever come along. All of them knew that they deserved a period of happiness after the events of that fateful year, but arguably none more so than the battered and bereaved Alice Hewitt.

One of the temporary jobs that she kept up to make the ends meet was in Reading and she was introduced to a man named Paul. He was slightly younger than she was, with dashing good looks and a charming manner about him which lit up the room every time he walked in. Paul Retter was tall with dark hair and he bore a passing resemblance to Geoff, but Paul seemed to have more charisma and less of Geoff's towering physical masculinity. Everyone loved his company, he was a loyal and good friend and he was, in every sense, a gentleman. He was a committed Christian; Alice would call it religious, but he assured her that it was merely a love affair like any other. He had something which she had always been attracted to, something that had always enchanted her, which was a razor sharp wit. She adored his sense of fun and his undeniable charisma and energy, and even the bleakest of situations could be overcome in an instant with his energetic and wonderfully rich way of expressing himself which put everyone in his company at ease. Whenever the two of them were together it was inevitable that before long Alice would end up shrieking and cackling towards the ceiling as she was bent double, tears streaming down her cheeks, her body channelling a torrent of pure joy.

Of course, it was their friends that noticed it before either of them actually did themselves. Whenever they would all gather in a group of work colleagues in the pub between shifts, whenever there was a birthday amongst their number and they would go out for dinner together, everyone was always quietly enchanted by the chemistry which was blossoming between Alice and Paul. All of his friends were relatively new and they did not really know much about where he had come from, but he was well liked and Alice's remarkable and admirable endurance of tragedy had made them the most popular of couples even before they realised that they were falling in love.

The reality of it was that she just treasured being in his company, and that she was infatuated by every move that he made. He had feelings for her; it was the start of something beautiful and they both knew it. She found herself unable to eat or sleep because her every thought concerned him and her mind could not wander far before she was led back, like Theseus through the Labyrinth, to be reunited with him once again.

After meeting a few times in a group, Paul asked Alice if she would accompany him to dinner. She agreed to it, although she still harboured a deep fear of people knowing that the two of them were an item because Geoff had drained all of her confidence out of her and these were unchartered waters for her. She hadn't dated since her teens and she was now approaching her sixtieth birthday, and there was a tremendous thrill in the prospect of romance. As she met him at the restaurant the adrenaline was pumping.

As she picked up the wine list, Paul noticed that Alice wore a diamond ring on the middle finger of her right hand. Perhaps she had misunderstood his initial proposal.

"You're married?"

She smiled at him blankly. "No, it's an engagement ring. I am divorced. I kept it because it is beautiful and expensive, and it reminds me of happy days."

"Oh," he said, "I'm sorry to hear that. How long has it been?"

"We separated twenty five years ago. We were married for sixteen years. At the time it was almost half of my life."

"Do you have children, Alice? Are you a mother?"

Alice beamed proudly as she corrected him. "I am a grandmother of two! But yes, I have three beautiful children. Kate, Jonathan, and . . . well Joy died when she was seven."

His eyes were huge with wonder and surprise. Confusion gave way to realisation. He cast his mind back over the decades, to the time when the Hewitt family was the most famous family in the nation, and he remembered reading in the papers the shocking story of suffering which had plagued the village and from which none of them had ever recovered. He saw the chanting crowds in Trafalgar Square and the pendulum of British justice swinging from life to death and back again. He remembered the newsreaders standing in fields and meadows below the village and the helicopter shots of the forensics tents in the churchyard. He remembered the agony of seeing the tiny coffin being carried into the church by just two pallbearers and the weeping sorrow of a young mother. Suddenly it was so obvious; suddenly he knew who he was talking to.

"Alice I am so sorry . . ."

She put a hand up to stop him. "No, Paul, I don't need your sympathy. I'm a strong woman and I have learnt to make my way through life without any help or any charity. I am a survivor and I'm fine."

He gazed down at her ring again. "May I ask what happened to your husband?" There was a silence. "You are allowed to say no if you like."

Infamy had been a funny thing for Alice Hewitt. As soon as the MLC campaign and the Restoration Bill had been abandoned the glare of the media had eased up over the family and their tiny village, and after the funeral they had been left in relative peace. The whole country mourned the death of her daughter, but there was nobody left when the time came to mourn the termination of her family. Nobody cared when Geoff began to lose his mind to the demon of alcohol, or when he became aggressive and began to hit her. Nobody cared when his business collapsed, or when they sold the home to ensure that the assets were divided equally. Matthew Brady and his publication who had promised to be with them "every step of the way" had left as soon as they knew that the push for the death penalty would fail and had nothing to say when Alice and Geoff were arguing over who could see their two remaining children at what times and on what days. For Paul, the whole story had begun at the murder and had ended at the funeral, but for the Hewitt family there was indescribably more to it than that. What the media had forgotten in a month they had to bear forever. It was only now, meeting her and hearing about her life in all of its wretched misery, that he understood the full magnitude of how a murder rips the heart and soul out of a family. He asked her to describe Geoff. Given how much she had loved him, how they had married when she was nineteen and how she had given birth to his daughter aged just twenty one, and then how spectacularly their relationship had imploded, it was not an easy thing to do.

"I heard rumours. You know, stories. Whispers, perhaps. He's a bad man and he did some bad things. He didn't treat us very well, and he decided to abandon us when it all got too much after Joy died. At first I thought he was the perfect father to the three of them but I guess you don't know people you've never been through trauma with. He surprised me a lot. He taught me a great deal and I will always cherish the time we were given together."

"Was it the right thing to divorce?"

"Yes."

Paul smiled at her. It was a knowing smile, an assured one, not mocking but rather questioning of the gravity of what she had told him. Above all things the smile was filled with love and his eyes shone with adoration as he looked at her. Paul thought Alice was wonderful. He looked like he was considering something before finally he came to a resolution.

"No. You won't convince me with that one."

He let out a cheeky little giggle. Although the words he was using were incredibly harsh his tone was light and playful, and she knew that he was using the words he was not speaking to reach out to her.

"It's not the most outrageous of stories that you could have told me. I think it deserves about a seven out of ten."

Alice looked at him in the eye and with an incredible surge of strength she made a joke for the first time in twenty six years. This was the jewel in Paul's crown of charm and charisma; he had gently encouraged her to lower her guard and remember the vitally important lesson of learning to laugh in all circumstances. Rather than scorning Joy's memory, Alice knew that she was enhancing it and simultaneously moving forwards into a bright and wonderful future.

"Seven!"

She feigned outrage, but she wasn't fooling anyone. Come and play, said his eyes. He knew that she was burning on the inside, but he implored her with his bottomless sense of humour. He had taught her the most valuable of lessons; a brighter day is coming, and so today's struggles will become tomorrow's faint memories. They were playacting, and she took on a role of irate defiance.

"It's an amazing story. You can't get better. I deserve to be recognised as the best storyteller of all time."

Paul attempted to summon the most ludicrous comeback that he could think of, something that would make the story really explosive.

"But I mean, he never abused you did he?"

Alice had no idea of how to react and she said nothing to him. She suddenly realised that because she did not want to outwardly verbalise how it felt to be beaten by her husband, Paul did not know anything about the situation. Her thoughts had become blended with her words and she had assumed that he had been able to deduce what had happened; from his naive jesting it was now obvious that he had not. A thick curtain of silence came down between them and the moment seemed to drag on for a very long time before either of them spoke. Her eyes were huge and frightened and the eye contact dropped between the two of them the second that he finished asking his half-sarcastic question. She wanted to say yes, to tell him everything that had happened to her idyllic marriage and her beautiful daughter and the way that Joy seemed to have accidentally destroyed Geoff in a clumsy act of desperate bad luck. She wanted him to know the very depth of her anguish and torment and the gut wrenching pain of the fact that she had eventually come to realise that the death of her daughter was by no means the end of the ordeal and the final moment of her immeasurable suffering. Paul should have felt the enormous height of the chasm that Alice was trying to climb out of, an almost hopeless reconstruction project of everything that she had lost in the chaos that consumed their lives over the past twenty six years. With no words she communicated to him every bruise which had long since faded and healed, scars and abrasions which stung like acid years and years after they had been rendered invisible by the passing of time.

"Oh Alice."

Paul pulled her in tightly towards his chest, cradling her head in his arms. She thought that he expected her to burst into tears as the memories came flooding back and swelled up within her soul, but the fact that she did not break down and weep into him did not mean that the recollections were slow to reach her.

In truth she did not really have any reaction in her mind that held any correctness or that seemed an adequate and appropriate response, and she was too emotionally exhausted to cry. Her well of tears was dry. He felt unimaginably awful and foolish; he had this tendency to attempt to impress people by the cleverness of his jokes and the unflinching search for humour in the face of the chaos of life but sometimes he knew that he did not have quite the limit that he should have done. Alice did not mind, even though she probably should have done. It would be far worse if everyone treated her completely differently by what she had been through, and she saw herself as a product of her past, every virtue in her character hard earned and slowly won. She could never bring herself to say that she was proud of or thankful for what had happened, but she knew that Leo and Geoff had made her into the woman that she was. They had bettered her, enhanced her, strengthened her and ultimately redeemed her. She owed them nothing but the changes for the better were ultimately down to them.

After a few dates, Alice invited Paul to come and visit the home in Salem Crescent which she shared with the Fergusons. It was a house that was clearly the beloved home of children; the bookshelves were filled with wondrous tales of faraway lands and fantastical adventures with triumphant heroes fighting dastardly villains. In the stories, good always won. The walls were decorated with imaginative drawings and paintings of animals and scenes of beauty, the dazzling colours swirling across the page like the splendour of a kaleidoscopic rainbow, and there were posters which explained the solar system, how the Romans lived, the alphabet and the countries of the world. Paul inspected this one closely; it was out of date because Minolia, the newest country on Earth, was not listed. The fridge was covered with magnetic letters and they were arranged into different words and basic sentences. There were magnets from Disneyland and on the windowsill Kate was clearly halfway through an experiment to show them how plants absorb moisture through their roots, because there were a series of flowers in glass pots filled with different coloured dyes in the water. There was yellow, and blue, and green, but not red. Never red. Red was forbidden.

They heard the door open, and knew that it was Kate and the children, coming home from school. Hope and William ran up the stairs ahead of their mother, dumping their coats on the end of the banister as they did so.

Kate came into the kitchen and Alice and Paul were there, ready to meet her. She took off her coat and laid it over the back of a chair, with her Mum giving her a kiss to welcome her home. After explaining that she had received a call from Tom to say that he had to work late and had changed his plans, she widened her eyes to wait for her mother to introduce her to the dashing stranger who was leaning against her sink. When Alice did her duty Kate took a great stride forwards to shake his hand, and as she did so she looked upwards and her eyes fell fully and firmly into the middle of his face. He spoke with a musical tone.

"I am Paul Retter. Your mother has told me all about you." He gave her hand a squeeze as shook it and his mouth settled into a satisfied grin. "It really is wonderful to meet you, Catherine."

For a split second Kate's head was filled with memories. His face was such that even though she was quite certain that she had never met him before, at the same time every pore and wrinkle and freckle and feature and landmark of that face which had been lived in so fully was incredibly and uncomfortably familiar to her. It was an intense and powerful sense of deja vu. Hope came up behind her and nervously hid herself behind her mother's hips, taking a good look at the handsome stranger and waiting for her mother's reassurance that everything was fine.

Kate, of course, was in every way the epitome of a professional working mother and had bloomed and blossomed into a strong and beautiful woman in the prime of her life and in total control of her destiny. She shook his hand, and as she did so she became suddenly aware that she was wearing a wedding ring. As she could feel the hands of Hope around her waist she felt a powerful tremble run up and down the length of Paul's arm and she could hear the speed of his breathing increasing sharply.

"Paul it's a pleasure. Mum talks about you all the time as well. I hope that you make one another very happy."

She was slightly hesitant to mention the trembling. "Are you alright?"

He laughed dismissively. "Yes I'm fine, thank you. I am just feeling the pressure slightly, that's all." His eyes narrowed and they were filled with sympathy and love. "I would hate for you to see me as an unflattering replacement for your father. I want this to work, and I want us to all be happy, most of all your wonderful mother.

Plus," He said, taking Hope by the hand and crouching down to make direct eye contact with her, "I wasn't expecting to be in the company of such a beautiful young lady." She blushed shyly, and he smiled kindly back at her, placing his hand on the side of her head with his fingers behind her ear and stroking her cheek with his thumb. "What is your name?"

"Hope," She responded.

"What a beautiful name! Why did your family decide to call you Hope?"

"Mummy says that it's because I am the little girl that my family has waited for for a very long time. They always had hope that one day I would arrive. I like my name. It is pretty and it makes me feel important."

Paul stood up again and looked at Kate, smiling in approval. "You chose very well, it's a beautiful name." He looked down at her again. "I am Paul. And you certainly are very important indeed."

He studied her face as fully as he could. It was astoundingly beautiful. She was dark haired, like her mother and father and unlike Alice and Jonathan, and her eyes were deep and rich and brown. Her skin was perfectly smooth and white. She had a small part of the stitching on the Velcro on her left shoe missing. Paul had waited years and years to become a father and it had never come to anything, but now he had a girlfriend with a granddaughter. Hope was so astoundingly beautiful that he suddenly had a desperation welling up inside him to be with Alice for the rest of his life just so that he would be able to see her again and again. He took her by the hand and he gave her a beaming, wondrous smile, his eyes filled with an electricity that he did not recognise in himself. She smiled back. Paul melted.

One night in the week Paul took Alice on another date. He had a place in London and he asked her to spend the night with him, and she accepted. They had a few drinks in the candlelight in the cavernous basement of Gordon's Wine Bar on Villiers Street one evening after seeing a show at the Adelphi, and Paul told her that it was one of his secret haunts that was almost unknown to people who had never visited before. Rumoured to be the oldest bar in London, Gordon's was a gothic riot of bare brickwork, rickety tables, steep staircases and an atmosphere that the owners had refused to change for more than two hundred years. The walls echoed with ancient conversation and the tables had the same delicate fragrance as the wine list. Alice was very impressed with his romantic showmanship but she was visibly nervous as they descended the staircase and found somewhere to sit and eat.

"Is something troubling you, my darling?" he asked tenderly.

She told him that her former husband had been an alcoholic and that she knew he had frequented bars and pubs such as this during his illness, which made it difficult to face because each glass of wine was filled with sour memories. But Paul was wonderfully reassuring, taking her by the hand and leading her assuredly down the staircase and into the future.

His love for her was deep, and she was happy to accept it and offer him the same love in return. Were they both delirious? It was a magical and beautiful time for Alice Hewitt, rescued at last; it would have come as no surprise to her if he had decided to whisk her away on his Pegasus horse, Alice burying her face in his cloak upon takeoff and the wind of the night sky whipping through her hair. She would look down and see the lights of distant towns embroidered against the darkness of the night, scattered like crystalline gems as though Aladdin's bag of treasures had a tiny hole in the bottom. Finally the dawn would break around them like a cool dream and Alice would look out ahead of her into a vast and evanescent expanse of sky to see his castle rising above a cloud, its misty turrets constructed of pink foam and guarded by soldiers made of sugar. Banners streamed proudly from the battlements and turrets, great flapping flags embellished with water, fire and sky. The highest tower was where they would retire; the bed would be a perfect circle of white sheets and lilies overflowing from the vases on the dressing table. Out of the arched window she would gaze over the smooth veneer of the sea towards the horizon to watch the sunset, peer down at the rock pools along the coastline and listen to the song of the mermaids as they brushed their hair and polished their technicolour scales and fins.

There would be no lovemaking. Alice's fantasy crumbled like the foam castle would in the rain. He made it clear to her that he would wait and that her body was worth a wedding ring, whether that be from him or from someone else. He had never married and he had never bedded a woman, because he explained that he needed something to offer his wife that he had never offered anyone else before her. If Alice was to be that bride, she would be his number one rather than linger outside of his top ten. The waiting would heighten the sensation of the moment when it finally came, the reward for a lifetime of battling for sexual self control.

Alice waited.

12   **EPIPHANY**

Nobody could be sure exactly where Paul was getting his money from. Quite unexpectedly he announced to everyone that he would be taking his girlfriend with him for a weekend to Paris to celebrate her 60th birthday, and when Friday came they promptly took the train to London and connected to the Eurostar, having booked a hotel room at the last minute. Everyone was very happy for them except for Kate, who expressed a concern at the reckless nature of the speed of the trip and the direction in which the stranger was taking his relationship with her mother. But why not? After years of hardship and pain, as well as the extreme carefulness with which she usually approached everything, Alice relished the chance to run away to Paris with an attractive man. It made her feel young again, letting herself be swept up in hedonism and romance as she ran away to France.

As they passed through St Pancras, Alice stopped for a second to gaze upwards at the vaulted glass ceiling and the enormous bronze statue of the two lovers meeting on the platform beneath the station clock. Watching them embracing, robed in a shining veneer of metal, their beating hearts and hungry spirits hidden from everyone save the other, Alice was overcome with a thankfulness that she did not recognise. Leo had made her cynical, and Geoff had helped him make her bitter, but now Paul had made her see the full potential of a world filled with opportunity and promise and her optimism was immeasurable.

Following a brief diversion via the champagne bar on the station's upper concourse where Paul had insisted upon a toast to her birthday trip, they finally made it to the check-in desks. Once they had passed through, the Immigration Officer at the security barriers took Alice's passport, opened it and looked at the photograph as she invited her to have her retina scanned by the computer. Smiling, she welcomed her through and wished her a pleasant journey. There was a small pastry counter within sight and as she walked forward Alice tried to see how much a croissant for the journey would cost them and whether she had the exact change in Sterling. When she looked back, expecting to see Paul immediately behind her, she saw that he was being questioned by the Officer and was looking hassled and stressed. Walking back over to them she came within earshot of the conversation.

"I am sorry Mr Retter but there seems to be something on your record which is a cause for concern to the French Government. It's a problem with your identity because the retina scan appears to be an exact match of someone else."

"Is everything in order, Officer? Will he be able to travel?" Alice asked her.

Paul interjected his reassurance. "It will be fine my love, there's just a problem with the scanner, that's all. I get this a lot, apparently I have unusual eyes. Can you buy me a coffee? I'll be over in a minute."

She walked over to the food outlet and bought two croissants, two coffees and a fruit salad. When she had taken off her coat and hung it on the back of her chair, she noticed Paul coming towards her and putting the passport back into his pocket.

"What happened?"

"Oh that? It's nothing to worry about; I get it all the time which means that I know how to operate the scanner better than she does. Apparently my eyes are suspiciously similar to someone else's and that means that they always think I'm some kind of impostor. I mean, seriously? Modern technology isn't perfect but we all rely on it as though it is. It must be like DNA, where family members are more similar than perfect strangers."

Alice sipped her coffee and gazed at him lovingly. "Is there anything you're not telling me?"

"Well, I don't know if you knew that I was born a twin?"

Alice looked surprised. Her eyes widened as she drank.

"Yes, I'm sorry Alice. I thought you knew that already. His name was James and he died when we were forty four in a car crash. It's been nine years. They must have got the records confused on the system. That must be it."

She smiled at him. "You failed to mention that, Paul."

"I know, I'm sorry. It isn't my favourite thing to talk about, that's all. James was my best friend. Aside from the tragedy of him being killed it was also a trauma for me because I was badly injured; I have scars on my body even now. There's a bad one on my chest where I went through the windscreen." He took her hand, raised it to his mouth and kissed it. "I guess that's it, that's my last secret that I had saved up for you. I will have to be inventive and think of some more."

Alice was thoughtful. "You reacted strongly when I told you about Joy," she said. "Why was that?"

"It was because of James," he said. "We have both lost people that we loved deeply and that we were very close to. It's something that we have in common. Your story about Joy brought it very close to home. You know what, Alice? I know how it feels. I know what you went through and what it felt like."

They both knew that to anyone else she would have exploded. He was testing her love for him to the limit; it was a statement of audacity, an outlandish declaration that lay down a gauntlet for her to challenge the depth of his knowledge about her story. Alice paused for a second, stunned by the impact of the words that he had said, and pondered over them in her head. After all I have been through how dare you tell me that you know how it feels to have your family destroyed! She was tempted to be angry, to shout at him as she had done to a thousand others who had claimed a starring role in her own very personal tragedy, but instead she gave him a very rare clemency. It was a touching moment, with Alice's guard gently eased down, but it was also very telling as to her feelings for Paul.

The train rushed through the dazzling white fields of snow at a blistering speed. Paul was reading his book and Alice, seated next to the window, gazed out over the battlefields of Northern France, the flashing trees and jagged battlements of tempestuous clouds crowning the horizon in magnificent peaks that gleamed like silver. They held hands for the whole journey and Alice put her head on Paul's shoulder as she gazed out of the window, for the landscape enchanted her.

Paul had clearly planned everything out very carefully. On the first evening, after they had had dinner in a beautiful and expensive restaurant beside the Seine at Place De La Concorde, they took the walk down the Champs Elysees, the most famous road in France, to the Arc De Triomphe. They climbed up inside, round and round the never-ending spiral staircase until they reached the observation platform on the roof. Her legs were getting stiffer and her bones more brittle, and she didn't really want to tell him why she didn't feel much affection for spiral staircases.

The view from the top was nothing short of spectacular. The Eiffel Tower was bathed in a golden glow from the light display which had been installed to celebrate the tower's bicentennial, and the whole of Paris stretched out far beyond them, blushing with thousands of lights as far as the eye could see towards the horizon. The business district in the faraway southern half of the city centre glittered with lights as the skyscrapers reached for the star strewn heavens, and the north and centre of the city were the more traditional style French architecture studded with lights like sequins stitched into a ball gown. The Eiffel Tower was fitted with a powerful searchlight at its summit and as it rotated the whole sky was filled with beautiful bright white light, visible from everywhere in the city, and flashbulbs were clearly visible from the top as tourists took photographs of Paris' majestic splendour; the Tower sparkled like a glittering diamond. Even now, Alice could not help but be reminded of the Leviathan Building a dream ago, bathed in a shimmering glow of brilliant and pure light.

Pausing to get her breath back both from the hundreds of steps they had taken up and the unbelievable view spread out far beneath her, she gazed out in the direction of Notre Dame and it took her a while to notice that Paul was not standing beside her. She turned and found him kneeling by her side, holding an open box with a glinting diamond ring inside it and gazing upwards at her beauty emblazoned against the starlit skies of France with a look of deep adoration. "My love," he began, his voice trembling with emotion, "I have known for a very long time that we have been brought together by fate. From the moment that I laid eyes on you I knew that you were the woman that I was always meant to be with. You are the most beautiful woman I have ever seen; I get fireworks in my stomach whenever I see your face. Your name on my lips is the sweetest sound to my ears and you have made me so wonderfully happy, and I now have the rest of my life to repay you that favour. Alice Hewitt," he began nervously, "please will you do me the great honour of becoming my wife?"

She barely listened to the question because she was already crying. She told him that she would, and finally he stood up so she could hold him in her arms. As she held him she lifted her feet off the ground and he span her around and lifted her above him, so that her stomach was level with his chin, and triumphantly exalted her into the starlit sky. She threw her arms upwards in delight, rescued and redeemed by the love he had given her, drinking in the significance of the moment after decades on her own.

Perfect strangers came up to them and began to congratulate them in French. Alice had always wanted to witness a spontaneous proposal because she never had done so and she understood their feelings completely. One woman had taken a photograph of Paul lifting Alice and had offered to email it to them, a token of spontaneous kindness which they were glad to accept. Alice and

Paul kissed again and all of the tourists at the top of the Arc de Triomphe burst into a spontaneous applause.

Their weekend was wonderful. Ever since Geoff had left she had always imagined being swept away in a foolish love affair, carefully pictured in her head a new husband and a new engagement, but now she looked back on her years of singleness and scolded herself for daring to dream. It was not because she was afraid that her imagination was too idealistic and would give her unrealistic expectations which would depress her when they turned out to be as elusive as shadows. Instead it was because she was angry with herself for not being as bold as she should have been to dream loftily enough. Her dreams were much more restricted and confined than she had ever envisaged and Paul's imagination was clearly a thousand times more vibrant and audacious than hers was; he had reached new heights for love that she never knew even existed. The naked truth was that he was more perfect than she had ever thought a man could be, and that birthday weekend was more wonderful than she thought was possible. She had dreamed, and at the time she knew she should not because of the crushing fear of disappointment after the dreams that she had had of Higher Pelham, but the reality was that even the most fanatical and outlandish of her fantasies would not even come close to the elation of experiencing the real thing. Love was the song in Alice's weary throat after all these years of darkness and despair.

On the night of her birthday they had gone to the Opera and the next morning they explored Versailles in the snow. The palace was so enormous that the mist and snow had meant that not all of the building could be seen at once; instead it faded away into the blinding whiteness like a painting that had yet to be completed. The frozen lakes and secret gardens enthralled them both, and even though Alice's fingers were cold she refused to wear gloves for any longer than was necessary so that she could see the glint of her diamond ring. The immaculate hedgerows and manicured bushes reminded her of Kate's adventures in the front garden of their terraced house in Rosevine Road, but the memory was like her view of the palace building in its misty incompleteness. She was at the end, and the beginning had vanished out of her sight.

The Grand Canal was totally frozen over with a thick layer of snow settled on the surface and Paul suggested that they should be reckless and walk on it. It was an exhilarating prospect, dancing across the water, in the middle of a lake with nobody watching them, perfectly alone in a frozen wonderland. Perhaps there would even be some particularly cold fish swimming in the water beneath their feet. Alice protested, remembering her reaction when her daughter had wanted to go skating on the village pond a lifetime ago, but she needn't have worried. The ice in Higher Pelham was cracked and fractured, like enormous shards of glass floating in the water, but here the sheet of ice was perfectly intact and the snow above it gleamed majestically. It was thick, and deep and strong. There was something so wonderfully beautiful about being together, quite alone, amongst the trees beside the Grand Canal with snow stretching as far as the eye could see ahead of them. There was not a single footprint in the flawless and pristine carpet of dazzling whiteness, stretched across the surface of the frozen lake like a vast harvest of crushed diamonds. Again he asked her, but she was having none of it; she told him that she was too old and aching to be fishing out a new fiancé from a freezing lake in the French countryside. She used an expletive, and he smiled at her. He understood her better than she understood herself, for he knew that Leo and Geoff had robbed her of her ability to trust people and he would gradually have to earn it from her, and his role as her husband would be to entice her out of her cynicism and teach her to regain her sense of faith. Alice was not ready to take his hand and step out into the unknown together, but there was nothing wrong with that. She had done so remarkably well and considering all that had happened to their family her pessimistic voice was astonishingly quiet. Alice liked to compare herself silently to Kate, and whilst Kate was a cynic, the flame of Alice's trust in the dauntless beauty of the world and the virtuous nobility of the people in it was strained and tested but never fully extinguished. The cold was beginning to get the better of her frozen hands but even as she put her gloves on she could feel the contours of the stone in the middle of her engagement ring through the leather, and at long last her hand was complete again. As the snow fell, Versailles echoed in a deep silence.

On the journey back from Paris, Alice phoned Jonathan as soon as the train came through the Channel Tunnel, telling him her news and he seemed genuinely delighted that his mother was so happy. When she had told him she phoned Kate next, telling her that he had proposed atop the Arc De Triomphe, and she sounded deeply cynical. "Of course he did, Mum, why else would someone take you to Paris to be alone together?"

In a tender act of inclusion, Paul and Alice began to make preparations to marry in St George's Church, Higher Pelham, so that Joy could be a part of the beginning of her mother's new life. It had been Alice's idea and Paul had given it his full approval as he had decided that it was his opportunity for an introduction to the little girl who meant so much to his loved ones but whom he himself would never meet. Kate had taken on the role of helping her mother select the wedding dress and the day it arrived was a great occasion of celebration as she opened the enormous box which it was delivered in, the satin and lace folded in great mountains of crinkled tissue paper, wrapped up in ribbon like a magnificent Christmas present. Everything was meticulously arranged over the next few months; the billowing flower arrangements laid out throughout the church, the antique wedding cars, catering for the reception at The Green Man, the outfits of the congregation, the photography, the music, the hymns and prayers and poems.

Alice awoke on the morning of the wedding with an unstoppable sensation of unyielding optimism. Today would be the day that her pain and sorrow ended, and the sunshine streaming in on her was a wonderful reminder of the steadfastness of his love.

Kate helped her with the dress, pulling the strings of the corset and tightly securing them into place, each one perfectly positioned. It had a stunning train, with great thick bustling layers of silk that flowed out from the hip of the corset top, and she had sewn in individual real white rose heads which formed a line down the middle of her train. She wore the diamond necklace that Paul had brought her back from Paris, a thick choker of rubies, and it was as cold as ice and sent a thrilling chill though her skin as it touched her.

"Are you ready, Mum?"

Alice gathered her skirts about her and ran a hand over the angelic veil and the tiny tiara on her head to make sure that it was all in place. "Yes, I'm ready." After all the heartache, all the tragedy, all the intolerable suffering and pain, her pursuit of happiness could resume twenty six long years after the murder of her daughter. After all of the pain of her last marriage, all of the stains and tainting, she knew that it was a statement of hope rather than of truth to wear a dress of a dazzling, whipped meringue white, as blemishless as the snow which covered the gardens at Versailles.

It was the most perfect day. The skies above were, finally and eventually, stunningly clear and blue. The couple were welcomed to the village by those with long enough memories to remember them and it was a huge local celebration as the cars swept into the Square and the local people clapped and cheered the bride who had once called this place home. It was the best attended wedding that St George's had ever had, on the longest day of the year in the golden midsummer, and there was standing room only at the back of the church. As the wedding car came through Higher Pelham, she felt a superstitious impulse to check exactly what had changed over the last quarter of a century. The A-road system outside of the village had changed so that it was not quite as remote as she had remembered it and the tiny school had been extensively modernised and expanded. For the first time the settlement was not entirely composed of thatched cottages, as the new developments on the outskirts of the village were new tiled semis and terraces but the ancient core of Higher Pelham was far to precious to destroy. The cobbles were still there, just as they had been that fateful summer a lifetime ago, and the old square with its war memorial and crooked little buildings that surrounded it. Some of the names of the shops had changed but the services on offer in the village were generally the same, and most of the people that were lining the streets were not the neighbours that she recognised as the ones she had had a hard time forgiving back then. Mr West was long gone.

The car came to a halt on the western side of the square where there was a gated entrance to the churchyard and a cracked stone path to the door. The chauffeur opened the door for her and she shifted herself in the leather seat, climbing gracefully to her feet, for there could be no clumsiness and no accidents today. Concentrating on the train of her dress, she was slightly taken aback when the crowd assembled in the square gave a mighty cheer when Alice Hewitt stepped into the warm sunshine for the final time. She gave them a wave, and they began to shout messages of congratulations and love to her; Alice was surprised that they even remembered the faces rather than just the names of the family who had lived here all those years ago. Instead they had come out and turn her second wedding into a celebration in the village which had almost been doomed by her daughter's murder and had become a byword for evil and tragedy. It had a low crime rate, that was to be sure, but Higher Pelham needed only one spectacularly infamous killing to be committed here for the village to be given an unshakeably gruesome reputation.

Having no father left, Alice had asked Jonathan if he would lead her down the aisle and give her away at the altar to the man who loved her. He was honoured to accept, and she held his arm as he led her to the door and waited for the signal to lead his mother towards her new husband and the destiny that waited with him.

The aisle seemed to stretch on forever through the tiny and ancient parish church. The anticipation as she waited to reach him was unbearable, and she was filled with a reckless desire to gather up the hem of her gigantic dress and charge forwards, leaping over the pews and the members of the congregation, making great athletic bounds towards the man she loved and flinging her bouquet of sunflowers up to the vaulted ceiling in an outlandish gesture of shameless romanticism, but unfortunately she was endowed with neither the boldness or the youthful agility to do so. Eventually she reached him, and took her place alongside him as Jonathan took a step back. He had not looked back, just as he had promised, and finally he turned his head and took a first look at his bride. "You look beautiful, Alice," he told her tenderly. "I have never seen a finer woman in my whole life."

She was awestruck as she cast an eye on her lover as he worshipped during the service. He had the emotional vigour and spontaneity of youth and yet at the same time she knew that her liaison with him had been an infant love affair compared to his relationship and service of God; this was a runner approaching his finish line, having run a triumphantly faithful race towards the prize, keeping his eyes fixed upon Jesus for his whole life. There was a glorious beauty in his steadfastness in his faith, the way that he knew that he had served the same Christ for decade upon decade but the flames of passion that consumed him were still burning every bit as brightly as the moment of his eternal rescue. It was a beautiful and tender thing to behold as she prepared to enter a union with him that would last for the rest of her life.

"And now it is my legal obligation to ask the congregation assembled here on this happy occasion if there is any known reason in law why these two persons may not marry each other then they are to declare it now."

As the preacher was speaking Thomas had reached his hand over to his wife, taking Catherine by the hand and whispering into her ear gently. "He isn't your dad and he never will be, but that's ok. Let your mum have her happiness." She had been seething, unable to pinpoint what exactly about Paul she refused to accept, and realised when she had met him that for all the steely charisma that she loved to show she had probably been affected by her father's departure much more deeply than she had realised. She smiled at him and nodded, and the silence was protected.

The vows were traditional, and when the crucial moment came and Paul was asked if he took Alice to be his lawfully wedded wife, he took her by the hand and knelt again like he had done on the Arc De Triomphe. His response was determined and bold. "Yes I do."

The wedding service lasted just under an hour and finally the moment came that the crowd outside had been waiting for. Mr and Mrs Paul Retter stepped outside into the warm summer sunshine, and the crowd in the Square erupted into applause as the couple emerged from the ancient church door and walked along the path to the gate, with hundreds of well-wishers showering them with confetti and rose petals. It was a joyous celebration, a conclusion of a fairytale, to see the woman who had lost so much and experienced such agonising hurt for a long time finally seal her happy future with the man of her dreams; people were openly weeping as they saw Alice's heroic story resume from where the rapture left off in this very village on the last day of May. The air was charged with hundreds of messages of love; surely there was never anyone who deserved this more. At *last*.

Surrendering to the pressure of the crowd, Alice and Paul enjoyed a passionate kiss as they walked across the Square to the waiting cars which would whisk them off into the countryside for a brief photo-shoot before returning to Higher Pelham for the reception dinner. They drove through the narrow country lanes and between the antique hedgerows to the very edge of Pelham Hill, the spectacular backdrop of Wiltshire and Dorset beyond it spread out far beyond them in all of its golden midsummer glory. It was a clear day and they could see the rustic folly of King Alfred's Tower piercing the horizon, and the unrivalled beauty of the vast expanse of woodland which stretched in an unbroken sweep all the way up to its base. Was she his Rapunzel, entombed within a doomed tower for decade after decade, waiting for him to ride on his muscular prancing steed to charge her impregnable fortress to miraculously release her and carry her off to his mythical kingdom? She was a Venus no longer, for her billowing and luscious golden hair had greyed and her glowing skin was wrinkled now, but Paul adored her unconditionally and he thought every aspect of her was stunningly beautiful. He had even asked her to not wear makeup for the service, claiming that he loved her face in all of its natural beauty, but she had ended up wearing it because the abuse from Geoff and the years of desolate singleness had led her to a crushing sense of low self esteem. Paul was working on it, committing himself to rebuilding her like some painstaking pre-Raphaelite restoration project, but his work was not yet completed. Every day in his arms was a success story on the road to recovery.

Alice and Paul posed for photographs on hay bales, in meadows and fields and in a local rose garden. The photographer told Jonathan that he had never worked at a more joyous wedding and that he even shed a tear when he took a close up shot of the rings on her finger. There were the traditional black and white shots which she so loved, one of which Paul selected as a photograph that he would order a canvas of and put it in pride of place in the cottage by the sea that he had always promised her. It was in a field of hay bales, with Alice holding her bouquet in one hand and Paul's hand in the other, with most of the frame filled with endless expanses of sky, huge and matchlessly beautiful. Standing on the edge of Pelham Hill, where years before two young girls had made their way home from school, the new couple gazed out on the vast expanse of countryside below in much the same way as they looked out on their future together as man and wife. It was unguessable and mysterious, but it was exhilarating and exciting and they could not wait to get exploring.

Finally the hours of whiling away the time until her husband bedded her came to an end. He carried her upstairs, her hand draped gracefully around his neck until about halfway up the staircase his back couldn't take the strain any more and he had to put her down. How they laughed; he was not as fit and strong as the knight in shining armour that he had promised her when they had met, the years had taken their toll on him but his romantic heart was as young and passionate as ever. Her flesh had also been eroded by the time that had passed; with a pang of regret she did not bleed as she had done when she was a maiden. Of all the gifts that she could give him, she could no longer offer him that and it was a heartbreaking regret that seemed to echo through her body; there was a time when I belonged to somebody else. Time was precious and every day that she spent with him from now on was a priceless gift. He thought differently to her; his life may have been easier, without the demons that had haunted her ever since Joy had gone, but he told her that the reason that he was wrinkled was from laughing his way through a good and happy life. If his hair was greying it was because he had walked along the beach a few too many times, the ocean winds stealing his breath and ripping through his hair with such strength that he could sing at the top of his lungs and nobody would hear him. He seemed like the kind of person who had always been old, who had always had a ripened and matured spirit within him. He knew that every day of his life was testament to the God who had loved him and known his name since the foundation of the world, who had moulded his eyelashes in his mother's womb a lifetime ago. Paul's faith was so simple, he loved God and God loved him, and there was little more to it than that.

When their marriage had been consummated they lay in a breathless state of wondrous tenderness. Both of them had scars that they had kept secret from the other until this night. Paul explained to her that he had been in the car with James when the fatal accident had occurred, and this was why there was a scar beneath his hairline and another at the base of his neck. Alice commented on the remarkable lack of damage that he suffered to his body considering his brother was killed in the accident, but Paul insisted that rather than being lucky, he knew that God had a purpose for keeping him alive and that it was a tremendously faith building experience to have been through. He pointed to a small tattoo for the shadow of a cross that he had on his left leg, right at the bottom next to the ankle bone. Every step I take I take on God's mercy and grace, he would say. Kissing her on her forehead, he told her that he was thankful to God for saving his life and that he believed that it was because they were destined to be together. Alice's scars from Geoff's attacks on her, the marks from smashed bottles and knives and the disfigurement on the back of her head hidden beneath her hair from the impact of the iron staircase were all gently uncovered with love. Some of the marks that they revealed were so personal and sensitive that they had never been seen by another before, and they navigated their way around their new spouse's body using the scars and lacerations as landmarks, much as a ship will navigate its way around a coastline using the lighthouses to guide the route. Even the dead skin of a scar can be infused with the thrilling sensation of erotic pleasure when you have been waiting your whole life to find your true soul-mate.

Right at the start of their married life together, they had both promised that there could be no lies and no secrets between them, everything would be uncovered and laid bare upon the marriage bed. Paul disclosed to her that before he had been saved and redeemed by Christ he had made love before, and she was not the first woman that he had lain with even though today had been his first wedding day. He told her that he had been convicted to wait in faith that God would be a provider and that He would give Paul the desires of his heart, which included a wife. He had never stopped waiting for Alice, even when his twenties came and went, then his thirties, then his forties. He held onto the hope that he had in Christ and he knew that his saviour would not fail him, and finally, today his ancient prayer was answered after all the waiting and pleading. He was incredibly happy and he would not have wanted it any other way, for she was worth waiting for but he also had an incredible testimony of love to show her considering he had waited all of his life for a day like today. Alice, as he knew, had been married to Geoff for seventeen years, sixteen of them blissfully happy and joyous. The wedding day had meant a great deal to both of them because they both had had many days when they thought that happiness had eluded them forever and they would spend the rest of their lives in desolate misery. The day had been perfect, but there was a definite feeling of squander as she had hoped and dreamed under thousands of skies for six long decades and gloomy days without the man that she had been created to love.

The honeymoon was sensational. Paul had organised it alone and it was a surprise to everyone until the morning of departure when he produced a pair of train tickets from Reading to Southampton telling his wife to pack clothes for hot weather. They embarked on a voyage around the Mediterranean on a cruise liner for two weeks and stopped off in Barcelona, Monte Carlo, Rome and Athens. As they came ashore for the stopover in Spain Alice remembered the problems with the retina scan that he had had as he had tried to leave London before the wedding. But this time they were ushered through the barriers with no problems, and Paul reassured her that the technology was faulty and it sometimes stopped him whilst on other occasions it was fine. Was this too good to be true? It seemed to be that way; the sunny days at sea, walking out onto the deck first thing in the morning to spread her bare toes across the warm teak of the decking of their balcony, exciting cities and countries, five star food and enough memories to last them both until their final day.

Paul took an enormous amount of pleasure in the days that they spent away from home. He was honoured to be given the chance to mimic his maker and to redeem her, to justify her, to rescue her and to take every day as an opportunity to bind up her wounds and push the pain of her experiences further and further into the past. He treated her in the way that he had felt God had treated him, not waiting for her to earn his love or judging her on virtues or flaws but instead to cherish her, to adore her, simply for being who she was. Alice was ashamed of her past, but Paul loved it. He absolutely loved where she had come from. He loved the way that his relationship with her helped him to understand better the wonderful gift of grace that God had bestowed upon him. His new wife mesmerised him. She was a learning each and every day to trust him more and more and Paul never failed to be moved by the amount that she had learnt and endured over the last quarter of a century and yet retained her hope and her unyielding optimism that a better day was coming. She had been taught by Geoff and Leo to be careful in all things, but she always worked hard to choose the good in people and she decided to believe that life, with all of the drudgery that comes with it, is truly a thing of immense beauty.

Alice loved Paul so much that it terrified her. She suddenly felt a youthful joy in the depths of her soul that restored to her consciousness aspects of her character that she had either forgotten about or had never known had existed. It was a beautiful thing and there was a colossal amount of freedom in it, a freedom that he remembered and empathised with from the moment that he had first accepted Christ as his saviour. All of the chains which had decorated her ankles for a small eternity, chains which she had lived with for so long that it was difficult to distinguish them as separate from herself, were suddenly and violently ripped off. It was a thrilling and adrenaline filled freedom, a reckless and audacious experience, and the world was filled with the sheer raw power of that most noble and conspicuous of birthrights endowed to humanity. She looked up from the bed and saw him standing on the balcony, overlooking the silent sea. He obviously did not think she could hear him.

"I scorn you, stars" he whispered into the night sky. "Surely I am more abundantly blessed and my wife more lavishly adorned than the whole sum of you."

13 CHASING SHADOWS

Paul loved Hope; that was clear for everyone to see. Kate could not explain it but she could not bear the thought of her mother being married to him because something about him which she could not identify made her skin crawl. One summer day in August when it was warm enough Tom got the paddling pool out for the children to play in and the garden was transformed into a blissful playground of ecstasy. Tom rubbed sun cream into his children's skin; it was a magical white cream that smelled of coconuts, summer and happiness. Paul used the sprinkler hose and he sent triumphant arcs of water high into the hot blue sky as he sprayed the children; Hope scrunched up her nose as the droplets ran down her face, holding her mouth open and letting her tongue loll out in the hope of catching some of the water in her cheeks so she could pretend to be a fountain. Her wet hair shimmered in the sunshine and she shrieked and squealed with delight as the freezing water collided with her and took her breath away. She began scooping up great handfuls of water and unleashing them on the skin of her brother and father. She found an old plastic bowl and filled it, waiting for the opportune moment before she dumped the whole thing over her step-grandfather's head. He was drenched in a thrilling sensation of shock as the freezing water ran over every inch of his skin and soaked his shirt. Hope shrieked with joy, caught red handed, and began running around the paddling pool as Paul chased her. Her father just stood there laughing at both of them, thoroughly entertained by the whole episode.

The heat of the sunshine was so strong that Paul decided to take his wet shirt off and he began to play with them wearing nothing but swim-shorts. It was the most picturesque scene of happiness and vibrant, abundant life for which they had waited for so long, the redemption which had been slow to reach them since the death of Joy and the shameful disappearance of Geoff.

Kate was reading her book in the lounge, and the stifling heat of the day was too much for her to be outside in the sunshine. She had a migraine, and she preferred to relax indoors, lying on the sofa with the crisp pages of an unread novel surrendering between her fingers. The house was refreshingly quiet and calm. She got up and went to pour herself a glass of juice from the kitchen to enjoy as she unwound from the stresses and strains of the week. The light from the kitchen floor as the sun shone in reflected upwards to shimmer across Kate's face, and it dazzled and blinded her for a second; as she walked over to the fridge the light readjusted itself and she saw the scene outside.

Her mother was sitting in a chair in the garden, wearing her sunglasses and laughing as she watched the children play. Alice was the epitome of glamour and elegance, still glowing from her wedding day, proudly wearing a wedding ring once again. A bare-chested Tom was carrying his son on his shoulders, standing in the paddling pool and kicking and splashing the water beneath his feet. The glittering crystal water shimmered between Tom's toes with astonishing beauty, and Kate saw the dancing shapes of the reflected sunlight swimming across her son's face, his young eyes ignited with wonder and chemistry.

Hope was running around the pool, screaming loudly. She was clearly being chased by Paul, who had taken his shirt off. She had never seen her stepfather's bare torso before and she did not expect to see a large scar at the top of his chest, illuminated on his shining skin as he ran after Hope. Why was his wife smiling as she sat there? Why was Tom not doing anything about this? Paul chased and chased the little girl until eventually he grabbed her by the arm and lifted her over his shoulder so that he carried her in a fireman's lift; Hope screamed and screamed, and Kate clearly heard her shout the word "no" several times. Once she was slung over his shoulder he began to spin, lifting her wet hair so that it thrashed about her head as though she was a rag-doll. Kate poured her juice into a tumbler, the cold glass pressed against the skin of her hands so that it felt like a communion goblet. Raising the glass to her lips as she looked out again into the sunshine she was overcome with an unimaginable sense of horror and dread, shocked by what she was witnessing. She dropped the glass onto the flagstone tiles of the kitchen floor, the shattered pieces clattering outwards and the blood red cranberry juice inside cascading in a spectacular stain which fanned out across the floor in the shape of a palm leaf.

She stared and stared to make sure that she was not mistaken, but she could not get another clean look and the first had only lasted for a fraction of a second. She could not be sure; if she had been convinced beyond all doubt she would have run outside and wrestled her daughter out of her stepfather's hands, but instead was left with a lingering suspicion, a half glance of something sinister. She thought she had caught a glimpse of the shape of Paul's male organ beneath his shorts. She had thought she had seen it standing erect as he chased her daughter around the paddling pool. She could only imagine the surging currents of passion which coursed through his veins, the heightened tenderness of excitement as the water dripped off her wet skin. Kate shielded the sunlight from her eyes and saw her daughter's shining hair, her glossy face, her fingers and teeth and eyes. Hope's legs were slippery. Suddenly Kate's mind was gripped by the image of her daughter licking him as though he were an ice-cream, of her holding the wet flesh of his chest between the gaps in her unfinished smile.

Was he a paedophile too? Was he charged with the same hellish energy as Leo had been, crafted and constructed from the same demonic fabric as the man who had killed her sister? Could it be that there was something about the young girls of this family, something inherent in their nature, which made them unnaturally attractive to men of a certain temperament? Kate tried to shake the migraine out of her head but it gave her no relief from the pounding and throbbing pain which was amplified by the pulsing sunlight searing against her body. As soon as she had entertained the idea in her head she was convinced of its irrefutable truth. She knew that he must be enraptured by Hope's virtuous beauty and that he must have fooled the whole family into thinking that he was innocent and that he really did love Alice after all. She had all the proof that she needed; that rushed half-glimpse, that half-remembered shadow of his phallus beneath the heavily patterned, psychedelically coloured shorts in blinding sunshine beneath a pounding, burning migraine.

Kate's hostility towards her stepfather doubled over the coming days. She began to scheme and plot against Paul, figuring out a way of bringing his dreams of Utopia with Alice crashing down. His menace, the unquestionable danger that he posed to the children was a grey and wraith like presence which tormented Kate day and night. She refused to speak to him whenever possible and she would not let her children be in the same room as him if she could help it. A heavy air of suspicion descended on the Ferguson household and Kate was very clearly extremely troubled by what she had thought she had seen and was deciding what should be done about his ghastly plans to rape the children.

When she caught Tom on his own she told him what she had seen. He looked at her with a total lack of recognition of what she was saying, as though she was speaking to him in a different language, and an undercurrent of horror which crawled beneath his skin like a maggot. Kate did not know how it felt to be a man, she did not know the ways in which the male body was subjected to the kinds of desires she was talking about; instead she knew theoretically, and from observing other people. Tom was extremely troubled by this suspicion of hers as he wondered if that may have happened to him, that her paranoia may have made a victim out of him had he been a little too careless in protecting his modesty in the presence of his own daughter. Sexual attraction was only one of many explanations for what she may or may not have seen; Kate clearly thought that a man has a far greater control over the position of his penis within his shorts than was actually true. The whole suggestion was completely absurd; had she not seen the amount of fun that they were having? Had she not seen that Alice and Tom were both in close proximity and had not seen anything, nor had Hope made any complaint after the event? Leo's legacy had been to implant in the tissue of Kate's brain a firm belief that every single person was out to harm her children, and Tom was concerned that it was about to claim another victim in the wonderfully sensitive and loving figure of Paul Retter. Perhaps, as Kate slowly lost her sanity, Tom Ferguson would become number fifteen. If she could turn on her mother's husband, she could surely also turn on her own.

Tom told her that both he and Alice had not noticed anything unusual about Paul's behaviour in the garden that hot day, and thought instead he had done remarkably well to insert himself into a tightly knit family with such ease. He was playing with the children with admirable enthusiasm and energy for a man of his age, and that the love with which he treated Hope and William was a beautiful thing to behold. Tom could not have asked for a more perfect, sensitive, carefully loving man to have joined the family and he was absolutely delighted that Alice and Paul had joined them briefly before finding a home of their own. At what point over the years of his marriage to Kate had it become unacceptable for the children to receive love? What was there about adoring Hope and William that was abhorrent and cruel, and where was the virtue in holding back and denying the children access to the love which they so desperately needed? To Tom cherishing children was the most honourable thing in the world, but the poison of Leo Faulkner had stolen Kate's ability to share in it, and her relationship with children was changed forever. It was such a tragic shame. Paul, surely, did not deserve to be victimised by the curse of a man that he had never met, a man who had tainted this family such a long time in the past and who should have been long forgotten.

As soon as Alice found out what was being discussed between her daughter and son-in-law she knew that it needed to be immediately addressed before it festered. Alice owed that to everyone.

"I think we need to talk, don't we Catherine?"

Kate knew that it was serious because of the few occasions when her mother addressed her by her complete name.

"The first thing that I want to say to you is that you have done so very well since your sister died. It must have been so difficult."

"It was difficult for all of us."

"I think that you have to confront the possibility that you have some issues hanging over you from all the things that you have witnessed and all of the things you have been exposed to over the years. You were the only witness and you were the one who had to give evidence at the Old Bailey. It is perfectly understandable and you have nothing to be ashamed about if you are finding things difficult now. Having the most important years of your life played out in a broken family will have an effect on you and it is unwise of you to ignore that."

Kate narrowed her eyes and looked at her mother with a combination of exasperation and deep confusion.

"You think this is about Dad?"

"It's about all of it, Kate, everything that you have been subjected to. From the day Joy died, when you were the only one to see that man, to the whole case resting on your testimony and everyone at the tabloids pressuring you into convicting him so that he could be executed. It was hard when you saw what happened to your father; I think Jonathan was a bit too young to fully appreciate what was happening but it hit you with full force. Everything that happened seemed to happen to or through you.

You were in the wrong place at all the wrong times, and I think it has made you paranoid."

Kate was horrified.

"Did you believe me when I said that I was sure that it was Leo Faulkner who killed Joy? Did you believe the testimony I gave or did you have to see for yourself when you went to Belmarsh to visit him?"

"What? Of course I believed you. Of course I trusted what you said."

"Well then why don't you believe me now? What's different? He was dangerous, Paul is dangerous. I was right then and I am right now."

"How do you know?"

"Mother's instinct."

"What about 'Leo's Thirteen'? Was it mother's instinct that condemned all of them to death as well?"

Kate sat in silence. Alice went on to apologise for the trauma that she had been subjected to, lamenting flamboyantly about the distress it must have caused and her failures as a mother to have exposed her to such evil. She suggested that her daughter was finding it difficult because Leo Faulkner had changed her outlook on the whole world; that would be his ghastly legacy.

"I think the most difficult thing about the whole experience is how uncomfortable I feel about knowing that all the people I love do not believe a word I say. I have told you that it is fine a thousand times. I'm strong, Mum, I have endured so much and I have survived because I am a fighter. I don't understand why you are not listening to me."

"You're seeing things in Paul that simply are not there. He does not deserve this, and I do not deserve this. I don't expect you to fall in love with him and be bowled over but I do expect you to be respectful to him, and to not accuse him of being inappropriate around your children when you have absolutely nothing to base that on."

"What I am trying to say is that the things that Leo has done to our family have had an effect on you which may only be surfacing now. There is nothing wrong with that at all. We all have our different methods of responding to something as tragic as what we have all been through together and there is nothing right and nothing wrong about the differences between each person and their way of coping with what we are faced with."

"What I don't understand is the fact that you're still so trusting of people, so optimistic about people's intentions after all that has happened to you because of others."

"That isn't wrong, Kate. It isn't a flaw or a fault of mine that I choose to see the good in everything that happens and choose to trust the ones I am close to."

"What I am saying is that you are laying yourself wide open to be abused again and I can see this all ending badly."

"How? What is it that you are predicting? There is no evidence that you have shown me to tell me that you are right about Paul, it is instead all smoke and mirrors and speculation. You know what? I said the same things once about Tom. I thought he would be a disaster for this family, because your father taught me that all men are violent, bullying thugs." Alice's voice became louder and stronger. "But I was wrong, because he was the best thing that ever happened to you, and when I realised I was wrong I loved him as my son and I accepted him into my family. I am not asking you to do anything that I have not done myself. I welcomed your husband, now you welcome mine."

"If my husband gets an erection when he is playing with one of the children then please, by all means, treat him how he deserves to be treated."

"The reason that I refuse to believe what you are accusing Paul of is the fact that Leo and your father took a great deal away from me. I had all that I had taken by their violence and hatred. It is simply too high a price to pay to carry on with the same attitude of bitterness. I can't hate Paul, I have no choice. He is the last shot I have at happiness and he is my last roll of the dice as I hedge my bets on the fact that life is worth living and that the world is a good place."

*   *   *

Kate decided that she would investigate in great detail the man that her mother had decided to marry.

She knew that he had a flat in London, and after the wedding he arranged for it to be sold so that he and Alice could use the money to buy a new house together somewhere that was away from the stifling oppression of the city. Alice had asked not to move in with him in the East End, because she had fought for so long and with such effort to move away in pursuit of her dream in Higher Pelham. There would be something so desperately incorrect about moving back to the city again, and her marriage to Paul and the new chapter in her life which was unfurling its splendour as a technicolour banner across bright skies was surely deserving of a new setting, a new backdrop, a new environment in which they could both continue the relentless and eternal pursuit of glory.

Whilst they were looking for somewhere else to live, Paul had moved into Alice's room in the Ferguson household and shared her double bed. The very first thing that Kate noticed was the fact that he seemed to have alarmingly few possessions. He had no photograph albums, and no framed pictures of his family were on the mantelpiece or windowsills as she had expected. The only time she had seen a photograph of his face was in the pictures which had been taken at the wedding. The beautiful one which they both loved of them posing with the hay bale and the open sky had been made into a canvas just as he had promised her and it hung in their bedroom before it could take pride of place in their new home. There was the other one on the Arc De Triomphe, her mother being lifted into the starlit Parisian sky, but no others. That was all.

Curious about the remarkable lack of photographs, Kate decided to ask him about it one Sunday over dinner when the family was all gathered together.

"Paul, do you have any family?"

Alice choked on a piece of her Yorkshire pudding, and quickly swallowed it and pretended that nothing had happened. Paul stared straight into his stepdaughter's eyes, trying to work her out.

"Not any more," he said humbly. "I am the last one. You are my family now."

"Oh really," she said politely. She had attempted to sound sincere but as it had left her lips it was soaked in sarcasm. "What happened, if you don't mind me asking?"

He was visibly uncomfortable, and attempted a smile whilst Kate attempted to look innocently curious. They both failed.

"Why do you ask?"

"I was just wondering why you don't seem to have any photographs with you. I'm sure we all have photographs of people that we love, and I am interested to see yours."

"Actually, Kate, I do mind you asking. I married your mother in an attempt to move on from a painful and difficult past, and the relationship that I have with your mother is my personal way of moving on from difficult times. It's the same for me as it is for Alice; we rescued each other. It's a painful and difficult thing for me to talk about. You are my family now, as I said."

"Mum said you have a twin brother."

Alice was horrified; he did not know that she had told Kate about James. She kicked her under the table, but Kate did not unfix her glare. "Kate," she said sternly, but Kate was not prepared to stop.

"No no, Mum, let me finish. Nobody has a twin brother who died in a car crash but doesn't own a single image of them. Have you ever gone by another name, Paul?"

Everyone at the table froze.

"No, of course I haven't. I have always been known by the name of Paul Retter."

"How curious," said Kate, "You don't seem to appear on any of the census records in the area where you claimed to live ten years ago. Nobody by that name has ever appeared in the phone book and there are no records of you attending local schools."

Paul excused himself and walked out of the room. The children looked confused, and William asked his mother what was happening. The air was electric.

"It's fine, darling, I am just trying to get to know Grandpa Paul, that's all. I don't think we know very much about him. When somebody comes into our family it's always nice to . . ."

Alice interrupted her with a burning fury. "Right Kate, that is more than enough from you. Don't you dare tell them those things about Paul. There is a logical explanation for everything that you have said; people don't appear on census records when they are living out of the country, for example. What's gotten in to you? Give him a break. If not for him, then do it for me."

A few days later, Kate was vacuuming her mother's room whilst alone in the house and noticed a photograph album laid out on the double bed, looking as though it was quite deliberately positioned. Intrigued, she could not resist opening it to see what was inside. She reeled back as she looked through the pages and found that he had written in the front of the album, presumably intending it to be read by his wife: "Here are the parts of my story that you missed out on. I love you." The album was filled with photographs of his life, beginning with him as a baby and going right the way through school and university, then on various holidays through his early adulthood, of him in the East End, growing into middle age and then finally a glorious final page shot of him with Alice, huddled together and giggling into their scarves as they walked through the gardens of Versailles hand in hand. It was a love story in a single photograph. She looked again at the baby photos and noticed that there was not a single one of him alone; there were always two baby boys together. Had she been wrong?

One night when Paul was sleeping Kate crept downstairs and found his laptop which he had left in the lounge. The laptop itself was not protected by a password, but all of his email accounts and bank account records containing sensitive information were. She guessed some of the possible passwords, things like his birthday or his name spelt out in numbers and symbols or her mother's name, but she had no luck. None of the combinations were correct, and she could not guess any different ones without the websites detecting an intruder and locking the account because of too many incorrect attempts to log in.

Frustrated by the lack of progress, she had a look through his internet history to see which sites he had visited frequently before and after his marriage to her mother. She did not really have a detailed understanding of what she was expecting to find when she searched, but she knew that it was not there. She couldn't find anything concerning children, pornography, drug use or criminal activity. It was the usual and expected information that any fifty three year old man would have on his internet history; some searches for holidays, some news articles, film and music files and some television shows that he had watched online. Kate was beginning to think that the only reason she had for suspecting him was in her mind, but she was agitated by compulsion and she could not stop now that she had come so far. She would never stop suspecting him, no matter what he did to convince her of his innocence, she knew that she was too far involved to let it go all the while that he was sleeping under her roof, sharing a bed with her mother.

Kate studied her stepfather's every move with fire in her eyes, meticulously learning everything that she could about him. Her job as a business manager was demanding and there were often long hours, but she took advantage of the few times when she was in the house without him such as at the weekend to go through his drawers and to search the bedroom as best she could. She bought a huge packet of business envelopes and would open his post every day, because she was usually the first one up as she prepared to go to work, then after she had checked through it and made a record of any important information she would repackage it and leave it for him to find. Alice became suspicious of the fact that some of the mail had no stamp affixed and so Kate bought herself a franking machine, stamping the envelopes as she repackaged them to make it look like the envelopes had come from the postman. Disposing of the old, genuine envelopes was difficult, so she would take them to work every day and shred them there to avoid detection.

She did some research online and downloaded some keystroke detection software onto his computer. It was surprisingly easy; no private investigators were needed as she substituted their services with her own brain and guts. She installed the software and used it so she could trace the letters that Paul typed into his keyboard when he was logging on to his email account, copy the password, and have a go at hacking in on her own to see what he was up to.

Eventually Kate had gathered enough information to record the passwords and she was able to log on to her stepfather's email account. She got what she was looking for; a book delivery which had an address on it to which the order was delivered. She made a note of his old address, and proceeded to trawl through his bank statements to see if there was a subscription for anything which would have seemed out of place. There wasn't a lot that surprised her, it was all the familiar mix of car insurance, groceries, train tickets, some books and magazine subscriptions which she already knew about, payments to electrical stores and a perfectly regular amount of cash withdrawals. It all looked perfectly legitimate, but she did not really know what to expect if she happened to come across something which was illegal or dubious. Would she be able to tell? She was quite certain that if he was paying for hardcore child pornography he would be slightly smarter than to allow it to be traced through his bank account. These were basic mistakes that Leo had made and she was sure that it was because he wanted to be caught, leaving a trail of breadcrumbs which led straight to his door. But what if Paul did not want to be caught? What if he was extremely skilled at concealing his secrets? What if he was a better paedophile than Leo had ever been?

The next night when she came downstairs to do some more of her investigations she noticed an icon in the corner which she had not remembered being there the previous night. She typed the name of the software into a search engine and she found that Paul had downloaded an anti-keylogger to detect and remove the software which had been installed on his laptop. All of her information had been deleted and she could no longer access his details through his computer.

Given that she had already thoroughly examined his laptop she went about going through the other devices that had internet access; she looked through his MP3 player and his mobile phone, but again there was nothing that came up which confirmed her suspicion. She was able to use the passwords that she had cracked from the laptop for a few days before he became suspicious and changed the passwords which gave access to any of his sensitive information, after which he was shrouded in darkness and secrecy once again.

Climbing into bed with her husband after a long day at work, Kate told Tom something she had been meaning to share but could not find the words to express.

"I've been stalking Paul."

"I know."

In the still and silent bedroom his reply sounded like a gunshot. She was dumbfounded. How could he know? She had been so careful, so subtle. Perhaps he was bluffing. But if he knew, did that mean Paul did too?

"It came to a dead end though. He has installed anti-tracing software on his laptop and changed all of his passwords."

"That happens all the time. He's just trying to make sure that nobody is trying to access his bank details. And the anti-tracing software is because he has probably found something suspicious on his system which has meant that he thinks someone is trying to hack in." There was an uncomfortable and tense silence. "And he would be right, wouldn't he?"

"No no, he knew that someone would come looking for him, he was expecting to be investigated. Nobody uses that kind of software on their home computer unless they have something to hide. There is something very strange going on in our house."

"Kate," he began, exasperated, "do you have anything which is more than just a hunch, a sneaking suspicion, that Paul has done anything wrong? That poor man, you are completely obsessed with him and we all need to forget about what happened to Joy. Just because it happened once does not mean it will happen again. It's time to stop."

Kate didn't stop. She began the process of filling out an application to the Criminal Records Bureau to check whether or not Paul had ever been convicted of a criminal offence. There were endless forms to fill in and she did so pretending it was him who had put pen to paper, then when it came to the appointment at the local police station she posed as a nursery school manager who was vetting one of her potential employees who had passed the interview stage and needed the clearance before he was legally permitted to work with children. She left the forms at the police station, even making a fake nursery manager's badge with her name on it and giving a fake name when she introduced herself, and making sure that she paid the fee in cash so that it could not be traced back to her. At first the officer behind the desk was unsure of whether or not they could take direct cash payments, but Kate Ferguson was an extremely gifted negotiator and the plan went ahead without a hitch. If there was any connection at all with a criminal record, whether spent or unspent, the police files would surely detect something. There was no way that the police force could fail her family the way that the justice system had so many years before.

A few weeks later Kate received a phone-call telling her that the police investigation into Paul Retter's criminal records was complete. She decided she should visit the police station to collect his certificate from them in person as if it was posted to the house then Paul would be able to detect what she was planning. She made the trip one evening on her way home from work and she felt a sense of elation as she walked up the steps to the police station, knowing that she finally would be able to prove that her suspicions about him would be right. What was it about paedophiles that made them attracted to Hewitts and Fergusons? She felt as though she had a bluebottle fly caught between her thumb and her index finger, and that he would come to his miserable end on her terms, when she was ready. She knew that she would enjoy the moment when it came.

The woman behind the desk was younger than Kate and she was wearing the familiar black and white uniform that the Hewitt family had been so accustomed to in the days after Joy died. Her hair was immaculate. She was wearing pearl earrings. She had a freckle just above her lip.

"Hope Williams?" Kate nodded, but found herself unable to maintain eye contact. "Here is your certificate, Mrs Williams," the woman said brightly, handing her a sealed envelope. Kate did not quite know how to react, like a squealing schoolgirl or like a steely, hardened predator closing in for the kill.

"Am I allowed to open it now?" she asked. The young woman examined her with her eyes for a few seconds, clearly not familiar with customers making this unusual request. "Yes, Madam. We would normally ask you out of courtesy to inform the employee of the outcome of the examination, but you may of course open it now if you choose to." She took a sip of water and glanced back down at her computer screen. Her eyes flashed an electroluminescent shade of blue as the screen was reflected in her irises. "Why? Is there something you suspect him of?"

Kate did not answer but instead ripped open the brown envelope and pulled out the certificate inside. It was wonderful to know that she was so close to finding out what he had been up to for the years that she did not know about. With an aghast sensation of horror she looked down at the certificate and saw that the police had found no trace of any criminal activity against the records of Paul Retter. He was completely innocent.

Kate did not know how to react or what to think. She was struck by an overwhelming doubt in herself; she had never been surer of anything else in her life, but she had been wrong. He was not a criminal, he was not a bad man who had been in trouble before. Might the legacy of Leo Faulkner and the memory of her sister be compelling her to see things which were untrue? She moved on from her accusations, knowing that she had no choice. But she could not extinguish from her brain the horrible image she had seen of him in the garden, aroused and reckless, and she promised herself that she would not allow him to be unaccompanied with her children ever again. He would not be permitted to take them anywhere and the sooner that Paul and Alice moved out of the house the better. She expected never to find him in any compromising situations again, but she knew how to react if she ever did. A mother's love is a powerful thing.

14   **FINGERS BURNT**

Paul had been thinking of buying a house for him to share with Alice, separate from the Fergusons, and he had been visiting estate agents and looking on the internet for ideas of where their new home could be. He had eventually found one that would be perfect; a small bungalow, two bedrooms, a pretty little garden, a veranda to sit under and the house was within walking distance of the sea. It was in Bournemouth, and he requested a viewing. When the estate agent offered him an appointment he decided to take Hope and William with him as a special treat for the summer holidays. He asked Tom if he could take the children with him for the trip, and wanting to prove to Paul that the family trusted and loved him, Tom gave him his blessing to take the children to the seaside.

Bournemouth was very busy with holidaymakers making the most of the good weather and the roads from Reading to the south coast were frustratingly overcrowded, but they got there in the end. Paul adored Hope, and both of the children loved him in return. They had managed to arrive in good time for the appointment and so they ended up on the beach, making sandcastles and digging vast and cavernous holes in the sand. The sun was bright and high and the coastline was deliciously warm as they enjoyed each other's company. Hope and William changed into their swimsuits in the car and raced each other to the water's edge, thrashing their arms and legs wildly in an attempt to get their sibling as wet as possible in a splashing contest. Paul followed them into the water, allowing the foaming crystalline sea to sweep up to his knees, delicately tracing his fingers along the surface of the exhilaratingly cold water. He had his rosary around his neck and he played with it with one hand, dragging the fingers of the other through the sea. He had friends in Bournemouth and he had visited here regularly as a child, the seven mile sweep of unbroken sand drawing him in time and time again. As his skin touched the surface and he submerged himself in the water, spreading his toes amongst the golden subaqueous sand, he felt as though he was making love to Mother Nature with every footstep he took along the golden coastline of Beautiful Bay. His feet penetrated the water smoothly and he thrust his toes under the sand as he waded out, further and further. Hope's wet hair glinted in the sunlight, and her brother's legs shone in the platinum water.

The little cottage was beautiful, and he asked Hope and William to help him in his decision. Can you imagine Grandma here, he would ask. They explored the garden together, and the children went on a hunt to see if there were any fairies lurking in the bushes and trees, and pretended to have a garden party for some of the teddies and dolls they had brought with them. Paul's imagination ran just as wildly as the children's, for he imagined his Alice sitting under the veranda, her pain only a memory now, shading her old eyes from the sunshine. It could be here that the two of them would eventually end their days together, the perfect end to the perfect testament of rescue and love.

*   *   *

That very same afternoon, Kate took some time off work to rest because the office was quiet. She walked into the house hastily, and slung her bag and coat on the kitchen table. "Tom?"

There was a moment of silence before he answered. "I'm upstairs, Kate." She walked up the stairs slowly, listening to the silence in the house that echoed loudly between her and her faraway husband.

"Where are the kids?" Tom was silent, as if gathering courage, and then he came out of their bedroom and answered her.

"Paul asked me if he could take them to Bournemouth with him so that they could look at a house together, he's trying to buy a place for him and your Mum. He said that they would be coming back tomorrow."

Kate's eyes widened with an unimaginable horror which sent chills through her marrow. It was with a dreadful terror that she suddenly had an indelible image on her brain, the clear memory of her sister and the paedophile's genitals inside her, of Joy's violently damaged body being repeatedly penetrated by the man who had stolen her flushing, youthful hue of abundant life. Was tragedy befalling this family for the second time? Would this man be sharing a bed with her children? Where would they sleep? Which places would he be taking them to on the way there and back? Was he even visiting a house that was for sale, or was it a lie to opportunistically whisk her children away from her so that he could murder and mutilate them? Something about house-hunting reminded her of Leo's attempts at asking her for directions to the train station.

Kate spoke with a strong, brutal aggression in her voice. "Who let him take them?"

Tom swallowed. "I did, Kate."

His wife raised her voice, screaming at him and trying to project the urgency of the disaster that he had allowed to happen to their children. "Do you have any idea who he is and where he is taking them? What makes you trust him with Hope and William? Why did you let them go?" Her eyes blazed with anger and fear.

"He's your Stepfather, Kate," he protested, "and you have seen how happy he has made her. You have seen how much he loves those children. He has never married, and he has always wanted to be a father, but by the time his time came they were both to old to make it happen. I think he has always wanted children to call his own."

"He's not having mine," Kate growled with the protective instinct of a lioness.

"You have some issues that we need to deal with," Tom told her frankly. "You have never got over the divorce and you have grown cynical of everyone else because you are used to things going wrong. It comes from being the witness to the crimes against your family and you need to let it go now. When Paul comes back tomorrow with the children, safe and happy, it will help you to learn that lesson."

Kate raised her voice to him, and she shuddered as she reminded herself of her father.

"You are putting our children in situations that are compromising their safety to teach me that I need to trust people more after what happened to us?" She was aghast. "Tom, are you insane?"

"We have absolutely no reasons to suspect him, and no evidence to prove his guilt. There is no conceivable reason on Earth why I should have said no."

"I'm finding more evidence every day."

At this Tom lost his cool for the first time, and shouted at her across the landing. "You have to drop this, Kate, it is time to move on. You have to let it go. You are deluded and stupid for thinking you have evidence against him, you must be having some kind of hallucination. The man has done nothing wrong and you have no right to treat him in the way that you have."

"I am going to phone him and tell him to bring the children back to me immediately. If he refuses, I will call the police. I am not prepared to let him hurt my children."

"Is that what this is about? Is it about an insecurity you have been holding on to for all of these years that you let Joy be hurt? That it was an act of neglect, and this is your way of compensating for it?"

She narrowed her eyes at him with a chilling coldness. "You have no idea, do you? Don't you dare accuse me of neglecting my sister! You have no right to judge me. Where's Mum?"

"She went out to the shops."

"Right, you tell her what has happened and that she needs to come back home immediately. I will call him and if he doesn't tell me what I want to hear I will get him arrested."

Tom was exasperated, but Kate pulled out her mobile phone and called her stepfather.

He was at the bungalow with the children, just as he had promised that he would be, and the agent was showing him the bathroom when his phone rang. He silenced it and apologised, but it rang again seconds later. He did the same thing again, and after a brief silence it rang for a third time. He apologised to the agent profusely and explained that he should probably take the call. It was Kate.

"Bring my children home to me," she demanded.

Paul was slightly taken aback by her bluntness. "I'm sorry?"

Kate raised her voice and strengthened her tone. "I said get in the car, with the children, and bring them home. Leave immediately."

"I can't really do that, Kate, I am at a viewing. I'm looking for a house that I want to buy for your Mum."

"If you don't get in the car in sixty seconds I am calling the police."

Paul was shocked to his core. He could not understand what was happening and why there was such aggressive urgency in her voice. "What? Why?"

"Because you have taken my children away from me without my permission and I'm doing what I can to get them back. Tom's on the phone to Mum, telling her what's happening, and I will call the police when I hang up on you in forty five seconds time. Hand me over to the estate agent."

He didn't know what to do. He was shocked and dismayed by Kate's astonishing accusations. The estate agent could tell that this was no ordinary phone call.

"Sir? Is everything alright?"

Paul was hesitant, and keen to minimise the damage. "It's my stepdaughter. She wants to speak to you."

He handed the phone to her. "Hello?"

"My name is Catherine Ferguson and I have reason to believe that the man in your company is holding my children against their will. I am about to call the police. Please tell me the address and postcode of the property that you are showing him."

The agent paused in a dumbfound silence. She opened the bathroom window which looked out over the back garden. Hope and William were sitting together in the sunshine, talking and smiling and laughing. They personified youthful happiness, and they did not seem to have a care in the world. Kate sensed the hesitation and doubt in her silence and she issued her with a challenge.

"I have access to the personal files on his computer and I am calling the phone company about the calls he has made in the last 24 hours. If you make my job of tracing my children harder I will contact your company and I will tell the police that I believe you are his accomplice. I can very easily find out who you are."

She looked at Paul, who was standing by the window and watching her every move. Kate knew this instinctively and was fast to continue instructing her. "Do not give yourself away to him. Do not let him suspect you. He is a dangerous fugitive and I don't want him to hurt you because he suspected you of helping me. He is very unpredictable and I think he may be planning a dangerous attack against my children."

"It's 12, Hunworth Road, Southbourne, Bournemouth, BH6 4DN."

"And your name is?"

"Ruth Pangbourne, I work for Lewis King Estate Agency."

"Thank you very much for your assistance."

Ruth handed the phone back to Paul. She was getting nervous, and she was planning a means of escape. Paul held the phone back up to his ear.

"I'm onto you, Paul," Kate told him sternly. "Get into the car, right now."

He could not decide what to do.

*   *   *

Alice came home, frightened and distressed by what she had missed, and very angry with Kate for ruining the surprise of where Paul had gone to choose her the house he had always promised. Kate had done what she always was guilty of: she drained the romance and anticipation out of every surprise because of her overprotective, relentless and obsessive pursuit of her stepfather.

The three of them sat at the dining table, arguing firstly over whether or not he was innocent of abducting the children and secondly over whether or not Kate was overreacting. She told her mother that she had demanded that Paul bring her children home and that if he did not do so immediately she would call the police.

"And did you?"

"No."

"Is he on his way back? Did he leave Bournemouth already?"

Kate had tears in her eyes. "I don't know." She looked at her husband. "How long do we give it?"

Tom was quietly seething with anger at his wife's hostility and he was worried that it could affect the marriage of Alice and Paul. "As long as he needs to get here."

The family did not believe a word that Kate told them. What was there to believe? She did not offer them a single piece of conclusive evidence which convinced them of his guilt, and there was a sense of sadness and loss which echoed through the home. Kate had been severely affected by the murder of her sister and the departure of her father, but the thing which had caused Alice so much pain was the fact that her daughter had developed a need for blame, a need for hatred and suspicion and a steadfast and chilling scepticism of the goodness of humanity. She had lost all of her faith, and Alice struggled to see where along the line it had happened as she had begun by dealing with everything so well. She felt within her the familiar doubt that only a mother can know; the wondering, the hopeless searching for anything that she may have done since the murder of Joy which could have damaged her precious daughter in any way and stolen so cruelly from her the belief that the world is inherently good before it is wicked. Could she have done any more? Could she have handled the situation differently, perhaps finding a way of preventing Kate from harbouring all of those feelings of hatred and bitterness which were only now overpowering her? She cast her mind back over the years and was deeply troubled by the idea that her daughter may have been suffering but that she held herself together because of any show of weakness that Alice may have given. She hated herself for the way that her daughter may have been struggling to keep her head above the water and that she was too submerged in her own suffering to notice. The way that she had been unable to read the signals before it was too late made her stomach turn.

And too late it now was. She had been consumed by her suspicions and overcome by her emotional disability, the lasting souvenir of that rendezvous with a paedophile. She saw paedophilia everywhere and it was robbing her of her ability to be a mother; instead of fruits of abundant life her ovaries were now cold and dead pebbles inside her abdomen. She had refused to let the children visit Father Christmas at the local shopping centres, a tradition which was integral to the experience of all of the other children during the winter celebrations, and she had attempted to take legal action against Hope's school when she was selected to help a magician during one of his performances. Hope laughed in all the right places and she was very honoured to have been chosen, but her mother exploded in rage when she discovered that the school had allowed her daughter to be in such close proximity to a man that she did not trust. During one of the nativity plays where Hope was given the honour of portraying a sheep Kate walked onto the stage in the middle of the performance and demanded that the play be suspended until she had personally confiscated every camera and mobile phone from the parents in the audience. Her logic was irrational and hysterical, and the school had assured her that the very tight British laws concerning children (which had, incidentally, been made even more stringent following the murder of her sister as a direct consequence of the MLC) meant that it was not possible for the magician to have performed with children without a special licence only available to people with a perfectly spotless criminal record. But nothing in their logical persuasion could overpower her wounded spirit thrashing out at a scapegoat for her unendurable pain and suffering at the fact that she would never know if she could have done more to protect and defend her sister in her hour of greatest vulnerability. The fact that she would not allow her children to have any interaction with solitary adults was a meagre attempt at reimbursement for her conscience. Hope had loved dogs, for example, and she would often ask if she could run over to a man who was walking a dog on his own to stroke the animal, but Kate was always fiercely protective and suspicious of everyone and she always refused. She was haunted, driven to the brink of insanity by what she had been exposed to as a fourteen year old so that she now regularly saw things which were not there and was utterly convinced of the fact that the world was filled with people waiting to have sex with her children. It was a type of agoraphobia which gave her a unique hatred and suspicion of absolutely everyone that she did not know. It began when she was directly with her children and playing the role of their mother, but the paranoia soon spread to all strangers who she came into contact with, which made her job as a business manager difficult when she was meeting clients. If they touched her on the back or shoulder for any reason, or lingered with a handshake for too long, the demons in her head instantly translated that into the fact that her well presented client must be a sex offender. She did not even notice it in herself but the role that she had played in sending a paedophile to Britain's provisional and hypothetical Death Row had actually allowed Leo Faulkner to continue to make her life a misery almost three decades after the crime that he had committed against their family.

Leo Faulkner had murdered one child, but his actions had directly led to the deaths of thirteen more. They had all been completely innocent of any crimes but they were desperately unfortunate to be caught in the crossfire between the furious mob and the disgusting beast released by a system which was shamefully liberal. Some of them had the misfortune of being a part of a MacGregor family, others were caught in the protests in London; Paul, who was next to join their number, was a man who was simply too close to the Ferguson children to avoid the burden of accusation falling heavily upon his shoulders. Perhaps it had been ignorant or naive of Alice and Tom to have closed off their minds to the possibility of this happening to any new family member, but now in hindsight it was obvious that Kate's fragile emotional state was not robust enough to deal with the pressures of accepting a stranger to come and live in her home as a stepfather. Alice and Tom felt so terrible for Paul; she had no evidence of any kind to prove his guilt and plenty to prove his innocence and yet she still despised him with the same burning hatred. Everyone else loved and adored him, and his charisma and sense of humour made him very popular with Tom. Alice, of course, was still deeply infatuated with her rescuer ever since they had met and she was relishing in her fortune of her painful marriage to Geoff being finally atoned for in the heroic figure of her new husband for whom she had waited for so long.

They had a takeaway for dinner to save the effort of cooking, and they ate from the foil containers without saying a word. They stayed at the table and only occasionally got up to use the toilet, and with an awful inevitability the night began to set in. The darkness fell like a plague and soon the symphony of stars was loud. The old grandfather clock which Alice had brought with them from Higher Pelham would chime every hour and eventually they all lost count.

Nobody had spoken for many hours when Kate cleared her throat to speak. It had been such a long and intense silence that she barely recognised the sound of her own voice.

"He's not coming home, is he?"

Alice and Tom both tried to be understanding of the pain that she was going through, trying to gently introduce her to the idea that her children had been taken away without her consent but that it was not the disaster that she thought it was. Kate was indignant, and as she slowly surrendered to the idea that she was extremely paranoid and psychologically damaged, she still had a question that she needed answered.

"You still don't think that his connection with Richard MacGregor is slightly suspicious?"

*   *   *

A week before the trip to Bournemouth, Kate had used the address of the London flat which Paul had been previously registered to in order to propel her search forwards. She made a request to the local council to determine a list of former residents who lived at the same address as Paul, and whether or not he had lived alone, and various other factors; to be safe she examined records over the past century. She was surprised by the ease with which this was possible, for British law at the time was very protective of present owners and current address details being disclosed to members of the public, but there was nothing which stopped her from investigating previous occupants. The privacy of the tenants to whom Paul had sold his home was stringently guarded, but Kate was not interested in the slightest in the current residents. She was interested in the past.

She did not need to go back as far as a century, in fact far from it. She found with remarkable ease that the flat which Paul had sold to marry Alice was previously the registered address of a Mr Richard MacGregor. Kate recognised the date of the tenancy beginning as the twenty fifth anniversary of the conviction which she had helped to achieve in the Old Bailey when she was fourteen. It was inherited from his mother, so there was no mortgage payment to be completed, and after approximately six months he had disappeared. The flat remained unoccupied for twenty two days and then the address was registered to Mr Paul Retter.

The name was familiar to Kate but she could not remember why. She tried to casually bring it up in conversation with her family to jog her memory but it backfired to spectacular effect. Alice and Kate were taking Hope and William to school one morning when in the car Kate decided, with a furrowed brow, to ask her mother a relaxed question. "Mum, do you know who Richard MacGregor is?" Alice clutched the sides of her seat on the passenger side of the car, hyperventilating like she was going into labour and letting her eyes bulge out of their sockets.

"What did you say?"

"I just came across the name the other day, it's familiar but I can't place it. I was wondering if you could help me put a name to a face, that's all."

"When Leo Faulkner was released from jail on parole after serving his twenty five year sentence he changed his name to Richard MacGregor under the Spent Convictions Protection Programme. They are the same person. Richard MacGregor was the new identity of the man who killed Joy."

Kate was taken aback by her mother's willingness to talk about it with the children in the car with them. They dropped William and Hope off at school and resumed the conversation in the playground. Young children were running around as they waited for the classes to begin. Kate felt sick as she turned over Joy's corpse in her mind, the rotting and seething flesh disintegrating between her fingers. She saw one little girl, around seven, who had the same golden hair that Joy had and Kate was reminded of the last time she ever saw her sister, threading that daisy chain with her top teeth held over her bottom lip in thorough concentration. There was a bittersweet truth in the direction that all this was going now, and she felt a strong sense of conclusion, that she was finally tying up mysteries which had plagued the family for more than a quarter of a century.

"Mum, why did you say that Richard MacGregor *was* his new identity? Is it now?"

"He was attacked by thugs who were wielding baseball bats, because the surgeon who changed his face sold his identity to the *Envoy*. They tracked him down and attacked him. I can only presume he died from his injuries."

"You don't know?"

"I don't need to know." Alice was very serene, and had become a master in the art of stomaching pain. She did not have any curiosity about her at all, which was where the two women differed. Kate could not deal with the murder until she knew everything; Alice could not deal with the murder until she had let it all go. "It doesn't matter any more."

"Yes it does," Kate scorned her, "I traced the movements of Paul before he married you. Twenty two days before he moved into his flat in the East End it was owned by the same man, Richard MacGregor."

Alice went cold. "You're certain?"

"Absolutely."

As soon as they got home they checked the internet for archived news stories about the attack on Richard MacGregor, but no matter how hard they looked there was nothing to tell them that he had died. He simply vanished from the record, disappearing completely after his hospital visit.

Kate phoned up the hospital where the news reports had told her that he had been taken, and she did something that she swore that she would never do. She used the legal powers given to a parent under the amendment to the Freedom of Information Act, commonly known as Joy's Law, which had been passed as new legislature following the murder of Joy Hewitt in Higher Pelham. It specifically gave parents of young girls the right to information about individuals whom they suspected of being sex offenders, and she asked if there was any information that she could reveal about Paul Retter. The woman understood the nature of the request and she promised to call back when she had released the relevant files through the authorities of her manager.

*   *   *

The phone rang. It was approaching 2am and they were still at the table, still going through the motions of waiting for Paul even though they had all silently accepted Kate's insanity and Paul's probably wise decision to defy her and stay on the South Coast. Just as it had done for Alice all those years before, Kate knew that the fate of her children would be decided by what she heard down the phone line. She answered it slowly, and the woman at the other end of the line began to speak.

"Mrs Ferguson?"

"Yes."

"My name is Gabrielle Wright, and I work with the medical records in Lewisham Hospital. You'll forgive me for phoning you so late, but I have discovered something which I think you should know about and so I am going to give you some news. I don't know if there are any family members with you but to save you the trouble I suggest you switch to speakerphone to avoid having to tell everyone yourself. Is Mr Retter with you?"

Kate switched to speakerphone. "No Madam, he is not."

"I have been looking through the medical archives," she began, "and I have noticed a pattern which causes me great concern. The beginning of the pattern you already know about, but I am interested in what happened later. Leo Faulkner murdered Joy Hewitt in Higher Pelham, was put on trial and found guilty, then was incarcerated in Belmarsh Prison for twenty five years. He was then considered for parole, and released under the SCPP. He was given a new identity and chose to have cosmetic surgery so that nobody would recognise him. Sadly for him the surgeon, Dr Shipman, released his details to the media and 'Leo's Thirteen' were killed in cases of mistaken identity. Leo himself, living under the name of Richard MacGregor, was attacked and admitted to us with severe injuries. He took three weeks to recover and when he did he was permitted to undergo the Spent Convictions Protection Programme a second time, in order to ensure that he did not get attacked again. He had more surgery and he was given a third identity. He moved back to his old home pretending to be a different person who had recently bought it, and he told all of the neighbours that Leo Faulkner and Richard MacGregor had both died."

"What was the killer's third identity? What was the name that he changed to when he was discharged from the hospital?"

"He changed his name to Paul Retter."

15 A BEAUTIFUL NECKLACE

Tom raced out to the car, sprinting at full speed and turning the lights and engine on with the key before he had left the front door. Alice and Kate were no less horrified and their movements were no less urgent, but they reached the car a split second after the traumatised father. It was the middle of the night and they had slammed the phone down as soon as the revelation was made; all had independently come to the conclusion that they should go and find Hope and William as soon as they possibly could. It was a conviction which had already claimed thirteen lives, because there really is no limit to what a parent would do to protect their child when they are in the hands of a paedophile. All three of them had in their minds the same agonising, stomach churning question; if he had murdered and raped Joy, what was he now doing to Hope? What would they find when they reached them?

In the seconds before they had left, Tom tried to be logical and think of everything they would need to take with them, but the women had been overcome with a dreadful realisation which had rushed through their bodies with all of the agony of cancer. It was not the fact that he was a man that allowed Tom Ferguson to hold it all together, but instead Alice and Kate were experiencing a horribly familiar scenario and their heads were filled with Joy whilst his was filled with Hope. Tom ensured that they had what they needed because they did not know how long they would be away for; he made sure that he had his phone on him, and that they had money, he pulled the thick blanket off of the sofa and grabbed the biggest bread knife in the kitchen before he ran for the front door. He didn't know why he took the knife and he did not know if he planned to use it, or if any attack on Paul Retter would be through aggression to reclaim his children or whether he was harbouring an underlying suspicion that Paul would become violent when challenged about his past. Tom had no idea what to expect and so he thought that having a knife on him would be a good idea. The blade glinted in the moonlight as he ran.

The car roared into life and Tom drove as fast as he could towards the motorway with a squeal of tyres and the snarl of the engine as he pushed the car to its absolute limit. Kate sat in the passenger seat and Alice was behind them.

Kate and Alice divided amongst themselves the tasks which needed to be completed, with Kate looking through the maps to find the fastest route and using the car's computer to search the internet and find out as much about the house as possible, and Alice making the phone-calls. She needed to get in touch with the hotel, the estate agency, the police and finally Jonathan, who she told to follow them. He told her that he was on his way. Tom decided to use the motorway for the whole duration of the journey because he could maintain his high speed, which was in excess of one hundred miles per hour the whole way. Eventually the time came for them to ask themselves an extremely painful and delicate question; should we tell Geoff? Alice immediately dismissed the idea, saying that she had meant what she had said and would never speak to her former husband again, but Kate was not so sure. She knew that there would definitely come a time when he would have to know, and she decided that it was better to phone him now. Surely it was better to tell him that they suspected her beautiful daughter, her wonderful and precious Hope, had been murdered and then posthumously raped in exactly the same way as Joy had all those years ago rather than prolong the agony and wait until it was a chilling certainty. She phoned her father and she told him who his former wife had married and what Paul had done to the children. It was with a cold and steadfast silence that he listened to what his daughter told him on the phone from a speeding car in the middle of the night. He asked to speak to Alice, but she refused to take the phone from her daughter. He asked Kate to tell her mother that he did not blame her for finding happiness and love with Paul and that he still loved her dearly in spite of the unfolding tragedy. He knew that Alice thought he was still suspicious of her over the mistaken arrest, but he reassured her that he knew it was not her fault, that nothing had been her fault, and that there really is nothing wrong with optimism even though it may transpire that this may have been the cause of further suffering to their family. He asked Kate to thank her for being a wonderful wife and an outstanding mother, and he asked to be kept updated with the news of the safety of his granddaughter.

The car raced along the M4 and connected with the M25, and soon they were racing southwest on the M3 towards Southampton. An altogether more troubling scenario presented itself when Kate suggested that they phone Paul. This situation clearly needed maximum stealth and sensitivity and they did not want to scare him into a chase. Even worse, he may be intimidated into a desperate showdown where he would be more likely to commit an act of recklessness and be spooked into hurting the children to try to protect and defend himself. They decided that it would be too dangerous to warn him that they were coming, and the element of surprise could be the advantage that they needed to reclaim their Hope.

As they approached the junction with the M27 Alice could see a police helicopter in the sky behind them, but Tom didn't care. He did not mind being arrested or even jailed for dangerous driving if it meant a few extra precious minutes to defend his daughter from the family's nemesis. A father's love is boundless and matchless, stretching across the world as comprehensively as the skies. Slightly further down the motorway they were flanked by two police cars and Tom accelerated. He sped up until he approached 120mph and the cars instructed him to pull over. He refused. As the car accelerated down the A31 one of the police cars managed to overtake them and slowed down in front of Tom so that he had to swerve into the hard shoulder to avoid a collision. All three of them leapt out of the car as soon as it came to a halt and sprinted towards the officers, which was the opposite of what the police had anticipated. Tom was hysterical, screaming at them in rage, whilst Alice had tears streaming down her face as she explained who she was and where they were going. Clearly the police force had not internally communicated the report that Alice had delivered by phone and the officers on the ground had seen a speeding car and had assumed that it was stolen so entered into a pursuit. Tom told them that he would happily hand himself over for arrest once they had rescued Hope, and asked for the cars to escort them at high speed towards the place where Paul and the children were staying. The officer understood his concern and told him that they would delay the discussion of arrest until after they had been escorted safely to the scene of the alleged crime. They would call the local Child Protection Squad who would make their way to the house and decide whether to arrest Paul.

Through the Freedom of Information Request made by Kate she had been able to trace his mobile phone without him knowing that they were coming. As it turned out he had been lying to them about his whereabouts but the reason was very simple; he was not the registered homeowner in Reading and his London flat had already been sold, and the estate agency would not let him use a hotel address on any of the documents needed for a viewing. He had an old friend in neighbouring Poole so had asked them if he could stay with them and use their address, and the group had enjoyed an unforgettable day at the beach and choosing a dream home for Alice.

The cars pulled up outside the house and skidded to a halt, leaving screeching skid-marks up the middle of the road. Kate and

Tom flung open the doors and sprinted to the house, pummelling on the front door with their fists and screaming and shouting for the family to open up. There were a few seconds of silence as the family inside stirred from their sleep; the policemen and the parents were too impatient and the door was promptly broken down. Torchlight flashed around the darkness of the entrance hall and the officers screamed and barked "POLICE" repeatedly as they trampled in over the smashed door.

Kate was breathless from the adrenaline pumping through her system and did not know where first to look. She remembered Leo being found in a hole after trying to leave the village all those years ago and so the first place she thought of looking for Paul was in the cellar or the garden.

It was Tom who found Paul. He was in the living room at the front of the house, cuddling William who was dumbstruck with terror at the raid. The child was trembling and crying, and Paul was cradling his head against his chest and calming him with the rhythm of his breathing. He made no attempt at escape. Tom found it difficult to keep the knife covered and hidden within his clothes. His voice crackled and trembled with emotion and simmering hatred. "Get your hands off my child," he said quietly. "Never touch him again."

Paul was indignant, protesting his good intentions and responsibility. "I am calming him down, Tom. I am trying to soothe him because he is distressed that the police have smashed through the front door."

"Shut up. Where is Hope? What have you done to her?"

Paul said nothing and simply nodded his head in the direction of the bed settee on the other side of the room. What looked like a pile of messy bed linen transformed upon closer inspection into his daughter, sleeping angelically through the chaos, her loveliness illuminating the darkness with bright lights of glimmering Hope. Tom did not notice Kate and Alice come into the room behind them until the girl's mother rushed forward, with tears prickling her eyes, to gather up her child in sweeping arms of relieved love. Kate buried her head in the sheets so that she could be close to Hope's face and called the policemen over, instructing them to inspect her daughter's body for any physical signs of sexual assault, but the officers refused to examine her. Hope stirred back into life, and Paul was horrified.

"No Kate, seriously, there is no reason for them to do that. She was asleep; do you have any idea how terrifying all this must be? Please, don't let them undress her. Put her down, it must be a dreadful shock. Honestly, she was sleeping so peacefully and now she's in a room full of policemen."

Kate fired him words of pure loathing and disgust, her voice straining under the volume as she shouted into the darkness. "Don't you dare try to cover your tracks, Leo. If you had sex with my daughter we will find the evidence and we will throw you back in jail where you belong. They should have executed you when they had the chance."

Paul started to weep, but he steeled his voice and the darkness shielded his tears. "You want to take her knickers off? Does she not have any dignity?"

"Shut up."

"No." Paul was surprisingly defiant. "I will not let them molest her. Her body is hers and hers alone and you shouldn't be doing things like that to her against her will."

Kate and Paul began arguing aggressively with raised voices in front of the police officers. She was convinced that abuse had occurred and she wanted to see herself proven right at any cost; he was determined to protect the dignity of the child that he had come to love. The policemen interrupted the argument, and one of them again told Kate that an immediate examination was out of the question.

"If she is to be examined she will be examined in a medical environment, not a criminal one. We are here to investigate and interrogate, not to examine the genitals of a child. Mrs Ferguson I think that you have misunderstood the purpose of the police force and what we are entitled to do. If we examine her it would not be him abusing her, but us."

"I don't care about that. Just do it. Take her knickers off, because I have to know. Do it now, while we are all together." Kate's mind was on the knife in Tom's pocket, and her mind was racing as she tried to decide what she wanted to do to him.

Paul's face was awash with horror and revulsion at his own destruction of Kate's logical rationality. She was trying to protect her daughter, but the effect was that she was achieving the complete opposite, exposing her to humiliation and shame. The police officer was firm and stubborn.

"That isn't going to happen, Mrs Ferguson. We are not allowed to be the ones to examine a child, and if an examination takes place at all it will happen in a hospital. This is not even your home. If you like I can arrange for Hope to be taken with me, and we can get her to a hospital and get her seen to, and an investigation can continue from there. But I have to tell you, this doesn't look much like a crime scene to me. She isn't showing any of the behavioural signs of abuse, and I find it hard to believe that anything has happened here. The only thing you have to go on is his identity."

Paul stepped forward. "You're not taking her," he declared resolutely. "There isn't any need. If you promise me that you will not examine her, I will hand myself in."

The police officer was taken aback. "But we have no evidence that a crime has been committed. This is only an investigation because Mrs Ferguson is demanding that we make it into one."

"I don't care. If you want to accuse me of a crime against children, then I'll plead guilty. All I ask is that you don't examine her. Kate, if you refuse to give permission to let your daughter be examined then I'll admit whatever you want to accuse me of and I'll go to jail."

Nobody knew it except for Paul, but he never did assault Hope Ferguson that night. He had made a promise to God, to Peter and to himself that he would not reoffend and he kept that promise to the bitter end. He did not care that his false confession carried with it a jail term that would see him die on the Captive Side, because he had learnt to see the value in humanity and he had chosen to place Hope and her wellbeing above his own. After living his life as he had done before Belmarsh he could not bear the thought of Hope being examined in a hospital, of her being poked and prodded and penetrated the way that he himself had been when the medics had begun his brutal course of testosterone reducing medication. It didn't matter to him that everyone would think of him as a failure and a devilish criminal; he cared for Hope so much that he could think of little else. A parent is endowed with an instinct to protect their child and endure sacrifice for them and Paul had that as well, even though Belmarsh had robbed him of his chance to be a father. He gave Hope everything he had, whereas Kate threatened to steal dignity from her daughter so that she could have her vendetta settled.

Unable to bear the pressure of walking in on her husband sleeping with her granddaughter, Alice had gone upstairs to explain what had happened to the terrified residents who were hiding in the bedrooms of the house. The blue glow of the flashing police lights was staining the edges of the curtains. Once she had explained the situation to them they all came downstairs and one of the officers told her that the girl was safe, upon which Alice finally summoned the strength to confront her husband.

"Fiend," said Alice, "I know what you have been hiding from me. Kate has been searching and she has spoken to the prison authorities and people in the hospitals. I know who you really are."

Paul stood beside the unmade bed, shrouded in darkness, and Alice stood in the hallway looking into the room with her head surrounded by the effervescent glow from the lampshade behind her. There was an astonishing silence that came down between the two of them as thick and black as crude oil.

"Alice," he said finally, rushing forward into the hallway to comfort her. She backed away into the kitchen, hurriedly searching for something to threaten him with. She backed up against the sink and took a glass from the drying rack, and with a swift blow she smashed the lip on the worktop behind her. Geoff had taught her many lessons in turning the most mundane of household objects into weapons. The whole kitchen was an arsenal aimed at the killer. She held the jagged top of the glass in his direction. Tears were streaming down her face but she kept her voice strong and full of gravel.

"You stay away from me. Don't come any closer. I need to know, once and for all, whether or not it was you who killed my daughter. If you love me you won't lie."

Paul opened his mouth to speak but nothing seemed to come out. He was trembling, his heart was pounding and unrecognisable chemicals and hormones were surging through his veins. He looked at his prize, the wife he had so longed for but had been denied by the siege of his sexuality, knowing that the future of their relationship depended entirely on what he said in the next few minutes. He had spent twenty five years alone in a jail cell waiting for her, dreaming of her, planning his meticulous conquest, and now she was slipping between his fingers after just forty days of marriage.

"I love you, Alice."

She grabbed a vase of flowers from the kitchen windowsill, threw the colourful bouquet into the sink and hurled the whole glass mass across the room at him. He ducked, and the vase hit the wall behind his head and smashed into a thousand glittering pieces. Neither of them noticed Catherine and Jonathan standing in the doorway. Alice screamed, spitting her words out in a ferocious rage.

"Did you kill Joy Hewitt twenty six years ago? Yes or no."

Paul's voice cracked and failed as he tried to find a way to answer her.

"Yes. I killed Joy . . ."

Alice let out a great roar of pain that she had waited to release for half of her life. The air was charged with emotion and she bent over, crouching to the floor and holding up a hand to support herself as she was crippled by a great deluge of pain exploding through her body. Her lips lost their colour as she screamed so loudly, and the whole house echoed from the sound of her anguished cry. She could not fathom it, even beholding in front of her the form of the abhorrent foe, that the man who had stolen her Joy all those years ago was the very same one who had swept her off her feet and slipped that cursed ring on her finger. She felt as though the bottom of her world had fallen away, slipping out into oblivion, a hopeless and endless agony. She raised her eyes to him again, eyes bloodshot with searing pain and heartache and brimming with tears, imploring him to tell her everything but not knowing if she had the strength within her to endure until the end of the revelation. She asked him specific questions but what she really wanted to know was how it was possible, how on Earth it could have happened, how the personification of their worst nightmares could have manifested himself within their home once again decades later.

"Why did you change your name?"

"I was given a rehabilitation benefit and was eligible for protection as a criminal with a spent conviction. They allowed me to have cosmetic surgery to change my appearance, change my name and change all of my details." A solitary tear ran down his cheek. "I am so sorry, I never thought you would ever find out and if I had even the slightest thought that you would then I would never have come back here."

"So why did you? What made you want to come to find me?"

His voice was trembling as he spoke, like the unsteady shimmer of a candle flame.

"Because I had to make it up to you; I know that I will never repay the debt of pain that I owe you but that isn't the point, I was beginning. I know, Alice, that you deserve so much happiness and that you have been given so little. It broke my heart when I found out that you were single, I couldn't bear to see your pain continuing."

"And it was you who I spoke to in Belmarsh?"

"Yes." He appeared deep in thought for a second, trying to recollect how it felt to be that man; in reality the identities that he had assumed were so completely different that he could not believe his answer was entirely truthful. He began to weep again, tears welling up in his electric blue eyes. All that Alice could remember was the poisoned rhetoric he had used to describe her body and his lack of sexual attraction to it across the barrier between freedom and captivity.

"Alice I am different now. I am not the same as I was back then. If I was still a danger to the public they would never have released me; I have turned my life around and I intend to start doing things right. I'm fifty three, Alice. It's a bit late, but I am living a good life now."

"What did the woman say to you when you gave her your passport at St Pancras?"

"It was a brand new passport with that name and they had not updated the retina file from when my name was Richard. The names did not match and that's what got her confused."

"Did you have a criminal record? Was that why she stopped you crossing the border?"

"No, I had it wiped when I was released. That wasn't why she stopped me. There's something called the Spent Convictions Act which means that they let me assume a new identity and not be recognisable as the person who committed the crime. They needed to do it after there were hate crimes committed against child murderers when they were released from jail on parole once the sentence was completed. I never lied, I just get a new criminal record once I am released from jail and any offences I commit are treated much more seriously than they otherwise would. They call it decline to declare."

Alice's eyes blazed with an intense and burning fury. She screamed at him at the top of her lungs, her heart an overflowing tinderbox ready to ignite, and she was completely overcome with a ferocious self hatred for being foolish enough to fall in love against her better judgement and her daughter's suspicions. She had been taken in, and the realisation swept across her body like a hellish rash.

"Don't you dare lecture me on the way that the law works, Paul, I know it better than anyone else and it has shaped and carved out my life in a way that you will never understand. What you have done to this family, what you did to Joy, was beyond what you could ever know and the damage will stay with all of us longer than any punishment you could ever be given."

Paul had tears in his eyes. He loved her so incredibly that it hurt; at first he couldn't eat, couldn't sleep, it was amazing. God had promised her to him since before any of the madness happened and he knew it must be impossible for her to believe him when he told her that she was the only one he wanted. How can it be that a killer who is sexually attracted to children chooses to take a wife, to honour her and love her forever? It sounded crazy to her because it was miraculous, a healing work of a god in whom she did not trust or believe, and there was no way that her mind could comprehend his change of character. But she didn't need to comprehend it because she had experienced it for the best forty days of her life, the redeeming love for which she had yearned and hungered. He had promised to rescue her and he had kept his word. He moved forwards towards her, gently and tenderly so as to not make any sudden movements which would have made her angry, slowly raising a hand to her and running a finger down her cheek. "Do you remember our wedding day, Alice? Do you remember Paris, and our honeymoon?" His voice lowered to a whisper. "I meant every word of the promises that I made to you. I meant every word that I said and every sensation that I felt when I was with you. The conversations that we had together, the journeys, the things that we taught one another, the memories we shared and the times we made each other laugh; all of those things were real." Paul's voice trembled with emotion as the reasons for loving her that he had clung to so determinedly throughout a storm of feral temptation surging through his body since his release flashed through his mind as he looked at his wife. So recently they had been together in the turquoise Aegean, and his impressive ability to make her love him was slipping through his fingers like the crystalline water had done a matter of weeks ago, with an unstoppable and inevitable certainty. He held her head in his hands and cradled her against his chest, but she was suddenly struck by the memory of Joy's dead body, struck not in her mind but in her flesh, remembering how he had held Joy in the same way. She remembered how the body and manhood that he had given her as a wedding present had been the very same as the weaponry with which he had wrenched off her head and stolen her virginity.

New revelations choked Alice with an overwhelming speed and a dreadful sense of cold horror.

"St George's Church," she whispered to herself, her eyes glazed over with revulsion, "we were married in the place where you killed her, the place where she was buried and where you raped her afterwards. Were you going to tell me if Kate had never found out? Would you have ever had the decency to say something?"

He had no choice but to be completely honest with her in the end. He shrugged and broke eye contact, every word slicing through his heart. "No, Alice. I would have never told you. I believe that you would have been happier if you had never known that it was me."

"And before you go on with all your stories about loving me," she hissed at him, "you have to tell me about why and how you were able to sleep with me when you are sexually attracted to little girls. Did you ever have a twin brother?"

"No."

"Were you ever in a car accident?"

"No."

"Then how did you get those scars?"

He pointed to each one as he explained to her. The ones on his chin, nose and beneath his hairline were from cosmetic operations on his face to change his appearance; the ones on his forearms were from laser surgery to remove distinctive tattoos, and the one on his collarbone was from an attack that he had suffered in jail from an angry inmate who had tried to kill him because the Crown would not. He held her hand tightly and raised her fingers to the scars which dotted his arms, neck and face, embracing her fingers with his and inviting her to trace the lines of flesh which rose like jagged mountain peaks from his skin. Some of the scars had reduced sensitivity in the tissue, but the love in her fingertips as she touched him made them ignite like touch-paper, overcome with sensation for the first time. He felt as if he was back in Versailles, running through the vast drifts of untouched snowfall, and he took two of her fingers and tiptoed them across the wound in his neck like they had wanted to across the vast and empty frozen Grand Canal on a happier day. It was different for Alice, however; she had the sensation of seeing Joy's corpse in him, and beneath her fingers the hue of the flesh which was thriving with life suddenly became ripe with the marbled texture of death, the flannel of his organic tissue disintegrating between her fingers as the decay and rancid rot overcame. Her fingertips became great blades of gleaming metal, and she excited herself by the thought of slicing through him as punishment for what he had done in the past. She could feel her pulse quickening through her chest; as she ripped him open and his blood flowed into the tiles of the kitchen floor below her, she could barely remember a time when she had felt more alive.

Kate came in and stood beside her mother, taking an enormous amount of pleasure in telling him exactly what she thought of his devilish plan to infiltrate their family for a second time. She demanded to know about the photograph album, and Paul told her that it was filled with photographs of his cousin who had died during his incarceration; the album had belonged to Lillith. Once all their questions fell silent there were some things that Paul needed answers for, and his frustrations were directed squarely at Kate.

"What made you chase me so obsessively? You hunted me down with much more conniving and venomous malice than I ever had in me when I was a paedophile. You claim that I ruined this family; no Kate, you were the one who did that. I rebuilt it. I worked so hard to recreate what I had broken, to repay my debt to your family. I could not bear to see your mother suffering and so because I was partly responsible for causing it and so the burden fell on me to fix this mess. Why couldn't you just let us have our happiness? You have prolonged your mother's agony when she was at her most joyful. Your curiosity, your hysterical obsession with protecting children has completely destroyed your family." Turning to Alice with passion blazing in his eyes he cried "I am a better husband than Geoff ever was. You claim I am the same man as the one who killed your daughter, but you are wrong. I have a different body, I have a different character, personality and soul, and I have a different name. I am further away from Leo Faulkner than you could ever imagine. She is right when she says that I broke this family but I succeeded in making you happy. Your first husband raped and beat you as he got smashed on alcohol every night, but I loved you and restored you and honoured you just as you deserved. I am nothing like the monster she accuses me of being."

Kate didn't even bother to take the time to listen to what her stepfather had to say. The Fergusons gathered up William and Hope and went to the car, leaving Paul to talk with the officers. Because he had admitted to assaulting and abusing Hope it meant that Tom would not be charged with dangerous and reckless driving because had satisfied the police officers' need for a genuine emergency situation in which he would be permitted to break traffic laws. Just as he had promised, Paul handed himself over to the Child Protection Squad and they led him in handcuffs to the waiting patrol cars. As Alice headed home she glanced out of the car window to take a last gaze at her husband as the Ferguson family sped past, but at the last moment she decided that she could not endure another look. He had murdered her Joy and in her mind he had assaulted her Hope, and there was nothing more that she wanted from him now. All the cars left, and the shocked residents of the little street were left wondering whether the whole episode had been an absurd dream. The police ordered the family's home insurance company to provide replacements for the door and glassware which had been damaged in the raid, and the home of a family they had never met before returned to a striking silence.

On the journey back to Reading, Alice sat in the back of the car between her two grandchildren. William was asleep but Hope's eyes were wide with wonder as her grandmother held her, and the little girl gazed out at the sleeping world beyond her window. The dull orange lights of the motorway streetlamps reflected on her face and she looked out in wonder on the silent, empty road speeding by. It was as still and sombre as a funeral procession, with the melody of the stars and moon quiet now.

Kate Ferguson had finally vanquished her old enemy, laying to rest the ghost of her sister as she protected Hope in the way she had failed to protect Joy. It was something she had never forgiven herself for and now she could breathe slightly easier about it. There was no smugness, no sense of accomplishment or satisfaction in the fact that she had been correct all along, no resentment of her family for having no faith in her whilst criticizing her for having no faith in her new stepfather, but the rest of the family were searching for that resentment even though it was not there. Her mother was trying to understand whether or not she owed her daughter an apology for telling her she was mistaken so repeatedly and yet inviting a child killer into her home to sleep and dine with Kate's children.

Alice was simply relived that her granddaughter was safe and that she had not become his second victim, but the long and silent car journey back to Reading gave her an uncomfortable amount of time to think.

The thing which had cut the deepest about the ordeal was the juxtaposition between Alice and Paul, the things that separated them in every way possible. Whilst killing Joy Hewitt had given Paul a quarter of a century in incarceration in a maximum security cell in Belmarsh Prison, it had also led him to find his faith, his new lease of life and had given him—with questionable success—the relief that he claimed that he wanted from his addiction to the abuse of pre-pubescent girls. He had found a new life, discovered an ability to love and find sexual satisfaction in women and had been swept away in a romance with the chosen woman that he had been waiting his whole life to find feelings for. He had taken her to Paris, been given unusually lenient conditions of release and had freely travelled around the Mediterranean Sea on his dream holiday. He had gained the granddaughter that he had always wanted and had distanced himself and found freedom from the ensnaring cords of passion which had bound him to girls of her age in a sexual and destructive way. Hope Ferguson was the first female child that he had been blessed with a normal and healthy relationship with; it was a tremendous demonstration of freedom in its purest and most magnificent form. He had been jailed and had become the closest prisoner in more than a century to being executed for a capital crime, but his life had been preserved by the vote of a single member of the House of Lords. Thirteen people had died as a result of the vote not being passed, through acts of violence and hatred against the perpetrators that the mob deemed responsible for the outrageously lenient clemency, but Paul had not been amongst their number. He had, through the attack by the gang in the street, been given an unprecedented ability and opportunity for metamorphosis and to distance himself even further from the horrific crime which had tainted his past. He had loved his wife as fully and completely as was possible for any man to love any woman, his wish to redeem and restore her and repay all the debt of pain that he owed the Hewitts and which he had been forbidden to pay back by that single member of the Lords had come cruelly close to being achieved. For a glorious moment he had made her truly happy once again. The wonderful beauty of it all was the fact that he had been set free; freedom in all of its truth and virtue, released from the incarceration he paid for his crimes which fell short of the standards of the British law and the Holy Commandments given by God to His people, and his chains which were both physical and spiritual had been broken. He was simultaneously the guiltiest and the freest person imaginable, which was a truth which was saturated with the beauty and wonder of the impossible, incomprehensible, miraculous Gospel of the cross.

Alice Retter had moved from her home in Raynes Park because she hated it and she wanted a better life for her family. They had moved to Higher Pelham with a great sense of optimism and hope, an uplifting symphony of opportunity and the beauty of the world ringing wonderfully in their ears. She had had a daughter murdered and the corpse raped repeatedly. She had endured the agony of being accused of the crime and arrested on suspicion of killing and sexually assaulting her own offspring, and had weathered the storm of negativity and accusation that had pounded her from the neighbours in the village. She had suffered the heartbreak of the trial, witnessed the courage of her daughter Catherine as she had defiantly taken the stand in the witness box at the Old Bailey, damning the killer to what she thought would be an execution only to have the sentence drawn out to include a Parliamentary vote which would last several long and painful months and eventually come to nothing. She had buried her daughter in the churchyard where her life and virginity had been stolen from her, committing her to the cold and lifeless earth when she had been made for so much more. She had been battered and beaten by the man she had loved, the man who had claimed her as his wife when she was nineteen, the man she had saved herself for and the one she had given the honour of fatherhood to. She had watched him drink himself to oblivion and destroy all that they had worked so hard to build for themselves and their children, violently assault her time and time again, and be dragged off to prison to serve time behind bars for attacking her. She had walked alone through the desolate valley of singleness for a quarter of a century, heartbroken and lonely, only to be rescued and redeemed by her faraway love, bounding over the mountains and fields to storm her castle and carry her away in a torrent of romantic dreaming. She had never lost hope or faith like Catherine had, and she had to endure the accusations from her daughter which would seamlessly transform themselves into revelations. As soon as the idea had nestled in her brain it spread though her as rapidly as a wildfire; it was soon completely undeniable that he had been the one to penetrate them both, the one to wreak sexual destruction on everything he touched, the feral monster who had yearned and hungered to be martyred as a champion of his minority.

The sickening truth of it all was the fact that he had been set free. Yes, he had needed to work for it and accumulate his bid for freedom which took years and painful abuses, but he had made it in the end. Alice had never made it. She had never reached her enlightened summit of glorious, wondrous freedom. It was a sobering thought that she had spent the time since the murder of Joy being far more of a prisoner than he ever had. She was a captive, chained to the corpse of her daughter and bruised from the spectacular disintegration of her family, and whilst his sentence had come to an end due to the parole board recognising his outstanding character transformation, her sentence was indefinite. She would never be truly free. It made her consider her words to him when they had met in Belmarsh Prison, how she had told him that she would take him with her to her grave.

*   *   *

Alice pulled the necklace over her head and she pulled at the knot until it was comfortably tight. There was a coldness and a correctness about the way it was happening now, but she felt inside of her a satisfaction that she had not felt in years. Gently she climbed onto, and then over, the old oak banister at the top of the staircase in her best dress. Standing on the edge, she smiled at the good times that had gone by and the glory to come. Her doomed wedding ring was loose and clumsy as it hugged her finger, and in turn her fingers loosened on the wooden rail of the banister behind her. With a rushing sense of relief and healing she spread her arms and leaned forwards. Joy flashed through her mind. The years of heartbreak and torturous suffering were undone in one glorious moment as Joy bounded across the infinite meadows of Heaven and Alice scooped her up in her arms, holding her high above her head as she spun around. The sunlight glinted off of Joy's beautiful blonde hair and the sky was an endless and ethereal blue. Neither of them had ever seen a more beautiful summer sky and its majesty was enhanced by the most wonderful reunion imaginable. For all those years of heartbreak and pain all Alice was really yearning for was to have her little girl back again, to hold her in her arms and give her kisses and cuddles like she had before the interruption. This was a delight that only a mother and daughter could know. The physical sensation of Joy's blooming flesh between and beneath Alice's now ringless fingers instantly made the whole ordeal worthwhile and all of her suffering vanished on the perfumed fragrance which scattered across the field, towards the far side of the place that she knew they both belonged in. Her bare feet climbed onto tiptoe and gently pushed her forwards and into the beautiful unknown, gradually losing contact with the edge of the landing. She felt as though she was leaning forwards into a wonderful embrace with someone, but suddenly it was not Joy. The hope with which she was moving was quenching her of the heartache of her past love affairs, it was removing the crippling disappointment and wrenching pain of two failed marriages and giving her the satisfaction in a relationship that she so craved and deserved but was always so cruelly denied as her toes came free of the floor above and she left all the pain behind. Glory.

For a delicious fraction of a second, Alice could fly.

ACKNOWLEDGEMENTS

I am forever indebted to the giants of literature who have inspired me to become a writer. I am particularly thankful to Annie Proulx, Ian McEwan, Angela Carter, Mary Shelley, Carol Ann Duffy, Elizabeth Barrett Browning, Thomas Hardy and William Shakespeare.

To Mike; I wrote you a letter at Forum 2009 about a talk that you gave and I signed it "Sarah" so that you wouldn't know it was from me! Thank you for your theological genius which inspired sections of this book. You helped Jesus to change my life and I'll always be thankful for that.

To my family; thank you for your support and love throughout this adventure. It's been quite a journey. Thank you for being there to share it with me, and cheers to the road ahead.

AUTHOR BIOGRAPHY

Michael Rogers studied English Literature and Journalism & News Media at Roehampton University in South West London, graduating in 2010. He has since worked as a journalist and a feature writer for local magazines before fulfilling a lifelong dream by writing novels.

This is his first novel. A second, Coconut Shells, followed shortly afterwards. He lives in Bournemouth, on the south coast of England.